ALSO BY ROSANNE BITTNER

LOGAN'S LADY

ROSANNE BITTNER

sourcebooks
casablanca

Published by Sourcebooks Casablanca, an imprint of Sourcebooks, Inc.
P.O. Box 4410, Naperville, Illinois 60567-4410
(630) 961-3900
Fax: (630) 961-2168
sourcebooks.com

Printed and bound in Canada.
MBP 10 9 8 7 6 5 4 3 2 1

PART I

ONE

London, England, April, 1870

"YOU HAVE DISGRACED THE FAMILY NAME BEYOND recovery!"

William Baylor looked away from his brother's dark, accusing stare, never sure how to deal with the man's fits of judgmental rage. He licked at his cut, swollen lower lip as he struggled for the right words to explain himself.

"This is the end of your foolishness," Lord Jonathan Baylor roared. He towered over William with a face as red as an overheated stove plate. William couldn't think straight.

He'd lived his whole life under his brother's stern rule and intimidating temper. Now the man leaned over him with fists clenched. "I...I cared about her," William finally answered.

"*Cared* about her? I asked one of my friends to go to that theater and ask about her. The woman's reputation with men is even worse than her profession! An *actress*! I'm not sure which is worse."

"She's just a woman, young and pretty and alone."

"She's a *slut*! No man who cares about his family and his reputation hangs out with actresses, let alone one who is talked about in smoking parlors. What am I going to tell my business acquaintances? It's bad enough you failed in your education—"

"I *told* you! I can't see letters in the right order!"

"Some people think you're slow in the head. And please, get up and face me like a *man*."

William slowly rose, glancing at the doorway to the parlor. His dear sister and best friend, Elizabeth, stood watching with tears in her eyes. "Jonathan, you know William has a soft heart for those less fortunate than we are," she tried to argue.

"I don't want to hear it," Jonathan snapped in reply, his gaze still on William.

Jonathan's wife, Caroline, also witnessed the argument, but her eyes showed the same cold disappointment as Jonathan's. Her husband suddenly whipped around to glare at Elizabeth.

"I am tired of you constantly defending your brother," he told her. "He needs to grow up and be a man."

"He *is* a man," Elizabeth answered boldly. "A kindhearted man who is brave enough to go into the poorer neighborhoods and—"

"And disgrace this family!" Jonathan interrupted. His eyes grew even darker. "Stay out of this, Elizabeth. With our parents dead, it's been my job to look out for *both* of you for six years. *I* will decide what is best for you and this family." He turned back to William. "I managed to get you a fake diploma to prove you have normal intelligence, William, and I've supported you since you finished school because your job at the family accounting business is a *farce*. We both know it. I've done all I can to save the family name and your reputation, even after that mess last year when you got drunk at your sister's cotillion and fell into the food table. But this…" Jonathan threw his hands into the air. "This is about as bad as it gets!" He glanced at his wife. "I'm sorry about this, Caroline. I can't begin to advise what you should tell your society friends. And here you have an embroidery tea tomorrow afternoon. By then, this story will be in all the newspapers."

Caroline heaved a deep sigh, glaring at William. "You have left me in a disgraceful position, William, having to defend you getting arrested for beating a man nearly to death, and over an actress and a *harlot*—"

"He was *hurting* her," William argued. "And she's not what you say. She's a sweet young woman who was left on her own at ten years old and—"

"Stop!" Jonathan demanded. "The fact remains that you were caught in the dressing room of a disreputable actress and in a fistfight with a drunken, low-class chimney cleaner who'd probably been sleeping with her. Have *you* slept with her, too? For God's sake, you probably already have a venereal disease."

Elizabeth again interjected. "Jonathan, he was just defending her."

Jonathan glared at her, the scolding look in his dark eyes as fierce as a slap. "Need I remind you that you are only nineteen years old and know nothing of that seedy side of life? Your brother has shamed and embarrassed the Baylor name since he was old enough to go out in public. It's time he stood on his own and learned true responsibility. I am kicking him out of this house."

Elizabeth's eyes widened in disbelief. "You wouldn't!"

"*Wouldn't* I?" Jonathan stepped closer to Elizabeth, flaunting not just his size but the power and influence that came with it. "I've had all I can take, Elizabeth. You should be upset, too, after what happened last year. I cannot go on like this. The man, if he can call himself that, has to leave this estate and this family and learn to survive on his own."

Elizabeth's eyes teared. "He's your *brother*," she reminded him. "His only problem is that he has a big heart, and that *you* have *no* heart."

"And you have no right talking to me this way after all I've done for *both* of you," Jonathan answered. "Your brother's big heart, as you put it, doesn't excuse the fact that he disgraced the family name yet again by hanging around disreputable people. I have babied him long enough. He's done too much damage this time." He stepped closer and grasped Elizabeth's arms. "And I might remind you that you are beautiful and have your own reputation to think about. You are a woman of honor and intel-ligence and talent, and as long as William is part of this estate and continues to bring shame to our name, the harder it will be for you to find a decent man to marry. Until you *do* marry, I will always care for you, but the best way to ensure a proposal comes sooner than later is to send William away."

Elizabeth jerked her arms from her brother's grip and faced the man squarely. "If William goes, *I* go!"

"Don't be ridiculous!" Jonathan shook his head and sneered. "You'd never survive away from the shelter of this estate."

"I am old enough to do anything I want. And I can claim my share of the money that is rightfully mine, and so can William. And mother left her jewels to me. All of that should be enough to survive just fine, out from under your rule and away from this depressing, boring life."

William spoke up. "Elizabeth, it's okay. I'll be fine."

"It's a matter of what is right and what is wrong," Elizabeth answered, still holding Jonathan's gaze, determination in her eyes.

"Don't be a fool," Jonathan told her. "I'll *never* allow you to leave this estate."

"I am free to leave any time I want."

"And your air of independence has always been as much of a burden to me as your brother's *stupidity*. You are Lady Elizabeth Baylor. A woman of your station should leave home only because she has a husband, and I might remind you that Lord Henry Mason is very interested in marrying you."

"And I'm *not* interested in that old lecher!"

"You are close to becoming an old maid, Elizabeth. Women whisper, and men wonder. I have had requests from others besides Lord Henry, men younger than he. I held that cotillion last year so you could meet other men. Why on earth are you not interested in such things? It's natural for a woman to want—"

"*I'll* choose whom I marry, and I will have to *love* him. I'm sure that is something a man like you would never understand, Jonathan. I'll not marry just for a man's title and money. Thanks to Father's connection to the monarchy and the approval of the Queen, you don't own me. And you are obligated to give me my share of this estate whenever I ask for it. I will not have what is mine used as a dowry for some old man who is already wealthy. I'll choose my *own* path."

Jonathan pressed his lips together in disgust. "You have no idea what it would be like out there on your own. I'll not allow it! You are my *sister*!"

"And William is your *brother*! You should be just as concerned about *him*. And don't talk about not giving him his fair share. If you insist he leaves, you are obligated to give him money to survive."

Jonathan stiffened. "How and when did you become so independently minded? That, too, is a disgrace! Women are not meant to make demands of those who keep them."

"*Keep* them? I'm not a zoo animal, Jonathan."

"Nor are you getting any younger. Think about what you are saying. Men swoon over you. And if you married Lord Henry, you would live like a queen, what with his money and your own. I have suffered enough disgrace because of William. How would I explain allowing my beautiful young sister to go off on her own when she knows nothing of the world outside this estate?"

"I'd have my brother for an escort. There is no shame in that."

Jonathan closed his eyes. "You're a *fool*. William can't care for you like I can, and you know it. To leave this estate would be to throw your life away."

"Staying here and marrying a man I don't love would be throwing my life away."

A new coldness moved into Jonathan's eyes. "You'll never have the courage."

Elizabeth put her hands on her hips and raised her chin. "*Watch* me."

William couldn't help a small grin. Elizabeth had a brave way of handling Jonathan that he himself had never possessed. More than once she had actually backed the man down.

Jonathan drew a deep breath, as though someone had socked him. He took hold of Caroline's arm and pulled her with him as he suddenly swept past Elizabeth with an arrogant air. "William, you have two weeks to decide what you will do and where you will go," Jonathan called as he walked out of the room. "And if you take your sister with you, what happens will be on *your* head, not mine. You think about that!"

Elizabeth watched him leave, then turned to William, arms folded. "There," she announced. "I've done it. William, we are leaving the Baylor estate. It's time to live our lives the way we choose."

William wiped at unexpected tears in his blue eyes. His thick, light-brown hair hung over one eye, and he quickly swept it off his forehead, revealing another bruise. "I'm sorry about all this, Liz. I'll be fine. You don't need to leave with me. Really. Jonathan's right about it being dangerous for you."

Elizabeth walked closer. "It's been six years since our parents died, but I remember Mother always seemed to understand your good heart. She had one, too, and she also was an independent woman. I remember her having a gentle way of bossing Father around." She smiled, and William broke down, covering his eyes as he wept.

"I miss them so much, Liz. I still feel them with us. If they hadn't decided to take that trip to France—"

"No one thought such a violent storm would hit the Channel in the middle of a lovely, calm summer." Elizabeth put her arms around him. "The fact remains we were left in Jonathan's charge, and I hate it as much as you do. I think he always resented the responsibility. He probably hopes both of us *do* leave. He was always the mean-spirited, spoiled firstborn, and since he inherited the estate, we have both felt like prisoners."

William sniffed and pulled away as he wiped at his eyes. "I don't mind leaving, Liz, but you shouldn't go with me."

Elizabeth shook her head. "You always say I'm the strong one, William. And I *hate* the fact that my future is mapped out for me as long as I stay here. I *am* strong, and I've already been thinking about leaving, *alone*, if I have to. Now we both have an excuse for going, and you can be my escort, so I won't shame Jonathan." She took a deep breath, summoning her determination and warding off any doubts. "And you and I aren't just brother and sister. We're good friends. We understand and trust each other. We've grown so close since Mother and Father died, and we both want to get out from under Jonathan. This is our chance."

William shook his head. "Where on earth would we go? By tomorrow, everyone in London will know about me. I'll be a disgrace, and you'll be looked down upon for leaving with me. I don't want that for you." He watched Elizabeth's brilliant blue eyes light up with excitement. A beautiful young woman with an alabaster complexion and thick, golden hair, she would catch any man's eye. "It makes me nervous to think of being responsible for you, Elizabeth. And people in London—"

"We won't stay in London. We'll go to *America!*"

William's eyes widened in surprise. "*America!* Are you crazy? I thought all your talk about gold and cattle and mountains and outlaws was just from those penny dreadfuls you read. Those are just silly, made-up stories, Elizabeth. I'm sure they make America sound more romantic and adventurous than it really is."

"They're called dime novels in America, and they're wonderful," Elizabeth answered, grasping her brother's hands. "Just think of it, William. With an ocean between us and Jonathan, we'd be completely out from under his control, and we'd have a lot of money. We could make investments in gold mines and maybe buy lots of land and—"

"Elizabeth, that's foolish."

"*Is* it? We'd be free to go where we please and make our own decisions. We will have enough money to go anyplace we want and live well. We can pay the best guides to take us to the gold mines in Denver once we reach America. I've been studying about all of it longer than you know. And I've been wanting to get away from here since our parents died and Jonathan took over." She squeezed William's hands. "If I stay in London, even living separately from Jonathan, I fear that somehow he will be able to force me into marrying some boorish man I don't love, and into a life of nothing but teas and cotillions and embroidery clubs and constant gossip. I have a need for adventure and independence, William, and everything I read about America tells me that a woman can have independence there that she could never have here. I'm nineteen and you're twenty-two. We have our whole lives ahead of us. Why not go to America and see what's there for us? If we don't like it, we'll come back to Europe, maybe France." She let go of his hands and smiled excitedly. "Once we're away from here, our futures are in our own hands. *Think* of it, William."

William smiled. "It does sound exciting."

"You can be your own man there. And you *are* a man, William. Don't listen to Jonathan when he insults you the way he does. This is our chance to be free from him."

William sighed deeply. "Are you sure?"

"Of course I am! We just need to buy passage on a ship to America, but first we'll need to set an appointment with the family solicitor to claim our inheritance."

William breathed deeply with a mixture of excitement and doubt. "You're so brave, Liz."

"I just want out from under Jonathan's thumb." Elizabeth leaned in and kissed her brother's cheek. "I'm going to my room to make plans and think about what I should pack. Tomorrow morning, I want you to take care of the solicitor and get some schedules for passage to America." She took his hands again. "Promise me, William. Don't change your mind."

"I won't. I promise."

Elizabeth squeezed his hands again before hurrying

off to run up the grand staircase to her room. William watched her go, his heart heavy with the knowledge that his name would be notorious by morning. He wanted to be strong for Elizabeth. He couldn't let her know he was scared to death to leave and go to America, but then he'd face just about anything to get out from under his brother's constant badgering and insults. Jonathan was right in saying he needed to stand up for himself, and he had to admit that going to a place like America sounded exciting. He'd read about the place, too, and he supposed there couldn't be a better chance at making a good investment than in a place that was growing like wildfire, where a man could do anything he wanted.

He sighed and sat down on the fainting couch, putting his head in his hands. "God, help me," he whispered.

TWO

Laramie City, Wyoming Territory, April, 1870

THUMP!

Sheriff Jack Teller awoke with a start when cold air rushed over him from an open door and something heavy hit the floor of his office. His first reaction was to reach for his gun.

"Leave it!" a deep voice told him. "It's just me." The intruder slammed the door shut. "Jesus, Teller, somebody could have come in here and helped a prisoner escape and you would have slept right through it."

Teller looked up at the tall man with long, sandy-colored hair that stuck out from under a wide-brimmed hat. His sheepskin jacket made his six-foot frame and broad shoulders appear even larger. And he was in bad need of a shave. It took a minute for Teller to realize who it was. "*Logan?*"

"I brought Sol Weber to you."

Teller turned to look beyond the end of his desk to see a man lying on the floor, still wearing a wool jacket, his frozen eyes staring up at the ceiling. An ugly hole in his forehead made Teller shake his head as he looked at Logan Best. "Is it possible that someday you'll bring one of these men back *alive*?"

Logan shrugged. "If the poster says dead or alive, I might as well keep things safe and kill him. Then I don't have to worry about feeding him and staying awake half the night watching him so he doesn't try to put a bullet in me and escape." He glanced at the dead body of Sol Weber. "Besides, when he robbed that bank in Sheridan, he killed two kids as he was trying to get away. He doesn't *deserve* to live."

"Says a judge and jury, in most cases," Sheriff Teller answered. He hoisted his too-heavy body out of his chair with a grunt. "Need I remind you yet again that your only job is to get wanted men back here? Let the right people decide if they should live or die."

Logan took a thin cigar from his pocket, then struck a match and lit it. "Why bother, with a man like that?"

Teller snickered, his belly jiggling when he did so. "You have the strangest set of values I've ever known in a man." He ran a hand through his thin, graying hair. "You kill a man at the drop of a hat with absolutely no regrets, but you worry about the right and wrong of what he did and get upset because a couple of kids died. Obviously, most men agree that's a terrible thing, but most men don't turn around and put a bullet in a man's forehead with no feelings at all."

Logan puffed on the cigar for a moment. "The weather helped. This sudden spring snowstorm froze his body pretty quick, so I didn't have to worry about burying him because of the smell. Besides, burying the men I go after isn't in a bounty hunter's job description."

"I didn't know there was such a thing as a job description for men like you," Teller grumbled.

Logan sniffed and ran his coat sleeve across his nose. "When do I get my money?"

Teller rubbed at tired eyes. "I'll wire the authorities in Cheyenne. It usually takes a few days, so stick around. In the meantime, get that damn dead body out of here. Frozen or not, it will stink damn quick." He studied Logan's sorry condition. "Or is that *you* I smell?"

Logan grinned. "Both, I reckon. I'm fixing to head over to Martha's place and let one of her girls give me a bath. I'm in need of a woman, or more than one. Maybe I can get two or three of them to scrub me down, all at the same time."

Teller walked around the desk and took his hat from a hook near the door. "I expect you won't have a problem there. The ladies at Martha's love you. I don't doubt you're well known at every whorehouse in Wyoming, and probably in Colorado and Kansas, too."

"A man's gotta do what a man's gotta do."

Teller put on his hat and looked up at the much taller Logan Best. "I've always wondered where you come from, Logan. What led you to do what you do?"

Logan kept the cigar between his teeth. "Lotta things. I come from everywhere and nowhere, and there isn't a person alive who gives a shit about me. Not since—" He hesitated, deciding not to finish the sentence.

Teller took down a wool jacket and pulled it on. "Since what?"

Logan frowned. "Never mind."

"You ever think about marrying and settling?" Teller asked.

"None of your business."

"Suit yourself, Logan, but some day you'll get tired of this life and want to settle. I don't doubt there are any number of women who would gladly oblige you."

"I'm not losing any sleep over it. I'm still trying to get over the fact that this territory allows women to vote."

Teller grinned. "Gotta agree with you on that one. In the meantime, I need you to drag that body out of here and have someone carry him to the undertaker. He'll dress him out and put the bastard on display for the newspaper. I'm going to the telegraph office to see about collecting your money."

The sheriff turned and opened the door for him. Logan kept the cigar between his teeth and reached down, taking hold of Sol Weber's ankles and dragging the man's stiff body out the door.

Teller left, and Logan closed the jail door, leaving Weber on the boardwalk. He nodded at two women walking past the jail. Both gasped at the sight of the dead body lying there with a hole in its forehead.

"Dear God!" one of them exclaimed. She looked up at Logan Best. "*You* again! You're a merciless killer, Logan Best! You're no better than the men you murder in the name of justice and only for money."

Logan nodded to her, taking the cigar from his mouth. "Believe what you want, ma'am. That man killed two little kids in a shoot-out after robbing a bank in Sheridan. Could have been one of your own."

The woman sniffed. "The man still deserved a trial."

"Maybe so, but he would have been hanged. I just saved the Territory a lot of money by taking care of things myself."

The woman shook her head in disgust and pulled her long, black wool coat tighter around her neck before stepping over Sol Weber and walking past Logan. Her friend stared at Logan a moment longer, then turned and followed.

Logan watched after them with a sigh, thinking about Teller's remark that he should settle. He doubted that a woman existed who'd put up with the kind of man he'd become. He'd settled once, and it had destroyed everything good in him. Whores pleased a man in all the ways he needed pleasing, and he didn't need to love a whore, so there was no danger of hurting anyone's feelings.

He turned to leave, and three men approached him with scowls on their faces. "Another dead one, huh, Logan?" one of them commented.

"Yup."

"Sheriff Teller told us to come and take him to the undertaker," the second man said.

"Be my guest," Logan answered. He shivered into his jacket and headed for Martha's Female Boutique for a hot bath and the best whiskey in town.

THREE

"I AM HAVING TROUBLE AGREEING TO THIS." IAN TYLER frowned at Elizabeth and William Baylor. "I have been the solicitor for your family for many years, long before your parents died."

"The Writ of Title to the estate includes me," Elizabeth told him. "That means I have a right to my share whenever I want it, whether you like it or not. I am over eighteen. Neither you nor Jonathan can keep me from what is mine, nor William from his."

Tyler leaned back in his large, leather chair. A streak of sunlight highlighted the many wrinkles in his very white skin. Elizabeth thought him so pale that he could easily be mistaken for a ghost. His shoulder-length white hair was thin and spindly, his pink scalp the only color on him. Even his eyes, which showed only a bit of blue, were pale.

"Lady Elizabeth, it would be one thing if you were marrying, or if you wanted to start your own separate account but remain living with Lord Baylor," the old man told her. "But to take this kind of money to a place like America is outrageously dangerous and foolish." He glanced at William. "And you, William, are nothing but a troublemaker, with no common sense whatsoever. Men belonging to a family like yours don't hang around on the wrong side of the tracks with lower-class people who have no standing among the elite of London."

"I refuse to look down on them. Some of them are good people who need help."

"They would rob you of every last shilling you own if they could!" Tyler, obviously angry, straightened in his chair. He turned his attention to Elizabeth. "It goes against every grain of good judgment in me to allow this."

Elizabeth caught the way the old solicitor looked her over. She'd often seen the same disturbingly hungry look in Lord Henry Mason's eyes when he talked of marrying her. She kept her hands folded properly on her lap. She'd worn a handsome silver-and-burgundy-striped day dress, with ruffled pagoda sleeves trimmed in burgundy lace, and a crinoline skirt with six rows of ruffles at the hem that matched the ruffles of the sleeves. Her tall, crowned hat in burgundy velvet sported one white feather, the color, she thought, looking splendid against her light hair. Her white gloves were decorated at the wrist with tiny burgundy buttons. She wanted to look mature and womanly, older than her real age. She kept an authoritative look on her face as she raised her chin, determined to have her way.

"And I could take you to court over this if you refuse to give me what is mine," she reminded the man. "That would make all the newspapers, and

Jonathan hates publicity. I have the necessary paper-work to prove my inheritance, and I want it. *Now!* William and I have already booked tickets on a ship to New York City."

"And then what?" Tyler asked with a hint of sarcasm.

"Then we will take a train to a town called St. Louis, where we will take one of those wonderful paddle steamboats on the Missouri River to Kansas and then a train to Denver, where there are gold mines in the Rocky Mountains and any number of other possible investments. Do not forget, sir, that I am well schooled. Not all women care about nothing but embroidery and proper dress and marriage. Some of us have loftier ideas, and under Jonathan's heel I will never be able to enjoy the kind of freedom I dream of. With the money we have coming, William and I can build our own home in Denver. We will have maids and cooks and all the other things we enjoy here. And they say that in western America everything is clean and beautiful, not like the smog and filth we have here in London."

Tyler glanced at William. "Is this what *you* want? You are not nearly as ambitious as your sister, William."

William glanced at Elizabeth and smiled. "Elizabeth has always been good to me." He turned his gaze to Tyler. "I want whatever *she* wants. I will be her escort and protect her along the way. And I think that once I am out from under Jonathan's control, I'll be stronger for it."

Tyler shook his head and leaned back in his chair, glancing at Elizabeth again. "And where did you hear all these stories about America?"

Elizabeth straightened her shoulders and held her chin proudly. "I *can* read, you know. The newspapers are full of stories about America, and some of my friends' fathers and husbands have already made investments there. I would not be surprised to learn you've looked into it yourself."

Tyler nodded. "I have considered it, but I am a man of wealth and experience. You, on the other hand—" He stopped and sighed when Elizabeth glared at him for trying to embarrass her and insult her intelligence. "Tell me," Tyler continued in a change of subject, "when you say you have read a lot about America, are you referring to those penny dreadfuls? Dreadful is the right word for those things. I hope you know those stories are a bunch of lies and exaggerations."

"They are exciting and adventurous," Elizabeth answered with a sure tone to her voice, "but I know better than to believe all of it. I must say, though, that it will be exciting to find out what is true and what isn't. Either way, I have studied about America, in books far more dependable than the penny dreadfuls. America has succeeded in supporting a democracy that promotes independence and entrepreneurship. We have little of that in England. Our lives are too controlled by the Queen's rule. And America just recently completed a railroad that goes all the way from New York City on the Atlantic coast to San Francisco on the Pacific coast. William and I just might take the whole trip. Who knows? San Francisco is another city that offers opportunities for investments, especially in shipping. They trade with China and—"

Tyler put up his hand to silence her. "Enough!

Have you considered the fact that America just got over a civil war? There is great unrest there now. And if you go anywhere beyond the Mississippi River, you will find life is very hard and very dangerous. There is little law of any kind in western America, or so I am told. Raiders and killers and robbers abound. Men get hanged for stealing a horse. Someone as young and beautiful as you would be in terrible danger. The only women in the West are cooks, laundresses, and whores. Is that what you want to become?"

"Of course not! I assure you, sir, that I have been secretly studying America longer and more thoroughly than you know. I have wanted to get out from under Jonathan for a long time, and to be free to do what *I* want to do. This is my chance."

"And what about Lord Henry Mason? Your brother promised you to him."

"He had no right to do so! I will not be a bride to that lecherous old man. I'd rather die."

"And die you might, if you go to America," Tyler answered. "Americans are nothing like the elite of England. They are barbaric, uneducated, far too independent, rough, and unruly. They have no proper manners. A young lady like you would be repulsed by most of them. At least let me find out if there is a proper family in New York who might be able to take you in for a while until you know what you want to do, where you want to go. You can't just land there with no plans for what you will do next."

"That is what makes it more exciting," Elizabeth answered. "We will stay at the finest hotel in New

York City and find someone to help us get to Denver—a guide of some kind."

Tyler turned his attention to William again. "I can see that your sister will be more in charge of this trip than *you* will be. Be that as it may, are you sure you can properly protect her in a new land?"

"I know how to use a gun and my fists," William answered. He straightened, with a proud look in his eyes. "I would do anything to protect her, in every way possible. In fact, we have decided that while we travel we will pose as husband and wife. That will keep away men who might have wrong thoughts about Elizabeth. We have it all worked out and have even decided what to pack in our trunks."

"And you just might need to use that gun and your fists more often than you realize," Tyler said, looking William over scathingly. "If any culprit finds out how much money you two have on you and that you have expensive jewelry in your possession, there will be a target on your backs. I am telling you that America is a dangerous place."

"We will be fine," Elizabeth declared. "And speaking of money, just how much exactly will each of us receive?"

Tyler closed his eyes and sighed in resignation, reaching for a heavy ledger and pulling it over in front of him. "I already did the figuring once Jonathan told me what you two were up to." He opened a drawer and took out something that looked like a receipt book. "I will give each of you a withdrawal slip from the Bank of England. Each of you will receive ten thousand pounds. In America, that comes to roughly twenty-four thousand dollars—*each*. That is a very large amount of money, especially in America, and it is enough to invest in a gold mine or whatever you choose to do with it. I hope you understand the enormous danger of traveling with that kind of money. I suggest once you get to New York you put most of it in a bank for safe keeping, along with any jewels you take along. Please tell me you will do at least that much."

"We will speak with a banker or investor when we arrive in New York," Elizabeth answered. "We will decide then how to handle the money."

Tyler handed Elizabeth and William withdrawal slips. "Whatever bank you choose to deal with in New York will know how to convert your money to American dollars." He rose. "I still think this is a dangerous and foolish idea, but you are of age and free to choose your own life, so all I can say is, God bless and protect you both."

Elizabeth looked at William, seeing the same excitement in his eyes as she felt. "We'll be fine. Thank you for your blessings and cooperation." She put the withdrawal slips in her handbag and rose, reaching out and shaking Tyler's hand. William did the same before walking out with Elizabeth and closing the door.

As soon as they were out in the hallway, Elizabeth turned and flung her arms around William. "We're free, William! Jonathan can't run your life anymore, and I can make my own decisions now!"

William hugged her gently, then grasped her arms. "Thank you, Liz. I have to admit, I wasn't sure we could really do this."

"Of course we can! We're free and rich and we're going to America!"

William sighed deeply. "Kind of scary, isn't it?"

Elizabeth shook her head. "I'm not scared at all, and neither should you be." She patted William's chest. "Come on. I can't wait to see the look on Jonathan's face when he realizes we are really doing this. And we have packing to do and plans to make. Once we get to America, maybe we'll see buffalo, maybe real cowboys and Indians. And I can't wait to see the mountains, and Denver." She took hold of William's wrist and pulled him along with her, heading down the hallway and outside, where their driver waited for them. They climbed inside, and Elizabeth turned to her brother. "Our lives are going to change completely, William."

He smiled a bit nervously. "Indeed they will."

"An adventure awaits us." Elizabeth looked out a small window at the crowded street. The sun was shining, but its brightness was blurred by smog, and the air smelled foul today. She couldn't wait to see the beautiful, clean American West and breathe deeply of that air, and to wake up in a new land where Jonathan could no longer control her life, where the threat of being forced to marry a man she didn't love no longer existed.

FOUR

Denver, Colorado Territory, late April, 1870

"Come on, Logan, tell me how you decided to be a bounty hunter."

Logan grinned as he fingered Tess Donavan's hair, then traced his hand down to the cleavage formed where her heavy bosom was pressed against his bare chest. "I don't care to talk about that, so quit asking." He forced back the flash of anger that always hit him when someone pressed him about his past. For a moment, he saw MaryAnne in bed with him instead of this whore. He could hear two-year-old Lilly call for him from the other room…so real that he turned his head to see her.

Reality hit and he rolled Tess over. "I'd rather feel your legs wrapped around me again while I have at you one more time."

Tess laughed. "Well, since you washed off the smell of a sweaty horse and old blood before you came to my bed, I don't mind. You clean up good, Logan Best. You're damn handsome when you wash up and shave."

"I figure when I'm on the trail, nobody cares how clean I am. Taking a bath wastes time when you're hunting a wanted man who tries his best to dodge you."

Tess shook her head. "You've picked a strange occupation, Logan. But to each his own." She wrapped her legs around him. "You gonna pay for the extra poke?"

"You know I will, although Stella keeps raising her prices for you girls. Good thing I collected a lot of money for delivering Sol Weber to Laramie City a couple of weeks ago." He shoved himself into her with a grunt.

Tess let out a gasp of pleasure. "I swear, Logan, your father must have been a big, big man."

Again...the anger. And again, he squelched it. It wasn't Tess's fault she didn't know a thing about his past, or what words triggered his anger. He pounded into her again. "Could be," he managed between thrusts. "I wouldn't...know." More thrusts. "Never... met the man."

"And I...suppose you brought Sol Weber in... dead," Tess said, managing her own words between his thrusts.

"As usual." Logan said no more as he moved in rapid rhythm, bending his head to again taste Tess's breasts while he relished the feel of being inside her. He'd tasted and explored every inch of her, needing to get his fill of a woman before leaving out again to stalk another prey. Tess Donavan was one of his favorites, still young enough to enjoy, although it didn't take much to please a man who'd just spent weeks on the trail. Her blue eyes were still bright, and she kept

herself clean and had all her teeth. Tess seemed to care
about him more than most, although he refused to get
too personal in return.

He kept up the pounding thrusts until every bit of
his release was out of him. He rolled away then with a
sigh. "Fix a pan of water so I can wash myself," he told
Tess. He threw his legs over the edge of the bed and
reached for a cigarette on a nearby stand. Putting it
between his lips and picking up an oil lamp, he leaned
over to light the smoke, inhaling deeply.

Tess rose and pulled on a flimsy robe, then walked
to a table where she kept a pitcher of water and a wash
bowl. "Where you headed next, Logan?"

Logan took a deep drag on the cigarette. "Abilene."

Tess turned in surprise. "*Abilene!* That's a long way
from here."

Logan shrugged. "A little far, but it's straight east,
through Colorado and into Kansas. Here in Denver is
where I advertise men can reach me for my services. I
went to the telegraph office and I found a wire from
some man with the last name of Rinker in Abilene,
asking for help finding a man who beat up on a whore
there and stole a lot of money from his saloon. I wired
him and found out the man Rinker wants still hasn't
been caught. Rinker is offering big money, so I'm
going to see what I can do."

"You ever been to Abilene?"

"Sure I have. I spent a few days there after the war
on my way out here. I was running from…things…
memories, you might say. I decided to see what might
be in store for me west of the Missouri. Had in mind
all along to maybe hunt outlaws. There were plenty

of them to go around after the war ended and folks started heading west…running from things best forgot. Hell, there are plenty of no-goods out here in this lawless land, from Kansas and Oklahoma all the way over the Rockies. I'd heard there was money in finding them, so here I am."

Tess brought over a bowl of water, along with a rag and a bar of lye soap. "Why don't you just be a sheriff or a marshal or something like that?"

Logan shook his head. "Sheriff Bales here in Denver says I could probably get a job as a U.S. Marshal. They're in short supply out here. But I make damn good money as a bounty hunter. I'm not ready to settle into a job that means following orders and staying in one area."

Tess set the bowl of water on the nightstand and wet the rag, then soaped it up. "Don't you ever think about settling?"

Again…the pain…the anger. "I wish people would stop asking me that." He lay back on the bed and listened to piano music and laughter from the saloon below, remembering a time when life was quiet and peaceful…back in Kentucky—a thousand years ago. "Some men are meant to be alone, Tess."

Tess gently washed him. "I suppose. But I sense you're a man who secretly would like to settle. 'Course I'm glad you haven't, because then you'd stop coming to see me. I just wish you would stop by more often."

Logan grinned as Tess dried him off. He sat up, grasping her hair in his hands. "I'll always stop by to see you, Tess. You're my favorite."

She waved him off. "Yeah, right. They all tell me

that. I know I'm losing my youth, Logan Best. Just remember that doesn't mean I don't enjoy a man in my bed, especially one like you. When a woman has been with as many men as I have, it takes a lot of man to really please her." She rose and set the bowl on the stand. "I generally have to fake it with a lot of them." She faced him, putting her hands on her hips. "But not with you. That's for damn sure."

Logan laughed lightly and reached for his long johns. He pulled them on and stood up, walking over to pick up his pants. He stepped into them and reached for his shirt, a clean one he'd just had laundered. It was blue. A woman he'd known once liked him in blue. That was also a thousand years ago. He tucked in the shirt and buckled his belt. After pulling on a leather vest, he sat down in a chair and pulled on socks and dusty, well-worn leather boots. Then began the process of strapping on his many weapons—first, a six-gun in a holster at his side, and a gun belt that held plenty of cartridges. He shoved another six-gun into his belt at the back, and a large hunting knife hung from his pants belt.

"You look like you're going to war," Tess told him.

"Sometimes it just about amounts to that." He reached for his hat. "And it helps to be well armed downstairs when you're playing poker. When you look like a man to be feared, men are less likely to accuse you of cheating."

"*Do* you cheat?"

"Hell no. I go *after* the cheaters, remember?"

Tess smiled, walking up to wrap her arms around

his waist. "You be careful out there, Logan. One man can only do so much."

"I'm always careful. Between the war and what I do now, I've had plenty of practice. You mind if I leave my rifle and shotgun and my extra cartridge belt here while I sit in on a poker game?"

"I don't mind. I'll be down soon." She looked up at him. "You have the most fascinating eyes. I've never seen eyes the color of yours—kind of a bright green, a little gold around the outside of the iris. And when you're angry, they turn a darker green."

"Are they darker green now?"

"No. They're just beautiful. It's too bad those eyes and that handsome face are hidden behind a beard and unwashed hair and trail dust every time you first get here. You're worth more than just out riding alone all over the country, Logan. You're good at what you do. You could work for the Pinkerton Agency, maybe even be the head of your own bunch of detectives. I've heard Pinkerton men were hired to protect President Lincoln during the war."

"Yeah? Well, look where *that* got him. If I'd been part of that, he wouldn't have got himself shot."

Tess couldn't help a laugh. "See what I mean? You're probably right."

Logan smiled and shook his head. "No thanks. I work alone. Besides, you need an education and have to read and write reports to work for a bunch like that. I work by instinct, and that's all I need. I figure wanted posters pretty good, but that's about as far as my reading goes."

"You underestimate yourself, Logan Best. I think

you could learn all that easily enough." Tess patted his chest. "Buy me a drink when I come down?"

He leaned down and kissed her forehead. "You know I will." A tiny part of him cared about the woman and her situation, but that was life out here. And he didn't dare let feelings creep into any part of his being. He was done with feelings, for anyone or anything. Feelings led to pain much worse than a bullet wound or a fist in the eye or a knife in the ribs. This life he led was perfect for a man with no feelings.

He turned and walked out. After tonight he wouldn't see Tess again for weeks, maybe months, maybe never. And that was the way he wanted it.

Don't get attached. Don't ever get attached.

FIVE

Early May, 1870

Elizabeth huddled into her wool coat, pulling the beaver collar around her neck and over her face so she could breathe her own warm breath rather than the cold air of the Atlantic. Tonight, the *SS Abyssinia* rose and fell gently on the now-calm ocean. Yesterday was a wild ride through an Atlantic storm, and she'd spent the day in her room, vomiting and shaking, fearful of meeting the same type of death her parents had met when they'd sailed the Channel to France.

"It was so warm at home when we left," William commented, shivering into his own ankle-length ulster. He wore the detachable cape around his shoulders for extra warmth and pulled his soft felt hat down closer over his ears.

Elizabeth opened her collar and breathed deeply once, then covered her mouth and nose again. "It's cold, but the air smells of freedom to me." She rested her head against William's shoulder and looked up at a black sky that glittered with a million stars. "We did it, William. Thank God we got through the storm and I've gotten over being seasick. Now all that matters is reaching New York and leaving Jonathan behind. I felt like a prisoner in that house."

William hugged her closer. "You don't miss your room? The servants? Your friends?"

"My friends, as you call them, were all spoiled snobs who were friends only because their families ran in the same circle of wealthy people as Jonathan. If I was poor, they wouldn't give me the time of day." She breathed in the cold air again. "Besides, we'll make new friends in America." She moved slightly away from William. "Where do you think we should go first, William? Do you think St. Louis is the right choice?" The wind ruffled some of the curls at the back of her neck, and she retied her beaver hat to keep it closer around her ears.

"I suppose so, but when we get there, we should go see a realtor or someone who can tell us the best way to find a guide to the gold fields in Denver. Maybe we should just go on to Denver first. That's where we'd find the best advice. There will be lawyers and real estate brokers and trail guides and all sorts of people who know the West and can advise us once we get there. A man I met in the smoking lounge told me so."

"We have to be careful, William. I am sure there are all kinds of devious people in those places willing to take advantage of those who don't know what they are about. And we shouldn't make too much ado about our wealth. Be careful whom you tell."

"This man already has investments in some of the

gold mines. He seems very successful, and he is also well spoken. He said Denver was founded on gold discoveries and it's growing fast. Maybe we could build our home there and simply invest in mining or grubstake some of the miners…make our fortune that way without even having to go into the gold fields or other dangerous places. The business opportunities in the growing gold towns are endless, according to this man."

Elizabeth smiled. "It's all so exciting, William. What's the man's name? Is he American, or English?"

"American, but he has an English title. Sir Robert Alexander. He's traveling first class, so he must have money. He's the descendant of English grandparents who sailed to America in eighteen hundred, so he knows the land. And, by the way, he is quite handsome and a pure gentleman. He deals in real estate and was in England to talk to possible investors. He might even be someone who could help us when we get to New York. That's where he lives, but he knows the West." William grinned excitedly. "It appears we aren't the only ones interested in the opportunities in America. He said more and more Englishmen are looking to do just that, so we aren't alone in this." He put an arm around her shoulders. "By the way, Sir Robert said he would like to meet my, uh, 'wife.' I thought it best, since I don't know everything about him, to keep to our story that we are man and wife while we travel."

Elizabeth put her head on his shoulder again, trying to stay warm. "Perhaps this Sir Robert could help us find decent servants who could travel west with us. He surely has connections. I must say, it isn't easy getting dressed and fixing my hair on my own. I'll be glad when I have a personal maid again."

"I'll make sure to look for good help as soon as our ship makes landing."

"Well, before that happens, I would like to meet Sir Robert. Perhaps he could dine with us tomorrow noon?"

"I'll ask him." William hugged her lightly. "I have to say, Liz, that he appears to be the perfect type of man for you. He has that adventurous American spirit, and he's single and wealthy. Perhaps we should eventually tell him the truth—that we are brother and sister. He is certainly nothing like that old sot, Lord Henry Mason. He just might take an interest if he knows you are available."

"I am not thinking about marriage or anything close to it right now. I want to see what I can accomplish on my own first."

"I should warn you that he does like to gamble, but he doesn't seem the type who would gamble away his fortune. Besides, a lot of men like to gamble, and it's pretty obvious he has the money for it." He let go of Elizabeth and huddled into his own coat again. "I need to get you out of this cold. I'll walk you to our room and then see if I can find Sir Robert in the gambling parlor. That will give you time to change and settle into your bed before I get back."

Elizabeth took his arm. "Thank you for seeking out someone who might be able to help us, William. You've been a dependable escort. I feel safe with you, my darling brother, and I'm sorry for all the years of berating insults from Jonathan and how he always made you out to be the lesser man. You have a good heart, and you're as brave and able as any other."

"Why should *you* be sorry? Jonathan is an arrogant brute who never understood either one of us. He has a heart of stone and no desire to live anything but the boring life of all men like him." He guided Elizabeth toward their stateroom. "You're the only person who made me feel loved, Liz. I'll protect you and defend you as much as necessary."

They left the walking deck. "In only about four days we will be in New York," William reminded her, giving her one more hug before sending her into their room. "Lock the door."

"I will." Elizabeth squeezed his hand. "Be careful, and don't stay long."

"I won't."

William left, and Elizabeth removed her hat and coat, then lit an oil lamp on the wall. She walked to a porthole and looked out at a calm sea that glittered from a bright moon.

She thanked God that William had already met someone who could help them once they reached New York. She looked forward to the day she could write Jonathan and tell him how wonderful life was in America. She hoped she would be able to lord it over her big brother about how much wealthier she and William had become from their investments. He thought a woman was incapable of managing such things on her own.

"I'll show you, Jonathan," she said softly. She turned to undress and put on her flannel gown and robe. She climbed into her bed and snuggled into the thick quilts only first-class passengers were afforded. William did not make it back before she fell asleep.

SIX

LOGAN GAZED AT THE VAST PRAIRIE BEFORE HIM. Sometimes it seemed odd that so much trouble could be going on here in the West when there were so few people, most of them in scattered pockets, while in between, the land stretched for hundreds of miles with not a sign of life. He added some buffalo chips to his morning fire and set a coffee pot on the hot coals.

He sat down on his bedroll and watched the flames grow larger as the fresh buffalo chips burned. This was one of those lonely times when memories plagued him, things he usually didn't allow himself to think about, things better left buried. But when a man traveled alone for days at a time with no one to talk to, it was impossible to put away hurtful thoughts. His only companion was Jasper, a fine buckskin that was sturdy and dependable and big enough to carry a tall man with plenty of gear and weapons. He'd trained the gelding to come to him on a whistle, and the horse could run like the wind. That came in damn handy when outlaws were chasing him, rather than the other way around.

Jasper stood untethered in the distance, nibbling at grass. Logan grinned at the memory of how the horse was named. He'd bought it down in Oklahoma from a breeder who let his little three-year-old girl name each horse that he sold. By now, that little girl was six, and he wondered if that man still let her name the horses. Some men probably changed the name once they left, but he'd kept Jasper's name because he couldn't forget that little girl. She'd had blue eyes and blond curls and a wonderful smile…and she reminded him of another little girl…same age…same blond curls… like her mother's.

One thing was for damn sure. He'd never love again. That is, if what he'd had for that short time was love. He'd never experienced it growing up, and now he knew if it *was* love, it hurt way too much.

Jasper suddenly raised his head and whinnied. Logan came alert and grabbed his rifle as he stood up. He could see riders on the horizon. He was in Cheyenne country, but he generally didn't have trouble with the Indians in these parts. Most of them had migrated north to fight with the Sioux against an influx of miners in Montana and the Dakotas, and more had been driven onto reservations or herded into Oklahoma.

He walked over and grasped Jasper's bridle. "Easy boy." He led the horse to the campfire. "Hold on." Setting the rifle aside for the moment and throwing a blanket over Jasper, he hurriedly saddled up in case he might need to make a run for it. He glanced over the top of the horse to see the riders coming closer.

He could make them out now. They were white men. Four of them. He leaned down and quickly rolled up his bedding and tied it onto the horse, then picked up his gun belt and strapped it on, tying the holster strap around his thigh. He threw his extra ammunition belt around the pommel of his saddle, then shoved his shotgun into its sling on one side of the saddle, keeping his rifle with him as he led Jasper over to a small, scrubby bush and tied the horse.

He waited then, keeping the coffee on the fire and leaving his saddle pack of jerked meat and biscuits nearby. Generally, white men meant no trouble and were always glad to share a cup of coffee. But he could read a man's eyes well, and he'd know pretty damn quick if these men were friendly or not. He preferred to wait and talk to them, because that's how a man learned what was going on in other parts of the country. Often, he even ended up with information about a man he might be hunting.

Jasper shuffled his feet and snickered.

"It's okay, boy." He kept his rifle in his left hand and his right hand free to pull his Colt .44 if necessary.

The riders finally made it to within just a few feet. Logan saw a motley bunch of men of various ages. All were armed. Logan noticed one of the horses was limping. Its rider was a heavyset man of maybe thirty years old with a red beard. Logan noticed the man glance at Jasper, and he immediately suspected what they were after. He rested his hand on his six-gun.

The red-bearded man spoke up. "Howdy."

Logan nodded.

"Got coffee?" the bearded man asked.

"Might be. Depends on who you men are and what you're doing out here."

"We could ask the same of you," one of the others said. He was younger and filthy. He wore a stained, wide-brimmed hat, and his teeth were brown when he smiled at Logan. He proceeded to spit tobacco juice to the side in that way a man had of showing his arrogance and supposed manliness.

"Name's Logan Best," Logan answered. "You?"

The younger man glanced at the red-bearded man, as though he knew he should let him do the talking.

"We're just a bunch of friends from up in the Dakotas," the red-bearded man answered. "Went up there to pan for gold, but there's too much Injun' trouble and the gold claims are all taken. Figured we'd head for Abilene or someplace where there's more civilization and maybe jobs."

Logan didn't take his eyes off any of them. "Pardon me, but none of you look like the type who cares about a decent job. You look more like the type who'd rather make money by just taking it. You won't find much on me, so maybe you should just ride on."

The red-bearded man stiffened. "Mister, I don't take kindly to insults. We only stopped by to see if you'd like to sell that horse of yours."

Logan grinned. "Why in hell would I sell my only horse when I'm out here in the middle of nowhere?"

The bearded man chuckled. "On account of the fact that you *are* alone in the middle of nowhere. You must realize if you don't sell us that horse, we can just shoot you and take it."

Logan nodded. "You can try, but you'll regret it."

The younger man snickered. "Hell, mister, there's four of us!"

"I've taken on more in my line of work."

"And what would that be?" a third man spoke up. He was a skeleton with weird eyes that didn't seem to really look straight at a man. Logan guessed him to be in the same age range as the others, all probably twenty to thirty years old, and all of them slovenly. He could actually smell them without even getting close.

"Bounty hunter," Logan answered. "Any of you wanted for anything?"

The bearded man guffawed. "Do you really think we'd tell you if we were?" He laughed again. "Mister, I need that horse, and you're gonna give it over unless you want to be fodder for the buzzards."

"Wait a minute," the younger man with brown teeth said. He sobered, glancing at the bearded man. "Seems like I've heard of a bounty hunter named Logan Best. I heard if a man is wanted dead or alive, he usually kills them."

The bearded man glared at Logan, and Logan gave the man his own hard look of warning.

"That be you?" the bearded man asked.

"It would be. And I suggest all four of you ride on. That's my last warning. My horse isn't for sale, and you damn well aren't going to steal him."

The bearded man shifted in his saddle. "Don't look to me like you have much choice," he told Logan.

"A man always has a choice, and unless you're looking to be the one to feed the buzzards, you'd better ride on like I told you."

The air hung silent. All of Logan's senses came alert. He saw it then—the sudden movement. In a split second, the red-bearded man's gun was drawn, and in that same split second, Logan drew his own six-gun and fired. He fanned his revolver at the other three when they, too, drew on him...but not fast enough. Within two seconds, all four men were on the ground. One of them was still alive...the young one with the brown teeth. He groveled in the deep prairie grass, grabbing some of it and using it to pull himself, as though he could crawl away.

Logan cocked his six-gun and walked up to the one man left alive. "You still want coffee?" he asked.

The young man grunted and managed to turn over. Blood poured from a bullet that had gone through his lower jaw. He could barely open his mouth, but he managed to spit out the word "bastard."

"I likely am," Logan answered. "Never knew my father. Grew up in an orphanage." He fired then, putting a hole in the young man's heart.

Logan proceeded to reload his .44 and put it back in his holster. He walked to each body then, rummaging through pockets to find identification. He packed whatever he could find into his saddlebags, then walked up to the lame horse and shot it. The other three horses whinnied and jerked, one of them running off.

Logan took the reins to the two horses and walked them over to tie them next to Jasper, then walked back to the fire and poured himself some coffee. He took some jerked meat from his food supply and ate it, calmly drank the coffee, and doused the fire with what was left. He packed everything up and untied Jasper and the other horses. As he mounted up, he glanced at the four dead bodies, his gaze resting on the red-bearded man.

"You seemed to be concerned about feeding the buzzards, mister. Now you have your wish. They'll have a royal feast over the next few days."

He patted Jasper's neck, a little part of him remembering when he was a different sort of man. Before the war, Logan Best would never so easily kill four men and leave them to rot in the sun. That part of him who used to know how to love and who respected another man's life was gone. Sometimes he wished he could find what was missing, but he didn't know how. The hurt and hatred ran too deep.

Besides, these men would have done no better for him if things had turned out differently. The code out here was survival, and there were no rules about that.

"Maybe we'll get lucky when we reach Abilene, Jasper, and learn that one or all of these men were wanted."

He rode off, leaving the unburied bodies where they lay.

SEVEN

ELIZABETH STIRRED, AT FIRST NOT SURE WHAT HAD woken her until she sat up and nearly fell out of her bed. The *SS Abyssinia* was pitching and rolling wildly!

"William?" she called.

There came no reply. How could her brother sleep through this? She quickly threw aside her blankets and rose, stumbling a little as she retied her robe. She reached over to wake William, but the rolling of the ship caused her to fall over his bed.

It was empty!

"William?" she called again.

She sat up straight and looked around, trying to see him, but the earlier bright moon was now covered with storm clouds, and the room was too dark.

"William!" She yelled his name this time.

Still no reply. She managed to get to her feet and stumble to the wall lantern. She took a match from the container, leaned against the wall for support, and managed to light the wick. She struggled against the terrible pitching of the ship to replace the glass chimney. "William!" she cried out again.

Another drastic roll caused her to fall onto her bed. She lay there a moment, clinging to the iron side supports to keep from being thrown off as she looked around the room. Memories of her parents' deaths from drowning in a shipwreck engulfed her still-confused mind. Was she going to die the same way they did?

And where was William? She managed to stumble her way over to her small, overnight carpetbag where she kept a pocket watch that once belonged to her father. Another wave caused her to fall onto her rump as she fished around in the bag for the watch. She finally found it and pulled it out to look at the time.

One a.m.! William never stayed out this late. It was nine o'clock when he'd left to see Sir Robert. Up until now, her brother had been almost too protective, seating her with the only other two women on the ship at mealtimes, always staying with her when she walked the promenade deck and keeping other men away from her. She'd not even met Sir Robert yet. William would never leave her alone for this long, most certainly not after the storm hit.

She shoved the watch back into the bag, then gasped when someone suddenly pounded on the door to her cabin.

"Lady Elizabeth! Are you all right?"

"Who is it?" she nearly screamed above the roaring ocean storm. She got to her knees and pulled herself up by grabbing a corner post of her bed.

"My name is Robert Alexander," the man yelled in return. "I'm a friend of your husband's. I must speak with you!"

Alexander! The very man William had gone to see. "Where is William?" she screamed. "I will not open the door to anyone but my bro—" She checked herself. "My husband!"

"I'm sorry, Lady Elizabeth, but that is why I've come here," the man yelled. "I know you're alone and must be terrified! Please let me in before I am washed overboard! I assure you, I mean you no harm!"

Elizabeth drew her robe close around her neck. Her heart pounded with the fear of what might have happened to William, and with uncertainty about whom she should trust.

The ship rolled again. "Please, Lady Elizabeth!" Robert again yelled. "I am soaked from rain and waves! You can trust me. Your husband and I struck up a friendship, and I cared very much about him!"

Cared? He'd spoken the word in past tense.

Elizabeth grabbed William's robe from a hook on the wall and managed to pull it on over her own, wanting to cover herself as much as possible. The ship rolled again and slammed her against the corner wall. She cried out from pain in her arm, then clung to furniture as she made her way over to the door. She opened it, and a man quickly stumbled inside. He took the door from her hand and closed it against the wind.

Elizabeth stepped back, grabbing hold of a bed post again. She stared wide-eyed at a very big, tall man with dark, wet hair that was plastered to his head and face. He pushed some of it behind his ears as he got his bearings. Water dripped everywhere from his soaked clothing. "Lady Elizabeth, something terrible has happened and you must be told."

Elizabeth stumbled a little again, and the man reached out and grasped her arm to steady her. "I'm so sorry," he told her, "but I come with bad news."

Elizabeth looked up into his dark eyes. "Is it William? Where is he?"

"Lady Elizabeth, I am Sir Robert Alexander, from America. I struck up a friendship with your husband over these past three days, and I gave him advice about land investments in the American West. I am so sorry for what has happened. I am at your service and can help you get settled with the right people when we reach New York."

The ship pitched again, but not as wildly as before. It seemed the storm was growing less violent now, and it was easier to hear Robert.

"Get me settled? Why would you have to do that?"

Robert let go of her arm and stepped back from her, as though to assure her he was a gentleman. "Again, I'm so sorry, my lady, but…your husband… has been washed overboard."

Elizabeth took a moment to let the news sink in. *No! It can't be! Not so many hours ago, William was with me and so happy.* "But…there was no storm when he left me to talk to you, and he promised to come right back."

Robert studied her with sincere regret in his eyes as the ship began to more gently rise and fall. "My lady, your husband and I were having a good visit and lost track of time," Robert told her. His voice was deep but had a gentle tone to it. "I was telling William about investment opportunities in America. Then we gambled a little and…I fear William had a bit too much brandy. By the time we finished talking and playing some cards, the storm had rolled in. These storms come up so quickly on the ocean, and at night it's very difficult to even see one coming."

Elizabeth put a hand to her stomach. This couldn't be happening!

"William was very worried about you, so he started back to your room," Robert continued. "I walked with him because the ship was rolling badly and he was a bit unsteady on his feet. A wave suddenly hit us both, and William slipped. The next thing I knew, he was overboard. I shouted that there was a man overboard, but the men handling the ship couldn't hear me because of the wind and rain. I couldn't find any kind of life preserver, and it would have done no good if I had. It is pitch-black out there, and almost instantly, I lost sight of William."

Elizabeth began to tremble. No! It couldn't be! William. Poor William. This was her fault. It was her idea to come to America. "It…can't be true," she cried.

"I'm so sorry, but it *is* true."

"But…William had vowed not to drink on this voyage. He never breaks his promises to me. And he…he wouldn't have stayed so long, knowing I was waiting for him."

Robert shook his head. "Lady Elizabeth, when a man is filled with the excitement of planning a new future, time goes by swiftly. I'm sure he didn't realize how long we talked. It was a wonderful conversation. And he told me all about you and how you share his dream." He reached out for her. "Please, sit down on one of the cots. When the storm is over, I'll see that the cook fixes you some hot tea and brings it to you.

You're all alone now, and you will need protection and advice when we get to New York. I truly want to help you."

Elizabeth shook her head. "It...can't be true." Her mind reeled with her situation. Alone. She would arrive in America alone and unescorted. She felt things going dark, felt herself slipping to the floor. *William! William!*

Someone lifted her. She felt herself being laid on a bed. A dark figure loomed over her. The ship seemed to be heaving and falling in an even slower rhythm now. "Please lie still," a voice told her. She felt blankets being pulled over her. "I'll be back as soon as possible with something to help you sleep and with some hot tea. I'll watch over you until we land in New York. Then you will have to decide what you will do next. If you wish to go back to England, I will escort you. I go there often."

Who was speaking? Someone tucked her in tightly, and then she was barely aware that whoever it was opened the door and left.

Alone. She was alone. Had William really drowned? Why hadn't he come right back? He always came right back. Should she believe he'd really gotten drunk and had fallen overboard? It was true that he never could handle liquor well, but he'd sincerely promised not to drink on this voyage. Could she trust the man who called himself Sir Robert Alexander? He seemed quite the gentleman and quite sincere.

She turned over and burst into bitter weeping, burying her face into her pillow. Her excitement and her dreams were shattered.

This was her brother Jonathan's fault. He was the one who'd kicked poor William out of the house. William would still be alive if not for Jonathan. Now what was she to do? She had no choice but to go on to America, for that's where this ship was headed and there was no going back. Nor did she want to. She hated Jonathan with every fiber of her being.

She vowed that somehow she would survive this. She would not go home…not to Jonathan…not to Lord Henry Mason. She would live the dream…for William.

EIGHT

LOGAN TIED HIS HORSE AND THE OTHER TWO TO A hitching post in front of the sheriff's office in Abilene. The air was heavy with the smell of cattle dung from pens near the railroad depot. Since the Union Pacific had completed its connection between the East and West coasts just a year ago, it was becoming more and more common for cattle to be shipped by train to slaughterhouses in Chicago and Omaha, which was a boon for ranchers and opened towns like Abilene for cattle auctions and buyers from the East.

Logan didn't doubt that ranching would be the "new" gold here in the West, with its vast grasslands and now a railroad that could transport cattle faster than herding them.

The weather had suddenly turned hotter than usual for May. He removed his hat and wiped at sweat on his forehead with his shirtsleeve, noticing how much Abilene was growing. Horses and wagons busied the streets, and there were more stores and saloons than the last time he was here just a few months ago. Then it was simply a new railroad stop, but it was sure to get even bigger, and he smiled at the thought of what a wild town it must be when drovers came in after weeks or months on the trail. He wouldn't mind being here for that. In fact, most ranchers should be in the middle of spring roundup right now, so he guessed within a month those ranchers closest to Abilene would be arriving, with others all through the summer.

"The West is growing fast, Jasper," he said to his horse as he patted its rump. He'd have to put all these horses up as soon as he delivered the belongings and identities of the men he'd killed to the sheriff. He brushed trail dust from his shirt and pants, then banged his hat against the hitching post to knock dust from that, too. He must not smell too good. His shirt and hat were both sweat-stained, and he needed a bath, a shave, and a haircut.

He unhooked the dead men's saddlebags from the two horses and carried everything inside the sheriff's office, dropping them on the desk and looking around the empty office. A man on a cot in one of three jail cells turned over and glanced at him. He was a disheveled mess, his eyes bloodshot. "Who the hell are you?"

Logan walked closer to the cell. "Name's Logan Best. Where's the sheriff?"

The prisoner rubbed at his eyes and sat up. "Shit, I don't know." He looked Logan over. "Logan Best. I've heard the name. Ain't you some kind of bounty hunter or something?"

"That would be me." Logan took a cigarette paper from his shirt pocket, a pouch of tobacco from a pants pocket, and started rolling himself a cigarette.

"Any chance you can roll me one, mister?" the

prisoner asked. "I just woke up from a bad drunk. I don't even remember anybody bringing me here. I could use a drink of water and a cigarette." He stretched his arms and rose.

Logan finished rolling the cigarette, then walked over to a bucket of water and dipped a ladle into it. He carried it over to the prisoner, who gladly took it and drank it all. "Thanks."

Logan handed him the cigarette and took a match from the same shirt pocket where he kept the papers. He struck it and helped the prisoner light the cigarette, then blew it out and rolled a smoke for himself.

"The sheriff is probably over at one of the saloons," the prisoner told Logan. "He ain't the best at his job, but out here folks have to take what they can get. His name is Adam White, and he's one of the few men in town who was brave enough to pin on a badge. You ever been here when all hell breaks loose?"

Logan took a deep drag on his cigarette. "Nope. I'm usually out in the middle of nowhere, hunting down wanted men." He turned as someone came inside. The man was perhaps in his late thirties and had a pot belly and a long, black beard. He looked Logan over, his gaze resting on the .44 Logan wore low on his hip.

"Somethin' I can do for you, mister?" He glanced at the prisoner. "Well, Hank, I see you finally woke up. This man here give you that cigarette?"

"Sure did, Adam, and I sure as hell needed it. This man here is Logan Best, bounty hunter."

Adam looked Logan over again, then nodded to him. "I'm Adam White, the sheriff here. I take it you're here on business?"

"I am."

The sheriff walked around his desk, noticing the saddlebags on it. "These for me?"

"They are. There is identification inside. The owners of the bags are all dead. I also had to shoot one of their horses that was lame. Another horse ran off, and I kept the two that remained. I brought them here for you to dispose of however you want, although I need an extra horse for a packhorse once I leave. I wouldn't mind keeping one of them."

Sheriff White frowned. "How did the four men die?"

"I shot them."

"All four of them?"

"Jesus," the prisoner muttered.

"Had no choice," Logan answered. "They were fixing to kill me and steal my horse. I brought this stuff in to report it and find out if any of them might end up being wanted men. If so, I'll collect the bounty on them."

White frowned. "Did you bury them?"

"Hell no. They meant to kill me and leave me for buzzard meat, so I figured that's how I'd leave *them*. Why should I go to all the trouble of digging holes deep enough to bury four bodies after what they intended for me?"

White just stared at Logan a moment while the prisoner chuckled and shook his head. "I sure am glad I've got no bounty on me," he said.

White removed his hat and hung it on a hook behind him. He rubbed at the back of his neck, then opened a desk drawer and threw some wanted posters on the desk. "Look through those. See if any of the names match. I guess it's my job to figure out what the hell to do with their identification and money and personals. Tell me where they are, and I'll send some men out to bury them."

Logan picked up the posters and sat down across from the sheriff's desk to look through them. "You know a man by the name of Sam Rinker?"

"Why?" the sheriff asked.

"He sent a wire to Denver. That's where I check for mail and messages. Those who know of me know to send notices there. I saw one from Sam Rinker, looking for someone to hunt a man who stole from him." He scanned through the posters, recognizing one face. He handed that one to Sheriff White. "This was one of them. I'm not good at reading, but that one looks like one of the four I killed. He has the same kind of beard and eyes. If the poster says he had a red beard, then that's him for sure, so I'll let you tell me."

White studied the poster. "Yup. Says he has a red beard. Name's Bob Adler, and he's wanted for murder and bank robbery. A hundred dollars bounty on him, dead or alive."

"Well, then, if you find the same name in the IDs I just gave you, I'll take the hundred bucks." Logan scanned the rest of the posters again while the sheriff looked through the saddlebags. Logan had seen enough posters to recognize the words "bank," "murder," "rape," and "robbery," not because he could read, but because they were such common words on posters. Sometimes a man was wanted for simple things, like abandoning his wife or drunkenness or petty theft, sometimes for cheating at cards. Those bounties were usually pretty small. "I don't see any of the rest of those men here," he told White after going through every poster. He kept the cigarette between his lips as he spoke. "I'll leave it up to you to find relatives of the men I killed."

"Gee, thanks," the sheriff answered. He met Logan's gaze. "Sam Rinker owns a saloon down the street, the Cattle Stop. He's probably wanting you to find a man who beat up one of his whores after the saloon was closed, then went downstairs and broke into the back office and stole a lot of money and rode off in the night. Rinker thinks he might be part of a gang of men who have been robbing other places along the railroad towns, maybe even involved in stealing women to sell farther west and in Mexico. This man bragged to the whore about such things—insulted her—said she'd be worth nothing because she's too used up."

Logan smoked quietly for a moment. "How long ago did this happen?"

"Heck, it's been two or three weeks now. I don't know how in hell you could track him after all that time."

"You'd be surprised. A man like that gets remembered by other people. If I get a good description of him and his horse, I'll try hard to find him, depending on what Rinker wants to pay." Logan quickly scanned through the posters once more, then folded them for possible future use. "Seems like the West attracts all the losers from back east."

"Yeah, well since the war ended and the railroad came through, people of all walks of life are coming out here: freed slaves, lots of immigrants, men running from the law or from a wife back east," White told him. "Then we have the leftover Chinamen and Irishmen who worked on the railroad, Indians who've decided to try to mingle with the whites and give up fighting, and the damn cattle drovers. You name it, it's come west—outlaws and decent folks alike. And with little law to hold it back, crime abounds everywhere. When the drovers come to town, I don't even try to walk out there and stop them from their wild celebrating. I'd get myself shot for nothing. Most of them don't mean much harm, but a drunk man, Christian or not, can do some pretty stupid things."

Logan nodded. "True. I've done some pretty stupid things myself." He rose. "Guess I'll go find this Rinker guy. How long will it take you to come up with my hundred dollars?"

"Come by tomorrow. Bank is closed now. I have to wait till they open, and I have to send a telegram to the authorities in St. Louis to get their okay. Did you come in on the train?"

"Nope. Costs extra for horses, and besides, I like to ride alone. More peaceful. Plus, you can track a man easier by meeting people along the way and asking questions. It's not so much a matter of speed when it comes to finding a man, Sheriff. It's more a matter of listening to people, keeping your eyes and ears open, and trusting your own instincts."

"Must get pretty lonely out there."

Logan shrugged. "I've been alone all my life. Nothing new."

"Never settled? Never got caught up in the war?"

Logan rose. "I don't talk about that." He stuffed the wanted posters into his pants at the waist. "I'll go find Rinker and then I'll be back here tomorrow noon for the money. Do you think it's okay if I keep one of those extra horses I brought back with me?"

"I'll write something up showing you legally own the horse." Sheriff White also rose. "There's a rooming house up the street—good food and clean sheets."

Logan grinned. "I think I'll see what's upstairs over the Cattle Stop. Might find some pretty good accommodations there and somebody to keep me warm tonight."

Both White and the prisoner laughed. "Oh, you'll be plenty warm, all right," the prisoner said. "Hey, Sheriff, when are you gonna let me out of here? I can show the man where to find Rinker."

"Never you mind. He'll be fine on his own. You have to stay in that cell till eight o'clock."

"Shit, that fight I got into was last night. I'm sober now."

"Makes no difference. Jail time is jail time. I'm going outside with this man to see which horse he wants to keep."

Both men started out. "I also need to know where the livery is so I can put up my horses for the night," Logan told the sheriff.

"Down at the end of the street, on the right," White replied.

"Not a bad way to make a living, Logan," the prisoner called out. "You kill four men and you get a hundred bucks and a horse out of it. I slave away on a farm every day and it takes a year for me to earn that much."

Logan waved him off and walked out with the sheriff. *I had a farm once, too, and I didn't mind working it. I didn't make much either, but I was a happier man than I'd ever been in my life.* That all changed…after the war.

NINE

"Mrs. Baylor? Are you up?" The voice came from outside Elizabeth's cabin door. "I have the captain with me. He needs to make a report on your husband's accident."

Elizabeth rubbed at eyes swollen from crying. She'd managed to dress, realizing that someone was bound to want to talk to her this morning. She walked to a small mirror on the wall and saw how terrible she looked. There were circles under her eyes, and her hair was a disheveled mess. She'd managed to keep it decently pinned into the upswept style it was in when she'd left London, but because of the ocean winds and all her tossing and turning last night, it had come completely undone.

What did it matter? William was dead. Dead! She still couldn't believe it, but there was his bed, the blankets wrinkled from when she'd fallen onto it last night in the storm, but still made, nonetheless. He really, really had not come back. He really, really was gone from her life. She would have to report his death to Jonathan, but she hated giving him the satisfaction of saying "I told you so." Besides that, he might try coming for her, or, more likely, for William's share of the money. She had to get out of his reach.

"Mrs. Baylor?"

She isn't *Mrs.* Baylor. She would probably have to admit that, too, so the record of William's death would be right. Her stomach tightened. She'd planned this whole trip thinking William would always be at her side. Now she was alone and unescorted, forced to trust a man she knew nothing about.

Her heart was so heavy over William that she simply could not gather her thoughts. "Just a moment," she answered. She quickly pulled back the sides of her hair and secured it with combs before opening the door.

There stood Sir Robert Alexander and the captain of the ship, whom she knew to be Steven Dorey. Sir Robert was far more handsome than she remembered by the dim lamplight the night before, and she'd been too upset to truly notice or care. "Gentlemen? I apologize for my appearance, but this news about William is almost unbearable for me."

"May we come inside?" the captain asked. "I have brought ink and a pen and paper so I can get the details about your husband."

Elizabeth stepped aside to allow them in. "I prefer to remain standing, since you two will need to sit somewhere, and there are only the two small beds to sit on. I made them up the best I could. I am accustomed to servants who do such things for me." She folded her arms nervously. "The quarters here are fine, Captain. My husband and I could have taken a bigger liner with better first-class accommodations, but we chose this slightly cheaper voyage because we wanted to save our personal funds."

"Of course." The captain sat down on William's bed and set a bottle of ink on a small table between the beds. Robert sat down on the opposite bed.

"I'm sorry about what happened, Mrs. Baylor," the captain told her with sincerity. "Please be assured that I will give you a free voyage back to London if you choose to go back home."

"No, I…I am going to stay in America until I decide where to go next. I need time to get used to this huge change in my life."

"I will set you up in the finest hotel, Mrs. Baylor," Robert told her. "And I have a sister in New York who can show you the best shops and introduce you to some other women of prominence. And whenever you need an escort, I will accommodate you."

Elizabeth nodded. "Thank you. But don't you have a wife and family?"

"No. I'm a widower with no children, so I understand some of what you are going through."

"I…" Elizabeth hesitated. "I'm not so sure you do." She turned her attention to the captain. "Captain Dorey, William was not my husband. He was my brother. You should know that for your report. We posed as husband and wife because we felt it would afford me even more protection."

Robert rose. "Mrs. Baylor—I mean, Lady Elizabeth—is that how I should address you?"

"Yes."

"Well, Lady Elizabeth, since you are truly an unattached young woman in a new country, you will most certainly need an escort. If you will allow it, I'd like to be that escort. A young woman unfamiliar with a city like New York should not venture into such a place without help and advice, as well as protection. I can provide all three. I live there with my sister and her family. I can introduce you to a banker who will help you safely put away any money and valuables you have until you decide your next move. I'm sure once I help get you settled and you meet my sister and her friends, you will feel much better about all of this."

"Thank you." Elizabeth wished she could fully trust the man. After all, he was "Sir" Robert Alexander, and a man didn't earn that title lightly. And William had quickly befriended him and seemed to like him. "I appreciate your offer, Sir Robert," she told him.

The captain wrote something down. "Your brother's full name and age, Lady Elizabeth?"

"William Leroy Baylor, twenty-two," she answered. "He was born March second, eighteen forty-eight. His death should be reported to our older brother, Lord Jonathan Baylor. I will give you his address. Jonathan should also be told that I have someone helping me get settled and that he need not come for me."

The captain frowned. "Are you sure? You are very young and beautiful and unattached, Lady Elizabeth, and you will be in an unknown city as well. I should think you'd *want* your brother to come for you."

"No. We…had a falling out. I prefer not to go back or to have him come here. Besides, I am of age and have the right to make my own choices."

The captain sighed. "As you wish. At least you have Sir Robert here to help you out for the time being.

It is imperative that you have protection and that you don't go out alone in a place like New York."

"I understand that."

"I'll make out a full report. You will need to sign it, to verify this is all true. Will your brother in London recognize your signature?"

"Yes. It's on all the legal paperwork I signed in order to—" Elizabeth hesitated. Perhaps she should not reveal that she traveled with a good deal of money. "In order to free me from my brother's control. My parents died in a shipwreck on the English Channel, which is how William and I ended up in Jonathan's charge."

"Oh, that is so sad," Sir Robert said. "The storm last night must have terrified you, and now your brother has also died at sea. I'm sure you will be glad to plant your feet on solid ground again."

"I most certainly will."

The captain asked Elizabeth for detailed information and wrote it down. "I'm sure you want to be left alone until we land in New York," he told her as he rose. "I will have your food brought to you here in your room. No one will disturb you until we make landing."

"Thank you, Captain."

"I'll have a steward bring you some tea, and you can tell him what you would like for brunch. He told me you didn't eat the biscuits he brought you last night."

"I couldn't eat. I was too upset, but thank you for the tea. That did help." Elizabeth glanced at Sir Robert again. She saw nothing but kindness in his eyes. "And I appreciate your offer, Sir Robert. I'll need a personal maid once I get settled. Do you know of one who could attend me?"

"Of course. My sister and her family have several servants. She will be glad to share one for a while, considering your terrible misfortune."

"Thank you." Tears wanted to come again over William. Elizabeth could still hardly believe any of this was real. "I would like both of you to leave now. Captain Dorey, please tell the steward to bring some biscuits and jam with the tea. I feel awfully weak and light-headed. I think that this time I should try to eat after all."

Sir Robert quickly approached her and grasped her arm, leading her to her bed. "You sit down right here, and I'll see that you get your tea and biscuits," he told her, patting her shoulder.

"Thank you."

"I am so sorry for your misfortune," he told her.

"I know. Thank you so much, Sir Robert."

"I truly did all I could to rescue William, but it was just hopeless." Robert stood up and turned to follow the captain out of the room, but when he reached the doorway, he glanced back at Elizabeth once more, his eyes moving over her in a way that made Elizabeth a bit uncomfortable. She dismissed the feeling, attributing it to her frightened and vulnerable state. The man had been so mannerly and gracious through her ordeal. He obviously had money and knowledge and was an experienced businessman. He gave her a wonderful smile that set her at ease, then followed the captain out, closing the door behind him.

Elizabeth bent over and shed more tears as the awful news hit her again, coming in waves of deep grief. William really was dead. She really was alone.

TEN

LOGAN ORDERED EGGS AND BACON. HE'D MANAGED TO find a bathhouse and a barber, figuring this next trip might take quite a while, so he'd better clean up before he had to scrape off the dirt with a knife. The man who'd waited on him returned with his order and poured him some coffee. "That's Sam Rinker coming in now, sir," he told Logan.

Logan looked up from his plate to see a nice-looking man. He didn't look like the type who'd own a saloon with whores upstairs, but so be it. Apparently, he owned other businesses in town, and a place where men could drink and gamble and sleep with whores was just one of them. After all, this was a cow town. Those were the kinds of things that made a man rich.

Rinker was of medium build and height, certainly shorter than Logan's six-foot frame. Logan rose to shake his hand. "Mr. Rinker? I'm Logan Best."

Rinker removed his hat and looked him over. "Well, I think I would have known who you are just by looking at you," he told Logan. "You certainly look like a man who knows his way around places where there is no law. The way you wear that gun on your hip tells me that." He grinned and hung his hat on the post of his chair, then sat down across from Logan. He asked the waiter to bring more coffee. "I see you found Drovers. Best steaks in town. Did my girl tell you about this place?"

"Yes, sir. She was real nice. I had a very pleasant night."

Rinker laughed lightly. "I hire only the best for the drovers who come through here, but if they abuse one of the girls, they get thrown out and sometimes go to jail."

Logan studied the man's common looks, his dark hair, his neat suit and paisley vest. Rinker spoke with a strong southern drawl. "Pardon me, Mr. Rinker, but you don't look the part of a man who'd be in the business of serving drinks and women to others."

Rinker smiled. "Mr. Best, I'm just one of those men who saw an opportunity in the West and took it. I used to own a plantation in the South. I lost all of it, as well as a wife and two daughters, to raiders during the war, so I don't much care what anyone thinks of what I do now."

Logan nodded. "I can understand that. I know what it's like to lose a wife and kid and not give a damn about anything after that. We have a lot in common."

Rinker sobered. "Apparently so." He drank some of the coffee the waiter had poured for him, then leaned back with a sigh. "I'm sorry I couldn't meet with you until this morning. I just got back an hour ago by train from Grinnel, where I made arrangements with a man who will run a supply store there for me. One thing I *didn't* lose in the war was my money. I never thought from the beginning that the South could win that war. I quickly moved my funds to the North. How about you? Did you fight for either side?"

Logan spooned some sugar into another cup of coffee. "I don't talk about anything to do with the war, Mr. Rinker. It's over, and that's that."

Rinker nodded. "I understand." He drank more of his coffee while Logan finished his eggs. "At any rate, I'm not a bad man, Mr. Best—"

"Logan. Just call me Logan."

"All right then, Logan. As I was saying, this saloon is just another business for me, and if I was a bad man, I wouldn't care how the girls upstairs are treated. But I *do* care, and one of them was beaten pretty badly three weeks ago by a man called Ben Rosell. He was just passing through, bragged downstairs in the bar about how he had plenty of money to gamble with and had business connections both in New York and in Denver. Never said exactly what he did for a living. Apparently, his occupation is stealing, because by the time Daisy came around the next morning and reported what had happened, Rosell had broken into my office downstairs and stolen four thousand dollars, then disappeared." Rinker's eyes grew darker. "I want my money back, Logan. And I want that man arrested for what he did to Daisy. I'll pay one thousand dollars—dead or alive. I'm told that you prefer dead, and that's fine with me, as long as you have the right man. Daisy seems to think he's involved with some other men who rob trains and coaches and kidnap and sell women. He laughed and joked about it when he was with her, then told her she wouldn't fill the bill for the kind of women he looked for because she was a whore. He said men who buy women want the fresh ones. I guess when she called him a few names for messing with innocent young women, he started beating on her. Choked her while he was doing it so she couldn't scream out for help. He choked her for so long that she passed out."

Logan finished his last piece of bacon and washed it down with the coffee. He leaned back then and lit a pre-rolled cigarette. "Sounds like a real son-of-a-bitch. What does he look like?"

"Daisy said he's a short man, shorter than I am, and I'm only five-foot-nine inches. The men he gambled with said he was a fancy dresser and liked to brag about being rich. They said he had kind of wide lips, at least they looked that way because he had a short chin. Black hair and likes to wear a top hat."

Logan nodded. "You've given me a lot to go on, but a thousand dollars sounds like a lot just to get back four thousand."

"It's not the money, Logan. It's the principal of the thing. I hate thieves and have no use for men who beat on women. Daisy can tell you more about Rosell, and I feel I should warn you that by the way he talked, the man works with others, so this could be more dangerous than you think. You could be going up against more than one man."

Logan shrugged. "Nothing new. I killed four men on my way here. They threatened to steal my horse." He smiled a little, and Rinker raised his eyebrows in surprise.

"All four at the same time?"

Logan took a long drag on his cigarette. "Well, within a half second of each other. They didn't understand that I don't take kindly to having my horse taken from me without my permission."

Rinker chuckled. "Well, then, I have a feeling I picked just the right man."

"I'll do my best, but I'd like to talk to Daisy."

"She's staying with a widow woman outside of town until her face heals. She's ashamed to let anyone see it, but I'm sure she'll talk to you since you'll be going after the man."

Logan nodded. "I'd like to see her today, because I want to stock up on supplies and leave out first light tomorrow."

"Fine. I'll pay you five hundred dollars now so you can keep supplied. I'll pay the rest when you get back."

Logan frowned. "How do you know you can trust me?"

Rinker rose. "Word gets around, Logan, and I have connections. I found out who's the law in Denver. When I got your wire from there, I contacted him and asked if he knew of you. He vouched for you and told me how to contact another lawman he knows up in Laramie, Wyoming. Said that man knows you better—a lawman by the name of Jack Teller. Teller said you were honest and one of the best at what you do."

"Yeah, I know Jack well. And I find it interesting how fast people can get in touch with each other now—Laramie, Wyoming being so far from Abilene.

You were just lucky the Cheyenne are mostly up in the Dakotas now, or you might not have got through. Indians have a habit of chopping down telegraph poles."

"Well, the way the West is growing, the Indians are going to all be pushed onto reservations eventually. I feel sorry for them, but we both know more and more settlement is coming, especially with the railroad going through the heart of the West. It's too bad, but that's how it is."

Logan nodded. "There have been times when the Indians actually helped me find someone. They're the best damn trackers a man could ask for. Some of them work as scouts for the army now."

"I've heard." Rinker put out his hand, and Logan took it. "Let's go see Daisy and then I'll take you over to the bank and get you that five hundred dollars. You can wire me right here in Abilene with your progress. If I don't hear from you every couple of weeks, I'll figure you're on the trail someplace where you can't get to a telegraph. If I go a full month without hearing from you, I guess I'll have to figure the worst."

"You'll hear from me." Logan shook his hand, then took his hat from the corner of his chair and put it on as Rinker did the same. He laid money on the table, and the two men walked together to the door. "The way the West is growing, things will get more civilized out here in time," Logan commented. "It might even get too civilized for men like me. I expect someday I'll be required to bring my man back alive rather than dead. That always makes things a little more difficult."

They walked through the door. "Well, by then you'll have met some nice woman and settled down, and it won't matter," Rinker told him.

"Farthest thing from my mind," Logan answered. *Damn, when are people going to quit talking to me about settling?*

Both men headed down the street toward the house where Daisy was staying. Logan noticed a curly-headed little girl skipping beside her mother along the boardwalk across the street.

There came that inner pain again. He wondered if it would ever go away.

ELEVEN

ELIZABETH STUDIED HERSELF IN A WALL MIRROR. Thanks to Sir Robert's sister, Helen Jennings, she had a personal attendant who'd done her hair for her, and she was pleased with how she looked. She would normally wear one of her finest dresses for a planned meeting today with Sir Robert, but for now, she wore black out of respect for poor William's death. Helen had taken her shopping at Dillard's for two black and one gray dress. She was in mourning and didn't feel right wearing any of the more colorful garments she'd brought with her from London.

She still had trouble believing her brother was gone and wasn't sure how she could have handled any of this without the help of Sir Robert and his sister. Helen's husband was a wealthy New York City attorney. They and Robert had insisted she stay at their lovely home in the upper west side of the city, but Elizabeth didn't feel comfortable there because Sir Robert lived in the same house.

With some of her own money, she'd chosen to stay at a hotel on Fifth Avenue. Sir Robert insisted she have a personal servant, and Helen provided one of her own, a full-time maid named Elsie Flag. Helen paid for a room right next to Elizabeth's, where Elsie could stay so Elizabeth had help whenever she needed it.

Helen could not have been kinder. Neither could Sir Robert, who was turning out to be quite the gentleman and proficient at business as well. They were meeting today for lunch, where Sir Robert would lay out his suggested plan for her trip west.

She used a hand mirror to study the back and sides of her upswept hairdo. Elsie had turned out to be very talented in styling hair. She'd twisted Elizabeth's hair into layers decorated with glittery combs. Tiny sausage curls hung at each side of her face, and a simple black pillbox hat was pinned to the crown of her head.

Elizabeth pulled on black gloves to match her black dress, thinking that it was time to leave New York and pursue her dream of heading west. She felt she owed it to William now to do what they'd planned to do together. She loved New York City and the luxury she'd enjoyed here, but she still wanted to explore the American West she'd read so much about, not just in honor of William, but because his death made it even more important than when she first left London. Besides, this city had turned out to be as smoggy and busy and noisy as London. The supposed healthy air and wide-open spaces of western America sounded fascinating.

Most of her money remained hidden in the bottom of one of her trunks and had not been touched. She'd hidden her mother's jewelry in the same trunk, still fearing Jonathan might show up any day to demand

William's share of the estate, which was why, after being here only six days, she'd told Sir Robert she wanted to continue her journey as originally planned, and as soon as possible. She'd seen all she cared to see of New York.

Sir Robert had escorted her to most of the important places on sightseeing trips, as well as showing her the carriage and wagon-making factory he and his sister had inherited from their father.

Others run the business so Helen can stay home with her children and I can travel to visit customers and find new ones, he'd explained. *Thank goodness I happened to be on the* Abyssinia *when you lost your brother.*

Yes, Elizabeth thought. It seemed fate was on her side. She would have been in a very vulnerable state right now if not for Sir Robert's help.

She turned when Elsie knocked on the adjoining door. "Come in." She stepped back and turned in a circle when Elsie entered the room. "How do I look, even though I'm wearing black?" she asked.

Elsie, a middle-aged widow woman, looked her over and smiled. "You are an elegant, beautiful woman, Lady Elizabeth."

Elizabeth walked to the dressing table and picked up a necklace. "Come. Put this on me, will you? It's a pearl-and-diamond necklace that belonged to my mother." She sat down in front of the mirror at her dressing table while Elsie hooked the necklace at the back of her neck. It hung perfectly at the throat of the white-lace bodice of her dress.

"It's lovely," Elsie told her. She suddenly frowned. "Lady Elizabeth, a single young woman of your stature shouldn't run around the country unmarried. It's dangerous enough out west. I will worry about you when you leave."

"But you shouldn't, Elsie. Sir Robert will be with me." Elizabeth looked at Elsie in the mirror.

"Well, he *is* a rich man and a gentleman," Elsie answered, "and he's never given his sister any trouble over the fortune and businesses they inherited from their father, but I feel I should warn you he's quite the gambler, in case you have intentions of marrying him."

"Oh, I'm far from ready for marriage," Elizabeth answered. "I didn't come to America for that. In fact, part of the reason I left London was to be independent, and to be free from my older brother trying to force me into marrying someone I didn't love. My goodness, I've only known Sir Robert a week. He *is* quite wonderful, but just my solicitor and my escort for now. As far as his gambling, I see no sign of it being out of control. And he is certainly wealthy enough to enjoy gaming when he wishes."

"Well, dear, if marriage does come up, remember, Sir Robert might be just wanting to replace the emptiness in his heart over the loss of his wife and baby. He lost both in a terrible accident, you know. Did he or Helen tell you?"

Elizabeth's eyes widened, and she turned around to look up at Elsie. "No! What happened?"

"Well, please don't bring it up to Sir Robert, as he does not like talking about it, so if he wants you to know, you must let him tell you yourself when he is ready. But if you have any thoughts about marrying him, you should know that he was married once before. The marriage only lasted six months. His wife became with child, and one night she tripped and fell down the long stairway from the balcony of their home to the bottom of the stairs. She and the baby both died. It was two years ago, and Sir Robert sold that house and never went back. He has never spoken of it, and he forbade anyone else to speak of it."

"Oh, how sad!" Elizabeth rose. "Did you know his wife?"

"Yes. She was very sweet."

Elizabeth turned and folded her arms, thinking how much she still did not know about Sir Robert, yet he was so easy to trust. "I don't even know how old he is, Elsie. Do you?"

"Yes, ma'am. He is thirty-seven."

Almost old enough to be my father, Elizabeth thought, *yet old enough to be well set, and quite the gentleman, let alone so handsome. And he is certainly still much younger than withered-up old Lord Henry Mason*. She could not ignore Sir Robert's kindness and accomplishments, nor his wealth; neither could she ignore his handsome face and physique. Still, at times she felt that odd sensation of danger when he looked at her in a way that made her a bit uncomfortable. It was a feeling she couldn't explain, and sometimes she wondered if it was just a new womanly desire she'd never experienced before… or was it an instinct to beware of the man?

Surely not! He seemed to adore her and would do anything for her.

There came a knock at the door, and she hurried to open it. There stood Sir Robert in a fine, black, lightweight wool suit jacket that had black silk lapels and was cut square at the waist, with tails at the back that hung nearly to his knees. He wore a silk paisley waistcoat and a black bow tie. A gold-chain watch was stuck into a small pocket of his waistcoat, and he carried a black top hat. He nodded and smiled.

"Lady Elizabeth, you look exquisite," he told her. "It's too bad you must wear black." He put on his hat and offered his arm. "Let me escort you to the restaurant downstairs. I've made some wonderful plans for you, exactly what you have been wanting for a trip west." He turned to Elsie and gave her a smile before leading Elizabeth to the hotel elevator. The Fifth Avenue Hotel was the first in New York City to install the wonderful new contraption that made moving from one floor to another so much easier.

"I can't wait to know what you have planned," Elizabeth told Robert.

"I've followed your dream, my lady, and I have to say that I hope I can be a part of that dream."

The elevator operator closed the doors and pushed a button. Elizabeth's stomach jumped a little when the elevator dropped, something she still couldn't quite get used to. They reached the restaurant level and exited. Sir Robert proudly paraded her down the hallway to the restaurant, where a maître d' led them to a table covered in fine white linen and decked with crystal glassware and polished silverware. Sir Robert pulled out a white, silk-stuffed chair, and Elizabeth sat down. Robert sat down across from her while a server poured water and took their order of baked salmon, buttered potatoes, steamed vegetables, and salads. As soon as the man left, Sir Robert reached over and grasped Elizabeth's gloved hand.

"My lady, I would like to call you Elizabeth, if I may. And I'd like you to call me Robert."

Elizabeth felt her cheeks flushing at the request. "I'm sorry, but it still seems a little soon, especially when others hear us address each other so intimately. Perhaps after we have known each other a little longer."

Robert squeezed her hand. "That's fine. I have to say I have so enjoyed helping you. And I think you will like my plan for you. I know you want to see Denver and visit a real gold mine. I've decided you chose right, and I have planned a trip there. We will leave in two days."

"Thank you! I was hoping you would say that."

"And I will personally see that you get there. And you should know that there is an area in Denver where only the very wealthy are building grand homes. That is where you should also build. The whole city is growing fast, and you will deeply impress the 'new' wealthy, as they are called in Denver. There is a big difference between old money, like your family inheritance, and those who were once poor but became suddenly rich from gold discoveries. The newly rich women in Denver will look to you as nothing less than the Queen of England, and they will turn to you for direction on protocol and manners of the rich."

The server returned with a silver pot of coffee and poured some for each of them.

"Oh, I'm sorry," Elizabeth told him. "I prefer tea."

"Certainly." The server took away her cup of coffee,

and Elizabeth turned to Sir Robert. "Thank you for your suggestions. I do dearly love New York, but I'd like to move on, as I have already told you. I do look forward to attending the opera tonight, though. Are we still going?"

"Yes. And to protect your reputation, my sister and her husband will also be going. We have to be careful, since we aren't man and wife, that people don't think there is something more between us than a business investor and his client."

"Of course." Elizabeth leaned back. "I truly appreciate everything your sister and her friends have done and the fact that Helen is sharing Elsie with me. But as you know, going to Denver has been my dream. And I so look forward to seeing the western landscape I've only read about and seen pictures of up until now."

"It's wonderful," Robert said. "New York's Adirondacks are spectacular, as are the Smoky Mountains, but there is nothing like the great prairies and plains of the West. And out west, you can see for miles and miles, wide-open landscapes you won't believe. And some of the Rocky Mountains are so high that snow stays on them all summer long. We'll go mostly by train, but we will also take a steamboat on the Missouri part of the way. That will be another new experience for you."

"Yes, it will!"

The server returned with Elizabeth's tea, then left to get their food.

"You will have to be careful with your money," Robert warned. "I still urge you to put most of it in a bank here in New York or get banknotes that can be exchanged for money once you reach Denver, so you won't be traveling with cash."

"That is probably good advice." Elizabeth hadn't told Sir Robert about her mother's jewels, nor did he know exactly how much money she carried. She would go with him to get the banknotes and handle the exchange herself. She was deeply grateful for all he was doing for her, but she told herself to be wary because of the short time she'd known the man, in spite of her unwanted attraction to him and her anxiety over being alone.

"Is there law now in Denver?" she asked aloud.

"Of course."

"I've been warned so often about how wild and untamed America's West can be," Elizabeth told him. "I've read so many stories about it in those penny dreadfuls."

Robert laughed richly. "Well, I suppose there is a hint of truth in some of those dime novels, but the West is becoming quite tame, I assure you. There are lawmen and U.S. Marshals who do their best, although some of the cow towns along the railway can get pretty wild when drovers come in with herds of cattle. They even have men who hunt outlaws for bounty. I suppose that, too, is a form of law and order, although some bounty hunters are hardly more than outlaws themselves."

"Oh, how dreadful! I can't imagine killing a man for money."

"To each his own," Robert told her.

"Well, I hope I never run into such a man."

"I'll protect you from such lowlifes, I promise,"

Robert answered. "The main thing we have to do is guard you and your money on the way to Denver. We will get those banknotes to protect your cash."

Elizabeth studied Sir Robert's dark eyes, so full of sincerity. She could not have been treated better since William's death than if it was William himself who accompanied her.

"What I have is English money that will have to be converted to American dollars."

Robert frowned. "All the more reason to get the banknotes here in New York, where it will be much easier to convert English money into American dollars. I'm not sure the banks in Denver would be able to do that. We can take your money to Hugh Becker, a banker in New York who is a good friend of mine. And he can give us the names of banking friends in Denver. Would that be acceptable to you? The banknotes would be no good without your signature, so it's a much better way to keep your money safe."

Elizabeth thought a moment as the server brought their salads. Getting banknotes did seem like a much safer way to travel, without real cash to worry about. "Yes, I think that is a fine idea."

"And I insist we bring a maid for you. Elsie can't go because she's one of Helen's favorites, but another one of my servants would be glad to go. Her name is Lora Means, and she is very good at fixing hair and such. She will attend to your every need."

"You're too kind, Sir Robert."

Robert sobered. "I deeply admire you, Lady Elizabeth. I want to show you my trustworthiness and sincerity. I'm excited, too. You can invest not just in gold mines, but in any number of other businesses in a fast-growing place like Denver. The opportunities are endless!"

Elizabeth nodded and removed her gloves to pick up a fork and eat her salad. Her heart beat faster at the thought of the wonderful trip soon to take place and the opportunities that lay waiting for her in the great American West. She was growing more confident in her decisions and enjoying her new independence. If not for William's drowning, everything would be perfect and just as she'd planned.

She held Sir Robert's gaze and smiled. He was, after all, handsome, accomplished, rich, and attentive. Knowing about the loss of his wife and child tore at her heart and enhanced her attraction to the man. She felt more at ease with him every day. "I feel blessed to have met you," she told him aloud.

"And I feel the same about you," Robert answered, reaching out and squeezing her hand again. "After lunch we will go to Helen's house so you can get your money. I will accompany you to the bank for safety's sake and you can procure those banknotes. After that, everything will be in order and we can leave."

Elizabeth felt her heart swell with joy and excitement, tempered only by the sad truth that William would not be with her when she headed west. *This is for you, William*, she thought, hoping he was "up there" somewhere, listening, and still watching over her.

TWELVE

May 20, 1870

Logan rode into the little town of Mirage, Colorado, or so said the small wooden sign about a half-mile back. Mirage was a fitting name, since you could see for miles and miles in this part of the country. Distances like that often led a man to see distorted images and sometimes things that weren't even there, especially on hot days when waves of ground heat mingled with distant clouds and hills. There were no mountains in eastern Colorado, so that made determining distance and formations on the horizon more confusing. There was no distinguishable terrain to go by in these endless high plains.

He was damned thirsty and hoped he could find a cold beer somewhere in this town. The wide-open country was hard on man and horse, with seldom one tree or even rocks under which a man could get out of the sun.

He'd decided that the best way to track his prey was to visit the saloons and bawdy houses in the rail towns between Abilene and Denver. Back in Abilene, Daisy had told him that Rosell mentioned heading for Denver. Since the man seemed to enjoy drinking and gambling and whoring wherever he went, Logan figured the bastard would likely stop at saloons along the way, maybe for two or three days at a time. He might get lucky and catch up with the culprit before he reached Denver.

An evening spent with his own favorite lady of the night, Brenda Lake in Hays City, proved his suspicions. Rosell was apparently in no hurry. He'd stopped in Hays City and stayed there four days, and Brenda certainly did remember the man. She was a good friend who always watched for anything that might help Logan if and when he stopped on one of his searches.

Said he and this other man dealt in selling young women for prostitution, Brenda had told him. *Said they weren't always willing. He actually asked me if I knew of any pickings he could go after. Said he and some man named Sir Robert Alexander from New York also dealt in stolen rifles, business scams, and talking unsuspecting people out of their money. He actually bragged about those things.*

Rosell had left Hays City about three days before Logan got there. That meant he was still hot on the man's trail, and Rosell would likely make a couple more stops before he reached Denver. Logan intended to catch up with him before that happened. Apparently, Rosell had no real job but somehow always had money and liked to brag about it. It was his bragging that caused people to remember him, and usually not in a good way. The sonofabitch didn't even seem worried about being caught and punished for beating up Daisy back in Abilene and robbing Rinker's saloon. He seemed to think he didn't need to answer for his crimes. Logan intended to see that he did. He also intended to find out about the man called Sir Robert Alexander and add him to his list of men to find.

He passed a livery, thinking to stop at the first saloon for that beer. Maybe he'd get lucky and find Rosell there. It irritated him that Rosell always seemed to be one step ahead of him. He drew Jasper to a halt in front of a large, empty lot just past the livery. Men were hammering away at what was very obviously a hanging gallows. *What the hell?*

Logan dismounted and quickly tied Jasper and his packhorse to a nearby hitching post. He walked up to the hanging platform and watched the men work for several seconds before approaching one of them. "What's going on here?" he asked.

The man he spoke to glanced at him, then straightened. He took a rag from his belt and wiped sweat from his face, then replaced the rag and looked Logan over more closely. "Pretty obvious, isn't it? We're building a hanging platform." He squinted. "You a lawman, or an outlaw? You're pretty well armed, and it's hard to tell."

Logan grinned. "I'm neither. I'm a bounty hunter, which probably puts me a little closer to lawman. There are times when outlaw is more fitting. Name's Logan Best." Logan removed his hat to also wipe at sweat, but with his shirtsleeve, as usual. "I was headed for the closest saloon for a cold beer when I noticed what's going on here. This town fixing to hang somebody?"

"Sure are, soon as we can catch him." The man put out his hand. "Stewart Klepp."

Logan shook his hand, after which Klepp removed his hat for a moment and scratched his mostly bald head. "Mr. Best, you just might be the man we need. We considered forming a posse, but nobody in Mirage is great at tracking. We've been figuring how we can catch the man we want to hang, and along comes a bounty hunter!"

Logan frowned. "What did this man do?"

Klepp shook his head. "The sonofabitch made off with a rancher's daughter. She was only thirteen. The ranch hands rode after him, but by the time they found the girl, that fucking snake had disappeared."

Logan frowned. "Do you know the guy's name?"

"Ben Rosell. I'll never forget it, because he was kind of an ugly little guy who liked to brag himself up. Know what I mean?"

"I know the type."

Klepp sighed and shook his head. "He abused that girl in the worst way. Know what I mean? He drugged her somehow in the middle of the night and took off with her on a horse he'd rented from the livery here in town the day before. Nobody even knew the girl was missing until the next morning. He snuck her out the bedroom window. He left good tracks but was just too far ahead by the time her pa and his men figured out the girl was missing."

Logan closed his eyes. "Shit!" He removed his hat again and whacked it against a stack of lumber. "That's the man I've been after. He's worth a lot of money to me."

"Well, mister, I have a feeling this whole town plus that girl's pa will add to what somebody else is paying you, if you can catch up to Rosell and bring him back here to hang. Fact is, just proof he's dead would be enough."

Damn it! Logan fumed on the inside. If he'd caught up to Rosell sooner, the man wouldn't have had a chance to hurt that girl. He walked a few feet away from Klepp, struggling not to punch something. "The bastard beat up a whore back in Abilene and stole money from a saloon there," he told Klepp, turning to face him again. "The owner of the saloon wants me to find Rosell and bring him back for punishment... or kill him if I want. He also wants his money back." He shook his head. "I'm damn sorry I didn't catch up to him sooner, but he had about a three-week start on me. I found out he'd stopped for two or three nights in just about every town on my way here, so I knew I was getting close, but I figured he'd made it to Denver by now. That was where I knew he was headed. I feel like a jackass for not catching up to him sooner."

"Yeah, that's too bad—because of the girl, I mean, not because you're wanting the bounty money. Know what I mean?"

"I think so." Logan could see that the term "know what I mean?" was just part of normal conversation for the man. He watched men hammer a crossbar onto the sturdy hanging post. "Don't think I'd go after Rosell just for the money," he answered. "The more

I learn about the man, the more I want to catch him and kill him just for the satisfaction."

"I can tell you he did have a lot of money on him. Some of it was probably what he stole. He won pretty big at cards, too, while he was here, before he left and decided to take the girl with him."

"How did he even know about her? I don't think he's from anyplace around here. How in hell did he get onto that ranch?"

Klepp shrugged. "He actually asked about her in a saloon while playing cards. He'd seen her earlier in the day, shopping with her father, Clive Macy. Later on, the father sent the girl home with a couple of his men and a wagon full of supplies and stayed here in town. He ended up in a saloon playing cards with Rosell. Rosell asked who the lovely girl was that he'd seen Clive with earlier in the day. Clive, he just figured Rosell was complimenting his daughter. Just a proud father, know what I mean?"

Logan nodded. "I know. How's the girl?"

"Linda Sue? She's pretty bad off, but she's strong and she's a fighter. We think Rosell meant to sell her to some whorehouse or something, but she gave him such a hard time he probably gave up because he didn't want to have to fight her all the way to wherever he was headed, so he beat on her and left her behind. Took off on that horse and caught a train and disappeared, so you might say he's also a horse thief, although the horse eventually found its way back to the ranch and got returned to the livery."

"The girl sounds like quite a scrapper."

Klepp nodded. "Linda Sue is tough—raised on that

ranch around a bunch of cowhands and knows her way around, know what I mean? She can do anything the men can do. Clive told us the only reason Rosell was able to get her out of the house in the middle of the night is he covered her face with something that made her pass out—at least that's what Linda Sue told him. Clive, he's beside himself that he didn't see through Rosell. The man stopped at his ranch when he left here and pretended to be interested in investing in Clive's cattle business—talked about a buyer in Denver who was paying good money per head for cattle and shipping them east to Omaha. Acted real friendly, know what I mean? Clive invited the man to stay overnight. Him and his wife are real nice—hospitable. That's how it is out here when you don't have neighbors and love having company. Know what I mean?"

Logan nodded yet again.

"Next thing he knew, in the morning Linda Sue was missing, along with Rosell," Klepp explained. "Sneaky as hell, that man is. He must have done something like that more than once, because he was good at it. Know what I mean?"

Logan removed a bandana from around his neck and used it to wipe at more sweat. "Any chance I can talk to the girl? I have a suspicion Rosell works for someone more important and a lot richer than he is. I'd like to track that man down, find out if there are more men involved in this whole thing than just Rosell."

"Why do you think that?"

"I have my reasons, and just plain old instinct."

"Well, you'd have to go ask Clive. I don't know

what he'd let you do. The girl might not want to talk, but then again, like you said, she's a scrapper. She probably wants you to bring Rosell back here to hang as much as the rest of us do." He looked Logan over again. "I'd suggest you go take a bath and get a shave before you go. And get rid of all those weapons. The way you look right now, the girl would be afraid of you."

Logan nodded. "I suppose. Where can I clean up?"

Klepp walked Logan to the street and pointed down past a saloon and a doctor's office. "There's a laundry and bathhouse up that way, just past a feed store. Sheriff Hart is likely at the Watering Hole, a saloon not far from the bathhouse. He's not much of a sheriff, but this little town doesn't need one very often anyway. You'd best talk to him about goin' to see that girl."

Logan tipped his hat. "Thanks." He walked back to Jasper and untied the horse. "Well, boy, I really messed this one up." He walked the horses up the street, hoping Linda Sue might know something that would help him find Rosell and maybe even the man or men he worked for. Men like Rosell were nothing on their own. Someone was behind that sonofabitch, and there could be more Ben Rosells out there with their hands in all kinds of dirty dealings they could no longer get away with back east.

"I'd better wire Mr. Rinker and tell him about this," he muttered to his horse. "I'll follow that bastard to Denver, and while I'm there, I'll see if I can find that man called Sir Robert Alexander. Maybe Mr. Rinker will pay me something extra for getting to the bottom of it all. And we just might make even more money if I can bring Rosell back here so the town can hang him. But you can bet your horse ass that he won't be in good shape when he gets here!"

A man walking past Logan looked at him like he was crazy.

Probably wondering who in hell I'm talking to, Logan thought. He realized he must have looked as though he was talking to himself. *Who cares? All I know is, money or not, I'm too damn angry over not getting here in time to let this go.*

Ben Rosell needed to be stopped—and soon.

THIRTEEN

—❧❧❧—

ELIZABETH STOOD AT THE RAILING OF THE *ANNA LEIGH*, watching how the bright moon made the Missouri River glitter at night. She couldn't get over a fascination with the huge paddle wheel at the back of the steamboat and how lovely the splashing water was as the wheel churned away, moving the boat forward.

She breathed deeply of the cool night air, feeling as though she should pinch herself to know this was all real. She'd fantasized about moments like this when she thought about coming to America all those years ago. It was just so sad that William couldn't be here now, and she felt deep regret that her dreams had cost her brother his life.

Sir Robert had been nothing but kind and attentive. She fully trusted him now. And how could she not be attracted to the man? She'd begun considering how exciting it would be to settle into a new mansion in Denver as the wife of respected businessman and investor, Sir Robert Alexander. Rather than doing everything alone, she and Robert could visit the gold mines together as husband and wife. They could buy large tracts of land—maybe develop a cattle ranch and hire men to build it—maybe open their own bank, perhaps start a supply business. Women would envy her for having a husband who generously allowed her to be a part of all his decisions.

The list of things they could do together was endless in a place like America's West, and Robert had only boosted her confidence and her desire for investing in America by adding his own excitement to hers, both of them often laughing in animated conversations about what the West offered to anyone who had money and the gumption to invest it wisely. She'd had no intention of marriage when she first left New York, but it was impossible not to think about it after traveling with Robert and knowing the lonely man had feelings for her and shared her dreams.

Robert called her Liz now, at least in private. And she called him Robert. She'd told him that yes, she would strongly consider a closer relationship. She suspected he wanted to marry her, but she felt it was much too soon to consider such a commitment. For now, they behaved very properly in public. People saw her as a young woman alone and unattached, traveling with her protector and solicitor. That was what they called Robert when around others, and in public, Elizabeth was always with her personal maid, Lora Means, whom Robert had chosen to take with them as they traveled.

Lora was only one year younger than Elizabeth. They got along famously, and Lora liked to tease her about how handsome Robert was and how she was sure he was in love with Elizabeth. Elizabeth smiled and looked up at the stars, feeling blessed to enjoy her own station in life. She knew she shouldn't be out here alone, but she was too excited to sleep. She needed to take a walk and drink in the beauty of a night on the Missouri River. She loved listening to the piano music that came from the main entertainment room, where she knew Robert would be now, smoking cigars with the men there and likely gambling. Lora slept in a room of her own, and Elizabeth didn't want to disturb her. She'd dressed on her own and re-tucked a few stray hairs with combs so she could come out here and enjoy the night.

She turned and let a soft breeze blow against her, wondering if life could be any better than this…free of the rules of London life, where women had no independence. She'd once daydreamed about what love would be like. She wanted the handsome knight on a white horse type of love, and she had begun to believe she'd found it in Sir Robert Alexander.

"Elizabeth!"

She turned to see Robert coming toward her.

"What on earth are you doing out here alone?" he asked.

"Oh, Robert, I just couldn't sleep. I wanted to come out here and enjoy the fresh air and watch the paddle wheel and see the moon shining on the river. I have already experienced so much here, and it's all due to you. Please don't be angry with me. I'm not all that far from my room."

Robert walked closer and put a gentle hand to the side of her face. "Please promise you won't do this again. You have to understand that there is a mix of people on this boat who are not like you, some of whom would stop at nothing to take advantage of you."

"I'm fine. We only have three more days on this lovely steamboat, and I don't want to waste or forget any part of this. The water is so sparkling and pretty at night."

"Liz, this is *America*. And not just that, but a part of America where there are few laws and even fewer men to enforce those laws. A lot of men on these steamboats heading west are running from the law back east or are out to get rich however they can, no matter if they harm someone else doing it."

What was that she saw in his eyes? Possessiveness? Ownership? Anger? It was a quick look that disappeared so fast, she dismissed her sudden alarm. Still, the way he'd looked at her reminded her of Jonathan when he was angry and ordering her to do as she was told. She also detected a strong smell of whiskey, but told herself that all men liked to drink, and he was behaving every bit the gentleman. Apparently, drinking didn't affect his manners.

"Please don't go running around on your own," Robert asked. "I should always be with you." Instantly, the look of concern and affection came back into his dark eyes. "I am only thinking of your safety, Liz. That's all. I'm not ordering you to do anything you don't want to do. I'm just reminding you that the farther west we go, the more dangerous it could be for you. In fact—" He hesitated.

"What is it, Robert?"

He sighed, a look of resignation coming into his eyes. "Surely you know how I feel about you. I want to be your protector and your friend, but I also want much more. I want...I want to be at your side all the time...as your...husband."

Elizabeth put a hand to her chest and stepped back a little, excited yet a bit confused about that quick look of anger she'd detected moments earlier. "Oh, Robert, I am so flattered! But I can't give you a decision instantly. Surely you understand. We've known each other such a short time, yet I cannot deny that I have had the same feelings for you. I consider it an honor that you asked." She studied him lovingly. "But you haven't actually said you love me. I won't marry just for money and position. I ran from that when I left London. I have to love the man I marry, Robert, and *he* must love *me*, just for me and nothing more."

He reached out and touched her face again. "Of *course* I love you." He hesitantly leaned in close. Before Elizabeth could agree or disagree, his lips were on hers, kissing her in a way that made her want him more. She let him pull her into his arms, ignoring the taste of whiskey on his breath.

"I do love you," he repeated softly into her ear. "That's why I was so worried when I went to your room and found you gone. In spite of the short time we have known each other, I don't know what I would do if I lost you." He pulled away and grasped her arms. "I'm sure my sister or one of the maids told you I was married once. I loved her dearly." Pain filled his eyes. "My wife—Alivia—tripped and fell down the grand staircase of our home and died. It was then the doctors discovered she was with child."

"Oh, Robert, I'm so sorry! I knew, but I wasn't

sure you would want to talk about it. I'm so glad you finally did."

"It's still hard for me to think about it. That's why…why I had a few drinks earlier. I'm sure you can tell, and I'm sorry, but I needed whiskey to get up the courage to tell you about Alivia and her awful accident." He sighed deeply. "I sold that house and never went back. I decided to live with my sister for a while, to be around family. It all happened two years ago, and this is the first time I've met a woman who actually has helped me forget my heartache, a woman who has made me realize I'd like to take a wife again." He looked at her pleadingly. "Say you will marry me, Liz. Please say you will marry me. I've been so alone."

Elizabeth touched his chest. "I can only say that I do love you, Robert. Please give me until we reach Denver to decide on anything more."

His eyes lit up with joy. "Just knowing you love me gives me hope. And I *do* love you. It's only you I want."

He pulled her close and kissed her again, this time harder. Why did his lips seem a little colder? His kiss more demanding? But what did she know about men? Perhaps they all kissed with a hint of commanding possession.

"And you will not go running off again without me, right?" he asked.

"I won't. Just remember that all of this is new and exciting to me, Robert. I want to experience so many things. Compared to England, this land is so big and wide and beautiful and full of wondrous new things. I need your promise that if I marry you, you will allow me those freedoms—that we can travel, and I can see the whole West. Maybe we could even go to San Francisco and see the Pacific Ocean!"

He squeezed her arm lightly. "We can do all those things. I promise."

They reached Elizabeth's room, and Robert leaned down and kissed her cheek. "Go inside and lock the door, dear. Three more nights on the river and we should reach Kansas City and board the train for Denver. We will travel in a very comfortable private car. And you just might see some real buffalo along the way."

Elizabeth smiled. "I can't wait."

"Sleep well—and lock this door," Robert told her. "I am going back to the main floor to play a few more hands of poker before I turn in. Remember that my room is right next to yours. Knock on the adjoining door any time you need me. And Lora's room is just on the other side of mine."

"I know. I'll be fine." Elizabeth gave him a smile before going inside and closing the door. She locked it right away and leaned against the door, thinking how, if he'd wanted, Robert could have snuck into her room any of these nights and abused her if he so chose. But he'd done no such thing. He was the perfect gentleman. And now he'd asked her to marry him.

She removed her hat and jewelry and took the pins from her hair, then sat down and flopped back on the bed with a deep sigh. What was it like to lie with a man? Robert was older and experienced and kind and gentle. Surely he would make it beautiful. She'd not planned any of this, but Robert Alexander was one of the most handsome, most charming men she'd ever met…and he had money. Though she did, too, a woman had to look out for her future, and the fact remained that a husband of means was important to that future.

FOURTEEN

May 22, 1870

THREE MEN RODE OUT TO THE GATE OF THE Two Hooves Ranch as Logan approached. Several hundred head of cattle were gathered in huge pens to Logan's left, and more were scattered about to his right, grazing far into the distant horizon. The air reeked of cattle dung, but out here men got used to the smell, which, Logan suspected, was why the men who worked these ranches didn't recognize their own smell. He couldn't criticize, since when he was on the trail for days at a time, he didn't smell much better himself. He'd cleaned up this morning because he didn't want to repulse the young lady he needed to talk to.

"State your business," the lead rider told Logan when he reached the gate.

"I'm Logan Best. I'm here to talk to Miss Linda Sue Macy. Sheriff Hart back in Mirage told me it was okay to come out here and talk to the girl."

The man held up his hand to the other two riders. "Go on about your chores," he told them. "It's that bounty hunter Clive said could come out here to talk to Linda Sue."

The men gave Logan a once-over, then turned their horses and rode off. The lead rider opened the gate, and Logan rode through. "I'm Pete Jeffers, ranch foreman," the ranch hand said. "We're all pretty worked up over Linda Sue, as you might expect."

"I can understand. I intend to bring back the man who hurt her. If you folks want to hang him, that's fine with me, long as I have the proof I need that I found him so's I can get paid by the man who sent me to find him in the first place."

"Mister, you'll get that much and more, because I have no doubt Mr. Macy will also pay you to find him, and Hart says the whole town is donating money as more bounty on the man."

"Fine with me."

"You'd better get rid of that gun you're wearing before you go see Linda Sue."

"I understand." Logan let Jasper amble along as he let go of the reins to take a pre-rolled cigarette from his pocket and strike a match to light it. "Pretty nice spread here," he said before taking a long drag on the cigarette.

"Yeah, but Mr. Macy wants to build it up more. Cattle is going to be the new gold, you know."

"So I've been told, more than once."

The two men ambled toward the main house, saying nothing more, both lost in their own thoughts. The house had wood siding and two big front windows. It was painted white, but dust from the cattle was already taking its toll, leaving the house looking more brown than white.

A tall, lean man came out onto the porch to greet them. His silver hair was neatly combed, and the stricken look in his pale-blue eyes told Logan he must be Linda Sue's father, Clive Macy. He nodded to the man before dismounting. "I'm Logan Best."

"Thought so," Clive said. "Take that gun off and come on in. Linda Sue says she'll talk to you, but not alone."

"That's fine." Logan unbuckled his gun belt and hung it over his saddle horn. He felt damn naked without it.

"Pete, see that the man's horses get fed and watered," Clive told Jeffers.

"Yes, sir." Jeffers leaned down and took the reins to Jasper as well as Logan's packhorse, leading them to a watering trough.

"Appreciate it," Logan said.

"Least I can do." Clive turned and led Logan into the house. "Sorry to make you take off your gun, but it might scare Linda Sue a little." Clive closed the door. "She's used to rough men and guns and all that, but right now she's pretty skittish around strangers. You gotta go easy on her. It won't be comfortable for her to talk to you, Mr. Best, but she knows you're after that sonofabitch who offended her. If she had her way, she'd put a bullet in him herself, and not in his head, if you know what I mean."

Logan couldn't help a tiny grin. "I think I do." He removed his hat and looked around a nicely decorated and clean great room that had three doors on the back wall, surely for bedrooms and such. A stout, graying woman turned from where she'd been cooking something over the fire in a huge fireplace. She smoothed back stray hairs that had fallen from the bun that once held them, then brushed her hands on her apron.

"You're that Logan Best, I suppose," she said to Logan, sounding tired.

"Yes, ma'am."

The woman was as plain as a piece of unused paper, her heavy face showing a shower of wrinkles. Logan guessed she was likely not as old as she looked. Hard work and the weather in this land had a way of aging a person real fast. He removed his hat and nodded as he hung it over the corner of a wooden kitchen chair. "You'd be Mr. Macy's wife?"

She nodded, looking ready to cry. "And Linda Sue's mother. She's in her bedroom, waiting for you. Clive will go in with you."

"Yes, ma'am."

"I'll have coffee and pie for you when you're done. Do you intend to stay the night?"

"No, ma'am. It's still early enough that I can get right on the trail when I'm done here. The man I'm after has stayed one step ahead of me all this time, but he's done eluding me. I won't let him stay ahead of me much longer, and I'm damn sorry I didn't catch up to him before this."

"Not your fault," Clive told him. "I blame myself for letting that bastard into my house."

The man's wife turned away. "That's what too much whiskey does," she muttered. "You end up trusting men you shouldn't." She faced Logan again. "I didn't like that man the minute he stepped into this house." She looked angry when she glanced at Clive. "But men will have their way." She turned to Logan again. "Women can sense a scoundrel when they see one, and that man was a scoundrel." She squinted a little and walked closer to Logan. "Now you, you're no scoundrel. It's true you're a man who will kill somebody for money, but that somebody has to deserve it. And I don't care if you kill Mr. Ben Rosell. I'm wishing you good luck." She turned away and headed back to the fireplace to stir something in a pot hanging on the fireplace crane.

"Thank you, ma'am," Logan told her. "I'll do my best."

Clive sighed and led Logan to the bedroom. "We're comin' in, Linda Sue," he said, opening the door gently.

Both men went inside, where a skinny, dark-haired girl sat in a chair in the corner. Logan was surprised by how thin she was, considering what a scrapper and tomboy men said she was. She wore a loose-fitting paisley dress that looked handmade. Logan could already tell that when Ben Rosell first saw her in town, a poorly dressed rancher's daughter, he would have guessed that she was young and too innocent of bastards like him not to trust him. He'd probably also figured that because she was so thin, she would probably be weak and easy to handle—an obvious target.

Her head was hanging when they walked in, but she looked up at Logan and her father as they entered. "Have a seat," she said to them.

Logan and Clive both sat down on the edge of the bed facing the girl. Logan thought her pretty, but she needed more meat on her bones. His heart ached at the bruises and scratches on her face and forearms.

Linda Sue met his gaze. "You're Logan Best?"

"Yes, ma'am. And I'm right sorry about what happened. I'm after the man who abused you, and I thought maybe you could tell me something I don't know yet—some clue—some friend of his—names—anything."

Linda Sue looked at her lap. "I ain't no bad girl," she told him. "I didn't go willingly with that man."

"I have absolutely no doubt about that. And when a man does something against a woman's will, it's not her fault and it doesn't make her bad. Fact is, I'm told you're quite a scrapper—know how to use a gun and ride a horse and round up cattle good as any man."

That brought a faint smile. Linda Sue nodded. "I can." She faced Logan again. "And I fought that man. I want you to know that. I fought hard."

"Anybody can see that by those bruises and cuts. I'm told by those who know you that you probably put up such a fuss that Ben Rosell gave up trying to steal you away with him."

Linda Sue returned to staring at her lap. "I...woke up at his camp, all groggy from something he gave me. By then I—" She hesitated. "I knew what he did on account of I wasn't dressed...and I hurt bad. I noticed he was sleeping by a campfire, and he wasn't dressed neither. I never saw a man with no clothes on before. It scared me. I thought he'd wake up and try to...do that to me again, so I hurried up and dressed and was gonna ride away, but he woke up and caught me... held a gun on me and told me to undress again." A look of anger and stubbornness came into her dark eyes then. "I sure as hell wasn't gonna do that! I told him no, and he told me he'd shoot me if I didn't. I walked right up to him and I said, 'Go ahead and shoot, cuz there ain't no woman alive, young or grown, who'd want you to stick that ugly little thing into them.'"

"Linda Sue, you shouldn't talk that way in front of a stranger!" Clive told her.

"It's fine," Logan said, keeping his eyes on Linda Sue. "Your daughter is really something. She's a brave girl." He could tell Linda Sue was fighting tears when she continued.

"Well, that remark made him real mad, and he hit me across the side of my head with his gun." She wiped at a quick tear. "Then he jerked me up and started beating on me, yelling stuff at me the whole time, things like…I was too bony anyway for him to sell to a…whorehouse. 'No man wants to bed a bag of bones,' he said." She wiped at another tear. "I'm awful sorry for the language, but that's what he said. And he said that some man he called 'Sir Robert' wouldn't want me on account of I don't appreciate men and I don't have big enough…you know…breasts." She swallowed. "But he called them something else— something real ugly. I knew what he intended to do if he could break me, so I grabbed a rock, and when he came at me again, I slammed it right into that ugly thing he used on me. He went down like he'd been shot." She faced Logan squarely again. "Do you want to know what I told him then?"

Logan couldn't help a grin. "I'm not so sure that I do."

Linda Sue smiled through her tears. "I told him maybe I didn't have big enough breasts, but he didn't have a big enough thing between his legs that any woman would want him either."

"Linda Sue!"

Logan couldn't help a bigger smile. "You do have a way with words, Linda Sue."

"I knew he'd hate that, so I said it, and I enjoyed watching him curl up in pain, holding his privates. Like I said, I never saw a man naked before, but I just had a feeling the average man ain't that..." She looked down again. "Little."

Logan struggled not to burst out laughing. He ran a hand over his mouth to hold it in. He'd been expecting a shivering, scared, devastated young girl when he came here. He could see what men meant by calling her a scrapper.

"I started for his gun," Linda Sue continued, "but he managed to grab me in spite of his pain, and he hooked an arm around under my chin so's I couldn't get away from him. 'I ought to kill you,' he told me. 'But I'll let you live so you can enjoy the pain and insults and embarrassment of some stranger doing—you know what—to me,' he said. He dragged me to his bedroll and fished around for something in his saddle pack—took out a little bottle of something and spilled it on his blanket. Then he smothered my mouth with the blanket till I passed out." She wiped at more tears. "When I woke up I was at least still dressed. I don't think he did that bad thing to me again. But he was gone—horse, bedroll, everything. I was left there with nothing to defend myself from wolves and such, and not even sure where I was. I just stayed there. I knew my pa would send men to track me down, which they did, but by then that man was too far gone to be found."

"Some of the men tracked him a ways," Clive told Logan. "But the trail led right to the railroad tracks at a water stop. He must have got on board a train there and gone on. That track leads to Denver. I don't have a man to spare, and finding him could have taken days or weeks once he got on that train. He could be anywhere."

Logan sighed and pushed some of his hair behind his ears. "I already know he's headed for Denver." He faced Linda Sue, who looked back at him pleadingly.

"I want him dead," she told Logan, "but I want him to suffer."

Logan nodded. "I have no problem making a man like that suffer, believe me." He leaned forward, resting his elbows on his knees. "You said while he was beating on you and dragging you around that he was shouting things. What did he say? Did he mention any other names besides this Sir Robert?"

Linda Sue thought a moment. "He said something about me not even being worth anything to the Comanche. 'I can get more from them for guns than I'd be able to get for the likes of you,' he said. And he said, 'Even Miss Betsy wouldn't want you.' I don't know who that is, but I guess maybe she buys women or something." A tear ran down her cheek as she faced Logan again. "He said he wasn't gonna be outdone by…I think he said the name Chad. 'Chad and his gang,' he said. 'They're best at robbing trains and stagecoaches,' he said, 'but I'm best at stealing women. Either way, Robert pays us real good,' he said."

Logan sighed and stood up. "I thank you for being so brave as to talk to me," he told Linda Sue. "I've heard the name Robert enough to know who I'm *really* after, but I'll get Ben Rosell first," he promised. "And I'll be looking for this man called Chad, too."

Linda Sue looked up at him. "Thank you." She stood up and suddenly flung her arms around him. "You come and tell me when you get him, okay? I want to see him shot or hanged!"

Logan reluctantly put his arms around her and patted her back. "I'll be sure you know." He grasped her arms and gently pushed her away. "You hold your head up and go back to doing what you always do, understand? I can tell by the men I've met here that they don't think one bad thing about you because of what happened. They all respect you, and they want Ben Rosell dead, too. You're a fine, brave young woman, and you'll be okay. I admire you for talking to me."

Linda Sue nodded and stepped back. "Ma wants to give you coffee and pie before you go," she told him.

"I'm grateful. But I'll be leaving soon as I finish that pie. And I'm betting you make pie just as good as your ma does."

Linda Sue smiled. "I do."

"That's what I figured." Logan gave her a smile and a nod.

"You be careful, Mr. Best. You're a right nice-looking man, and you speak real nice, too. I think that if you find the man who did this, you'll have some of his friends after you. If they're all as mean as this one is, you'll have a fight on your hands."

Logan reached out and patted her head. "I know what I'm doing. I'll be fine." He turned and walked out of the room with Clive.

"You can leave the door open," Linda Sue called out.

"Okay, darlin'," Clive said.

Logan walked to the kitchen table, where Clive and his wife insisted he stay a few minutes and have the pie and coffee. Logan obliged, but he was more anxious than ever to get onto Ben Rosell's trail. The man would regret what he did to Linda Sue Macy. He was equally anxious now to find one Sir Robert Alexander. The sonofabitch was likely behind men like Ben Rosell. And now he had yet another man to find—someone called Chad.

FIFTEEN

ROBERT KNOCKED SOFTLY ON THE DOOR TO LORA Means's room. Lora opened the door slightly, then fully, reaching up as Robert pulled her into his arms and kissed her roughly. He held onto her as he closed the door and locked it. "I see you were ready for me."

Lora laughed lightly, turning in a circle for him. She wore a see-through negligee that softened curves that didn't need softening. Robert could see her pink nipples and the dark spot between her legs that hid what he'd come for.

"Get that damn thing off," he told her as he began undressing.

Lora slowly pulled pins from her long, dark hair and let it tumble, then turned and let the negligee fall, knowing Robert liked looking at her firm bottom. He tore off his clothes even faster.

Lora sauntered closer and touched his already-bare chest. "Let me help," she told him.

Robert gladly allowed her to kneel down and untie his shoes. He stepped out of them, and she pulled off his socks.

"Are you sure she will go to bed and not be looking for either of us?" Lora asked.

"Yes. I took her to dinner and then back to her room. I heard her lock the door. I don't think she'll venture out on her own again."

Lora looked up at him and smiled. "She's been excitedly talking about you and how handsome you are and how she thinks she has fallen in love with you. I have no doubt that she will marry you, but then we both know that's not really what you have in mind." She raised up on her knees and gently massaged Robert's swelling penis before unbuckling his belt to let his pants down. "I almost feel sorry for her. She has so many other plans," she said.

Robert grinned wickedly. "Good. She still trusts me then. It kills me not to rip those clothes off her and force myself on her, but she's worth so much more if she's untouched. It's almost comical how 'proper' she tries to be, insisting on waiting to give me her answer about marrying me."

Lora laughed. "And you would like to be very *im*proper with her, wouldn't you?"

"Even more improper than I am with you, you little wench."

"Mmmm-hmmm." Lora took hold of his underwear and jerked it down. For the next several minutes, all plans he had for deceiving Elizabeth Baylor took second place to what Lora Means was doing to him. He grasped her hair and hung on until he could no longer hold back his ejaculation.

Lora swallowed and flung her head back as Robert picked her up and carried her to her bed, then threw her onto it and dove on top of her. He sucked at her breasts wildly, moving down to lick and explore until she, too, could not hold back the utter ecstasy he drew from her. Still, he'd gotten a little more demanding and hurtful over the last year, since he began gambling and drinking even more than usual. Drinking made him more violent, and as he began ravaging her roughly, she knew he'd drunk more than he should have. She was surprised he'd been able to hold back from forcing himself on Elizabeth last night. He'd drunk a lot then, too, and he'd been just as forceful as he was now…almost too forceful.

Lora was well aware that Robert Alexander had an evil streak, knew about his heavy gambling and that he'd often cheated on his wife, including with her when his wife was asleep. He'd sometimes talked about how easy it was to swindle people out of their fortunes, mostly unsuspecting single or widowed women who needed help. He enjoyed the power of knowing he could get away with it, using his looks and wealth to charm them. He'd mentioned once that the only reason he'd married was because he would legally inherit his wife's personal fortune, which she'd in turn inherited from her deceased father, a wealthy supplier to the railroad.

He worked his way back up her body, tasting her breasts again before shoving himself inside of her, ramming hard over and over until she had to ask him to slow down.

"Slow down?" Robert pinned her arms down. "You know better than to tell me how to have you. You're here to service me whenever I need it. Remember that."

He rammed harder until she cried out in pain.

"Fine," she grimaced, clearly and suddenly not enjoying the tryst. "Just let go of my arms, Robert. You've had too much to drink again."

Robert squeezed harder. "No one gives Robert Alexander orders, especially not a street urchin like you!" He leaned down and ravaged her mouth, biting at her lips as he surged into her almost violently.

Lora grimaced. "You're hurting me!" she complained.

Robert let go of one arm and slapped her hard. "I *want* to hurt you. I'm frustrated as hell holding back with Elizabeth Baylor. I'm sick and tired of being the proper gentleman with that snobby, tight little virgin." He raised up and grasped her hips, digging his thumbs into her hip bones and squeezing painfully as he kept thrusting into her. "I intend to have at you every way there is, and you're going to enjoy it, or I'll throw you into this boat's paddle wheel later tonight when no one is looking!"

Lora knew the man meant exactly what he said, drunk or not. After all, when she was only fourteen and a street orphan, he'd hired and trained her as a maid to his wife, but it wasn't long before he came to her attic room one night and made sure she understood her "real" duties. After that, he visited her there practically every night. He'd talked about how he was already bored with his wife and how he hated her for getting pregnant, as though she did that all on her own. Worse, Lora had witnessed Robert Alexander throw his wife down the great, wide stairway of their mansion, screaming at her that he *didn't want any damn babies*.

No one questioned the death of Mrs. Robert Alexander as being anything but an accident. Robert pretended great mourning, but he quickly had her buried, and that was the end of it.

The man meant business. Lora never told him she saw him kill his wife, fearful he'd do the same to her if he knew she'd witnessed the murder. Besides, who would ever believe the word of a lowly, uneducated street girl over the suave, respected, successful Sir Robert Alexander, who had friends in high places, including judges? His own brother-in-law was a well-known attorney.

From then on, she'd done everything he told her to do. She desperately needed the money he paid her and the free place to live. He'd often taken trips west, and she didn't doubt he was up to something, but it wasn't until this trip that she realized he was involved in running guns and selling women.

She could tell this was going to be a long, humiliating, painful night, but letting the man have at her was better than being thrown back into the streets…or worse, being tossed into the paddle wheel of the *Anna Leigh* and dying somewhere along the Missouri River, her bloody, dead body washed up on shore in the middle of nowhere and eaten by wolves or coyotes. She was an unknown and would never be missed. And Robert damn well knew it.

SIXTEEN

LOGAN BOARDED THE KANSAS PACIFIC JUST SOUTH OF Mirage later the same day, figuring he had no choice if he wanted to catch up with Ben Rosell. He'd taken the slower way by horseback initially because he'd needed to inquire at every town along the way. If he'd traveled by train all the way to Denver from Abilene, he might have gone right past Rosell in one of the towns and lost track of him. Now he knew for sure the man was on a train headed for Denver.

He got off the train for a half hour delay to fill the engine's boiler with water. The first water stop after Mirage, where Rosell had likely boarded a couple of days ago, was empty, so the train had stopped here instead. Logan carried his usual weaponry, and people on the train had looked at him as though they thought he might be part of a gang of train robbers. Men watched him carefully, and women stared with a mixture of fear and curiosity. Logan didn't much care what they thought. A man of his profession made enemies. He wasn't about to go anywhere without his sidearm and his rifle. Still, when he climbed down from the train, it felt good to get away from the scrutiny of so many strangers. Another reason he preferred traveling alone.

Others disembarked to stretch their legs at the tiny stopover that had nothing more than a water tower, a livery, one supply store, and a saloon. He headed to the saloon for a quick beer, since the conductor had told them that the next part of their trek toward Denver would take several more hours before another stopover.

Men turned to look at those who entered. It was always that way in small towns. All saloons had their faithful patrons who sat there every day, usually in the same place at the bar or their favorite table, drinking, smoking, playing cards, and gossiping, looking for anything to break up a boring day.

He strode to the bar and ordered a beer. Before he lifted it to take a drink, loud laughter from a table where six men were playing cards caused him to turn and look.

Holy shit!

"Deal 'em again," one man said loudly. "I couldn't run out of money if I tried."

"Well, now, ain't you just the big man," another man answered.

"If you have that much money, I'd be damn careful bragging about it in front of a bunch of strangers," another said. "Not a lot of law out here, you know."

The first man took a look at his cards. He had a glass of whiskey in front of him and a fat cigar stuck between his lips…*lips wider than the norm for the average man*, Logan thought.

"You just remember that I have men behind me who would deal some pretty bad luck against any man who brought harm to me or took what's mine," the man answered.

"Bullshit," one of the others spoke up. "Just play your cards, Rosell, and shut your fucking mouth."

All senses came alert for Logan. If he'd prayed for good luck on this trip, he couldn't have received a better answer. The sonofabitch was again taking his time getting to Denver. He'd stopped at this nameless little settlement just to play the role of rich man in front of what he knew would be a bunch of unsuspecting wanderers with no money—people he figured he could impress. The man was sitting there bragging himself right into a noose.

Logan walked over to the card players, beer in one hand and rifle in the other. He leaned against the wall nearby and watched the game, eyeing Rosell and taking several long sips of beer. The man fit all descriptions others had given him—short, thinning black hair, thick lips, and a braggart. Best of all, he'd told these men his name. Logan didn't even have to ask. While he waited for the hand to play out, Rosell glanced at him a couple of times, looking both curious and worried. Logan enjoyed making him uncomfortable.

Rosell finally folded his cards then and looked straight at him. "Something you want, mister?"

"Could be."

Rosell snickered. "If you're thinking about robbing me, think twice. I have people behind me who'd tear you to pieces."

"That so?" Logan downed his beer. "I don't see one damn person behind you at the moment."

Rosell took the cigar from his mouth and set it in an ashtray, then finished his drink. "Who the hell are you?"

Logan slammed his beer mug on the table between two card players. Every man at the table jumped in alarm and scooted back to get out of Logan's way.

"Name's Logan Best," Logan answered, keeping a steady gaze on Rosell. "Bounty hunter."

The look of confidence in Rosell's eyes faded. "I've got no bounty on me."

Logan stepped closer, holding his rifle in his left hand and resting his right hand on his sidearm. "You brag too much, Rosell. I've been on your tail ever since you beat up that whore back in Abilene and stole money from that saloon owner. He's the one who put a bounty on you. And it seems you upped the bounty when you kidnapped and raped a thirteen-year-old girl back in Mirage."

"Oh my God," one of the women serving drinks in the saloon muttered.

"We knew there was somethin' fishy about you, Rosell," one of the card players told him.

Rosell slowly rose. "Now you just wait a minute!" he ordered.

"The owner of the saloon in Abilene is paying good money for you," Logan informed him, ignoring Rosell's objection. "Dead or alive. And that girl's pa is paying even more money for me to bring you back to Mirage, only *he* wants you *alive*. The whole town of Mirage wants to hang you." Logan grinned. "I figure

I've got the best of both, since the man in Abilene doesn't care if you're dead. I'll take you back alive to Mirage and let them *hang* you, and then I'll deliver proof you're dead to that saloon owner in Abilene, along with whatever money you have on you, because most of it belongs to him anyway. That way I'll collect *both* bounties."

Rosell swallowed, and sweat beaded up on his forehead. "You need some kind of paperwork to take me anywhere with you," he declared. He glanced at one of the card players. "Go get the sheriff!" he demanded. "This man can't just take me away on his word and with no paperwork."

The card player grinned. "I just told you a few minutes ago that there's not much law around here, Rosell. This place is just a short stop for the train. In fact, we aren't a legally formed town yet, and we don't have a sheriff."

"Considerin' what this man here says you did, we don't much care if he does take you away, you ugly little braggart," one of the other men told Rosell. "If you took advantage of a thirteen-year-old girl, you *deserve* to hang." He looked at Logan. "Go ahead and take him," he told him. "Ain't none of us gonna stop you."

Logan never once took his gaze off Rosell. "Obliged," he answered. He started toward Rosell, but Rosell reached into the jacket of the silk suit he wore. In half a second, Logan's six-gun was about an inch from Rosell's forehead. "Don't even think about it," he warned. "I don't necessarily have to take you back to Mirage alive, Rosell, remember? But I'd like to satisfy those people's need to hang you. I promised Linda Sue I'd bring you to her, and I aim to grant her wishes." He pulled back the hammer of his .44. "Still, it won't break my heart to blow your brains out instead. Unload that piece you were reaching for."

Looking ready to cry, Rosell pulled a small pistol from his jacket and laid it on the table. "Sir Robert Alexander will have your hide for this!" he growled, seething.

"Well, now, I was just going to ask you about the man, since you've been spouting off his name all the way here. But we'll save that conversation for our trip back to Mirage. Right now, you can take that top hat hanging on your chair post and shove your winnings into it. That money will be a gift to Linda Sue, seeing as how you stole something from her that's much more valuable. I'll be asking one of these men here to carry the money for me and ask the conductor to hold the train up while I get my horses off it. You and I are going to head back to Mirage, but not by train. Might be you'll have to walk part of the way. My packhorse is carrying a lot of weight, and I hate to add you to it."

"Walk? I can't walk all the way back to Mirage!"

Logan shrugged. "I can drag you behind the horses if you prefer. Makes no difference to me. I just figured we'd take our time so's I can learn a little more about this Sir Robert fellow and what the hell you're really up to out here…besides beating up whores and robbing people and raping innocent little girls, that is."

One of the card players walked around behind Rosell and took his hat, scraping the man's winnings into it for him. "I'll help you, Mr. Best," he told Logan.

"Appreciate it," Logan replied. He turned to one of the card players. "Follow me out, if you don't mind. I have rope on my horse that can be used to tie this man's hands behind his back."

"I don't mind at all." The man walked around behind Rosell and gave him a shove. "Let's go, mister."

"You sonofabitch!" Rosell cussed at Logan. "You can't do this!"

"Seems like I just did," Logan answered. He waved his pistol, indicating the front door. "Let's go."

Rosell was visibly shaking. "You can't do this!" he repeated.

"Shut your damn mouth while you're still able to walk," Logan demanded.

The man behind Rosell gave him another shove, and the three of them walked out, followed by the card player who'd collected Rosell's money in his top hat. No one questioned Logan's right to take Rosell away with him.

Logan grinned inwardly. Luck was still with him. Ben Rosell was going to hang, Rinker would get his money back, and Logan would be a fairly rich man after collecting all his bounty. And on their way back to Mirage, Ben Rosell was going to tell him all he knew about those he worked for—or suffer the consequences.

SEVENTEEN

ELIZABETH HUNG ON TO HER WIDE-BRIMMED STRAW hat as soon as she exited her room. The *Anna Leigh* had landed in Kansas City on a windy day, and even though her hat was tied under her chin, she could feel the tug at the ostrich plumes that decorated it as a rather hot wind tried to tear it from her head.

"Oh my!" She laughed. "Robert, is it always this windy out here?"

"Not always." Robert grinned as he took hold of her gloved hand. "You look incredibly beautiful today, Elizabeth. I'm so glad you agreed to wear that pretty blue dress instead of black or gray. Your brother would have wanted you to be your most beautiful on this trip and celebrate your joy and independence."

Elizabeth let out a little yelp as the wind whipped the skirts of her heavily ruffled dress. "Robert, I'll be blown away!"

"Not if you hang on to me."

Elizabeth realized right away that muslin mixed with wool was not going to be comfortable here in Kansas. The trip on the Missouri had been cool and refreshing. This Kansas air was far from that. Thank goodness, the dress had a low neckline. If she'd worn the first dress she'd put on, which had a neckline at her throat, she would be miserable.

"My trunks!" Elizabeth looked backward.

"I have taken care of everything," Robert told her. "The boat has men who will unload our things and make sure all we need is stored at our hotel. The rest will be guarded all night and loaded onto the train in the morning. I'll hail a buggy soon so you won't have to walk on the dusty streets."

"Hotel? Won't we get right onto a train?"

"Goodness no. It's already three in the afternoon, my dear. The train for Denver doesn't leave until the morning. Just stay with me and you'll be fine, I assure you."

Elizabeth wrinkled her nose. "Goodness, what is that smell?"

Robert laughed. "Elizabeth, every town we hit from here on will smell like that. It's from cattle. Remember we talked about ranching as a possible investment?"

Elizabeth smiled and hugged him. "Of course." She leaned back and looked up at him. "But I still want to see the gold mines."

Robert kissed her cheek. "Whatever you want." He teasingly touched the end of her nose. "But first I want an answer to my proposal."

Elizabeth laughed. "I am almost sure I will marry you, but I still want to wait until we reach Denver. There is so much more left to see and do on this trip. I want to settle a bit first and make sure I have my head on straight and my feet firmly grounded before I take such a big step as marriage."

Robert embraced her again. "Please don't break my heart by saying no," he asked her softly. "I'll be such a happy man with you for my new wife."

"Oh, Robert, you know that I love you. I just need time to settle my thoughts and take a breath. This trip has been so busy, and I've hardly gotten over William's terrible death. I want to wait just a little longer out of respect for poor William. Surely you understand."

There it was—that quick flash of anger in his dark eyes—gone as fast as it appeared. "Of course I do," Robert told her with his usual charming smile. He took her arm and helped her down the stairs to the lower deck, where they carefully made their way down the plank to the loading dock. Elizabeth looked around at the bustle of disembarking passengers as well as others waiting to board as soon as the *Anna Leigh* was unloaded. She could see that the city beyond the docks was quite large, but of course, it was nothing like New York or London. She knew everything would be very different out here, and she couldn't get enough of the sights.

"Now, you wait right here, my dear," Robert told her after leading her to a bench on the dock. "There are a lot of good people getting off and also waiting to board. No one will bother you in front of so many people. You'll be fine for a few minutes."

Elizabeth frowned. "Where are you going?"

"Elizabeth, from here on, I have a lot of people to see, so there will be times when I'll have to leave you for just a short while. Someone who has news of ranch land for sale near Denver is waiting for me."

"But—how did he know you would be here today?"

Robert gently forced her to sit down. "For goodness' sake, haven't you heard of the telegraph? I was able to contact him all the way from New York City. We've done business several times."

"But...Lora. Where is she? Shouldn't she sit here with me?"

"We'll talk about that as soon as I get back."

Robert quickly left, carrying one of his suitcases with him. Elizabeth watched after him, feeling a bit alarmed by his remark about Lora. Lora should be here with her, but she didn't see her anywhere. She stood up to try to see where Robert had gone. She couldn't spot him at first, but she did see a church on a distant rise, and from here she could see that Kansas City had a newspaper office, a clothing store, and a sign that said *Pharmacy*. She also caught sight of a sign that read *Doctor's Office* and *Guns and Ammo*. The street went on much too far for her to see all the businesses, although she then made out a sign that said *Lady Luck Saloon*. There were a couple of buildings built higher than the others. She supposed those were the hotels.

She caught sight of Robert then. She realized he must have been telling the truth about meeting someone about a ranch because he was talking to a man wearing dusty pants, a paisley shirt, and a scarf around his neck, as well as a wide-brimmed hat. His blond hair was shoulder length, and from here it looked as though he was as tall or taller than Robert. He was standing next to a horse. Behind him were several other men on horses, all dressed similarly.

Cowboys! she thought. They looked just like the drawings in the penny dreadfuls she'd read back in London.

So, this was the American West! It was alive and bustling and growing, just like she'd imagined. But it was also dusty and windy and full of people unlike any she'd seen before. There were black men unloading the *Anna Leigh*. She thought the recent war between the states had freed such men, but these looked just as much like slaves as she would have pictured. They were poorly dressed and were ordered around by white men.

She gasped when she saw a man that might be a real Indian. He was dressed like a white man, though poorly, and his hair was straight and long and black, with beads in it. He wore earrings, and she saw a knife at his belt. He glanced at her, and she stepped back, sitting back down on the bench. To her relief, he turned away and walked on.

What a strange and wonderful place this was. People everywhere, dressed in ways she'd never seen. Most of the women were so plain, their hair either hanging long or tied into prim buns at the base of their necks. Most wore cotton dresses with hardly any slips and petticoats underneath, and no bustles. They didn't wear gloves or carry parasols, and their hats were fitted to their heads and tied under their chins, with huge brims at the front. She glanced up at the very blue sky and very hot sun.

Of course, she thought. *Out here a woman must protect herself from the sun and dry wind*. There was little of either in London. Most days were gray, and it rained often.

She wished Robert would have introduced her to the cowboys he was meeting. She waited, taking in the sights and sounds, wanting to remember it all.

Finally, a fancy buggy approached, causing people to have to move out of the way as it drew closer. A black man drove the buggy, and Robert sat in a velvet, cushioned seat behind the driver. He was all smiles as the buggy pulled up in front of her, and he stepped down and took her arm. "I'm here to take you to our hotel," he told her.

Elizabeth excitedly climbed into the back seat. "Shouldn't Lora be with us?" she asked again.

"Well, dear, I didn't want to tell you right away because I didn't want to alarm you, but I am sending Lora back to New York. She missed the city, and I don't feel right taking her all the way with us."

Elizabeth put a hand to her chest. "But…Lora never said anything about going back."

"It was my decision." Robert put an arm around her. "My darling, you will be fine. It won't take long at all to find a servant for you once we reach Denver. It will only take a few days, and we'll be on a train the entire way, so there won't be much chance to worry about baths and getting your hair done and such. Believe me, when we reach Denver, you will have the best accommodations possible. And there are so many wealthy people there now that any number of them can help us find the proper help for you. You won't have just one attendant. You'll have several. I'll see to it."

Elizabeth suddenly felt lonely. A tiny voice tried to tell her something wasn't right. "Robert, we can't be seen traveling alone together."

"All people will know is that I am your solicitor and escort. I am taking Lady Elizabeth Baylor to Denver, where she intends to make investments." He squeezed her shoulder. "You needn't worry about one thing." He ordered the driver to take them to a hotel, then took hold of Elizabeth's chin, forcing her to look at him. "Elizabeth, once you settle in Denver and have a few days to rest, we will be married, so it will no longer matter that we are seen alone together." He kissed her gently.

Elizabeth studied his dark eyes. "Robert, we mustn't be seen kissing in public. If we want people to believe you are merely my solicitor, we have to behave as such."

"Haven't I been every bit the gentleman this whole way? Haven't I provided you with every single thing you needed ever since we got off the ship in New York? I am no longer worried about what others think, and neither should you be concerned. We are in the Wild West now, where there is little law and few social rules."

Elizabeth reasoned she was being foolish not to trust him. "I'm sorry, Robert. This is all so very new to me. This place…it's not like anything I've ever experienced."

"And isn't it just as different and exciting as those penny dreadfuls said it would be?"

Elizabeth smiled and faced him again. "Yes! And I don't mean to sound ungrateful for all the wonderful things you've done for me, Robert. And I…I *will* marry you after a bit of time. I still need to grieve William properly. Once we are married, we will no longer have to hide our feelings for each other. I want that as much as you do."

The carriage driver got the horse into motion and drove away from the dock. Elizabeth looked back again at the steamboat. "What about our trunks?" she asked yet again. "Nothing was loaded onto the buggy."

"I told you what we need will be delivered to our hotel and the rest will be guarded until it is all loaded onto the train. I've taken care of everything."

"But earlier you had one of your suitcases with you. You didn't bring it back."

Robert frowned. "You ask too many questions, Elizabeth. Why are you so worried? You know I'll take good care of you. And I gave that suitcase to the men I met with. It had money and contracts in it for a cattle deal." He patted her hand. "You just worry about enjoying yourself. I told you I'll have a few business dealings from here on."

He kissed her cheek, and Elizabeth turned to look at all the businesses and people they passed as the driver snapped the reins. "I wish you would have introduced me to those men," she told Robert. "I saw you in the distance. They looked like cowboys."

"There will be plenty of time for you to meet real cowboys," he told her. "These men were in a hurry. We will meet up with them again in Hays City in a day or two. You can talk to them there."

"Oh, that's exciting!" Elizabeth settled into her seat, ready for the next step of her journey into the Wild West she'd read so much about.

Chad Kreiger left his horse with the seven men who'd ridden with him into Kansas City to meet up with Robert Alexander.

"Sounds like Alexander has brought us a real beauty this time," he told the others. "And she's rich! Carryin' banknotes for nearly fifty thousand dollars. Alexander suspects she's got real jewels with her, too—a real, for sure, titled lady from London. I'm supposed to go to the woman's cabin on that steamboat and put everything of any value she's got with her into this suitcase."

He held up the case, and the others whooped and hollered. Chad spit tobacco juice, some of it catching on his short beard. "She's some prim and proper young thing," he continued. "Trusting, and as virgin as they get. We'll meet up with Alexander again in Hays City and get a good look at her." He tied the suitcase to his saddle horn. "You boys go on up to the Lady Luck for drinks and wait for me there. I have to get that money before the lady's trunks are loaded onto the train."

"Sure, boss," one of the other men answered. He and the others headed for the saloon, while Chad made his way through the crowd onto the *Anna Leigh*. He had more to do than retrieve Lady Elizabeth Baylor's valuables. A young woman named Lora was waiting in her room for Alexander to bring her tickets to head back to New York. Chad would meet her instead. He'd been given orders and paid a lot of money to make sure Miss Lora Means never made it back to New York.

"She knows too much," Robert had told him. "I want her silenced."

Chad knew exactly how to silence her.

EIGHTEEN

"COME ON, YOU SONOFABITCH! PUT ME ON A HORSE!"
Ben Rosell struggled to keep up. His wrists were now
tied together in front of him instead of behind, and
Logan had in turn tied Rosell to the packing cords of
his extra horse.

"You have to earn it, Rosell," Logan answered. He
sat astride Jasper in front of the packhorse, a cigarette
dangling from his lips as he spoke.

Rosell fell to his knees, then scrambled to get back
up again, having no doubt Logan Best would otherwise drag him for a while. "My feet are killing me.
And I'm sweating to death," he protested. "The man
I work for will have your hide for this!"

Logan halted Jasper and turned around to eye
Rosell. "Mister, if your feet are killing you, it's because
you insist on wearing fancy duds and expensive shoes
just to show off. It's not my fault they aren't made for
long walks. And until you give me the information I
want, I'll not give you any breaks or any water."

"But…you can't do this! It's against the law!"

Logan shook his head and turned around to kick

Jasper into a slow walk again. "Right now I *am* the law, Rosell, and I really don't give a damn what you think the rules are. Besides, you don't seem too sorry about breaking the law yourself."

"You bastard! I'll not tell you a damn thing. You said they'll hang me in Mirage anyway, so why should I talk? What would it get me?"

"It will get you a canteen and a ride on my pack-horse," Logan answered. "It's true they will hang you, but you could at least make the trip to Mirage a lot easier on yourself. I can stretch this out for days, and you can suffer the whole time if you insist. I'm in no hurry. Got no special schedule, so it's all up to you. You can walk for the next five or six days, or you can get on my packhorse."

Rosell did not reply. He simply struggled along. He could tell his feet were already bleeding inside his shoes, but if he kicked off his shoes, it would be worse. The prairie grass would cut into his feet, and there were rocks all over this land, let alone snakes. His silk suit was already dirty and grass stained from other falls, and there were several tears in his jacket and pants. "What did you do with my belongings?" he demanded.

Logan finished his cigarette and crushed it out against his canteen, making sure it was completely out before tossing the butt into the dry prairie grass. He was surprised at how little rain had fallen on this trip. It was getting close to the end of May, the season when several spring storms usually hit this part of the country, and sometimes even a tornado or two. He was caught in a tornado once, out on the wide-open prairie. That was something he preferred to never experience again.

"You won't need your belongings," he finally answered. "And what money I found in your goods on the train is safely packed away in my own gear. Your card winnings are going to Miss Macy, and the rest will be returned to Mr. Sam Rinker in Abilene, the man you stole it from. I expect he'll give some of it to that whore you beat on, and he's paying me good money to come back with evidence of your death."

"Whores don't count when it comes to beating on a woman," Rosell protested.

"A woman is a woman, Rosell."

"And this country has come a long way!" Rosell coughed on dust and shook some from his hair. "We have laws now. Courts! I deserve at least a fair trial, hanging or not!"

"That's up to the folks in Mirage. They all like Clive Macy and his wife, and they all like Linda Sue. They won't be feeling too charitable toward you."

"Have you no feelings? No conscience?"

Logan didn't answer right away. He stopped to drink some water out of his canteen, deliberately taking a long swallow in front of Rosell. He capped the canteen and hung it back over his saddle horn. "My feelings went out the window when I lost my wife and daughter to bastards not a lot different from you," he said. "I still have a conscience…sometimes… especially when it comes to a man beating up on a little girl." There it was again—that sharp pain Logan felt in his chest whenever he thought about his little girl's cruel, senseless death.

"Linda Sue Macy was no little girl. She was the *devil*! I've never known a woman to fight like she did. She's mean and feisty and talks like a man in a saloon!"

"Maybe so, but she was a virgin and saving herself for some nice young man, not for an ugly sonofabitch like you." He turned to look back at Rosell and grinned. "You know, that girl said she'd never seen a man naked before, but even at that, she by God realized they had to have bigger peckers than yours."

Rosell's eyes grew wide with rage. "What would that little snit know?"

Logan chuckled and got Jasper into motion again. "Plenty. She's helped breed her pa's bulls and has been around animals and ranch hands her whole life. I'm sure she's heard plenty of jokes around the corral when the men on that ranch didn't know she was around. She likely had a pretty good idea how a man should be built." He reached into his shirt pocket for another pre-rolled cigarette. "Now that I think about it, if you're small enough, maybe you didn't even take her virginity."

Rosell went into a tirade of name-calling, screaming at the top of his lungs about Linda Sue not being old enough to know what she was talking about, and defending his manhood.

Logan chuckled and rode a little faster, enjoying Rosell's protests and curses. Rosell finally fell, unable to keep up. Logan dragged him for several hundred feet before finally stopping and dismounting. He walked back to Rosell, then pulled out his .44 and knelt down to ram it against Rosell's privates, making the man cry out.

"You're going to talk, Rosell, or this will be the most miserable trip of your life! By the time we get to Mirage, you'll be *begging* them to hang you, just to put you out of your misery."

Rosell grimaced and curled up his legs, tears in his eyes. "You don't realize…who I am," he whined.

"I know *exactly* who you are. You're a little man with a big mouth…a little man who beats on and rapes women just to feel like a *big* man! You brag about how rich you are to other men because that's the only way you can look important in their eyes. You're a braggart who probably wouldn't have a shirt on his back if it wasn't for the man behind you who pays you for whatever it is you do. It's likely you were running *out* of money on that trip to Denver, so you decided to *steal* some from the man who owned that saloon back in Abilene. Who is your backer, Rosell?" Logan jammed the pistol harder, and Rosell screamed. "Who's behind you?" he asked again. "And what the hell do you do for him? Is it Sir Robert Alexander? You've mentioned his name to others often enough. And tell me about a woman called Betsy, and a gang of men led by someone called Chad!"

Again, Rosell screamed when Logan jammed the gun into his privates. "All right! All right!" Tears streamed down Rosell's face. "Just promise me you'll give me some water and let me ride."

"I'll do all of that, but if you lie to me or refuse to talk again, the deal is *off*, understand?"

"Yeah! Yeah! Just let me…sit down somewhere in the grass. And let me take off my jacket and my shoes for a while. Please!"

"Is please the word that whore used when you were beating her up? Or what Linda Sue said? *Please stop!* Is that what they said?"

"I...I don't remember. Just do what you said you would do. I'll tell you what you want to know."

Logan jerked the man to his feet, then walked up to his packhorse and untied the rope. He led Rosell and the horses to a lonely cottonwood tree that had somehow managed to sprout in the middle of nowhere. He tied the horses beneath it while Rosell sat down under the tree, grunting as he hit the ground. He continued crying while Logan took his canteen from Jasper and walked over to Rosell, uncorking it and handing it out. "One swallow," he told him.

Rosell grabbed the canteen and took a long drink, then handed it back. Logan corked it, then yanked off Rosell's shoes. He took out the knife he wore at his side then, and Rosell's eyes grew wide as he lowered the knife. "You want that jacket off, but I don't intend to untie you, Rosell, so I'll *cut* off that fancy jacket."

Rosell grimaced. "Do you know how much this suit cost me in New York?"

Logan just shook his head. "Jesus, you're the most worthless bastard I've ever met," he grumbled. He took the knife, and Rosell cried out with shock and fear when Logan ripped through the jacket with the knife and pulled it off, piece by piece. He also ripped off Rosell's once-fancy paisley vest and tossed that aside. Then he ripped open the front of the man's shirt. "That ought to be cooler for you," he growled. He pulled off Rosell's socks and enjoyed seeing blisters on the man's feet, some of them bleeding.

He sat back then, taking a puff on his partially smoked cigarette. He waved the gun at Rosell. "Start talking, unless you want me to ram this thing right up your ass. Who the hell is Robert Alexander?"

Rosell struggled to stop crying. He raised his hands to his face to wipe at his tears. "He's...a wealthy man from New York City."

"What's his role in all of this?"

He spoke haltingly. "He's a...professional gambler...doesn't like to work, so he lives off...the money he gets from his dead father's businesses... back in New York. But that's not enough to cover his gambling. He's involved...in other things—other ways to make money. He started coming west three or four years ago. I...can't remember. He figured this was where a man could find ways to get money, legally or illegally, because there's hardly any law out here. I...met him at a card game, and he...talked about how he liked to visit the whores...said it was too bad they were mostly not much to look at. He likes women, but he said something like 'the young fresh ones are the best.'" Rosell sniffed and wiped at his nose with the back of his hand. "I told him lots of men out here...would like that, too...on account of there aren't many women out here that aren't already married or are used-up prostitutes. I said there were men out here...who would pay good money for young, pretty women." He forced a grin. "I know I would. Wouldn't you?"

"Willing is one thing. Unwilling is something else. So, you offered to find fresh women if he'd pay you for them?"

"No, I…well…yes. And I told him the Apache would take guns in return for…captured white women."

"So, he runs guns, too?"

Rosell nodded. "I need…another drink."

Logan handed him the canteen and let him take another swallow of water. Rosell poured some over his head before handing it back. "It's not just women," he continued. "He does have legal investments out here. He owns a couple of gold mines, but I think he got them by swindling whoever owned them out of their claims. He owns some land, too. The man you called Chad…he helps. He runs the guns for Robert— picks up the women and delivers them to a whore-house down in Oklahoma. They also rustle cattle for a ranch Robert owns. He saw how the beef business was growing because of the trains, so he got started in that, too, with stolen cattle. The man has all kinds of ways of making money, some legal—most not so legal. He spends most of his time gambling. He'll do anything to make sure he has money for that. He comes out here two or three times a year to check on his investments and get hold of whatever money he's made."

Rosell sniffed again, grimacing as he curled up his legs, still in pain from sore privates.

"Keep going," Logan told him, waving his gun again.

Rosell swallowed before continuing. "When he's in New York, Robert visits his father's businesses and pretends to be involved, but he doesn't do much. He said this last time that he was going to go overseas to London. Said he wanted to see about finding wealthy men there who might invest in his ranch and gold mines. Europeans—they're real interested in America and how it's growing. I've seen some come west to invest or to settle." He sniffed again. "Anyway, I got a wire from Robert a few weeks ago, saying he was back and had an investor, and he was bringing her out here."

"*Her?*"

"Yeah. Said he thought he'd found a good source of new money and had a pretty woman to sell to boot. Said this one was going to be worth a fortune. I was... when I took Linda Sue...I was just wanting to have a woman ready to sell when he got here. You were right about me getting low on money when I robbed that saloon. I like to gamble, too."

"And spend money on fancy clothes. It's your way of trying to get some respect, Rosell, but it doesn't work that way. Were you supposed to meet up with Robert in Denver?"

Rosell leaned his head back against the tree trunk. "That's why I was going that way. I rent a little house there. I was going to keep Linda Sue there till Robert arrived. I expect he already met up with Chad and his gang somewhere. They would have headed for Denver, too. I'm not sure. He's likely already robbed the woman of her money. I have a feeling she was pretty rich. I don't know how he got his hands on her, but Sir Robert is a very good-looking man who shows off his wealth. It's easy for him to woo a young, unsuspecting woman. I expect he'll try to have his way with this one before he turns her over to Chad and his gang, but then again, maybe not. Virgins are worth a lot more money, but the man likes women. He won't go without for long."

Logan jerked Rosell to his feet. "Where would he likely dump her off to this Chad? And what is Chad's last name?"

"I think it's Krieger," Rosell answered with another grimace of pain as Logan half dragged him to the pack-horse. "He has a gang of seven or eight men, all mean as hell. You wouldn't have a chance against them."

"You'd be surprised. And you didn't answer my question. Where does Robert usually meet up with the man?"

"I have no idea. Honest. It's always someplace different. I doubt Robert is any farther than Kansas City right now. He might even still be on the Missouri River. He said he wasn't leaving New York till May fifteenth. It takes about eight days to get from New York to Kansas City, a lot of it by steamboat."

"*Describe* him."

Rosell shook his head. "Damn you! I hope the man makes sure you *die*, Logan Best!"

Logan pulled him close. "*Describe* him, or you won't have any balls left by the time we reach Mirage."

"Tall, like you," Rosell answered through gritted teeth. "Dark. Handsome. Dresses like an English Lord or something. You won't have any trouble recognizing him. And he'll likely be with a beautiful young woman with an English accent."

Logan gave Rosell an angry shove against the horse. "I have to hurry up and get you to Mirage before the man manages to get past me," he told him.

"Ouch! My feet!" Rosell protested.

Logan lifted the man and threw him belly-first over the packhorse.

"Wait! You promised me I could ride to Mirage!"

"And I'm keeping that promise," Logan growled. "I never told you *how* you'd be riding." He took the rope that was tied around Rosell's wrists and pulled it under the horse, tying the other end around the man's ankles.

"You can't take me back like this!"

"I can do anything I want. Soon as we reach a spot where we can hop a train, we can be in Mirage by tomorrow if we're lucky."

"Then what?"

"Then I watch you hang, collect my bounty on you, and head east along the rail lines. I have a good description of this Sir Robert Alexander now, although I doubt he is really titled at all. The sonofa-bitch probably just made it up to sound important."

Logan picked up the reins to the packhorse and mounted Jasper, kicking the horse into motion.

"Are you going to speak up for me in Mirage?" Rosell literally screamed the words. "I gave you a lot of information! That has to be worth something!"

"I'll tell them to make sure the rope around your neck is tied right so's your neck breaks right away, and you don't suffer," Logan answered. He smiled at the string of curses that came out of Rosell's mouth.

NINETEEN

May 25, 1870

ELIZABETH STROLLED THE BOARDWALK OF KANSAS City's main street with Robert holding her arm and keeping himself between her and the street for protection. She jumped when she heard a gunshot, and Robert moved an arm around her waist and pulled her closer.

"You wanted to see the real West, my dear," he told her. "You are now getting a taste of it."

Elizabeth huddled closer. "I did say that, didn't I?" She laughed lightly.

"Things get pretty wild out here, especially after dark. We'd better get you to your room."

Elizabeth realized she was actually getting a little more accustomed to the smell of thousands of cattle. "Are you sure I'll be safe at the hotel?"

"Of course you will. Just stay off the streets. I'll be doing some gambling this evening, so keep your door locked. I'll be staying in a room next to yours when I get back."

They passed a saloon where someone played a rousing tune on a piano. She could hear laughter and whistles. When she glanced over at the swinging doors, through a haze of smoke she could see painted women dancing with men.

"Robert, are those women…you know…"

"Prostitutes?"

Elizabeth covered her eyes. "What an awful word!"

Robert chuckled. "Those women are all over out here. I'm sure many of them have stories about why they do what they do, but some of them make good money. You're lucky you are rich, my dear. You certainly don't want to ever be destitute out here—not a beautiful young thing like you."

What a wild, fascinating place. But Robert's words frightened her. She was already beginning to see how dangerous it would be out here for a woman alone, especially one with no money. Marriage was beginning to look like the best way to keep herself safe.

"We could marry right now," Robert told her, as if reading her thoughts, "if it will make you feel better about traveling alone with me."

Three riders went charging past on horseback, shouting and laughing. They dismounted and tore into the saloon. Robert hurried Elizabeth farther down the boardwalk and across the street, heading for the hotel.

"No. I still want to take a little time and marry in Denver," Elizabeth answered, "in a nice church in the best part of town. I want to buy a wedding dress there, or have one made for me. And I want to find a personal maid first to help me with all of it."

"Whatever you wish."

Elizabeth stopped walking and looked up at him. He looked even more handsome by the light of an outdoor oil lamp. "Thank you for the wonderful meal, Robert. I am so full, and so tired from this long day. I think I will turn in as soon as I get to my room."

"I don't blame you. We will be leaving by train in the morning. Our next stop will be Abilene. You wanted to get a taste of everything out here, so you will get to see every crazy cow town all the way to Denver, all from a very comfortable private train car."

Elizabeth smiled as Robert walked her into the hotel lobby. "Are you sure my trunks are safe?" she asked.

"They are being well guarded and will be on the train in the morning. How many times must I tell you that?"

"I have so many valuables in those trunks, Robert."

"I am well aware of that, which is why I came along with you this whole way—marriage or no marriage. I want to protect you."

"And I'm so grateful."

Robert walked her up the stairs to her room. "You won't find luxury hotels in these towns," he told her, "not like what you are accustomed to. But you will enjoy all the luxury you deserve once we reach Denver." He stopped at her door and pulled her close when they were out of sight of people in the lobby. "I do love you so, Elizabeth. I can hardly wait until we can marry." He leaned down, and Elizabeth allowed another kiss. Again, his lips seemed cold, but the kiss was gentle. She was sure he would also be a gentleman in her bed. She could hardly believe she'd met such a wonderful man at a time when she needed him most.

"And I love you," she answered sincerely. "I'm sorry to make you wait until we reach Denver, but it just seems right."

"I understand. I was just offering the idea of marrying sooner because I know it bothers you that we are traveling alone together. I would never want to soil the reputation of the woman I intend to marry."

Elizabeth smiled, and he kissed her again. "You stay in your room tonight and lock the door. Tomorrow will be another exciting day for you."

"Yes, it will. Good night, Robert."

He smiled at her. "Good night."

Elizabeth reluctantly left him and went into her room, closing and locking the door. She heard more gunshots and hurried to a window to look out at more men whooping and hollering as they rode up and down the street. A moment later, she saw Robert exit the hotel and head across the street and into a saloon, the very same saloon where she'd seen those painted women dancing and cavorting with the men.

He's just going there to gamble, she told herself. Sir Robert Alexander was far too much a gentleman to visit those sinful painted women.

TWENTY

May 26, 1870

LOGAN LEANED AGAINST THE WALL OF THE CLOSEST building and watched as Clive Macy pulled the lever that opened a trap door under Ben Rosell. With a front-row view, Linda Sue held her head high as Rosell's body plunged through the floor of the hanging platform and his neck snapped so loudly everyone heard it. Gasps and groans moved through the crowd in unison, and some looked away, but not Linda Sue. After standing there staring at the taut rope for a moment, she turned and headed toward Logan. The crowd parted ways for her, most of them silent except for a few whispers.

Logan watched her closely. He tossed away a lit cigarette when she marched right up to him and threw her arms around him again, as she'd done when he'd first promised to find Ben Rosell.

"Thank you again," she told him.

"My pleasure, Linda Sue."

Linda Sue pulled away, looking up at him with big, dark eyes that had circles under them. "You're some man, Logan Best. If I was older, I'd be setting my sights on you. I'll be praying for your future conquests and hoping you don't ever get hurt."

Logan grinned. "I appreciate that. And if you were older, or me younger, I'd be *proud* to have you set your sights on me. You just make sure the man you settle with some day deserves you and treats you right. I have to say, he'll have to be pretty brave to hold up against the likes of Linda Sue Macy."

The girl grinned. "Yup." She grasped one of Logan's hands. "Can you come back to the house for pie and coffee again?"

Logan squeezed her hand and pulled away. "I'd like to, but I learned a lot from Rosell about the men who are part of his dirty dealings. I aim to find them. I'm thinking the leader of the bunch is headed this way with a woman who might be in trouble and not even know it. I'm heading east toward Abilene, hoping to catch him coming this way. I expect if I make it to Abilene, I'll go ahead and collect my bounty on Rosell from that saloon owner he stole from."

Linda Sue nodded. "I understand. You be dang careful, Logan. I suspect those other men you want to find are real mean. You let us know when you're done, so's we know you're okay. Promise me."

"I promise."

Linda Sue turned to her father as Clive reached out and shook Logan's hand. He reached into his left pocket and brought forth a wad of bills that he handed to Logan. "Me and the people in Mirage raised three hundred dollars for you, Mr. Best. You did a good job trackin' down that no-good."

"And we enjoyed watching him beg and cry," one of Clive's cowhands told Logan. "Made watching his hanging even more enjoyable."

"I've never seen such a sniveling excuse of a man," another put in.

"And we're glad you made him suffer some on the way here," Clive added.

"I figured on extra bounty, but it just doesn't seem right to keep it in this case," Logan said. He handed the three hundred dollars to Linda Sue. "You put this with that money I gave you from Rosell's card game. Use it to buy the things you will need to set up a household of your own someday."

Linda Sue's eyes widened. "But you *earned* this money."

"What I earned is the satisfaction of getting rid of a cheating, swindling sonofabitch who can't hurt young girls anymore. That's enough for me."

Linda Sue looked down at the money in her hand. "I don't know what to say, but thank you."

"That's good enough."

"That's right nice of you, Mr. Best," Clive said.

"Did Rosell tell you about that man called Sir Robert Alexander?" Linda Sue asked.

"That and more. There's a gang of men involved also. They deal in stolen cattle and swindling men out of their mining claims, as well as selling guns to the Comanche for captured women."

The couple of women present drew in their breath and turned away.

"We all wish you luck, Mr. Best," Clive told him. "I expect you want to get after the others soon as you can."

Logan adjusted his hat. "I do, which is why I'm leaving right away." He headed for Jasper, already saddled and ready, as was his packhorse. He'd only stayed to watch the hanging.

The whole crowd followed him. Logan felt embarrassed. He didn't usually get such a friendly reception when he turned a man in. Usually, it was simply a matter of delivering a dead body, or once in a while, a live one, to the closest lawman. Most often, no one cared one whit about him or his prisoner. He almost felt guilty for the heroic way these people were treating him. He sure as hell wasn't any hero. He was just a man out to earn more bounty money.

"Come back any time," Clive told him.

Others in the crowd voiced their own welcomes in various ways.

Logan glanced at Rosell's drooping body. The man's head hung in a weird, rather grotesque position. It almost looked as though it might fall off. *Good riddance*, he thought. He glanced at Linda Sue. She'd lost an innocence she'd never know again. He was glad to see how strong she was. She wouldn't let what had happened get the better of her, and a girl like her didn't lose any respect over her situation. She'd do okay.

"You take care, Linda Sue. Don't break too many hearts."

She smiled. "I'll try not to." Tears suddenly formed in her eyes. "Don't you go doing something stupid and getting hurt, Logan Best."

"I'll try not to."

Linda Sue and Clive stepped back as Logan turned his horse. It was time to head for Abilene. Maybe he could reach Robert before he did more harm to some innocent woman. It still bothered him that he hadn't caught up with Ben Rosell before he hurt Linda Sue.

Not this time, he told himself. He kicked Jasper's sides and headed east.

TWENTY-ONE

May 28, 1870

ELIZABETH SLIPPED HER NIGHTGOWN ON AND LOOKED out the small window of the luxurious Pullman car Robert had purchased for their journey on the Kansas Pacific railway. There were bedrooms and bath facilities at each end of the car, and in between, a lounge area with stuffed chairs and chandcliers. The car was as comfortable as any luxurious hotel room. She'd traveled once in a similar train car in England, but she was surprised they were already available here in America, since the railroad was so new in the West. The Pullman car she enjoyed now was such a contrast to the rugged country they were traveling through.

She could see nothing out the window. It was already dark. Although she and Robert shared this car, Elizabeth felt perfectly comfortable in the fact that the sleeper compartments were far apart. Besides that, she could lock her sleeping area from the inside, although she felt that wasn't needed. On this whole trip, Robert had made sure they had stayed in the best hotels, and her room on the riverboat had been beautiful and comfortable. A Pullman porter waited on them hand and foot, running and getting her anything she needed, and bringing their meals, which she and Robert shared in the lounge area, drinking tea and talking about their plans for the future. The only upsetting thing she'd witnessed was men shooting down buffalo when hundreds of them caused the train to stop yesterday.

She thought the great beasts were beautiful and was thrilled to see them for the first time, but she hated watching them being shot for no reason at all. Robert had simply said it was the best way to get rid of the Indians, who relied on the buffalo for everything they needed. *Kill the buffalo and you kill off the Indians.* His remark seemed so cold, as though the Indians were worth no more than flies or snakes to be eradicated from the earth.

This was their third night on the train. In just a few days they would be in Denver, where they would have a grand wedding and build their mansion. Just as Robert had promised, her personal trunks were in the car waiting for them when they boarded in Kansas City. She hadn't even bothered to check the trunk that carried her jewels and banknotes. Most of her things of immediate need were in the other two trunks. All three trunks were well guarded when transferred from the riverboat, and from then on they had been right here with her. Robert had made sure they were safe as they traveled through more of what Robert called "cow towns" on their way to Denver.

Tomorrow they would be in Abilene. She'd enjoyed every stop along the way, drinking in the sights of this very different world called America. And big! Everything was so big!

She brushed out her hair several times over, having heard that the more a woman brushed her hair, the fuller and shinier it became. She studied herself in the mirror, remembering Lora telling her what handsome children she and Robert would have. She missed Lora and hoped she made it back to New York with no problems.

She thought about what she should wear tomorrow, perhaps the lovely deep-pink dress she'd not worn in a while. The material was lightweight cotton and would be cool in the hot Kansas weather, and the neckline was just low enough for a tempting reveal of her cleavage. She wanted to be beautiful at breakfast for Robert, and she remembered a pearl necklace she'd brought with her. It was another piece of jewelry that had belonged to her beloved mother.

William wouldn't mind her dressing this way, and he would love to see her wearing the pearl necklace. She stood up from the dressing table and walked to the trunk that carried her jewels. It was yellow, with a white, deep-satin lining into which was sewn her banknotes. Her jewels were in the bottom of the trunk. All she had to do was uncover and open the door at the false bottom to get to them.

She knelt and opened the yellow trunk. It was full of dresses and petticoats packed tightly, things she'd decided she wouldn't need until they reached Denver. She thought how wrinkled they would be by then. She would have to find someone to press all her clothes. She carefully removed each dress and laid it on her bed neatly, so it would be easy to put them back into the trunk and still get it closed.

She finally managed to empty the trunk of most things when she noticed the lining at the sides had been ripped away. "What on earth?" she muttered.

Had someone stolen her valuables? She quickly tossed out the rest of the dresses to see the lining at the bottom of the trunk was also torn away. She flung open the trap door, and her jewels were also gone!

She drew in her breath and covered her mouth in shock. Robert had told her the trunks had been guarded this entire trip. She rose, still staring at the ripped lining.

"Robert!" she screamed. He had to know about this and report it. Her money. All her money. And her mother's jewels! "Robert!" she screamed again.

There came a knock on her door, and Elizabeth hurried to open it, forgetting she wore only her nightgown and no robe. Robert stood at the door in a silk house coat.

"My dear, what is it?"

Elizabeth grabbed his arm. "Robert, my jewels and money are gone!" she cried. "Look!" She dragged him over to the trunk. "You have to report this right away!" She looked up at him. "What shall I do? My entire wealth was in those jewels and the banknotes."

Robert looked at her strangely. He reached out and touched the side of her face, glancing down at her bosom. Elizabeth realized he could tell she wore no camisole or any other kind of underwear beneath her nightgown. She suddenly felt embarrassingly exposed.

"You won't need your money and jewels," Robert told her. "It's all taken care of, my lovely."

What was that look in his eyes? Dark. Hungry. Dangerous. He'd never looked at her like this before. "What are you talking about?" she asked.

Robert shook his head, grasping the back of her neck a little too tightly. "You are so damn innocent and trusting, Elizabeth Baylor."

All senses came alert. Elizabeth tried to back away, but his grip on the nape of her neck was too firm. "What…what do you mean? Let go of me, Robert."

He grinned. "Didn't you wonder even once about how your brother managed to fall overboard on that ship coming over here?" he asked.

Elizabeth blinked. "I… The storm…"

"He was drunk, my dear. And I'm the one who *got* him drunk…so it would be easier to cause an accident."

Elizabeth's heart pounded so hard she could hardly get her breath. "You…*pushed* him?"

"And didn't you wonder why I sent Lora back home?"

So you could get me alone, Elizabeth thought. She stiffened defensively. "Did you kill her, too?"

"I thought you might figure all of this out sooner," Robert answered. "You are clever and industrious and schooled, Elizabeth Baylor, but you don't know a damn thing about real life, or about men, or about living in a lawless land. You never even asked how I got my title."

"I… You—"

"I don't have a title, Elizabeth." He squeezed her neck almost painfully now. "I use it because it brings respect and makes me appear a high-class gentleman. Even my sister doesn't know it's not real. I told her I was awarded the title on one of my trips to England, for contributing to business there. Helen knows nothing about the life I lead away from New York."

Elizabeth shook her head, backing away when he finally let go of her. "My God! You killed your wife, too, didn't you?"

Robert folded his arms and shrugged. "I got tired of her. Lora serviced me in all the ways a man needs whenever Alivia was asleep. And when Alivia got pregnant, I had to do something about it. I have no time in my life for a child."

Elizabeth was not so much shocked by what he'd done as she was shocked over his cool attitude about it. His wife and poor, trusting William had meant nothing to him! He spoke of killing them as though it meant no more than dumping garbage. "Did you really send Lora home?"

His dark eyes grew even darker. "Lora knew a little too much. A man who helps with my businesses out here got rid of her for me. He is also the one who has your jewels and your banknotes."

Elizabeth struggled to think straight. "It was that man you met in Kansas City, wasn't it?"

"At last, she is waking up to reality," Robert gloated, smiling.

Elizabeth wanted to cry for Lora…for William…for being so stupid as to fall for this man's treachery…for losing all of her wealth because of her own stupidity… her own innocent trust of a man just because he was wealthy and respected and he'd been kind and attentive and helpful. He'd even proposed to her!

She felt as though someone had just punched her in

the stomach. This man had seemed like any woman's dream for a husband. Had she seen only dollar signs after all? Would marrying this man have been any different from marrying Lord Henry Mason just for money and status? No. It would have been much worse. She might have ended up suffering the same fate as his first wife.

But she'd *loved* Robert Alexander. She'd given her heart to him. All her wealth. All her trust. All her confidence.

"What are your intentions?" she managed to say. Her mouth was bone dry. Already she realized he'd told her too much. Surely he wouldn't let her live after admitting to murdering people. And here she was alone in this train car. Reality moved through her like a vile disease tearing through her veins. All trust and innocence vanished, and her initial instincts about protecting herself as a woman alone came rushing to the surface. *Think!* she told herself, facing Robert squarely.

"Can't you tell, my dear?"

Elizabeth backed up even more, her legs against the trunk. She could go no farther. She quickly glanced around. The train windows were too small to climb through. And since they were on the last train car, no one in the other cars could possibly hear her screams. "Where are my jewels and the banknotes?" she demanded, putting on a stance of bravery and a determined fight.

He stepped closer again. "I told you. Chad has everything. And you will be meeting him very soon. It won't be enjoyable, I assure you. You are worth a fortune. Nineteen. Beautiful. Untouched—or at least taken by only one man. *Me!* Even so, men will pay a fortune to bed the likes of an English lady. In the meantime, those jewels of yours will bring a lot of money, and before we left New York, I made sure I have full rights to sign and cash in those banknotes. That banker and I are very good friends."

Elizabeth refused to break down in front of him. He would get too much pleasure from her tears. "You won't get away with this! My brother in London will come looking for me."

"*Will* he? I think not. From what you told me, he doesn't care much that you left, and he's been told by now that your brother drowned at sea. I told the captain of the *Abyssinia* to tell your brother in London that you are in good hands and he should wait to hear from you when you reach Denver. It will take a while for him to realize something might be wrong. By then, you will have disappeared, my love. After I break you in myself, I'll turn you over to Chad and his gang when we reach Hays City. I can't guarantee they won't all take a turn with you, but then you wouldn't be worth quite as much, so maybe they will do no more than strip you just to get a good look at those beautiful curves."

Elizabeth felt her blood run cold. This couldn't be happening. It just couldn't. Not Robert! This had to be a bad dream. Yet now it all made sense. Sir Robert Alexander could do anything he wanted with her now, and no one would hear what was happening. He'd waited until just the right time. He could make her a prisoner in her own sleeping area and no one would know it. All he had to do was gag her or knock her out or drug her and tell anyone who came into the car that she was resting. He'd just been waiting until they were far from civilization.

"So, when we reach Abilene, you will hand me off in the middle of the night to this man called Chad."

Robert smiled. "Maybe Abilene. Maybe Hays City. They left the day I met up with them in Kansas City, so they have a head start. Actually, I told them Hays City, but you never know. They know we will be stopping in both places."

Elizabeth's eyes teared. "*Why?* You could have had me the right way, Robert. We could have married, and you wouldn't need to tell me any of the dastardly things you have done. We could have just gone on and lived as a happy, wealthy couple in Denver and had the world at our fingertips."

A *tsk*, *tsk* slid through his lips. "And what fun would that be? I would have become bored with you in no time and would have cheated on you with the whores in Denver. And it would have been harder then to get rid of you without being found out. It's so much more exciting this way." He untied his robe and dropped it.

Elizabeth's eyes widened, and she gasped. He was totally naked under the robe. Not only that, but his private man part was swollen and sticking out. She didn't need any feminine counseling to know what she was looking at and what he intended to do with it. She dived onto the bed, intending to climb across it and run for the door, but Robert was a big, tall, strong man. In a moment he was on her. He flipped her onto her back and pinned down her arms.

No! She was not going to let this man take what

was only hers to give willingly! He tried to wedge her legs apart with his knees. Her mind rushed with ways to stop him, and when he came closer to plant his mouth over hers, she reared her head as quickly and as forcefully as she could, slamming her forehead into his nose.

She heard a crack, and he cried out. Blood instantly dripped onto her face and neck, and he let go of her.

Elizabeth quickly rolled away, dropping to the floor and scrambling to the second trunk that had been loaded onto the train.

"You bitch!" Robert yelled. "You broke my nose!"

Elizabeth flung open the trunk and desperately rummaged through it for the pistol William had packed before they'd left London. She frantically felt around to the bottom of the trunk, and just as she felt the gun handle, Robert was on her again. He yanked her to her feet and threw her back onto the bed.

"I'll show you how it feels to take a man for the first time, you stupid child! And I'll do it as often as I want until I hand you over to Chad Krieger!"

His face covered in blood, he shoved her nightgown above her waist and yanked her legs apart, then settled that hard, naked part of him against her.

Elizabeth was desperate. She felt for the gun hammer. She'd never fired a gun, but she'd gone with William on shooting practices. She damn well knew how a gun worked. Robert came down close and she pulled back the hammer of the pistol and held it against his chest.

"Get off of me!" she growled.

Robert hesitated, then grinned. "Where in hell did you get that pistol?"

"It was *William's*! What better pistol to use to kill you than my poor *brother's*?"

"You're too young and innocent and trusting to pull that trigger," Robert snarled.

"*Am* I?"

Before Robert could answer, Elizabeth fired. The gunshot was muffled because it was so close to his chest. Robert stared at her a moment, astonishment in his eyes. Elizabeth felt blood running down her hand and onto her nightgown, quickly soaking through.

Robert's eyes rolled back in his head, and he collapsed on top of her.

Elizabeth broke into screams. "Oh my God! Oh my God, Robert, how could you do this to me?" She shoved him off of her, and he tumbled over the side of the bed and to the floor.

Elizabeth looked down at his bloody body, then looked at the pistol, the blood on her hands. She tossed the gun and stumbled to the door, practically every inch of her soaked in blood.

So, this was the wild, lawless American West! She'd wanted to experience all of it, but she never dreamed it would be quite this realistic. She was supposed to get a look at a real outlaw, not be the victim of one or become one herself!

She opened the door to her sleeping room and ran out into the lounge. She began to panic even more at the realization that maybe no one would believe her when she told them what had happened. Robert Alexander was a well-known, respected, wealthy businessman. This was the Wild West! Maybe she would be *hanged* for this. She had no idea what had happened to the man called Chad, or to her jewels and banknotes. Maybe Chad and his men would be waiting for her in Abilene. She knew absolutely no one out here, and in most places, there wasn't even any law. Maybe a U.S. Marshal would come for her. Maybe a mob would attack her and drag her off to a hanging tree, if the one called Chad didn't get hold of her first. After all, that's how it happened in the penny dreadfuls! Killers were always hanged! Robert Alexander was an important man. Maybe people would think she'd intended to rob him, that she had seduced him and then murdered him.

She sank to the floor. She would arrive in Abilene with blood on her hands and a dead man in her sleeping quarters. She would look like a harlot and a murderer, and she had absolutely no one to defend her.

TWENTY-TWO

May 29, 1870

Logan strolled into Sheriff Adam White's office in Abilene and handed him a letter. White looked up at him and frowned. "You again?"

"Yup." Logan noticed the man had a few crumbs in his long, black beard, probably from breakfast. "I already checked at Rinker's saloon, and he's out of town again, so I'm bringing you proof that I found the man Rinker was looking for. Rosell still had over three thousand dollars on him." Logan handed out a leather satchel. "The money is in here. That letter is from a Mr. Clive Macy and a few citizens of Mirage, Colorado, saying I brought them Mr. Ben Rosell. The town promptly hanged the man for kidnapping and raping Clive Macy's thirteen-year-old daughter."

White looked into the leather satchel, then back up at Logan. "You actually *found* the man? He had a good three-week start on you."

"He was easy to track. He was a braggart, and every place he stopped people remembered him. He also spent a few days at each stop along the way to Denver—liked to show off. That slowed him down."

White shook his head. "I'll be damned."

"I want you to give all that money to Mr. Rinker and tell him I'll be back to collect my bounty. Right now, I'm in kind of a hurry because I intend to find the man behind Rosell. His name is Robert Alexander. Have you—"

"*Alexander?*" White interrupted, speaking the name as though in shock.

It was then Logan heard an odd whimper from a jail cell behind the wall where the sheriff sat. White got to his feet.

"Logan, you have no idea—"

"Do you have a *woman* back there?" Logan interrupted.

"Well…yes. That's what I started to tell you. We didn't quite know what to do with her. She just rambles crazy when she talks." White leaned in closer and dropped his voice. "Logan, she shot a man on the Kansas Pacific. Bloodiest mess you ever saw! She claimed he attacked her, but heck, they were traveling alone together, so I don't know *what* to believe. We found the mess just this morning on their Pullman car when the train came in. The man's identification says his name is Robert Alexander."

Logan stepped back. "*What?*"

"Yes. And he was layin' in a sleeper car buck naked and covered in blood. There were dresses all over the bed in the back bedchamber, and they were covered in blood, too. We found a small pistol laying on the floor, and the woman—she's a young thing—she was just sitting in a chair in the parlor area wearing a nightgown and covered in blood—her clothes, her face, her hands—it was the most god-awful mess I ever saw. We've been trying to decide what to—"

Logan left him and hurried around the corner, and there in the jail cell sat what he thought might be a very beautiful woman with blond hair. He couldn't be sure because she was covered in so much blood. Even her hair was stuck together in places from dried blood.

His rage knew no bounds. After what Rosell had told him about Robert Alexander, he could just imagine what this woman had been through. He turned to Sheriff White when the man followed him to the cell.

"Why in hell is this poor woman sitting in there unwashed and unattended! Can't you see she's been through something awful?"

"We just weren't sure what to do with her—what to believe. She could be a murderess."

"*Murderess!* Hell!" Logan roared the words so loudly the sheriff stepped back defensively. "I know all about this Robert Alexander, and I can tell you if she shot him he damn well *deserved* it! Get that woman out of there."

Sheriff White shrugged. "What the hell are we supposed to do with her? She doesn't talk any sense."

"*Look* at her! She's shaking from shock. And she's probably scared as a baby rabbit. I guarantee Alexander brought her out here under false pretenses, and then he took her for every dime she has and was going to sell her to a whorehouse. Get her out of there. There are more men behind this, and I need to know what *she* knows and what Alexander took from her."

"You sure—"

"Get her *out* of there!" Logan raged.

White ran for the keys. Logan's shouted words made the woman look up. Her eyes widened, and she quickly curled up onto the cot where she sat and shook even harder.

"It's all right," Logan told her. "I'm going to get you some help."

She just kept staring at him as White returned with the keys and opened the cell door. Logan stepped inside.

The woman shook her head. "Don't let him touch me!" she screamed at the sheriff. "He's here to take me away to someplace awful!"

They were the first coherent words she'd spoken since Sheriff White had pulled her off the Pullman car.

Logan stepped closer. "Ma'am, I'm not going to—"

"His name is Chad!" she screamed at the sheriff. "He's here to pick me up and take me away. He rides with a lot of bad men! Robert told me about him!"

"Ma'am, this man isn't called Chad," the sheriff tried to assure her. "This is Logan Best. He's a bounty hunter, and he was after that man you killed. He wants to help you. His word is good, so we won't hold you any longer. Logan claims Alexander was a swindler of some kind."

"Don't believe him! He's Chad Krieger, and he's going to take me someplace where I'll never be found again. Look at him! He's filthy and wears guns and— he looks like an *outlaw*! Don't let him take me!"

White stepped closer and leaned down to look into the woman's eyes. "Ma'am, I *assure* you, this man isn't

Chad Krieger. He's a bounty hunter. He *hunts down* men like Chad Krieger. His name is Logan Best, and he wants to get you some help. You'll be safe with him."

The woman buried her face in her bloody hands and wept.

Logan turned to White. "Where is the closest doctor's office?"

"Couple of doors down. Doc Billings. This is the best time to catch him sober. It's still early. The man is pretty useless by eight o'clock or so at night."

"I'll carry her. You lead the way."

"Sure." White stepped back, and Logan walked closer to the woman. She shrank back again. Logan knelt in front of her.

"I'm not that man called Chad," he assured her again. "My name is Logan Best, and I was here in Abilene to collect bounty on a man called Ben Rosell. You ever hear that name?"

She shook her head.

Logan looked her straight in the eyes and hesitantly reached out to touch her arm. She didn't pull away. "Let me help you. What's your name?"

She watched his eyes, and her shaking stopped. "Elizabeth Baylor."

"Let me guess. Are you British? I mean, your accent tells me you are, but I need to know for sure."

Elizabeth nodded.

"And this man called Sir Robert Alexander duped you into trusting him—offered to bring you west and then managed to steal your money and turn on you. Right? He was taking you to someone. He was going to leave you with the man called Chad."

Elizabeth swallowed. "How—do you know all that?"

"It's a long story. But I'm not this man you call Chad Krieger. I'm *hunting* for Krieger."

Elizabeth broke into tears. "I'm alone out here. I don't know what to do. I killed him! I killed Robert!"

"And I'm betting it was for a damn good reason," Logan told her. "We need to talk, Miss Baylor. *Is* it Miss?"

Elizabeth wiped at her tears, smearing the blood on her face. "Lady," she answered, showing a spark of pride. "I am Lady Elizabeth Baylor...from London." She cried even harder. "I loved him! I was going to marry him! Why did he...do this?"

"Because he's a swindling sonofabitch," Logan answered. He rose. "Come on. Let me get you to a doctor." He looked at White. "Where are her things? She needs to wash up and get dressed. For God's sake, how could you leave her in this condition, and in a jail cell to boot?"

"We were going to have a meeting soon to discuss what to do with her."

"Common sense should have told you this woman didn't do anything wrong. *Look* at her! She's been abused, and she was probably just defending herself. If you weren't a lawman, I'd land a fist into your face. Where are her things?"

"They're still down at the depot."

"Then have somebody go get them and bring them to the doctor's office." Logan reached out for Elizabeth. "Can you walk?"

Elizabeth crossed her arms over her breasts as though

she thought Logan might be able to see through her gown. "I don't want people out there to see me. And…I'm barefoot."

Logan grasped her arms and pulled her up. He noticed she winced.

"Are your arms bruised?" he asked.

Elizabeth nodded.

Logan reached down and yanked a wool blanket off the cot. He wrapped it around her shoulders, covering her completely before lifting her into his arms. He thought how small and light she was. Her situation reminded him of what had happened to MaryAnne. He'd killed every last one of the men who'd hurt her before coming out here to hunt down every damn wanted man he could find.

"Let's get her to a doctor," he told the sheriff.

White obliged, heading out the front door.

A few people gathered to watch Logan Best carry the strange, bloody woman who'd killed a man to the doctor's office.

Elizabeth curled against him, her head on his shoulder. At least he could get help for this woman. He'd never had the chance to help MaryAnne.

TWENTY-THREE

May 30, 1870

ELIZABETH OPENED HER EYES TO A BLURRY FIGURE sitting in a chair across from her bed. It took a moment for her to focus her thoughts and her vision. A man sat there, wearing a six-gun and a big knife in a sheath at his belt. A second belt of cartridges hung over the corner of his chair, and a rifle was propped beside him. He wore a wide-brimmed hat, but she couldn't see his face well because his head was drooped in sleep.

She turned onto her back and looked at the ceiling, slowly remembering the horrors of last night. Or *was* it last night? How long had she been on this cot? She raised her hands to see there was no blood on them. She felt under the blankets and realized she wore a flannel nightgown. It felt clean and soft. She suspected it might not be hers because it felt too big. She touched her face and hair. It all felt clean, and she could tell there was not one pin or comb in her hair.

Voices. A big man talking to her, telling her she was safe. *I'm not Chad*, he'd told her. It must have been true, because here she lay, clean and fresh, in what smelled and felt like clean bedding. The room was quiet but for the soft ticking of a clock. The light outside the curtained window was dim, but she couldn't tell if it was from a sun coming up or a sun going down. She glanced at the ticking clock, which sat on a table beside the sleeping man. Seven o'clock. Was it a.m. or p.m.?

It struck her then like a sword in her heart. Robert! She'd killed Robert, the man who'd been so kind and attentive and gentle and understanding this whole way. He'd treated her like a queen. He was handsome and well set, and it would seem he needed nothing more in life. Why would he do the dastardly things he'd told her about? He'd killed his own wife and pushed William off the ship and let him drown. He owned businesses in New York City and had a lovely sister. Why did he feel he needed to swindle and murder his way to prosperity? Could pure evil exist in a man's heart? Poor William! She felt even more responsible now for his untimely death. And how awful for Robert's poor, pregnant wife, to be thrown down a flight of stairs by her own husband. And what had happened to Lora? She was so young. Had she trusted Robert, too? Or did she live in fear of what he could do to her if she didn't obey his every command?

Thank God she hadn't already married Robert. What kind of horror would she have gone through on her wedding night? She wasn't sure she could now ever trust *any* man, let alone give herself to one.

She remembered the big man who'd come into her jail cell, yelling at the sheriff to get her some help—remembered him wrapping her into a blanket and picking her up in his arms, demanding someone show him the way to a doctor. She remembered a stout, older woman helping her wash and talking soothingly to her. The doctor had given her something to drink to help her relax and sleep. Whatever it was, it must have worked, because she remembered little after that.

The big man. She thought she remembered him calling himself Logan. She looked at the man sleeping in a chair beside her bed. She was pretty sure he was the same man. If she could trust her memory, she thought he'd said something about being a bounty hunter.

Bounty hunter! What a horrible occupation. Surely he couldn't be a man with any feelings or a man to be trusted. Still, he'd been so upset by her situation when he'd found her in that jail cell. And he'd been so gentle when he'd picked her up and carried her to the doctor's office. He'd even seemed to understand she didn't want people looking at her, so he'd wrapped her in a blanket first.

The man started awake then, and Elizabeth pulled her blankets up to her neck and just stared at him as he cleared his throat. He removed his hat and ran a hand through shoulder-length, sandy-colored, very unkempt hair. He sorely needed a bath and a shave. He looked at her, only then realizing she was awake.

His eyes! They were sort of a brilliant green that seemed to have a light behind them. She'd not expected such eyes. There was something rather magnetic about him—his size, his weapons, his dangerous occupation. Though her feelings about men had been shattered by Robert Alexander, her womanly side told her this man was different, in spite of looking and behaving as different from a man like Robert as could be.

She'd come here wanting to experience the excitement of the American West, the cowboys and Indians, the gold miners, the buffalo hunter, all glorified in the penny dreadfuls. Once in a while, one of those little books would mention the bounty hunter, and here sat one, right in front of her. Everything about him spoke danger and "hands off." Why wasn't she afraid?

"So, you're finally awake," he told her in a deep voice. "I was beginning think maybe I should just leave and go have a beer somewhere." He grinned, and a handsome smile it was. Still, he was so disheveled.

"I... You're Logan Best, right?"

"Yes, ma'am."

"A bounty hunter?"

"Yes, ma'am."

What was it about those eyes? He looked at her in a way Robert had never looked at her. And Robert's eyes had always had a rather cold look in them. This man's eyes spoke warmth. "How long have you been sitting there?" she asked him.

"Most of yesterday and all last night."

So, it was seven a.m. "You mean—"

"You've been out since yesterday morning when I brought you here."

"But why did you help me? And why are you still here?" Her eyes widened with fear. "Is there a bounty on me? Will they try to hang me?"

He shook his head and grinned. "No, ma'am. It

was pretty obvious what happened to you. Nobody is going to hang you." He stretched his long legs out in front of him and crossed his ankles. Elizabeth noted he wore big leather boots, worn and dusty. "I didn't like the way you were being treated in that jail, so I took you out of there," he continued. "I know all about Robert Alexander. I'm still here because I was after Alexander and some of the men who work for him. I'll explain more in time, but right now you need to rest—a lot. There's no sense going into a long story for now. All I want to know is if Alexander stole money from you."

Elizabeth turned her head to stare up at the ceiling again. A tear slipped out of one corner of her right eye down her cheek. "Yes. Close to fifty thousand American dollars. He also stole my mother's jewels, which I had brought with me from England. I think I know who has both."

"Chad Krieger."

Elizabeth let out a light gasp and faced him. "How did you know?"

"I know a lot more than you think. I have a lot of questions for you, as you likely do for me, but right now I want you to sleep some more. Now that I know you're for-sure okay, I'll leave you alone for a day or two and go get that beer and find a place to sleep." He brushed at his shirt. "Sorry about my condition, but when a man is on the trail for days, he doesn't look or smell too good. I dragged a man to a distant town for a hanging a couple of days ago and then made my way here to Abilene as fast as I could, because I already knew Alexander might be on his way west." He stood up, much taller than Elizabeth expected. "I think I can get your money and jewels back, Miss Baylor, but that's something else we need to talk about another time. I just want your promise that you will stay right here and not try to move on alone. No woman as pretty and penniless as you should be traveling around out here by herself."

Elizabeth covered her eyes. "I learned that the hard way. And you should call me *Lady* Elizabeth, not Miss."

"Well, ma'am, I'm not much for fancy titles. I'll likely forget to call you anything but Miss Baylor, unless you don't mind if I call you by your first name."

The comment brought back memories of Robert. *May I call you Elizabeth?* he'd asked. So gentlemanly. She felt like the most ignorant fool ever born. Why did the request from this rough-hewn bounty hunter not offend her in the least?

"Like you said, we can talk about all of that later, Mr. Best," she answered.

Logan nodded, turning and putting on his hat. He stared at her a moment. "Either way, I'm sorry I didn't find Robert Alexander before you had to go through all this hell."

Elizabeth blinked back more tears. "It's not your fault." She faced him again. "It's mine, for being so incredibly trusting and ignorant."

He shrugged. "Maybe, but I still feel responsible. A very young girl suffered greatly at the hands of another womanizing, swindling bastard not long ago—right before I caught up with him. I found him and they hanged him, and that made me feel pretty good, but still, if I'd caught up with him sooner, things might have been different." He sighed. "He's the one who told me all about Robert Alexander, and about the man called Chad Krieger. Like I said, I think I can help you—at least maybe get your money and jewels back."

"Thank you, but why would you do that?"

He adjusted his hat. "Ma'am, for one thing, I don't like what these men do. For another, you're an innocent young lady who's been stiffed, and that makes me real angry. The biggest reason I'd help is because, if they stole practically fifty thousand dollars from you, I'm figuring I might collect a good bounty if I get it back for you." He grinned, this time a rather teasing smile.

Elizabeth couldn't help a tiny grin in return. "You would be right."

Logan nodded. "You get some rest. You're in the back room of a doctor's office. Doc Billings is his name. It was his wife, Ethel, who cleaned you up and dressed you. The doc will look in on you soon. I'll be leaving for a day or so. I have to collect a bounty, but I'll be back. That's a promise."

"All right."

Logan Best nodded and walked out, closing the door behind him.

What a strange man, Elizabeth thought. She wanted to know more about him, why he did what he did for a living. And was she wrong to trust him? How did she know he wouldn't ride off with her money and never come back?

"I'll not let you go after my money alone, Mr. Logan Best," she muttered. "I will darn well go with you." She started to turn over, but every muscle in her body ached. She grimaced and then noticed the purple bruises on her forearms. Her anger and terror and deep disappointment returned, and her hands moved into fists. She decided she had better rest, like Mr. Best had suggested, and get her strength back as soon as possible. She was going to ride out of Abilene *with* Logan Best—or die trying. She would not let Robert Alexander or the men who'd taken her valuables win.

PART II

TWENTY-FOUR

May 31, 1870

"HEY, LOGAN, YOU IN THERE?"

Logan rolled onto his back and stretched. The prostitute lying beside him made a little moaning sound and curled against him. "Who is it?" Logan called back.

"Sheriff White. Doc Billings says that woman is awake and dressed and wants to talk to you and me both."

"What the hell time is it?"

"Nine a.m."

"Miss Baylor should still be resting. What the hell is she doing up already?"

"How the hell do I know? I'm just delivering the message."

"Well, tell her I'll be along in about an hour. I had a rough night. Too much to drink. Too tired from being on the trail. And the woman beside me kept me up later than normal." Logan turned his head to face Rose Lopez, a dark beauty who did business above Rinker's saloon. She grinned, and they both chuckled.

"She's pretty adamant we come now, according to the doc," White announced through the door.

Logan frowned and sat up. "Sheriff, right now if the President of the United States summoned me, I wouldn't go. Tell her one hour. I have something to attend to first, and her name is Rose. Besides that, she has to give me a bath and a shave."

There came a moment of silence. "Damn it, Logan, yesterday you were all upset about what happened to Miss Baylor. Now you act like you don't care."

"I *do* care, and I still intend to help her. But that doesn't mean she can summon me like a servant. I have a feeling she's used to things like that. I'll get there when I get there."

"All right then."

The sheriff left, and Logan turned to Rose. "*Lady* Elizabeth Baylor has ordered me into her presence," he told her.

Rose laughed. "I think perhaps you were very attracted to that woman, and that is why you came to see *me*," she purred in a soft Spanish accent. "You needed to get rid of those thoughts."

Logan chuckled. "Get a bathtub ready for me, woman."

"All right." Still smiling, Rose got out of bed.

Logan studied her naked backside as she pulled on a robe. She opened the door and asked someone to bring hot water for the tin bathtub she kept in her room.

"I will tell you something, Logan Best"—she sauntered back to the bed—"you talked a lot last night. Whiskey does that to a man."

"So?"

"So, you kept saying that English lady looked very much like your dead wife. You said it really hurt to see her in all that trouble. You even said when you held her—"

"Don't say it!" Logan ordered, losing his smile. "Forget everything I might have said last night, and don't ever bring up my wife again."

Rose raised her eyebrows. "I hit a sore spot."

"Yes, you did."

Rose smiled sadly. "I'm sorry, Logan."

Logan reached for a can of pre-rolled cigarettes Rose kept beside the bed for her clients. He pulled one out and lit it. "I'm surprised Miss Baylor is already up and dressed. What she went through was pretty awful. I expect you couldn't find much more contrast in living than a pampered lady from England who probably lived in a mansion, to now out here in a wild, dusty cow town in America. I can't imagine why she even left England and ended up out here."

"Well, soon you will find out."

Two other women came in, each carrying two buckets of hot water. They wore thin nightgowns and gave Logan sweet smiles as they dumped the water into Rose's tub. Giggling, they looked him over and waved to Rose as they left.

"There is a bucket of cool water over there in the corner," Rose told Logan. "Dump that in. Otherwise the water will be too hot."

Cigarette still between his lips, Logan got out of bed, completely naked. He picked up the cool bucket of water and poured it into the hot water, then lowered himself into the tub, bending his knees to fit. He scrubbed himself, then let Rose give him a shave. He said little through it all, irked that Rose had brought up the subject of his dead wife. Usually he could bury the memories, but finding Miss Elizabeth Baylor… holding her in his arms…seeing the terror in her brilliant blue eyes…seeing that beautiful blond hair…

Shit! Rose was right. He'd made a beeline for too many drinks and then spoke too sharply to Rose. "I didn't mean to yell at you a few minutes ago," he told Rose, trying not to move his jaw too much while she shaved him. It might not be wise to anger a woman who had a straight razor at his jawline.

"I understand," she said. "I am the one who is sorry." She stroked the razor upward. "So, what do you think this English lady wants?"

Logan leaned his head back against the edge of the tub, and Rose pulled the razor away so he could talk. "She wants her valuables back, and I don't blame her. I already intended to go after the men who stole them, but I'm sure she wants to talk terms or bounty or whatever."

Rose smiled and kissed his forehead. "Wait until she sees how handsome you are under all the dirt and sweat and the overgrowth on your face. It is too bad she is so proper. She has no idea how much fun it is to be *im*proper with you."

Logan took the cigarette from his mouth and grinned. "And I enjoy *im*proper women," he answered. He reached up and grasped her hair, bringing her closer to kiss her gently.

Rose laughed and pulled away. "You are getting me all wet! And do not get me wanting you again.

Right now, you must get yourself bathed and dressed and go see the pretty young lady from England." She finished shaving him. "And you be careful, Logan Best. I know you will go after those men whether that fancy lady likes it or not. Always you put yourself in danger. It makes me wonder if you have a death wish. You make all that money, but you never settle down. What is all the money for if you are always alone?" She laid the razor aside.

Logan washed off his face. "I don't even know, Rose. Most of the time I just sort of go on day by day with no idea what I want and only my horse to talk to." He rinsed off the rest of himself. "I expect the day is coming when I'll have to make a decision. Then again, maybe some man with a gun will make it for me."

He climbed out of the tub and dried off, then began dressing, as did Rose. He strapped on his gun, shoving the second .44 into his gun belt behind his back and picking up his rifle. He stuck his hat on his head then put out his arms, still holding the rifle. "How do I look?" he asked Rose.

She smiled. "Like a man I would like to get back to bed with, but also like a warrior."

Logan chuckled and shook his head. He shoved his left hand into his pants pocket and pulled out ten dollars. "You're an expensive woman, Rose, but worth it." He handed out the money, and she gladly took it. "Rinker is supposed to be back today. Tell him I'll be back later to pick up my bounty. I'll give you another twenty when he does."

"*Twenty!*"

"He's paying me damn good."

"Well, I guess!" Rose walked up to him and offered her mouth. Logan leaned down and kissed it. "Thanks for putting up with this drunk last night."

"It certainly wasn't the first time I've had to do that," she answered. She gave him a little shove. "You were very sweet to me. Now, go to your fancy lady and see what she wants. I think perhaps you should not keep her waiting much longer."

Logan grinned and left, heading down the stairs, unsure what to expect from Lady Elizabeth Baylor.

TWENTY-FIVE

LOGAN MET SHERIFF WHITE OUTSIDE THE DOCTOR'S office. Together, they walked back to the small room where Lady Elizabeth Baylor had spent the last three days. After knocking lightly on the door to her room, both men were struck by what they saw when Elizabeth opened the door. She looked beautiful, and surprisingly calm and sure. Logan half expected the weeping, shaking, frightened woman he'd carried out of a jail cell two days ago. His biggest shock was how similar her looks and build were to his dead wife. He felt a quick, sharp pain in his heart.

Elizabeth turned and sat down in a straight-back chair and watched both men closely as they entered the room. Holding her chin high, she sat prim and proper, gloved hands folded in her lap and a somewhat arrogant air about her. There was no smile on her face, and her pose seemed too deliberate, as though to assure them she was just fine, even though she likely wasn't.

Logan didn't miss the way she looked at him, with both surprise and a hint of fear. He figured the surprise was because he'd actually cleaned up, and the fear was from his size and his weapons. She had, after all, recently suffered greatly at the hands of another man his size. What a horror it must have been for someone like this refined, proper woman to kill a man. He would not himself have wasted one minute of regret over blowing the man's head off, and he wished he could have been the one to do it, but death and blood and attempted rape had to be a shock to this delicate woman's system.

He'd seen Robert Alexander's dead body yesterday before the undertaker buried him in a plain, wooden coffin. It was obvious even in death and with a broken nose that Alexander had been a big, handsome man. Logan couldn't help wondering how the lovely, petite woman he was looking at now had managed to break the man's nose, but then maybe she was a scrapper like Linda Sue Macy. Still, Elizabeth Baylor was now alone and confused and penniless. It all showed in her big, blue eyes.

"Please sit down," she said, nodding toward two kitchen chairs the doctor had brought into the room earlier.

Logan could smell her, a delicate, soapy smell that stirred senses better left latent. Elizabeth wore a lovely blue dress, rather plain compared to the kind of dresses he'd seen in her trunk last night. Her skirt hung close to her body, meaning no petticoats. He suspected she was a woman who normally never went without them. He couldn't get over how beautiful she was, even though she wore no paint of any kind, no jewelry, no fancy hairdo.

The room suddenly seemed too small…the woman too close. She never took her eyes off his as he sat down across from her.

"You're late," she told him.

Logan hardened a little at her snippy attitude. "What?"

"I asked you to come right away, Mr. Best."

Logan glanced at the sheriff, who shrugged. "I told you to hurry it up," White said.

Logan looked back at Elizabeth. "Ma'am, I'm not a man who takes orders. And I was on the trail several days before I came here and—I might remind you—helped you. I was damn tired last night, so I slept in."

"You probably drank too much and slept with one of those awful painted women. I know about men like you. I've read about them in penny dreadfuls."

Logan could hardly keep from bursting out laughing. "In *what*?"

"Penny dreadfuls. I've learned here in America they are called dime novels."

Logan couldn't control a little gasp of laughter. "You *believe* those things?"

"Was I wrong about where you were last night?" she replied.

Never in his life had Logan struggled so hard to stifle a true guffaw. "No, ma'am, you were not wrong, but life out here isn't *always* like what you read in those little books. I've heard about them and they're food for a lot of jokes among men like us. Believe me, there aren't many heroic cowboys or lawmen out here."

"Have *you* ever read one of those little books?"

"No, ma'am."

"*Do* you read, Mr. Best?"

Logan still felt sorry for this poor young lady, but already he wasn't fond of her as a person. The "princess" from London had an air about her he did not like at all. He bent his leg and put a foot up on his knee, then placed his hat on his bent leg. "Ma'am, whether or not I read is nobody's business, and it has nothing to do with what I do for a living or how well I do it. I have a good idea how to find the men who took your valuables, and I am willing to help you find them, but I didn't come here to be questioned about personal things that don't matter. How about just telling me what the hell I *am* doing here."

Elizabeth drew in her breath and suddenly looked ready to cry. She looked down at her lap. "I'm sorry. I was rude. I just—" She looked at Logan again. "I'm just not used to places like this, or how people behave out here. This is all so different from how I grew up. I don't want you to think I am some weak, fainting flower you can take advantage of."

You were pretty much a weak, fainting flower when I found you in that jail cell, Logan wanted to tell her. "Apology accepted. As far as being late, I wanted to take a bath and shave before I came here, out of respect for a nice woman who's been through hell. I might add you sure do recover fast, considering what you suffered."

One thing Logan knew was women, and this one was pretending strength and determination. He could tell she was still scared to death of everything and everyone. She took a deep breath and sat up straighter, looking him over in a way that told him she felt a bit of an attraction she didn't expect. It was the same for him, in spite of her haughty attitude.

"I appreciate your thoughtfulness," she told him. "And I'm sorry for my appearance." She shifted her gaze then to Sheriff White. "I am accustomed to a personal servant who helps me dress and always fixes my hair and helps me pick out my jewelry." She looked at her lap and smoothed her skirt. "But, of course, I have none of those things now." She pulled some of her hair behind her shoulder. "And I am still rather weak. I couldn't find the energy to put on the proper...petticoats and such." She turned to Logan again. "I must look quite plain and pitiful compared to those painted women."

Logan looked her over. "Ma'am, if I may say so, you don't need to fix that hair fancy and paint your face or wear baubles on your ears to be a lovely woman. You're all of that just the way you are. There is no comparison between you and those painted women, as you call them. Everything about you demands respect, and I believe you damn well deserve it."

A look of sudden confusion came into her eyes. She'd intended to be all business, Logan could tell, but she was starting to crack.

"Why don't you just tell us why we're here," he repeated.

Elizabeth swallowed nervously. She began to twist her fingers in her lap as she spoke, addressing Sheriff White first. "Sheriff, the way you treated me the other morning was reprehensible! I know this is rough country, but manners and a sense of decency should still prevail."

White nodded. "I know, and I intended to get you some help just when Logan came inside. I just wasn't sure at first what had happened and what your role was in the whole thing. And you were all mixed up and not even talking straight."

"That shouldn't matter. However, there are apparently things I don't understand about the way you do things out here. My first intent is to tell you I have written down all that happened to me and why I shot Sir Robert Alexander. I have also written a letter to Mr. Alexander's sister in New York City. Helen will be devastated, and I fear she might try to blame me. She might think I'm lying and that I killed Robert for whatever money he had on him. I have no idea what she might do." She shook her head. "I feel sorry for her. I am pretty sure she had no idea of the things her brother was up to out here."

Logan studied her. For all her bravado, she was suffering inside. Damned if he didn't want to hold her and tell her everything would be all right—that she was safe now. *Stop comparing her to what happened to MaryAnne*, he told himself.

"A reporter tried to talk to me already this morning," she continued. "I thought him very rude. Please tell him I don't want to talk to him. If he wants to read the explanation I wrote down, that is fine. He can use that for his lurid story."

Logan noticed her hands were shaking a little as she kept twisting the handkerchief in her lap.

"I just worry it will make the news in New York City," she continued. "Robert was well known there. If that happens, the story might even travel all the

way to London because of who I am. My brother
there might come looking for me. I'd rather he didn't,
but that is not your problem." She looked at Logan.
"Or yours." She turned back to Sheriff White. "I'd
like to know what was done with Robert's…body,"
she asked.

"He was buried yesterday morning. We have a
graveyard north of town. If his sister wants to come
and claim it, we can always dig it up."

"Did someone pray over him?"

"Yes, ma'am. The local preacher said a few words."

"Good. Robert doesn't deserve to go to heaven,
but that is God's decision, not mine."

"Yes, ma'am."

"I have no money for a headstone. I suppose you
will have to have a wooden one made. I don't even
know the date of Robert's birth, nor do I care. The
man was a reprehensible cheat and liar."

She glanced at Logan again, looking him over
as though judging his looks and, Logan figured, his
trustworthiness. She picked up some papers lying on
the bed and handed them to Sheriff White. "Here
is my written explanation of what happened, as well
as the letter for Mr. Alexander's sister. I know the
address, because I stayed with her a few days when I
first landed in New York. Be sure she gets the letter."

"Yes, ma'am."

"Now, Sheriff," she continued, "I need you to
verify something for me."

White scratched at his beard. "What's that?"

"How well do you know the man sitting beside
you—Logan Best?"

Logan turned to White. "I'd like to hear this myself," he said with a grin.

White gave him a disgruntled look before turning back to Elizabeth. "Good enough to know he can be trusted. I've only met him once before, but I've heard plenty, and I read men pretty good. I figure he's as honest as they come. He went after a man who'd robbed one of this town's citizens and who had beat up on a—pardon me, ma'am—a lady of the night, if you get my meaning."

"I most certainly do."

"Well, Logan came back here yesterday with proof he'd caught the man. He brought back all the money the man had on him. Logan could have kept that money. It was more than what he will collect in bounty money, but he returned it anyway. I call that being pretty damn honest. I also know that Logan Best is one of the best trackers around."

"And he kills men for money."

"I *am* in the room, in case you didn't notice," Logan reminded them both. "And I've never killed a man who didn't deserve it or who wasn't wanted—dead or alive."

Elizabeth glanced at him. "I just need to know you're a man to be trusted," she told him. "I want to hire you."

Before Logan could say another word, Elizabeth looked back at Sheriff White. "So, I have your assurance that this man *is* Logan Best, a bounty hunter, and not someone named Chad Krieger, an outlaw and a killer."

White sputtered a short laugh. "Hell yes, he's Logan Best."

"Can he be trusted alone with a woman? I mean, out on the plains where there is no help?"

Again, Logan struggled not to laugh. He glanced at White and could tell the sheriff was also in a bind not to let loose a knee-slapping howl.

"Well now, ma'am, no man can vouch for another man in that department. All I can tell you is this man goes *after* those who would abuse a woman. I've learned that the man he tracked down had also abused a thirteen-year-old girl. Logan brought the man to her home town to be hanged. That's where he'd just come from when he came here and found you in that cell. Add to that the fact that he saw you in that jail cell and went into a rage as to how you were being treated. He demanded I get you out of there, and he carried you to a doctor. I'd say that's a man who can be trusted alone with a woman out on the prairie. Anything I've ever heard about Logan Best is that he's a good, trustworthy man and a good tracker. And though he kills men for money, he's not a bad man. I'd say he's more like a lawman. And I've never once heard he'd abused a woman."

"Again, I'm in the room," Logan reminded them.

Elizabeth turned her attention to him then. "Mr. Best, I have been duped and lied to by a man who was supposedly a pure gentleman, well dressed, wealthy, knowledgeable, experienced, handsome, gentle, sweet, and full of promises. He was a man no woman in her right mind would ever dream could be the monster he turned out to be. Is it any wonder I am having trouble deciding if I can trust another man who has...well... questionable ethics? You already admitted to drinking in a saloon and sleeping with one of those horrible women, let alone the fact that you carry enough weapons for an army. However, your behavior after finding me in that jail cell was commendable and that of a gentleman."

Logan shrugged. "Well, ma'am, compared to the man you described earlier, I can say I am far from the fancy gentlemen you're used to, but I am respectful. I am definitely not well dressed, and I have almost no education." He smiled. "The handsome part is for others to decide. And I don't believe I've ever been called gentle and sweet, especially by the men I go after. I have my own reasons for what I do, and it's not because I enjoy killing. One thing I *am* is experienced in tracking men, and my only promise is that if you're asking me to hunt down the men who have your valuables, I can find them. *That's* my promise. I say things straight out, and I don't put on airs. I very often smoke, drink, cuss, and visit loose women. But never in my life have I abused a woman in any way, either by physically hurting her or by breaking her heart in some way. What the hell else do you want to know?"

Elizabeth frowned, studying him closely. "I want you to know that Sir Robert did not"—her cheeks flushed visibly—"he did not…abuse me in the…well, the worst way. I killed him before he had the chance. Some men think that once a woman goes through something like that, she is somehow soiled and easy."

"Where in hell did you hear that?"

"I…well, I don't remember. I just supposed it, I guess. I want you to know that is not true in my case."

Logan wondered why it mattered to her. After all, he was going after the men who might have her money, and he wouldn't even see her for the next few weeks. "Ma'am, I never gave it much thought," he told her. "I figured how far that man went in attacking you is your business to say or not say. The point is, he *did* attack you, and I don't abide by such treatment. I wish I had found him sooner. It would have saved you all of this."

Elizabeth nodded. "Thank you. Tell me, Mr. Best, have you ever been married?"

Logan shifted in his seat, then put his foot down and stood up. "I'm done with questions."

"I only meant…well, a man who's married just seems more trustworthy and—"

"I don't like people doubting my word, and I don't like anybody bringing up my personal life." He leaned closer to her. "And you look pale and ready to pass out. I suggest you lay back down. You want me to go after those men, so when you're ready to talk about that and only that, you send someone for me. I'm going to get some breakfast, and then I'll be at the Cattle Stop saloon to get my bounty money. And I sleep upstairs at the saloon, which I'm sure horrifies you, but you have a lot to learn about men…and painted women. I assure you I am a hundred times more trustworthy than your fancy lord or duke or whatever you call the man you were traveling with."

He turned to go, and Elizabeth broke into tears, covering her face with her gloved hands. Logan glanced at Sheriff White and tilted his head in a sign that he should leave. White grinned at him and shook his head before going out of the room. Logan sighed, feeling like an ass. "I'm sorry," he told Elizabeth.

"It's not what you said," she sobbed. "Robert told me…that a woman left penniless out here…had only one choice if she wanted to survive. He said I would have to…sell myself to men. And I *am* penniless! I can't even pay for something to eat or pay the doctor…or even get a decent room somewhere. And I can't pay you unless you find my valuables. I just don't want you to think I should pay you some other way."

Logan wanted to reach out and touch her beautiful hair. Instead, he reached into his pocket and pulled out a wad of bills, kneeling near her and placing the money on a small table beside her bed.

"There," he said. "Keep it. Believe me, I don't need it. I have a lot more coming from Mr. Rinker. And I don't expect anything back for it. You have my word that no matter what happens, you will *not* have to sell yourself to me or anybody else to get by. I'd shoot myself before I'd force myself on some unwilling woman. And when this is over, I'll make sure you get back to New York or London or wherever you want to go, whether or not I find your valuables."

Elizabeth wiped at tears with her gloves and looked over at the money. "It…it looks like too much."

"Don't worry about it. You get some more rest. I'll come by around five and we'll have supper someplace decent, then get you a hotel. How does that sound?" Logan's heart ached at the devastation in her eyes.

"Surely you understand why I have trouble trusting anyone."

"I do. We'll talk about all of that later." Logan rose and headed for the door.

"Mr. Best, I...I'm sorry if asking if you were married upset you."

Logan stared at the door. "I *was* married once. She's dead. So is my little girl." He opened the door. "I'll be by at five." Without further explanation, he walked out.

TWENTY-SIX

It upset Elizabeth that the best she could do with her hair was pull it back at the sides and secure it with combs, then secure it into a tail at the back of her neck using a piece of ribbon. She smoothed the velvet skirt of her dark-green dress and made sure the scoop-necked bodice was buttoned right, the lace trim fluffed. At least she had the dresses that were in her trunks, although several of them were now bloodstained and useless. Since her jewels were gone, she had no necklace to wear, and only one pair of tiny diamond drop earrings for her ear lobes. She pinched her cheeks for color and wondered why she cared how she looked.

She heard Doc Billings talking to someone at the door and recognized Logan Best's deep voice. It was irritating to feel so nervous. Or more to the point, she was scared…scared of everything…scared to trust. The only way she could sleep was to take the sleeping medicine the doctor gave her. Otherwise, the minute she closed her eyes, she saw Robert Alexander's naked body coming for her—saw his leering smile and that ugly, swollen man part—heard him laughing about killing poor William.

"Mr. Best is here to walk you to a restaurant," Ethel Billings told her from the doorway. She looked Elizabeth over. "You look lovely, dear, but are you sure you are up to this?"

"I'm fine, Mrs. Billings. Thank you for everything. I will be back later for my things. I am getting a hotel room for the night."

Elizabeth smiled at the woman and walked past her to greet Logan at the front door. Immediately, she was hit with the odd new feelings she'd experienced when talking to him earlier today, feelings she'd never had around Robert. She'd never suspected violence from Robert, yet Logan Best wore violence like a sign on the front of his shirt and it didn't frighten her. She had a feeling he simply knew how to keep it leashed until it was necessary to use it. She met his eyes, and the look they shared was more like a collision than a greeting.

"Hello, Mr. Best."

Logan removed a wide-brimmed hat and nodded to her. He wore no fancy suit or top hat, no ruffled shirt or gold watch. He was at least clean, though a shadow of a beard was beginning to show. His blue calico shirt was clean and unbuttoned at the neck, where he wore what must be considered in the West a tie. It was more like a long cotton scarf in a paisley design and tied at his throat. His tan trousers looked new, and she could smell leather, probably from the vest he wore, which also looked new. He wore the same dusty boots she remembered from the other morning when he'd stretched out those long legs. He wore a six-gun at his side, attached to a wide gun belt packed with cartridges.

"Do you always wear a gun, even when dining?" she asked.

"Yes, ma'am. A man like me has a lot of enemies, mostly friends and relatives of men I've killed."

Again, Elizabeth wondered if she really could trust this man. "I see." Those eyes! He had a way of making her wonder if he knew her every thought and knew what she looked like naked. He'd been with one of those painted women last night. Was he wondering what it would be like to do those things with a woman like her? She nearly gasped out loud when she realized those were *her* thoughts about him instead! She was perfectly aware of what men enjoyed about women, but after what Robert had tried to do to her, and seeing him naked, she couldn't imagine enjoying such things in return.

She shivered with the thought of Robert's kisses, sick that she'd ever let him touch her at all. She shook off all thoughts of the lurid details and walked through the doorway, brushing past Logan Best and getting a whiff of him. Was that men's cologne he wore, or was it just the smell of soap? Somehow, she suspected men like Logan Best didn't bother with fancy colognes. The scent was huskier than that…perhaps simply the scent of the man himself, mixed with that leather vest.

She waited as Logan closed the door. He moved to position himself between her and the street, as though to make himself a protective barrier as they walked. He took hold of her upper right arm, and his gentleness surprised her. He looked like a man who wouldn't know the meaning of the word "gentle." It reminded her of how it had felt to be carried in his arms three days ago.

It secretly embarrassed her to realize that for that short time he'd carried her, she'd felt safe and had even curled against him, trusting a total stranger to help her. She remembered that he'd not smelled so clean then. He'd smelled of horses and hay and leather and trail sweat, and yet she'd almost liked the smell. It was natural and all man and real...honest. She realized now Robert always smelled fake...too clean...too much expensive men's cologne. Her stomach lurched when again, she saw that leering smile, his handsome face suddenly ugly, like a demon coming for her.

"You look really pretty," Logan told her. "Are you okay for a few hours up and walking?"

"Yes. I know you see me as a pampered rich girl, Mr. Logan, but I am much stronger than I appear. It took courage to leave my older brother in London and come to America."

"I'm sure it did. You can tell me more about it when we get to the restaurant, where you can sit down. I suppose you will want tea rather than coffee."

"Yes. How did you know?"

Logan shrugged. "I've just always heard English people like tea."

"I didn't think a man from the wild American West would know that."

"I've been around more than you think."

Two women passed them, nodding to Logan, then looking at Elizabeth curiously before passing.

"I suppose to the people here in town, I am a murderess," Elizabeth told Logan.

"Most know what really happened, and they feel sorry for you," Logan said. "But you are obviously a curiosity in a small town that lacks for entertainment. Those women probably wonder what it's like to go through what you went through. Some probably want to help, but they're pioneer women who've seen and been through some pretty rough times themselves. They're a little put off by a fancy lady from England. They aren't sure how to talk to you." He led her through the door of a clean but small restaurant. Elizabeth didn't even look at the name of it before they went inside.

More people looked up from their tables and stared. Elizabeth nodded to them proudly, trying to dispel their wonder. Logan led her to a table in one corner and offered her a chair that faced the corner and not the people. She appreciated his consideration.

She looked around, thinking how common and small this restaurant was compared to the places Robert always took her. "I'm not terribly hungry, as you might guess," she told Logan. "I'll just have soup and toast, and tea, of course, if they have it."

"That's fine. But I have to warn you the tea won't be served in fancy china cups like you are probably used to," Logan warned. "It will come in a common mug, just like how the coffee is served. And it will be plain black tea—nothing delicate or fancy. I'm sure they can bring cream for it if necessary, and sugar."

"That will be fine."

A waiter approached their table. "Hey, you're that

bounty hunter, Logan Best, aren't you?" he said with a wide grin.

Logan remembered he should have taken off his hat. He removed it and hung it on the corner of an empty chair beside him. "I am."

"That's quite a thing that happened, isn't it? I mean, that lady they found on the train—"

"This is Miss—I mean—Lady Elizabeth Baylor," Logan interrupted. "She's been through a lot and doesn't appreciate being talked about."

The waiter reddened. "Oh! Sorry, miss. I thought you were one of them ladies from over at Rinker's—"

"Take the damn order!" Logan interrupted yet again. "Miss Baylor wants a bowl of soup—whatever kind you have. Make sure it's good and hot. And she wants toast and tea. You *do* have tea, right?"

The waiter gave him a disgruntled nod. "We do."

"Thank you. Just bring me coffee and a steak and boiled potatoes, after which you can make sure the lady's tea is kept hot."

The waiter glanced at Elizabeth. "I'm sorry, ma'am. It's good to see you up and around and feeling better." He left, and Logan glanced at Elizabeth.

"You won't find a lot of fussy manners out here, Miss Baylor. Men in general respect women—a lot— but they aren't bred as high-class gentlemen. People wear themselves right out in the open, and men like that waiter often speak before they think."

Elizabeth smiled softly. "I am learning a lot, and fast." She sighed. "Mr. Logan, I'm sure you're wondering what I'm doing out here in the first place. I came to America on a passenger ship with my younger brother,

William. My older brother had kicked William out of the family mansion because he didn't agree with William's behavior. William was...a little slow in learning. But he had a big heart and tried to help people worse off than he was. Jonathan hated that. It embarrassed him. William got into a fight one night over an actress, and Jonathan was mortified. He kicked William out, and I decided to go with him. We were always close, so I told him that once we legally procured our share of what was due us from the estate, we could leave London together. I'd been reading those penny—I mean those dime novels, and I was excited to go someplace new. We were going to invest our money, mostly in buying up land, and perhaps in gold and silver mines and cattle ranching." She blinked back tears and waited as the waiter brought her tea and Logan's coffee.

Logan took a sip of his coffee. "What happened to William?"

Thinking about William made Elizabeth's throat tighten. "I don't suppose they have any lemon for my tea?"

Logan drank more coffee. "Fruit is pretty hard to come by out here," he answered.

Elizabeth nodded. She dipped a spoon into a bowl of sugar and sprinkled a little of it into her tea, then added a little cream and stirred it. "Robert killed my brother," she told Logan. "Of course, at the time I thought it was an accident. There was a storm on the voyage over, and William fell overboard, or so Robert told me. He was on the same ship. The night Robert...attacked me...he told me the truth—he'd gotten my brother drunk and shoved him overboard so I would be alone. I now know that in me he saw an opportunity to make money, by stealing mine and selling me to the highest bidder."

"He was an expert at swindling people, or so Ben Rosell told me," Logan said, "and in dealing with captured women. He also was involved gun running, mostly with the Indians. I don't doubt he dealt with the same thing during the war."

Elizabeth drank some of her tea, fighting tears. "Yes." She sniffed before she continued. "Obviously, I had no idea the man was such a devil. When William drowned, I was completely alone, and by then Robert had learned all about our situation and knew we were traveling with a lot of money. I'm sure you can figure out the rest. He treated me like a queen, helped me, befriended me, then began professing his love for me, making all kinds of wonderful promises, telling me he would take me to Denver, where he would help me with investments." She swallowed more tea. It helped keep her from crying. "You know the rest."

Logan sighed, saying nothing for the moment as the waiter brought their food. Elizabeth ate some of her beef-and-potato soup, which was a bit too greasy for her liking, but she ate it anyway. "I want my valuables back, Mr. Best. I learned Robert made arrangements with a man called Chad Krieger, a roughneck who runs with scurrilous other men and kidnaps and sells women. He told me Chad had my money and my jewels. Robert was supposed to meet him someplace farther ahead...Hays City, I think he said."

She waited while Logan cut his steak and ate some of it. She could tell he was thinking...planning.

"I'd like to hire you to go after those men, Mr. Logan. There is enough money involved that I can pay you a very generous bounty." She sipped a little more soup. "I will not let Robert Alexander win. I will never forget how it felt to be swindled like that, lied to, attacked in an ugly, filthy way. And it makes me feel ill to think of how my poor brother died. I feel so responsible, because it was my idea to come to America." She raised her eyes. "Look at me, Mr. Best."

Logan met her gaze, and again Elizabeth felt an air of power and recklessness about him, mixed with extreme confidence, and again...violence. "I will never again allow a man to touch me wrongly, or be so innocent and trusting as to let a man I hardly know lie to me and cheat me like Robert did. Yet here I am trusting you. I have no idea why, but if you make off with my money and jewels, I will make sure the law hunts you down with a vengeance."

Their gazes held, and Elizabeth suddenly felt like a silly child talking this way to a rugged bounty hunter like Logan Best. Everything about him spelled man and brave and the kind of Wild West character she'd often fantasized about. Who was she to tell this man she would come after him if he made off with her valuables? Of course he wouldn't. But if he did, no man who walked would catch him or overcome him. He was too good at what he did. A seriousness came into his bright-green eyes, not a dangerous warning look but rather an intense sincerity.

"Let me tell you something for once and for all,

Miss Baylor. I have never harmed a woman in my life and never will. I have never lied, cheated, or stolen. I've killed, and I've beaten men, but they damn well deserved it. If any man I ever went after seemed to be innocent, I never harmed him. I brought him in to let a judge decide. But when I know for sure a man is guilty, I find it difficult to let him live, especially if it involves abusing a woman. I have my reasons. And you can bet that if I had reached your fancy Robert Alexander in time, *I'm* the one who would have killed him." He took a drink of coffee, then plunked down the cup. "I'm sorry as hell it turned out the way it did for you. Knowing this Chad Krieger and his gang have your valuables, and knowing what they intended to do with you, an innocent young woman who had big dreams about this country and had them thrown in her face, I would damn well have gone after them whether you asked me to or not. I told you that the first morning you woke up to see me sitting by your bed. I sat there watching you and thinking about what all this must have been like for you, and thinking how cruel it had to be to find out this land isn't anything like you must have pictured it, and I thought how bad I wanted to go after those men. I'm leaving tomorrow. I wanted to let you know that."

Elizabeth drew in her breath and struggled for the courage she would need for her next statement. "I already knew you intended to go after those men. The reason I agreed to meet with you is to tell you I am going with you."

Logan raised his eyebrows in surprise and leaned back in his chair. "The hell you are."

"If you leave without me, I will rent a horse, and I will follow you!"

"No!"

"I will! I mean it! I know you can be trusted, yet part of me—the part that was so viciously lied to through a handsome smile and gentle treatment, tells me I shouldn't trust *any* man with that much treasure." She raised her chin. "I am going with you, and I am taking my pistol with me."

Logan struggled to keep his voice down. "Well, you'd better buy a *bigger* one, because that little thing you used on Robert Alexander would never have stopped a man that size if it wasn't fired point-blank, I assure you. And if you get a bigger gun, you'll first need to know how to *use* the damn thing. I don't intend to get shot by accident by some debutante who thinks she's suddenly able to do what it takes grown men *years* to learn!"

Elizabeth reddened and felt tears wanting to come again. How could she travel for days or weeks with this wild, sometimes violent man who knew all there was to know and would resent her being along? "You...you can teach me."

Logan closed his eyes and shook his head, then leaned closer, still keeping his voice down. "Miss Baylor, I can't *begin* to teach you everything you will need to know. And you will slow me down. On top of that, you have no idea the kind of ruthless men I'm going after. What if they get the better of me? You'd be at their mercy."

This time a tear did slip out of one eye. She quickly wiped at it. "I know how to ride."

"A western saddle? There are no side-saddles out here, lady."

"Then I'll find one of those riding skirts and ride like a man. But I *do* know horses."

"Western broncos? Or fancy, groomed jumpers that servants take care of?"

"I...don't know what you mean."

"That's my point. Out here, there are all kinds of wrong plants and grass a horse can get into—and sometimes water that's no good for them. You need to groom them yourself, find a blacksmith if they lose a shoe, know how to get a stone out of a hoof, saddle your own horse. It's a long list, ma'am, and that's just the horse. You need to learn to use a gun, good enough to help me defend myself if need be. You'll sleep on the ground and eat over a campfire, and sometimes the biscuits will get worms in them. There won't be any fancy tea—just stiff black coffee. We could run into buffalo, or worse, buffalo *hunters*, men who haven't seen a pretty woman for weeks. They don't even know the *meaning* of the word gentleman. And there are mountain lions and snakes...let alone the likelihood of Indians. I can't take a woman like you into something like that."

More tears came. Elizabeth sniffed and wiped at them with her napkin. "Mr. Best, I left England with big dreams about America, especially the West." She wiped at her nose. "I can't begin to explain my excitement, nor my pride at the plans I had of investing in the growth of this country. I lost my brother, and then Robert Alexander shattered every dream I ever had. I have already learned a good lesson about life out here, and believe it or not, I look forward to learning *more*, even the hard lessons. You have no idea how stifled I felt back in London. I hated my domineering brother and the boredom of living among London's wealthy. I am ready to give up that life and give up fancy dresses and servants…*all* of it. I want to *learn*. I want to experience this life. And I want the satisfaction of helping you. I am *begging* you to take me."

Logan leaned back and drank more coffee, then took a pre-rolled cigarette from his vest pocket and lit it. He studied her a moment. Elizabeth could tell he thought her a fool.

"All right," he finally told her. "I'll give you one day to get together the things you will need. I'll have to take you around and *explain* what you need. I'll pay for everything because you'll make it up to me once we get your valuables back. I will also have to give you a quick lesson in shooting. And once we set out, I want no complaints, and you'd better keep up. And remember, a bullet can kill me just as easily as the next man, and you'd be left out there alone. And I need to point out that we will traveling alone together—a *lot*. I'm just a man, Miss Baylor, so there might be times we stop at a saloon where there are obliging women upstairs. I'll likely pay them a visit. Can you handle that?"

"Oh, I *do* understand about men, Mr. Best. Robert taught me well, or have you forgotten?" Elizabeth scooted back her chair. "Thank you for the dinner, but I have lost my appetite. If I am to spend tomorrow shopping for what I will need, I had better go find that hotel room and have someone get my trunks for me from the doctor's office. I will have to find a place to store them while we are gone."

She saw a look of anger and resignation in Logan Best's green eyes. Neither of them had finished their meal. He drank down a last swig of coffee and threw some money on the table, then stood up and grabbed his hat. "Come on," he told her, taking her arm. "I'll show you to the hotel."

He walked a little too fast, and Elizabeth had to hurry to catch up.

"You're taking me with you then?"

"I told you I don't lie, which means I also don't break promises. Yes, I'll take you, but we'll be doing things *my* way, understand?"

"Yes. Thank you."

They headed down the boardwalk toward a hotel, but Elizabeth's heel caught on a loose piece of wood and she nearly fell. Logan kept hold of her arm to keep her from going all the way down. She broke into tears. "I'm so sorry, Mr. Best, but I'd go crazy waiting here for you to come back, and I'll feel safer going with you than staying here alone. And I don't mean to cry, but every once in a while, it hits me that I killed a man. I *killed* a man, and it was a man I thought I loved! I can never forget it!"

"You did what you had to do," Logan assured her, "and if you go with me, you might have to kill again."

Elizabeth nodded. "I understand." She wiped away her tears. "Thank you for befriending me and getting me out of that awful jail cell. I don't mean to seem ungrateful and demanding."

Logan pulled her around the corner of a building. "Come here." He put his arms around her, letting her cry against his chest. "I can't abide a woman's tears," he told her. "Sorry I got short with you, but I was only thinking of your safety and comfort."

"I'll manage," she wept. "I won't be a burden."

"We'll see," he said.

Elizabeth breathed in the scent of him. Why was it she felt so safe in his arms? She hardly knew the man, yet the safety she felt here was far different than what she'd felt in Robert's arms. With him, she'd always felt that tug of ownership and that odd, threatening feeling she couldn't put her finger on... the feeling she'd so often ignored because he was so handsome and gentlemanly. Why hadn't she followed her instincts?

"Let's get you that room," Logan said. He pushed her away and let her find a handkerchief in her handbag. Walking her to the hotel, he paid for a room and left, assuring her he would send men with her trunks, and he would be back in the morning.

Elizabeth watched him walk out, realizing she'd told him nearly everything about herself. Yet she knew next to nothing about Logan Best—how he was raised, if he had family, what had happened to his wife and daughter. He'd made it clear he didn't want to talk about himself. He certainly didn't want to talk about his wife, and she suspected it had something to do with the way he lived now.

She wondered if he would spend the night with that saloon woman. Why on earth did that bother her? She went to the window, but she didn't see him anywhere. *Who are you really, Logan Best? Why do you do what you do?* Piano music and laughter came from one of the saloons not far away.

She finally spotted Logan heading inside that saloon.

TWENTY-SEVEN

*LOGAN BEST, YOU'RE THE DUMBEST SONOFABITCH WHO
ever walked.* Why had he allowed Lady Elizabeth Baylor's
tears get to him and allow her to make this trip with
him? "Put your left foot in this stirrup and just swing
yourself over," he told Elizabeth. "Grab the pommel."

They stood inside the livery, preparing to leave.

"This saddle is so different from what I'm used to,"
Elizabeth said, "and this horse is so big." She reached
up for the pommel.

"She might be big, but she's dependable and fast, yet
gentle. At least that's what the livery owner told me."

Elizabeth put her left foot in the stirrup, then
strained leg and arms to get herself into the saddle.
Logan was very tempted to give her a boost, but that
would involve grabbing her bottom…not a good idea,
although he wouldn't mind it at all.

She didn't make it the first try.

"You want a boost?"

Elizabeth looked up at him. "I certainly do not!"

She tried again, this time managing to get her leg
over the horse's back. Once in the saddle, her feet

didn't reach the stirrups. Logan adjusted each stirrup to fit, and Elizabeth settled into the saddle.

"There," she said. "I'm fine."

Logan handed her the reins to her packhorse, then mounted Jasper and took up the reins to his own packhorse. "You're going to hurt in places you never thought possible," he told Elizabeth, "till you get used to riding that way. Your rear end will give you a hard time the first few days."

Jasper was behind her horse, and Logan took a quick look at how her small bottom fit into her seat. *Good God, I'd better always ride in front once we're out of town*, he told himself.

"Let's go!" he said louder. He headed for the livery entrance, ducking his head as he rode through it, pack-horse in tow. He glanced back to make sure Elizabeth made it out, then turned his attention forward.

He smiled inwardly at how clean and prim and proper Lady Elizabeth looked, wearing all brand-new clothes, a wide-brimmed hat, riding skirt, new boots. She actually wore a gun belt, though a much narrower one than he wore. A woman her size probably couldn't even carry the weight of his belt full of cartridges and his .44. It hadn't been easy, but they'd finally found a belt small enough to fit her, which created another disturbing memory for Logan. He'd had to feel how the belt sat on her hip bones, making sure the damn thing wouldn't fall right off her. Touching her hip bones made him want to touch other things. Too bad she was so damn inexperienced and, for now, hated the touch of any man.

He'd picked out a gun for her—a Manhattan navy

revolver, much smaller and lighter than his .44 but big enough to kill, or at least put down a man from a few feet away. He'd also bought her a lightweight .22 rifle.

"Once we get away from town, I'll give you a few lessons with that gun and rifle," he called back to her.

"You will find out I learn fast," Elizabeth answered, urging her horse into a faster gait to catch up and ride beside him. "William occasionally let me shoot his rifle when he went skeet shooting. In England, it's all but forbidden for a woman from a prominent family to be allowed to shoot guns. Did you know that, Mr. Best?"

"You'll find different out here," he answered. "Pioneer women are taught to shoot from a young age. Sometimes the husband dies and the woman has to do the hunting." He looked at her, noticing how she filled out the calico shirt she wore. Even with a vest over it, any man could see how full-breasted she was, let alone the fact that certain body parts bounced fetchingly. "And a woman has to be ready to defend herself," he finished.

"I am well aware of that, Mr. Best."

Townspeople stared at them as they rode out of town together, all still wondering about the truth behind the English lady who'd killed her lover, Logan figured. Now she was riding out of town alone with a bounty hunter known not only for a penchant to kill the men he hunted, but also a favorite of prostitutes in practically every town he set foot in.

"Hey, Logan, I bet you'll enjoy this trip, ridin' with a murderess who seduces her men before she kills them," one man nearby called out. "Your favorite whores are gonna be jealous!" The man guffawed and guzzled whiskey from a bottle in his hand.

Elizabeth covered her mouth in shock at the words. Logan halted Jasper and reached over to grasp Elizabeth's horse. "Hold up," he told her. He dismounted, walked up to the drunk man, and landed a big fist into the man's cheek, sending him sprawling halfway across the street. Women gasped and men backed away. "Get this straight!" Logan shouted at them. "This is a fine lady who was horribly abused and robbed! She is going with me to find the men who stole from her, and I'll make sure she finds them and brings them to justice. If I have my way, they'll all die. Either way, that's what this trip is about and nothing more. The next man who insults this lady will answer to *me*."

Men stepped back as Logan climbed back onto Jasper. "Let's go!" He headed out of town and Elizabeth followed. Once away from others, Logan slowed Jasper and looked at Elizabeth. "You okay?" He noticed her quickly wipe at tears.

"Yes, but you really didn't need to hit that man, Mr. Best."

"Yes, I did." He wasn't about to tell her it wasn't just because of her honor he'd clobbered that drunk. It was his own frustration at having to share days and nights with a beautiful woman he couldn't touch. "And I wish you would call me Logan," he finished. He reached into his vest pocket for a pre-rolled cigarette and a match. He lit the cigarette and inhaled deeply.

"Using first names just seems too familiar so soon," Elizabeth replied. "I've known you all of six days, and

I spent a couple of them sleeping, so I didn't even speak with you then."

"Well, we don't much care about rules for addressing each other out here," he answered. "Using Mister and Miss just makes it more of a mouthful. Logan and Liz is a lot easier, but since you insist, what should I call you?"

"Miss Baylor is fine, but in England I am Lady Elizabeth."

"Yeah, well, we aren't in England, and Lady Elizabeth is a bit more of a mouthful than Miss Baylor, so I'll go with Miss Baylor. Personally, I don't have much use for fancy titles, especially for men. Titles don't make a man. You found that out."

They rode on without speaking until they made it well beyond the outskirts of Kansas City. Things grew quiet, with only the sound of squeaking saddles and gear, the snorting of their horses, the gentle plodding of horse hooves into soft prairie sod, the buzz of a bee at times, and occasionally the sound of birds. There wasn't even any wind today.

Logan heard a sniffle or two behind him, and he knew the man's words in town had hurt Elizabeth deeply. He'd just made things worse with his remark about useless titles.

Elizabeth finally spoke up, as though to open a conversation about something else. "I like this horse. She's quite gentle. Does she have a name?"

"Livery owner called her Suzy Q. I don't know if that's her name or if he calls all horses that."

"Then I will call her Suzy. Just Suzy."

More silence.

"May I ask why we are going by horseback rather than train?" Elizabeth finally asked. "We already know these men will likely stop at Hays City."

"They could stop anywhere, and I'm betting they travel strictly on horseback. When you're up to no good, you don't want to be caught some place where you can't make a fast getaway. A train can't go anywhere but on its tracks. A man running from the law can disappear on a horse real quick. And with the telegraph and most of these small railroad towns having their own newspapers, they might have heard about Robert Alexander by now and are trying to figure out what to do next. Alexander was probably the only one besides you who could cash those banknotes. Otherwise, he wouldn't have left them with men like Chad Krieger and the others. And it won't be easy finding some place to hock your jewels. My bet is we will find them on the trail headed for Denver, the only place they might find a way to unload all of that. They might even be looking for you—not just because they intend to sell you, but because they think they can force you to sign those notes. You'll never be completely safe until I find them and do away with them. They probably blame you for Alexander's death."

"If you're sure they are headed for Denver, why don't we just take a train there?"

"Because I aim to stop them *before* they get there. It's the only way to be sure of saving what they have with them. Once they reach Denver, there will be a lot more opportunity to unload stolen goods." Logan smoked quietly for a moment, forcing himself not to glance at Elizabeth Baylor too often. She looked beautiful in the morning sunlight, her blond hair tied with a ribbon at the nape of her neck and hanging long down her back. Her little bottom bounced temptingly in her saddle. "I don't suppose you cook, do you?" he asked.

"No. I've never needed to cook. Even if I learned, I doubt I could ever match one of those pioneer women you keep talking about, let alone cook over an open fire."

"I was afraid of that." He smoked quietly again. "You'll have to get used to hardtack, beans out of a can, and biscuits most of the time. If you want a really decent meal, you'll have to wait till we reach the next town."

"Fine." She glanced at Logan and smiled. "I wanted to experience this life, Mr. Best, and now I am. I want to see everything I read about in those dime novels. Back in England, I would be reading or embroidering right now, and then I would go to my room, and my personal attendant would help me change into the proper clothes for dinner. Then we would eat each course as it was served to us, after which the women would retire to the knitting room and the men would retire to the smoking room. The women would talk about frivolous things and sew, guests would later go home, and we women would retire for the evening. In the morning, we would dress for breakfast, eat, sew, or read or take piano lessons and such, then have our midmorning tea, change for lunch, eat, then shop or go to some female activity, come home and nap, then read some more, dress for dinner, and do the same thing we did the night before all over again."

"Sounds boring as hell."

"It is. That is why I'm here now. I felt stifled, and my petulant brother's tight control over me made things worse."

Petulant? Logan had no idea what the word meant. *Jesus, is she going to start throwing around big words the whole way?*

"You can imagine why those dime novels sounded so exciting to me," she continued.

Logan finished another cigarette. "Just don't put me into any of the characters in those stories. I don't fit."

"Oh, but you do, Mr. Best. You are just like those wild, bronco-riding cowboys they show in the drawings. I just can't figure out if you come closer to the dark and devious outlaws in the stories, or the heroic lawmen."

"I'm neither. I'm just a man out for bounty."

He rode several feet ahead of her, and they continued for a good four or five miles, until they were completely alone in wide-open country, no civilization in sight…not even a farm or a ranch.

"Let's stop here and let the horses rest," Logan suggested. "This is a good place to let you practice a little shooting. There's a tree down not far ahead. You can aim at some of those branches sticking up. If you miss, you miss. If your bullets go flying off, there sure isn't anything to hit for miles around." He drew Jasper to a halt and dismounted. He thought to help Elizabeth down when he saw her hanging on to her saddle horn, feet dangling over the left side of Suzy. She released her hold and jumped down, then managed to pull her rifle from its boot. Logan just shook his head and led her over to the downed tree while the horses grazed.

"Won't shooting spook the horses?" Elizabeth asked.

"Not those guns of yours. They don't make a very loud shot. That pistol you have won't do a lot of damage either unless a man is pretty close, so we'll get closer to the tree for that one." Logan walked up to the tree trunk and found a few rocks to set on the branches, then had Elizabeth come up within six feet of the stones with her pistol. "Try hitting that pink colored rock," he told her.

Elizabeth raised her pistol and aimed.

Logan saw the gun dip a little. "Use both hands for a steadier aim," he told her. He walked up behind her and grasped her wrists, having to bend down a little to show her the best way to grip the gun and take aim. She felt good in his arms. It would be so easy now to lean in and kiss her cheek, her neck. *Keep your mind on what's important*, he told himself.

The next few minutes were difficult. It would be easier if he didn't feel so damn sorry for her. Feeling sorry made him want to hold her close and let her feel his strength and tell her everything would be all right. She took a few shots, hit some of the rocks, got excited over it. She even hit a few with her rifle from farther away. It seemed to lift her spirits after the insult in town, and he was glad for that, but having to help her position the rifle, leaning close to show her how to take aim, it all led to pure frustration on his part. How in hell was he going to keep this trip strictly business?

"We'll ride on farther before we make camp for the night," he told her when they finished shooting. "I'll show you how to build a fire and make coffee.

There will be times you might have to do things like that instead of me." He turned to see her struggling to get back up on Suzy. The stirrup was too high since he'd shortened it before they'd left. *Damn!* He walked over and bent his knees a little. "Here. Step up on my hands, and I'll boost you up."

"But I can—"

"No, you can't. Just do it, or I'll have to grab your ass and send you up that way. Which do you prefer?" There. He'd properly offended her. Keeping her a little bit angry would help him harden up his feelings in return.

Elizabeth gave him a look of disgust and stepped onto his hands. He pushed up, and she climbed onto Suzy.

"Why do you seem to find ways to humiliate me?" she asked. "After standing up for my honor in town?"

"Just trying to help you onto your horse," Logan answered, mounting Jasper. He rode off, keeping his eyes straight ahead, but unable to put away thoughts he shouldn't allow. He slowed Jasper, letting her catch up. "I didn't mean to offend," he apologized, feeling like an ass again. How in hell was he going to handle these damned mixed emotions this woman caused? "And you did a pretty good job back there," he added, hoping to soothe her after the embarrassment he'd caused her.

"Thank you," she answered. "I had a good teacher."

Logan urged Jasper farther ahead again so he didn't have to see how her bottom fit her saddle. *Lord, help me.*

TWENTY-EIGHT

"HOW DOES THIS THING WORK?" ELIZABETH ASKED, feeling silly not knowing how to manage a bedroll. "It's just one blanket. Do I sleep on top of it and put another one over me?" She laid out the bedroll.

Logan finished lighting a cigarette, then came over and lifted the end and side of the bedroll that were not sewn together. "You sleep *inside* of it," he told her. "That's why there are ties along the edges. You can tie yourself up into it nice and tight or leave it loose. I leave mine loose because you never know when you'll have to quickly get out of the damn thing and find your gun."

Elizabeth put her hands on her hips. "Well, that's reassuring. I should sleep well knowing some culprit could come along any time and murder me in my sleep."

Logan grinned, the cigarette still at the corner of his mouth. "That's life on the trail." He walked back to his own bedroll. "Put your saddle at the head of your bedroll and use it for a pillow."

"But it's *hard*!"

"Like I said, that's—"

"Life on the trail," she interrupted. "I know. And I

feel like I've already *been* on the trail for a week and it's only been one day!" She glanced at him. "And by the way, where on earth do I…you know…relieve myself?"

Logan sat down on his bedroll and stretched out his legs, leaning against his saddle. "Anyplace you want. Nobody to see but the bugs and the snakes."

Elizabeth glanced at him. "And *you*."

"I won't look."

"And I'm supposed to *trust* that?"

"Well, if I was your husband, I might accompany you for protection. But I'm not your husband, so I won't unless you ask me to. Simple as that. I told you I never lie. There's paper in the supplies on your packhorse. Just don't let a snake bite you in an unmentionable place."

Elizabeth gasped. "Never in my life have I been around such a…a… I don't know *what* to call you."

"Anything you want. I doubt there is any word you could use that would upset me."

Elizabeth shook her head and went to her tethered packhorse to search for paper to clean herself. She marched far enough away to be out of the light of the fire.

"Not too far," Logan warned.

"Far enough for you not to see me," Elizabeth declared. She kept her eyes on him as she dropped her riding skirt and hurriedly finished her business, wondering how she would be able to do this in daylight. She'd held herself all day for that very reason, but she wouldn't always be able to do that. She quickly dressed and walked back to her bedroll.

Logan still just lay there smoking quietly as she

carried her saddle over to place it at the head of her bedroll. The heavy saddle was no easy job, but she was determined to do these things by herself. She removed her boots and climbed into the sleeping bag, pulling it around her.

"You're not going to undress and put on a nightgown?" Logan asked.

"Certainly not!" She heard Logan chuckle.

"I'm beginning to like you, Elizabeth. It's fun teasing you. When are you going to learn to trust me?"

"I'm not sure."

"Didn't I defend your honor back there in town? And aren't I risking my life to save your valuables?"

"That is yet to be proven. This is, after all, our first day out here alone. However, I'm glad you *like* me. And thank you. You did stand up for my honor today. Actually, that was quite a punch. Have you been in many fistfights, Mr. Best?"

"Too many to count, and most from too much drink. Some were with men I was hunting." Logan sat up and removed his boots, then climbed into his bedroll. "As far as risking my life for you, I'm really just thinking about the bounty you're going to pay me when I get your money back."

Elizabeth frowned. "I don't believe it's just that. You're too… I hate to say it, but in your own strange way, you are too gentlemanly, in spite of some of the rude things you say."

Her remark brought a loud laugh. "I'll be damned if the woman didn't call me something nice."

They lay there, the campfire dwindling. "You didn't eat much," Logan told her.

"I'm not used to beans and coffee, but I suppose I won't have much choice once I get hungry enough. Besides, I'm still too upset over what's happened to me the last few days. And I truly do realize you could be risking your life going after Chad Krieger and his men. Believe it or not, I am as much afraid for you as for myself."

"Well, the woman said a *second* nice thing. Thank you, but don't ever worry about me. I can handle myself."

"That is very obvious."

Another long moment of silence. Elizabeth tried not to think about how it had felt yesterday when Logan helped her find a gun belt that fit. The feelings that ran through her when he positioned it on her hip bones and stuck his fingers between the belt and her person to make sure it wasn't too big, had brought a rush of desire she'd never felt in her life. It was nothing like anything she'd felt for Robert. She didn't even know a woman could *have* such feelings. Everything about the man—the way he wore his gun, the way he sat a horse, his bold talk—totally open and honest— his disturbingly masculine build, and those eyes. It was like he could look right through her. When he'd helped with her gun belt, she'd made sure not to look up at him. He might have read her mind.

And earlier today, the way it felt when he reached around her to help her shoot. Part of her wanted him to fold those arms completely around her so she could relish the protection she was sure she would feel there. And now, lying here in the dark after the mention of culprits who could be prowling around them, she had a desire to crawl into his bedroll just to feel the strength and shelter and safety she would find there. The man knew everything there was to know about this way of life. Then again, maybe she wasn't safe with him at all. He slept with whores and had openly admitted having manly needs. She most certainly was not going to have any part of satisfying them.

You're just confused and scared and out of your element, Elizabeth. How could she possibly think straight when her world had been turned completely upside-down? She warned herself to be careful of her emotions.

"How do you like lying here looking at the stars?" Logan asked.

The night was dark and still, billions of stars sparkling overhead. "It's quite nice. It gives you a peaceful feeling."

Logan finished his cigarette and smashed it out solidly in the dirt beside him before tossing it. He stared at the sky quietly for a few minutes. "I like to think that one of them is my wife and one of them is my little girl," he told her.

Elizabeth's eyes widened in surprise. She wanted to know what had happened to them, but she didn't dare ask. If he was going to tell her, he'd tell her in his own good time. They were actually getting along at the moment, and she didn't want to spoil it. Should she say anything at all? "I'm…I'm sure they are always with you in spirit." She waited for his angry words, but he said nothing. Moments later, he began snoring lightly.

Elizabeth raised up on one elbow and looked over at him. By the light of what was left of their campfire, she saw his gun belt and six-gun lying beside him, along with his rifle. He'd pulled his hat down over his eyes.

Well, Logan Best, for all your womanizing, you apparently can be a one-woman man, and you are actually capable of loving someone. She felt strangely jealous of his wife, even though she was gone from this earth. Logan was so different—more man than any she'd known—and that was what made him so dangerous.

She lay back down and winced with the pain of what she was sure were a couple of blisters on her bottom. Logan had been right. She was sore in places she didn't even know existed, but she was not about to admit it.

TWENTY-NINE

Logan gladly broke camp, keeping busy while Elizabeth walked off to relieve herself. He'd had a restless night lying half awake, partly because a beautiful young woman slept two feet away from him, and partly because it was his job to *protect* that beautiful young woman—not an easy job in a land filled with far more men than women. Now he had to force himself not to look as she dropped her riding skirt in daylight. He knew she still didn't trust him not to look, but Mother Nature had a way of forcing a person to ignore his or her fears.

Elizabeth finally came back and walked up to Suzy. "Thank you for saddling my horse," she told him.

"Not easy for someone your size to throw a saddle over a horse a little too big for her," he answered. "She was the smallest horse at the livery that was also gentle and easy to control, so we didn't have a lot of choice. Sorry about that."

"Well, I have to be able to mount her on my own. I can't rely on you to help all the time, so let me do this."

Logan waited, determined not to embarrass her by

laughing when it took her four tries. She finally managed to keep her left foot in the stirrup and hang on to the saddle horn, grimacing with determination as she pulled herself up and flung her right leg over Suzy's back. "There!" she said proudly.

"Good job," Logan told her. He mounted Jasper, and they left, each of them leading a packhorse again.

They rode a good two or three miles in awkward silence, Logan wishing he hadn't mentioned his wife and daughter being in the stars. The thought had broken open bad memories. He figured Elizabeth probably didn't know what to think of the comment, let alone what to think of their moment of closeness when they joked about liking each other.

"I don't suppose you will tell me why you do what you do?" Elizabeth asked, as though it might be best to break the silence.

"No."

"Don't you even have a place of your own somewhere?"

"No. I live wherever I land for the night."

Elizabeth rode up beside him. "Well...I know you lost your wife. But don't you have parents? Siblings?"

"What's a sibling?"

"You don't know?"

"I don't have your fancy education."

"A sibling is a brother or a sister."

"None that I know of. I was raised in an orphanage and was loaned out to work on farms till I ran away at thirteen years old."

"Oh my! So you have no idea about your lineage."

Logan was getting irritated with her fancy words

and her line of questioning. "Tell me what lineage is, and I'll let you know if I have any," he answered.

Elizabeth shook her head in wonder. "You really *do* lack education, don't you?"

Logan halted his horse, almost glad for her uppity attitude. It helped keep him from wanting her. "Are you going to spend this whole trip talking about my lack of education and asking personal questions?"

"Well, I just—"

"Let me explain, Miss Baylor. I never knew my parents. They or someone else took me to an orphanage when I was just a baby. I endured a lot of beatings and was turned out to work on farms at eight years old. No schooling. I grew up knowing nothing about normal life and even less about family and love and feelings in general. And maybe I can't read, but I damn well know *survival*, Miss Baylor, and I know how to hunt men. I can sniff them out as good as any dog or mountain lion. I know guns and horses and life in the open, and it's likely what I know could save your slender little neck before this trip is over. I don't like talking about myself or my past, so I'd appreciate it if you stopped asking questions. In fact, you need to stop talking—period. When you talk, I can't hear certain sounds I might need to hear, like the distant sound of men's voices or the whinny of a horse or the crack of a gun."

Elizabeth pressed her lips together like a spoiled little girl who'd just been reprimanded. She let out a little whimper, then suddenly charged ahead of him at a full gallop. Logan kicked Jasper's sides and rode hard to catch up, coming close and grabbing the reins to her horse.

"Let go!" she ordered.

"Not until you promise never to do that again!"

"Do what? *Insult* you?"

"That would be a good start!" Logan yelled. "But I wasn't talking about that. I was talking about suddenly riding off like that. You need to stay beside me or *behind* me. *Behind* would be best."

"What difference does it make?"

"It could make a *big* difference." Logan kept hold of Suzy's bridle. "You should never do something that could get you noticed and leave you exposed." He yanked on Jasper's reins when the horse snorted and tossed its head, a little confused by its rider's anger.

"Get one thing straight, Miss Baylor. You need to do what I say out here. Sometimes things happen that I'll have to give you a real quick order of what to do. Don't *ever* question me. Understand? Our lives could depend on it. If I tell you to hightail it out of here, or get down off that horse and hit the dirt, or to just plain take out that gun and shoot somebody, you *do* it—understand?"

Elizabeth sniffed and pouted her lips. "Yes."

"Good. Now get off that horse so you're not such an easy target. There is a small band of Indians up ahead, in case you didn't notice. I was about to warn you when you suddenly took off. On top of that, you lost your packhorse."

"I...what?"

"Just get down!" Logan let go of her horse. "And take these." He handed her the reins to his packhorse and rode after hers, catching it quickly. He turned back, and she was standing beside Suzy. She'd removed her hat and had taken a handkerchief from a pocket on her riding skirt and was dabbing at sweat on her forehead. Logan dismounted and tied the reins of his packhorse around Jasper's pommel. "We'll walk a while, slowly. We might have to get low to the ground real quick. They won't shoot at us once we're down, because all they'll see is the horses. Indians won't shoot horses to kill their riders. It's the other way around. They shoot the *riders* so they can steal their *horses*."

He handed her the reins to her packhorse. "Let's walk to that lone elm tree and cool off under it. Those Indians are likely harmless. If they're coming our way, we are better off letting them come than trying to outrun them. No white man on a fully outfitted horse can outrun a Plains Indian, believe me."

They started walking. Suddenly, everything seemed too quiet. There was only the sound of insects and again, the soft plodding of the horses.

"We need to rest anyway," Logan explained. "Jasper is a little lathered from that hard run." He realized Elizabeth had said nothing because she was trying not to cry. "Sorry I yelled at you," he told her, always torn by a woman's tears.

She swallowed. "I'm the one who is sorry. I wasn't meaning to insult you. I've never met anyone who grew up like you did. It must have been terrible for a little boy." She sniffed. "I was just making small talk because I am nervous and scared. I want very much to impress you."

"You don't *need* to impress me. And I don't give a damn if I impress you either. I am simply here to help you get your valuables back. Then you can pay me and go wherever you intend to go once you have your things."

They reached the tree and pulled the horses under it for the shade, positioning themselves so they could see the small band of Indians far in the distance. Logan pulled his rifle from its boot and retracted the lever, keeping it in hand as he leaned against the tree.

"By the way, what's petulant?"

"What?"

"Petulant," Logan repeated. "Yesterday, you called your older brother petulant."

Elizabeth smiled. "It means crabby—grumpy."

Logan lit a cigarette. "Just wondered. I thought a little conversation would help us keep our minds off losing our scalps."

Elizabeth swallowed. "It didn't really help."

"Me either."

After several quiet, tense moments of not even looking at each other, Elizabeth took a deep breath and spoke.

"How did you know they were there? I never saw a thing."

"It's part of being good at what I do. You learn to sense things. That's why it's best not to talk too much out here. Save your talking for when we make camp. Even then, you have to be careful."

Elizabeth sighed. "You *are* an educated man, Mr. Best—educated in things like this."

"And that's all I need for what I do." Logan kept his eyes on the Indians. They were inching closer. "And for your information, running from Indians only draws them to the chase. And once they are on the chase, they are harder to deal with. We're better off waiting for them peacefully."

"I see."

More silent, tense waiting.

"I didn't know you never knew your parents, or I wouldn't have asked about your lineage, Mr. Best," Elizabeth said quietly. "And if you'd like to know, lineage is about the same as heritage, which is simply knowing your blood lines…where your parents and grandparents came from. Judging by your looks and build, I would guess you were from Scottish descent, or maybe Irish." She finally looked up at him. "Maybe even British."

Logan managed a smile. "Guess I'll never know. And you are talking too much again."

Elizabeth turned her attention to the Indians. "Sorry. Actually, my heart is pounding so hard I fear they will hear *that*."

"Just let me handle things." The Indians came even closer. "And by the way, I only yell because I feel so responsible for you," Logan said. "I would never go so far as to get violent, if that's what you're worried about. I save my violence for the men I hunt." He walked over to Jasper and rested his rifle on the horse's saddle, taking aim in the direction of the Indians. Jasper snorted and moved a little. "Easy, boy," he soothed. "Take the reins to the other horses and hang on to them," he told Elizabeth. "If they are startled, they might break away and run. If they do, those Indians will get them. That's likely what they are after anyway."

Elizabeth didn't answer. She simply untied the

other horses and wrapped the reins of all three tightly into her fists. Logan turned to look at her and saw terror in her eyes. *Damned if she doesn't make me want to yell at her one minute and hold her the next.* He turned his attention back to the Indians.

"Don't worry. We'll be okay," he assured Elizabeth. "I brought extra tobacco and whiskey with us. They might settle for that. The only thing that worries me is that they are all men. It's better when they are traveling with women and children. That's a sure sign of peace. They don't like putting their women and kids in danger, but just men means a possible war party." He looked back at her again. "You wanted to see some real Indians. Now you'll get your chance." He watched the approaching warriors again and leveled his rifle. "Welcome to the world of your dime novels, Miss Baylor."

THIRTY

ELIZABETH HUNG ON TO THE HORSES AND PEERED around the tree trunk at six nearly naked Indians, all of them heavily painted. Even their horses were painted. A seventh man wore buckskin pants and a vest. Their hair hung long and was decorated with feathers and various ornaments. All seven warriors looked fierce and intimidating.

Three held rifles and two others had quivers of arrows slung over their shoulders. The other two appeared weaponless except for knives at their waists. Logan waited until they came within fifty feet or so before calling out.

"Hold it right there!" he shouted. He still stood behind Jasper, his rifle resting on the horse's saddle.

The Indians pulled up short and stared silently at Logan. It reminded Elizabeth of the way a deer once looked at William when she was allowed to go with him on a hunting trip. The buck simply stared at William at first, as though trying to determine if he was friend or foe, wondering if it should stay, or run.

"What do you want?" Logan asked.

The one who wore buckskins moved in front of the others. "You have fine horses," he said.

"I do, and I intend to keep them."

The one who had spoken moved his eyes to Elizabeth. "The woman with you has hair like straw."

"She's my wife."

Elizabeth's eyes widened at the remark. Logan must feel she'd be safer if the Natives thought she belonged to him.

The lead Indian nodded and looked around. "You are one man alone."

"And I killed four men at once not all that long ago. They, too, wanted my horses. I made sure they didn't get them."

Four at once? Elizabeth was surprised at the remark. Just how good *was* Logan Best?

"If you try to take anything I have with me, several of you will die before it's finished," Logan added.

The Indian turned his head and said something to the others. A couple of them laughed.

"What are you called?" their apparent leader asked Logan.

"Logan Best. I hunt men for money, and I damn well know how to use this rifle. I have extra tobacco, the chewing kind, and whiskey. I can spare that and a few biscuits and hardtack. I'll give you that much if you'll ride on by."

The leader looked around, then back at Logan. "I am Walks Away—Cheyenne. I am the only one here who speaks your tongue. We are going to a place where more of our people have gathered on the Smokey Hill. We will head north then, to the

Dakotas. We will join the Sioux and fight the white men there who come into lands promised to only the Sioux and Cheyenne."

"And you want fresh horses."

Walks Away smiled. "*Aye.*"

"Well, you won't get them here. I told you what I have. Take it or leave it."

One of the others raised his rifle, and Elizabeth thought her heart would leap right out of her chest when Logan fired, knocking the Indian's rifle out of his hand. The Indian cried out as his rifle flew sideways and whirled once before landing in the dirt. The horses Elizabeth held onto all jolted, but she kept a tight hold, glad she'd worn leather gloves, or the reins might have cut into her hands. It all happened in perhaps a second—the shot, the rifle flying away, the horses snorting and moving. The Indians looked surprised and exchanged words as they tried to settle their horses.

Logan instantly cocked his rifle and aimed again. "The next one goes into someone's heart," he announced, "and the next one and the next one. I told you you can't have my horses or my woman. All I can spare is the whiskey and tobacco and a little food. I could easily shoot some of you, but I understand where you are headed and why, and I don't blame you. But you won't be taking my horses or my woman with you. If I was an Indian killer, that man who tried to shoot at me would be dead right now instead of his hand stinging. You make the choice."

Walks Away turned to the others, who were all obviously nervous and upset. Walks Away spoke to them in their own tongue. One of them seemed angry and said something to Walks Away in a very determined voice, but Walks Away shouted back at him with an air of authority.

"*Nohetto!*" he yelled at the angry Indian. He said it several times over before the man calmed down. "*Hopo! Hopo!*" Walks Away shouted then, pointing to the east. Five of the Indians rode off, whooping and shouting as though to show Logan he hadn't frightened them at all.

The Indian who'd lost his rifle stayed behind, looking very disgruntled. He jumped off his horse and picked up the gun, but the butt of the rifle had broken away from the rest because of Logan's shot. He said something angrily to Walks Away.

Walks Away turned to Logan. "We will take tobacco and whiskey and some food," he told them, "and a rifle. We will need the gun where we are going. Give us those things and we will leave you."

Logan kept his aim on the leader. "Elizabeth, tie those three horses to that low branch near you and then bring your rifle here."

Elizabeth started to object, then remember Logan had said she'd better do everything he told her. She retied the three horses and pulled her rifle from its boot, walking around the horses to Logan.

"Go hand it to the one who lost his rifle."

"*What?*"

"You heard me."

"But he might—"

"Indians keep their word. They won't hurt you."

Elizabeth could hardly make her legs move. Hoping

she wouldn't sink to the ground from fear, she walked up to the wounded, half-naked warrior and handed out the gun. He yanked it from her hand with a grunt. Elizabeth eagerly hurried back to Logan.

"Find some of your cartridges and give him those, too," Logan told her.

Elizabeth obeyed, reaching into her saddlebag and taking out a box of cartridges. She hurried over to the scowling Indian who held the rifle and handed it up. Again, he yanked it from her hand.

"Give the leader two cans of tobacco, a small bottle of whiskey and five or six biscuits," Logan told her then.

"If you say so." Elizabeth walked over to one of the packhorses and fished around in a gunny sack Logan had kept separate from their other supplies for just such an occasion. She put all the things he told her into a spare gunny sack and hurried back to hand it up to Walks Away, hardly able to believe she was so close to a real Indian. When she looked up at him, he grinned.

"Be lucky your straw hair is not decorating my war lance," he told her.

Walks Away turned his attention to Logan. "*Ha-ho*."

Logan nodded. "*Ha-ho*," he replied.

Elizabeth hurried back to the horses, and the two Indians rode off, whooping and shouting like the others had done. The one with the rifle let out an extra loud cry, holding the rifle in the air like it was a grand prize.

Elizabeth leaned against the tree for support, her legs wanting to buckle. Logan watched the last two

Indians catch up with the others and they rode on, still letting out shrill cries of what they considered victory.

Logan finally relaxed and shoved his rifle into its boot. He turned to Elizabeth. "You all right?"

She breathed a deep sigh. "Just give me a minute to feel my legs again."

Logan grinned. "How's that for getting to see real Indians?"

"Oh, I don't even feel like joking about it," she answered.

"Just part of everyday life out here." Logan walked over to untie the other three horses.

"Jasper hardly moved when you fired that shot," Elizabeth told him.

"He's used to me and gunfire," Logan explained. "He's a damn good horse." Logan stood looking down at her while he held the other horses. "I'm proud of how you hung on to these other three. And thanks for remembering to do what I told you. You did a good job."

Why did that comment make her so happy? "Thank you, but if at all possible, don't make me do something like that again."

"I'll try not to. I just didn't want to turn my back to get those supplies. I had to be ready with my rifle."

"I understand."

"Can you walk yet?"

Elizabeth couldn't help a smile. "I think so." She moved away from the tree, stretching her shoulders and neck. "I'm stiff from fear and stress."

"Happens to all of us at one time or another."

Logan kept the reins to the two packhorses and

handed her Suzy's reins. He waited while Elizabeth made three attempts before managing to climb back onto her horse. She took the reins to her packhorse, and Logan urged Jasper out at a slow trot.

"We'll ride till almost dark," he called to her. "We'll be in Hays City in about four days."

"Those men might be gone by then."

"They won't—not till they know what is and isn't true about Alexander. They will be wondering if he or someone he appointed is still bringing them a beautiful, young virgin. Plus, they won't be sure what to do about your banknotes and jewels. Until they know for certain Alexander is dead, they'll stay put in Hays City. They know it will take Alexander a while to get there, if he's still alive."

Elizabeth rode to catch up. "Mr. Best, you called me Elizabeth back there when you told me to get those things together for the Indians."

"I had to. If I'd called you anything else, they might have realized you weren't really my wife."

I'm not so sure being your wife would be such a bad thing, Elizabeth thought. She thought how fetching he'd looked when he'd ridden off at a fast gallop to catch her packhorse earlier. He sat a horse like he was part of it. He was so sure and dominant in everything he did. She'd not detected an ounce of fear or doubt in him when he stood against those seven Indians.

"I thought I was going to faint back there," she said. "Weren't you scared?"

"Only for you, not myself. And you can usually dicker with Indians. I wasn't fond of giving up a brand-new rifle, but I'll trade one any day for my scalp.

And Indians respect bravery. They didn't expect me to shoot at them like that. It surprised them enough to change their mind about trying to take our horses." He looked over at her and grinned. "Or my woman."

Elizabeth reddened, but for some reason, she wasn't offended. "If they wanted to take your woman, Logan Best, they would have had to kidnap every painted lady in every saloon in every town from here to Denver."

That got a big laugh out of Logan. She liked his laugh.

"It's good to see you are finding your sense of humor, Miss Baylor," he told her.

Elizabeth smiled, and they rode on for several silent minutes before she spoke up again. "I think I don't mind if you just call me Elizabeth," she said. "I am already learning formalities out here mean nothing. May I call you Logan?"

"Some men have several other names for me, but you can call me Logan."

"Please tell me you don't chew tobacco. It's such a filthy habit."

"No, ma'am, I just smoke it."

"And you won't delve into that whiskey when we are alone?"

Logan looked sidelong at her and grinned. "I'll try not to."

"Don't forget I have already killed a man, Logan."

Logan chuckled. "Oh, I wouldn't forget something like that, Elizabeth."

"Then we understand each other?"

"We most certainly do."

THIRTY-ONE

June 4, 1870

LOGAN NOTICED ELIZABETH WINCE WHEN SHE MOUNTED her horse the morning of the third day of their journey. "Getting a few blisters?" he asked.

Elizabeth scowled at him. "You told me not to complain if you let me go with you."

"Just asking a question. Admitting you hurt in new places isn't complaining. It's just a fact. I have something that might help."

"I'm afraid to ask what that might be." Elizabeth looked straight forward and kicked her horse into motion, holding the reins to her packhorse. As always, to avoid having to watch her backside, Logan kicked Jasper into a faster trot to catch up and ride beside her.

Logan wondered how much longer he could survive with little sleep. All he could think about was how soft Elizabeth Baylor would feel under a flannel nightgown, how nice she probably smelled. It didn't help having to turn away every time she relieved herself. He had to fight his baser instincts to keep from looking at things he shouldn't, which brought him back to the fact that she surely had a couple of sores on that little, round bottom. He caught up and answered her original comment. "It's called buffalo grease. Stinks like hell, but the damn stuff will heal just about anything. If you're really hurting, you might want to put some on the sore spots."

"It *smells*?"

"If a man, or a woman in this case, is hurting badly enough, he or she puts up with the smell. Besides, where you'd have to put the stuff, no one would notice." *Unless you were lying naked beneath him.*

They rode on silently for several minutes. Logan lit a cigarette and scanned the horizon.

"And how do you propose I apply this buffalo grease?" Elizabeth asked. "It would involve…you know…getting to unmentionable places."

Logan shrugged. "I can always apply it for you."

"I'm sure you would thoroughly enjoy that."

"I thoroughly would."

Elizabeth didn't answer right away. Logan took a side glance at her and saw her face was red. It was too early for the redness to be from the sun. She actually looked ready to cry.

"Hold it," he told her, reaching over and taking hold of Suzy's bridle.

"What's wrong?" Elizabeth asked.

"You."

Elizabeth met his eyes and quickly wiped at a tear as she did so.

"You're hurting more than you're letting on," Logan said.

"So what? Do you actually think I'd all but undress to put something on a few sores when I am out here in the middle of nowhere with a near stranger—who, I might add, is a womanizer?"

Logan frowned. "A womanizer? What the hell does that mean?"

"Well, it didn't take long to figure out you hang around with those awful kind of women every place you stop. Isn't that womanizing?"

Logan took the cigarette from his mouth as he drew Jasper to a halt. "You sure have a lot to learn about men and life." He dismounted, and at first, Elizabeth watched him as though she needed to worry about what he was going to do. He walked around Jasper and around Suzy to take the reins of Elizabeth's pack-horse out of her hand. He walked behind her and tied her packhorse to strappings on Suzy, then walked back to Jasper and tied his own packhorse to Jasper's straps. He mounted Jasper then.

"What are you doing?" Elizabeth asked him, a nervous shake to her voice.

Logan met her gaze. "A womanizer is a man who cheats on his wife," he told her. "I don't *have* a wife, so I'm not a womanizer. I'm just a man, and if I *had* a wife, I wouldn't cheat on her or hang out with those awful women—who, I might add, aren't awful at all. Some of them are pretty damn nice and deserve to be *treated* nice. And believe it or not, sometimes all we do is *talk*. And if you have to drop your drawers around me, I'm not going to attack you just because you're a woman. If I was going to do that, I would have already done it. The fact remains you have a sore ass and you need to do something about it or some of those sores will start bleeding, and they will get so bad I *will* have to do something about it myself."

Now the tears came. "Surely you understand I can't...I just can't half undress out here in these wide-open spaces. Please don't get angry. Maybe tonight after dark—"

"That means riding all day with those sores."

"Then that's what I will have to do," Elizabeth told him obstinately. She cried harder. "No matter how much it hurts!"

Logan closed his eyes and sighed. He crushed out his half-smoked cigarette against his canteen and reached out for her. "Come here."

Elizabeth did not obey. "What do you intend to do?"

"I intend to make sure you take it easy on those blisters until tonight. We're stopping at Fort Harker for the night. They will have some kind of accommodations where you can sleep inside, probably even wash up a little. You can take care of those blisters then, in *privacy*."

"Really?"

"Yes. Now get over here. You can sit sideways in front of me and relieve the pressure you're feeling in all the wrong places. I'll take Suzy's reins, and she can walk along beside us and tow your packhorse."

Elizabeth wiped at her tears and hesitated. "That will...it will be uncomfortable for you, having to ride with an extra person."

"What do you weigh? A hundred pounds, maybe? That's nothing for Jasper. And I've half lived on a horse for years. I'll manage just fine."

"But it will mean—" Elizabeth didn't finish.

"Being close to me? I promise to keep my hands to myself."

Elizabeth squirmed uncomfortably in her saddle. "It just doesn't seem right."

"And if you don't start trusting me, I'll leave you at Fork Harker and finish this little journey by myself."

"Please don't!"

"Then get over here."

Still she hesitated. Logan reached over and wrapped an arm around her. Elizabeth let out a little yelp when he jerked her off her horse and plunked her in front of him sideways. "Wrap one leg around my saddle horn, kind of like sidesaddle," he told her.

"But what do I hang on to?" she pouted.

"*Me.*"

"But I can't—"

He grabbed her right arm and pulled it around him. "There. It's pretty simple." He reached over for Suzy's reins and placed them in her left hand. "Push your hat behind your back and lay your head against my shoulder," he told her, "then just hang on."

Elizabeth had little choice but to obey.

Jesus, a full day and night on the trail, and her hair still smells good, Logan thought. He kicked Jasper into a gentle walk. "I'll ride easy for a while, but we'll have to speed it up later if we want to make it to Fort Harker by nightfall," he told her. "And I might remind you that you've already dropped your riding skirt with me around. I haven't done one thing inappropriate yet, have I?"

"Well, at least when *you* go, you don't have to— you know—"

"What? Drop *my* pants?" Logan chuckled. "Men do have an advantage that way."

Elizabeth sniffed. "If you understood my background, how I was raised, you'd know how humiliating this is for me."

"I can guess." They rode in silence for a while. Logan felt Elizabeth beginning to relax a little more as she settled against him. But then again, she didn't have much choice. "I'm not trying to embarrass you, Elizabeth. I know you're hurting and I want to help. That's all."

"Then I guess I should thank you," she answered.

"I guess you should." *Except I don't mind riding this way at all. If you didn't look so damn much like MaryAnne, this would all be easier.* "I'm going to tell you something I haven't told anyone in a long, long time," he said. "Usually even then it's only if I'm drunk. It takes whiskey for me to be able to talk about it."

Elizabeth straightened a little and looked up at him. "What is it?"

God, she's close enough to kiss. It would be so damn easy, but it would scare her to kingdom come. "My wife," he answered.

She rested her head on his shoulder again. "You don't have to tell me if you don't want to."

"I think I do, just so you'll rest easier being around me."

She tightened the arm around him a little, as though she sympathized with him. "All right," she said softly.

Logan wrestled with the memory. "After I ran off from that orphanage in Pennsylvania, I worked odd jobs all over the place. I was thirteen and didn't know a damn thing about love and family and all that. By nineteen, I was broke and going nowhere, didn't know how to read or hold a real job, so when the war broke out, the one between the states over slavery, I decided to join the Union Army just for something to do. I ended up wounded someplace in the South. I didn't even know where I was, and most of the men in my Company were dead or had run off. I crawled to the closest house for help, and it ended up being MaryAnne's folks' house."

He cleared his throat. "By MaryAnne, I mean my wife. She and her family were Southerners," he continued, "but real Christian people. Even though I wore a blue uniform, they helped me. Nicest folks I ever met. MaryAnne was sixteen. She did most of the nursing, and for the first time in my life I knew kindness from someone. I learned what love was supposed to feel like. We got married. I went back to my Company because I was healed and didn't want to be considered a deserter, but leaving MaryAnne was the hardest thing I'd ever done."

He stopped and looked around. "Thought I heard something," he told Elizabeth. He listened a moment longer. A gentle breeze blew a piece of Elizabeth's hair against his face. He wanted to hold it against his nose and breathe in the smell of it. "A lot of hills in this part of Kansas," he said. "Makes it harder to see or sense someone coming." Finally, he kicked Jasper into motion again.

"Damned if I didn't get wounded again," he told Elizabeth. "Not as bad as that first time, but it was enough to get me discharged for being wounded twice. They gave me some kind of silly medal and I rode back to MaryAnne as fast as I could. By then, she was eight months pregnant and the prettiest sight I'd ever seen. Her pa gave us some land to farm and we settled in. MaryAnne gave me a daughter…and I found out what being a father felt like…and what it was like to be part of a real family. That was the happiest I'd ever been in my life. I finally felt like somebody cared about me."

Again, they rode on in silence. Logan searched for the courage to continue. "Right after the war, the South was a mess," he said, "full of outlaws and people out to take what they could from ravaged plantations and such. One day I was out plowing a field when I—" He struggled to keep finding his voice. "There were five of them. Raiders. Southern men who'd lost everything they had and were out for revenge. One of them used to be a neighbor of MaryAnne's pa. MaryAnne was scared of him because he sometimes threatened her. He knew she had married a Union man, and that was his excuse for attacking our place… attacking MaryAnne. I heard her screams and had to run from that field. Seemed like it took forever, and I had no gun with me. By the time I reached the house, it was on fire, and that man and all four others were taking their turns with my wife."

"Oh dear God!" Elizabeth tightened her hold on him even more. "I'm so sorry!"

Logan fought the rage that always visited him when he allowed the memories to come to the forefront. Why did he feel he needed to tell Elizabeth? "When I got closer, one of them saw me and shot at me. He got me in the left leg. Broke a bone. I did everything in my power to get back up, but I couldn't. All five of those men came up to me and beat me into unconsciousness. The last thing I remember was that man calling me a Yankee and laughing, saying now he'd had a piece of my wife for himself and so did all his friends. He told me he'd cut up her woman parts so she could never make love to her Yankee husband again."

He couldn't control the choking sound he made then. "I, uh, I managed to crawl to MaryAnne. I've never seen so much blood in my life. She looked at me with a kind of begging look in her eyes, such horrible sorrow. I heard a scream from the burning house, and I knew it was…Lilly…but I couldn't get to her."

He cleared his throat again and sniffed.

"I passed out from loss of blood. When I woke up, I was in a neighbor's house and a doctor was working on me. They had to hold me down because I kept trying to get back home. They told me MaryAnne and Lilly were dead and there was nothing I could do, but I could go after the men who'd taken the only love and family I'd ever known. The worst part was not being able to help my wife and daughter or tell them one last time that I loved them. After I healed, I visited their graves, and then I went after those men. They were easy to find—they had left a bloody mess every place they went. I guess when I hunted those bastards, it was my first lesson in tracking men like that."

He breathed a deep sigh before continuing.

"I found them, one by one, and I killed every last one of them. I've been killing men like that ever since and have enjoyed taking money for it." He halted

Jasper again. "When I saw you in that jail cell and found out what had happened to you, I felt the same rage all over again. And I know what Chad Krieger and his bunch had in mind for you, so that's why I'm hunting them. You never needed to offer me money for it. I just want you to understand I'd never force myself on you. I figured if I explained about my wife, you would understand why I'd never do that, so you won't be so scared all the time. I forget what kind of world you come from. Out here women understand I'm just teasing—like when I said I'd gladly help you with that buffalo grease." He sighed again. "So, there you are. You should feel damn special because I've never talked about my wife since it all happened—not the full story anyway. And when you look at me like you're scared of what I might do next, I see that look of terror in MaryAnne's eyes and it bothers me."

He kicked Jasper into motion again. Elizabeth kept hold of Suzy's reins as she moved her left arm around Logan, hugging him tightly and saying nothing. Since he'd met this unusual, haughty, wealthy, proper, educated woman from another world, he'd felt MaryAnne with him, and that was driving him crazy. Something was happening to him, and he wasn't exactly sure what it was...or that he even liked it.

THIRTY-TWO

ELIZABETH OPENED HER EYES. IT TOOK HER A MOMENT to realize where she was and that she'd been riding for who knew how long with her arms around Logan Best and her face close to his neck. She'd fallen asleep against him as though it was as natural as breathing.

Oh dear God! She stayed still a moment, thinking how comfortable and safe she felt here. Only then did she realize she'd never truly felt that way around Robert. Both men emitted power, but there had always been that sense of danger around Robert that disturbed her. But here in Logan's arms, she felt none of that. She gathered her thoughts, remembering his story about his wife.

How did a man bear such horror? Now she understood the bounty hunter, the man who was always going after the men who'd brutalized his wife and child. Every man he killed or watched hang was one of those who'd taken his wife and daughter from him.

She straightened, rubbing at her eyes. "My goodness! How long did I sleep?"

"Judging by the sun, I'd say almost two hours," Logan answered.

"Oh no. I'm so sorry."

Logan grinned. "Believe me, I didn't mind."

Elizabeth started to feel defensive, then remembered what he'd told her about trusting him. She met his eyes, those yellow-green eyes that sparkled through lines around his eyes from too much living in the sun, and trail dust that highlighted the lines.

Close! He was so close! She was sure that for a moment he was going to try to kiss her. She looked away. "How old are you, Logan?"

"Not sure. When I kicked one of the teachers at that orphanage for using a strap on me, I was told a thirteen-year-old boy who would kick a woman was a terrible sinner and needed some sense beat into him, so one of the male guards proceeded to do just that. That's the night I ran away, and also the first time anybody there bothered to tell me how old I was. I just figured that's the age I would use, so that would make me twenty-eight. You?"

Why did she not want to vacate his arms? "I'm nineteen. And speaking of dates, I am realizing I don't even know what day of the week this is, or what the date is. I have never *not* known." Elizabeth laughed lightly. "I always lived a very regimented life. Not only did I always know the day and date, but I also knew the *hour*, because back in London, everything is scheduled, from the moment you wake up through the time you are supposed to go to bed—*everything*."

Logan chuckled. "Sounds even more boring than what you've already told me."

"I never realized just *how* boring until I got onto that boat to America."

"Well, as far as I know, it's around June third or fourth—and by the sun, I'd say it's about ten a.m. We got up at six, according to a watch I keep in my gear. We ate a decent breakfast and drank too much coffee, then left around seven."

"Oh my goodness! I never kept such hours in London either. I never rose before eight a.m." Elizabeth frowned. "Shouldn't we rest the horses for a few minutes?"

"We should. I just didn't want to disturb your beauty sleep. I know you didn't get much last night, worrying if I might crawl into your bedroll and take privileges."

Elizabeth gasped, sitting up even straighter and putting her hat back on. "You aren't helping my trust, Logan Best. Just don't forget I keep my gun in that bedroll with me."

"That's the only thing that kept me away. You've already killed one man for daring to touch you. I don't want to be the second." He met her gaze and grinned.

Elizabeth smiled. "That was one of those jokes, right?"

"Don't people tease and joke in London?"

Elizabeth put on a stern face. "Oh no. It's not allowed. Everyone is very serious."

"Then I'm glad I don't live there." Logan pulled Jasper to a halt. "We'll give the horses a break." He had to grab the pommel and keep his arms around Elizabeth as he dismounted. "Come on down," he told her, reaching up to help her. Elizabeth grasped his shoulders, and he planted big hands around her waist and lifted her down as though she weighed nothing. Why did his strength and his touch bring these odd desires again? Damn the man! All the properness and inhibition she'd known her whole life seemed to go out the window every time she was close to him. She found herself wondering how different a kiss from Logan Best might be from Robert's kisses.

"We should reach Fort Harker before sunset if we ride at a faster pace after this," he told her.

"Whatever we need to do. Why Fort Harker? Is it a real army fort?"

"Yup. Used to be Fort Ellsworth, but they built a bigger and better fort next to that one and closed Ellsworth. Named Fort Harker after some general from the Civil War. I'm stopping there to see if anyone who fits Chad Krieger's description might have stopped there for supplies."

Elizabeth searched for a biscuit in her pack. She still couldn't get over the fact that the very private, and, she guessed, sometimes brutal Logan Best had been so open with her earlier. She decided never to be first to bring up the subject of his wife. If he wanted to talk more about her, it had to come from him.

Suddenly Logan pressed her shoulder from behind. "Grab the horses," he told her.

Elizabeth turned at the order to see Logan pull his spare six-gun from behind his back.

"Stay in between the horses so you're less visible," he said. "Out here the land looks flat when it really isn't. There is a rise to our right, and some men just rode up from the other side of it and are headed this way. They look like buffalo hunters."

Elizabeth's heart tightened. "Is that good, or bad?"

"Bad. You'd have been safer with those Indians." He stepped out from behind the horses and waited.

Elizabeth counted them. Five. And all five were burly, rugged men with long, unkempt hair, riding big horses and wearing buffalo and wolf-skin coats in spite of the heat. They carried the biggest rifles she'd ever seen. She remembered reading about buffalo guns in one of those dime novels she'd loved. Was that what these men were carrying?

"Jesus, it's Roy McBain," Logan muttered. "Stay inside those horses and get your gun ready. If they take me down, use that gun on yourself."

Oh my God! Logan *knew* them, and it obviously was not a friendly relationship!

THIRTY-THREE

"Well, if it ain't Logan Best."

The statement came from the man who appeared to be in charge of the rest. Elizabeth thought all five of them the most reprehensible, filthy men she'd ever seen. Even though they were several feet away, she could smell them, and the smell was akin to rotten meat. Compared to the men who sat their horses right in front of her, Elizabeth judged the Indians they'd come across yesterday to be far cleaner and now, as she watched these men, far less dangerous. Logan and the man who apparently knew him exchanged a look that made her blood run cold.

"Roy McBain," Logan declared. "I haven't seen you since I took your brother in for a hanging."

McBain grinned through rotten teeth. "That's right. And you've always been one step ahead of me, Logan. I've had to keep up with the buffalo to earn my money, but whenever I get the chance, I ask about you and where you might be so's I can kill you. I took some hides in to Abilene yesterday and heard a real interestin' story."

With crusted, bloodshot eyes, McBain moved his gaze to Elizabeth. "This the woman who murdered a man back there? I heard you took off with her." He turned his attention back to Logan. "You takin' an attraction to murderesses now?"

One of the others laughed. "Hell, *look* at her! Wouldn't matter to me if she killed *ten* men if I could get under them skirts!"

"You pickin' European princesses now, Logan?" McBain joked. "Seems like you should have made it to Fort Harker by now. What's got you so slowed down? We've been ridin' like hell to catch up, figurin' you had an extra day on us. And yet, here you are." He laughed from somewhere deep in his belly. "Must be the woman who slowed you up. Everybody knows how much you like women." He looked at Elizabeth again. "Fact is, I'd stay in one nice, shady place and fuck her all day long if she was mine."

Elizabeth felt a numbness through her whole body when Logan cocked his spare six-gun and aimed it at McBain. The movement was so fast she couldn't believe what she was seeing.

"Look at her one more time and you're a *dead* man," Logan told McBain flatly.

McBain's smile faded. "We'll all do more than *look* at her after we kill you," he told Logan in a low snarl. "Then again, maybe we'll just wound you so's you can watch."

"Try it. I'll gladly shoot all of you in self-defense. That will be my excuse."

Elizabeth's eyes widened in terror. Logan Best was challenging five men holding huge buffalo guns and all apparently eager to kill him! She hoped she wouldn't pass out with the terror that engulfed her.

The others spread out a little. Elizabeth moved behind Jasper and pulled out her six-gun, secretly begging God to let her hit at least one of them if it came to that. She decided if these men killed Logan, she would do what Logan had told her to do and use her gun on herself before she would let them touch her with their vile hands.

"I might die here today, McBain," Logan warned, "but you will by God be the first one to go down before any of these other men get a shot off! You willing to take the risk?"

McBain backed his horse a little. Elizabeth could see the fear in his eyes. Apparently, Logan Best had a reputation the man wasn't sure he wanted to deal with. McBain moved his gaze to Elizabeth. "Might be worth the risk," he told Logan. "You might be good, but not that good. There's five of us and one of you, and a pretty piece of ass standin' there all fresh and tight."

"And I told you not to look at that woman again." Logan fired, and a hole burst open in McBain's forehead.

Elizabeth gasped. There was no way to remember the timing of things after that. Her world became a hail of gunfire, Logan's six-gun and the hunters' big buffalo guns. Logan got off five more shots in rapid succession, then pulled his holstered gun and kept firing.

Three of the other men fell from their horses before they could even get their rifles up into position. After that came two big booms. Elizabeth's packhorse went down…and so did Logan, still firing. A fourth man fell from his horse just as his buffalo gun went off again with another loud boom.

"Oh my God!" Elizabeth cocked her pistol and took aim at the last man. She missed. He came for her, but another shot was fired, and he screamed when a huge gash opened at the side of his head. He whirled his horse and aimed his buffalo gun at what Elizabeth was sure must be Logan. She couldn't see him because of the horses.

Another boom, and then another shot from a six-gun. The wounded buffalo hunter fell from his horse.

"Logan!" Elizabeth screamed, running out from behind Jasper.

Logan was grimacing with pain as he got to one knee. Blood poured from his right thigh. Elizabeth stood frozen when he actually managed to get to his feet. He stumbled to each man to make sure he was dead. One was rolling around in pain, blood pouring from his stomach. Elizabeth held her own stomach when Logan used his good leg to stomp onto the man's wound. The man screamed and stared up at Logan.

"Was this risk worth a good fuck?" Logan snarled at the man.

"I never...said nothin'!" the man objected.

"No, but you *thought* it!" Logan fired, opening a hole in the man's throat. The man made a horrible, gurgling sound as blood gushed from his neck. In seconds he quieted.

Logan stepped back, then collapsed.

"Logan!" Elizabeth holstered her gun and ran up to him. "What should I do?" she asked frantically. "You're bleeding awful!"

Logan, who Elizabeth could tell was weakening fast, untied the scarf he always wore at his neck and yanked it off. "Tie this…tight as you can…above the wound," he told her. "Real tight…or I'll…bleed to death. Buffalo guns…make big holes."

"Oh dear God!" Elizabeth's heart rushed with panic and devastation. She took the scarf and moved it under his leg, then wrapped it around and tied it as tightly as she could.

Logan cried out with pain.

"I'm sorry!" Elizabeth agonized. "You said to tie it tightly!"

He touched her arm. "It's okay." He groaned. "I… should have spotted them…or at least…*smelled* them. They must have been…downwind. I usually…never let a man…get the drop on me like that! It was that damn hill. I didn't hear them. I wasn't paying enough… attention." He gripped her arm again. "You all right?"

"Yes, but they shot my packhorse."

In obvious intense pain, Logan cried out, then spoke through gritted teeth. "You need to get my rifle…shoot the packhorse in the head."

"What?"

"*Do* it! That horse…won't be any good now. You'll be doing it…a favor. And I need you to try to…pack most of those supplies onto the other packhorse. Bring all three horses…over here. I'll try to…get onto Jasper. We have to…try to make it to Fort Harker before dark…find a doctor. And bring me my guns."

Elizabeth was stunned by what had just happened, her ears ringing painfully from all the gunfire. She blindly did as he told her. She found his six-guns, surprised by how heavy they were when she picked them up. She laid them next to him, then looked around at five dead men. She'd never seen anyone fire a gun so fast, and she realized if Logan hadn't done what he'd done, she'd be at the mercy of the horrid men who lay scattered around them now, all dead.

Logan! She'd almost lost him, and it struck her how devastated she would have been if he'd been killed today. She felt sick at the realization that he could still die, and all because of her. She hurried to the horses and pulled Logan's rifle from its boot. It was bigger and heavier than the .22 she'd practiced with. She cocked it. That much she knew how to do.

She walked up to the wounded packhorse. A large, gaping hole bled at the horse's right shoulder. The animal lay struggling and whinnying, terror in its eyes. Tears filled her own eyes as she lifted Logan's rifle and took aim at the horse's head. "I'm sorry," she told the mare. She fired. The gun jolted against her shoulder, and she stumbled backward. She stood transfixed for a moment as she stared at the hole she'd just put in the horse's head.

The animal stopped struggling.

Feeling removed from her body, she shoved Logan's rifle back into its boot and struggled with the ties on the dead packhorse. She had to hurry. Logan Best could be dying! She retrieved what bags of supplies she could, unable to get at the ones under the horse where it had fallen. She quickly retied what supplies she could salvage, then looked around to see that the horses belonging to the buffalo hunters had run off. Three of them stood several yards away grazing on prairie grass.

There was no time to worry about any of them. She had to save Logan! Praying Logan wasn't already dead, she took the reins to Jasper and led the horse over to where Logan still lay. She heard a soft groan. *Thank God he's still alive!* She noticed the blood on his pants looked as though it was drying a little. She figured that must be a good sign, but how long could a man go with no blood to his lower limb before the limb itself died? Did she dare untie the scarf a little so blood could get to his extremity?

She knelt beside him. "Logan! Logan, can you hear me? You have to try to get on Jasper." She put a hand to the side of his face. "Logan, you have to try to get up!"

He grasped her wrist and kissed the palm of her hand. "MaryAnne?"

Elizabeth felt her heart breaking in two. "No. Logan, it's me—Elizabeth. You have to get up, Logan. Try to climb up onto Jasper."

His eyes were closed, and all he did was groan.

"Oh, dear God, help me!" Elizabeth leaned down and wrapped one arm under his neck and the other around and under his left arm, trying to lift him, but it was impossible. He was too big and too far gone to be of any help. She rested her face against the side of his, talking into his ear. "Don't die, Logan! Please don't die! Tell me what to do!"

No reply. Elizabeth held him and wept, then struggled to stop her sobbing when she thought she heard the sound of horses' hooves. She quickly let go of Logan and wiped at tears with her forearm.

Yes! She heard horses! Was it Indians, or more

buffalo hunters? She quickly rose and pulled out her pistol, frantically turning in a circle to see who might be coming. Several men on horseback came over a rise, riding from the west. She pointed her gun at them, until she realized the men were soldiers. Relief flooded over her, and she put her pistol back in its holster.

Someone ordered the men to halt.

Someone was suddenly at her side.

Someone was ordering others to pick up the dead men and haul them "back to the fort for identification and burial."

"Get their horses!" the same man shouted.

Someone picked her up in his arms. "We'll get you some help," a voice told her as he plunked her onto a horse. "Make up a travois for that man and we'll get him to a doctor!" the same voice ordered.

Someone mounted up behind her, putting his arm around her. Was it Logan? She felt the horse start moving. "Please help him," she told the soldier who was helping her.

"We will, ma'am."

"He's Logan Best. He's a bounty hunter."

"I know," the man answered. "I've met Logan more than once. I'm Lieutenant Whittaker from Fort Harker."

"Don't...let him die."

"We'll try our best. But it's quite a ride to the fort. Our medic will do what he can to keep him from bleeding to death, but we also need to make sure some blood reaches his lower leg."

Elizabeth's head swam with all that had happened... so fast...so horrible. "I'm...Lady Elizabeth Baylor...from

London." *Or am I?* The young "lady" who'd left London only a little over a month ago seemed like a totally different person now. It was as though she no longer existed. Maybe she'd drowned along with William and this was all just a strange dream.

THIRTY-FOUR

ELIZABETH SAT NEXT TO LOGAN'S COT IN FORT HARKER'S infirmary, thinking how strange it was to see such a big man like Logan Best lying there so still. He'd seemed invincible, but she remembered what he'd said before they'd left. *I'm just a man. A bullet can kill me just as much as the next man.* He'd been worried about what would happen to her if she was left alone in the middle of nowhere.

She wondered that herself. If the soldiers hadn't happened along and found them, Logan could truly be dead by now, and she'd be left at the mercy of the land and the weather and whoever might come along—men like those buffalo hunters.

Logan had saved her virtue and probably her life. His shirt was open, and she studied his physique with curiosity. His broad, muscled chest quietly rose and fell with each breath. His stomach was flat, and its rippled muscles were interrupted by an ugly scar near his belly button, most likely from the wound he'd suffered in the war. She'd stayed with him through his cries of pain until chloroform finally quieted him.

She'd struggled with an urge to vomit as the doctor first probed Logan's right thigh for the bullet. She'd learned most buffalo guns were called Sharps rifles and used black powder .45 cartridges meant for big animals, not for men.

He lost a lot of blood, the doctor had told her. *Good thing you managed to tie something above the wound or he wouldn't be with us. It was really just a flesh wound. He's lucky. That bullet could have broken his thigh bone. I think he'll be okay as long as infection doesn't set in.*

The words "or he wouldn't be with us" struck deep. Why did she care so much about the life or death of a man she'd known all of seven days? Why had she taken such comfort and safety earlier today when he'd made her ride on his horse to keep her sores from getting worse? And *was* it only this morning?

She'd been so dazed and confused. Gunfire. So much gunfire! The ringing in her ears only recently had subsided to a bearable decibel. Was Logan's wound her fault for missing that man she'd shot at? She couldn't remember if he fired again at Logan after that, or if Logan had already gone down.

She'd now seen Logan at his best when it came to gun play. No wonder he was so good at what he did. The ugly things the buffalo hunters had said about what they wanted to do to her likely helped him. In his mind, he was protecting his wife.

She touched his hand, hoping for a response, but there was none. She wondered what life with him had been like for his wife, what it was like to sleep with him, to be held by him, to make babies with him.

She closed her eyes and squeezed his hand, feeling

ashamed that such thoughts plagued her. Not only was he likely determined to never love again, but how could she even think about that kind of a relationship with someone so vastly removed from the world she'd known?

Still, she wanted to cry just at the thought of someday having to part ways. She couldn't help the strong feelings that came to her heart as she studied him. He was like a warrior, a wolf on the hunt, much like the brave knights of old England. He was the hero of those penny dreadfuls. He'd lifted her down from her horse as though she were a mere child. He could shoot down five men and face Indians.

She felt torn in a thousand directions. She knew she must be careful of her feelings because she was out of her element. It seemed like she'd left London years ago instead of just weeks. That fight between William and Jonathan was like something she'd read in a book and was no longer real. It was that fight that had started all of this and led to poor William's death…and now here she sat—beside a ruthless bounty hunter who'd been gravely wounded because of her—at a fort in the middle of Kansas, which in turn was in the middle of America. She'd killed a man she thought loved her. She'd lost her money and her servants. Maybe she'd lost her mind.

"Miss Baylor, you really should go to a different room and clean up and rest."

Elizabeth looked up at Captain Rodney Loomis, the fort medic. He was not much older than Logan, nice-looking and caring; and from what Elizabeth had seen, he seemed to be good at what he did.

"I want to stay with Logan."

"You look worn out." The captain walked closer and listened to Logan's heart. "His heartbeat is plenty strong. He'll sleep for quite a while, so I insist that you go into the room next door and wash up. I'll have someone bring you a bowl and pitcher. My wife will bring you something to eat and give you some linens so you can make up a cot for yourself. You can change out of those clothes, and I'll give you something to help you sleep. Would you like some coffee? Maybe you prefer tea."

"You have tea?"

"Yes. I can't promise we have any of the fancy, high quality teas you might be used to, but we do have some."

"Plain black tea will be fine."

"Good." The captain frowned. "You have been through quite an ordeal, Miss Baylor. Are you sure you're all right? No wounds you aren't telling me about?"

"I'm fine. Really."

"May I ask why you were traveling with Logan Best? He's a pretty rugged and sometimes ruthless man, or so I'm told. A lot of people out here know about him, including my commanding officer, Lieutenant Whittaker."

"I hired him to hunt for some men who stole my valuables after I arrived in America. In the short time we have traveled together, I've learned enough about Logan to trust him completely."

"Oh, I'm sure you can trust him, but it's just… riding with a man like that, hunting down dangerous men…it's just not a good idea for someone so young and inexperienced as you. Look what happened with those buffalo hunters. If Logan hadn't been as good as he is, it would have been awful for you. It's just so dangerous. Why on earth did you come along?"

Elizabeth glanced at Logan. "Because at first, after what I had been through, I *didn't* trust Logan. I was worried he would find my valuables and then just ride off with them and I'd never see him again. The sheriff back in Abilene assured me he could be trusted, and Logan was all I had when it came to finding my money. I need it to survive."

Logan groaned again, and Elizabeth's heart ached for his pain. "And in this short time we have traveled together, I have learned the sheriff was right." She looked up at the doctor. "I'm not in danger, Captain Loomis, not as long as I'm with Logan. I've never known anyone so good with a gun and so brave."

The captain grinned. "Feckless is the better word. The man lives as though he doesn't care at all about his own life."

Elizabeth thought about what he'd been through over his wife and daughter. "Maybe he doesn't," she answered, looking back at Logan. "That's sad, isn't it?"

Captain Loomis walked closer and gently took her arm. "Come on. Let him sleep. If you don't eat and rest, you won't be able to continue your journey once Mr. Best is healed. He's a strong man. He could wake up tomorrow and want to leave, although I would strongly advise against it. Either way, you should be rested and strong."

Elizabeth nodded. "Yes, I suppose." She finally left Logan and did what the doctor asked. After she washed, she realized how good it would feel to put on her flannel gown. She took it from the supplies the men had brought in from the remaining packhorse, her heart aching at the memory of having to shoot the wounded horse.

She slipped on the nightgown, and it felt like the most luxurious thing she'd ever worn. The doctor's wife, Amy Loomis, a lovely woman about the same age as the doctor, brought her a tray with buttered biscuits, a bowl of corn, and hot tea. Because Amy was a woman, Elizabeth got up the courage to tell her about her only physical malady—the sores on her bottom from riding a western saddle for the first time in her life.

Amy laughed. "I know exactly what you are suffering," she told Elizabeth. "I'm from New York. I missed my husband so much that I came out here to the middle of nowhere just to be with him. It's a hard life. Anyway, I learned to ride, and I had the same problem. I'll get something from Rodney that you can put on those sores."

"Thank you so much!" Elizabeth studied her, noticing how pretty she was—and she was from New York. "Aren't you afraid of Indians?" she asked.

Amy put the linens on Elizabeth's cot. "Of course I am. It's an everyday fear. Mostly I'm afraid for Rodney. There isn't usually a problem right here at the fort. I just worry when Rodney rides out with the troops to look for renegades. I'm so afraid he won't come back."

"This life has to be hard for a woman."

"It's very hard, and it can age you fast." Amy tucked

in the blankets and rose to face Elizabeth. She didn't look all that old, but her dark hair showed some gray, and lines were beginning to form around her brown eyes. "A woman will put up with a lot to be with the man she loves." She patted Elizabeth's arm and headed for the door. "I'll get you that salve."

Elizabeth sat down with the tray and ate as much as she could, enjoying a real cup of tea. *A woman will put up with a lot to be with the man she loves*. She supposed that was true. Originally, her plan was to be with Robert Alexander, living a rich life in a mansion with servants in Denver. That would never happen now. Would she end up living like a pioneer woman—wearing plain muslin dresses, her hair in one big braid or wound into a bun at the base of her neck—needing slat bonnets to keep the sun off her skin, which would still age too fast because of the dry air—living in a log cabin and doing all her own cooking and sewing? She knew nothing of such a life. She'd never cooked a meal, even depended on Logan to build their campfires and make the coffee and heat food. The only type of sewing she knew was embroidery, which certainly wasn't anything that was needed to survive out here.

Why was she even wondering about such things? What made her think Logan Best would ever want to settle? And why on earth did she care? She reminded herself again that once he found her money and jewels, they would go their separate ways. She would go to Denver and take up the kind of life she'd always known before all this horror visited her. She would move into a fine home, hire servants, live among Denver's wealthy…and Logan Best would go back to hunting men for money. A life of wealth and comfort was all she knew, and hunting men was all Logan knew.

Amy brought the salve. Elizabeth finished her meal and set the tray aside. She closed the door and proceeded to apply the salve to unmentionable places, smiling at how Logan had teased her about doing it for her, then wanting to cry at his kindness of making her ride sideways on his horse so her sores wouldn't get worse.

Darkness fell. She carried her tray to the kitchen at the back of the infirmary and heard light laughter from behind the door of what she imagined was the doctor and his wife's sleeping quarters. What did a man and wife do deep in the night in their bedroom?

She knew very well what they did, and it stirred womanly desires she felt were wrong. Still, Amy Loomis was laughing. Did women really enjoy a man's touch?

Don't do it, she told herself. *You are letting your heart go into dangerous territory.*

She couldn't help it. She felt so sorry for Logan, sorry for his pain, sorry it was all because of her. After hearing about his wife, she thought how terribly lonely the man must be. He shouldn't wake up alone. He wouldn't even know where he was.

She headed back to her cot, then hesitated at the door to Logan's room. She quietly opened the door and peered into silence. By the dim light of a lantern she walked up to his cot.

"Logan?"

There came no reply—just a steady rhythm of breathing.

He was such a big man that he filled the bed, but for one narrow area on his left, away from his wound. All she could think about was how the poor man shouldn't wake up alone.

She crawled in beside him, keeping to the very edge of the cot. She put her head on his shoulder and an arm across his solid chest. She wanted to comfort him. After all, his pain was because of her. She wanted to be there for him in case he woke up and needed something. Most of all, she didn't want him to wake up alone.

THIRTY-FIVE

June 5, 1870

LOGAN AWOKE TO THE TWEETING OF A SONGBIRD outside the window. In his sleepy and still drug-induced state, his mind wouldn't quite relate to reality. For a moment it seemed he lay in bed with MaryAnne on a sweet Sunday morning. She was right beside him, on his left, where MaryAnne always slept. He could feel her hair against his face, smell its soapy scent. She was nestled into his shoulder, like always. He moved his right arm to gently pull her closer as he grasped some of her hair in his hand, then turned his face and kissed her sweet, full lips as he felt for her breasts, always so comforting and warm and soft in the mornings.

"Logan!"

MaryAnne suddenly pulled away from him and got out of bed. He reached for her, but terrible pain shot through his leg when he moved. He cried out and came fully awake. He tried to sit up, but a woman pushed him back down.

"Logan, you're hurt. Lie still."

He groaned, then rubbed at his eyes and looked at MaryAnne, but it wasn't MaryAnne. It was Elizabeth. She stood there blushing, wearing a flannel gown. Was it *her* lips he'd kissed? *Her* breasts he'd touched? "Jesus, I'm sorry," he told her. "I thought—" Maybe by some miracle it was all a dream and he never touched her at all.

"It's okay." Elizabeth reached for her robe, draped over a nearby chair. She quickly pulled it on and tied it. "I was scared for you, so I…I decided to lie down with you last night in case you woke up and needed something."

Jesus, God Almighty, it wasn't a dream. He tried to sit up again as he struggled to remember all that had happened the day before. "Where in hell are we?"

"Fort Harker. After you passed out from loss of blood, soldiers came along and found us and brought us here. Logan, it was like God knew we needed help."

"Those buffalo hunters…"

"You killed them all. I don't know how, but you did it. Then you passed out. I had to shoot my packhorse because she took a bullet from one of those buffalo guns. I used your scarf to tie off your wound, but I couldn't get you onto your horse. Then the soldiers came."

Vague memories began coming back. "You did… all that?"

"I was doing what you told me to do before you passed out. I wouldn't have known what to do otherwise. I feel like your pain is all my fault, because if I had been better with my gun, maybe you wouldn't have gotten shot." Elizabeth closed her eyes and took a deep breath. "I'm so sorry I couldn't do more. I thought I'd lost you, Logan, and it was the worst thing I've felt since finding out my brother had drowned."

Elizabeth looked at him apologetically and with… what was that? Love? Hell no! Deep affection, maybe, but surely not love. Good God, she was already feeling dependent on him. He reminded himself how they had ended up here. He was hired to find her valuables and nothing more. He tried again to sit up and again Elizabeth pushed him back down.

"Logan, you have a lot of stitches in your right thigh." She sat down on the edge of the bed. "You took one of those big bullets from a buffalo gun. The doctor said it's only a flesh wound, but it hit an artery and bled badly. He said you're lucky it didn't hit the bone, or it probably would have broken it. You lost a lot of blood, but you'll be okay as long as there is no infection."

It hit him then that she hadn't jumped up and screamed "how dare you!" at him when he'd touched her breasts, and now she stroked some of his hair back from his face almost lovingly. *Good God, the kid is becoming attached!*

"How do you feel?" she asked him.

Was that desire in her eyes, or just true concern? Something was different. "I don't know yet. Get the doctor. I need help getting up."

"I can help you, Logan."

"Not for this. I need to do something you *can't* help me with."

She jumped up at the remark and blushed. "I'll get him!"

Logan felt under the blankets and realized he had only a towel over his privates. How much had she seen? What a crazy, mixed-up situation they'd both gotten themselves into! Damned if he didn't want the woman, and damned if he didn't see a little bit of want in her own eyes.

The doctor came inside and introduced himself. Logan managed to sit up with the man's aid. Loomis walked him behind a small, curtained-off room where he could use a chamber pot, then helped him back to bed.

"Lie down and let me look at that wound," the captain told him.

Logan obeyed.

The captain carefully unwrapped Logan's wound. "It was Lieutenant Whittaker and his men who found you yesterday. Whittaker says he knows you, said he wasn't surprised you got yourself shot."

"Yeah, we know each other," Logan answered. "I've been here before to pick up supplies."

"Well, I'm pretty new here, but the lieutenant had plenty of hair-raising stories to tell about you." Loomis got the bandages off and studied the stitches in Logan's leg. "You're a lucky man," he said. "If some of our soldiers hadn't come along and found you and Miss Baylor when they did, I don't think you would have lived. Miss Baylor tied off the wound, but you still could have lost your leg from lack of blood."

The doctor began rewrapping the wound with fresh gauze. "Miss Baylor is quite a strong young lady," the man continued as he worked. "She was a bit confused when the men first found her, but after some water and the reassurance they were there to help, she came around—told us everything. You went up against five mean buffalo hunters, Logan. Remind me to never get on your bad side."

Logan grinned in spite of his pain. "There are a lot of men who wished they hadn't. Most of them are dead."

"I have no doubt." The doctor tied off the bandages. "I put several stitches in your leg, but this is just a flesh wound. It was the bleeding that made things serious. I'm surprised I don't see any fresh bleeding after you got up." He straightened. "I'll have my wife fix you some soup. She can feed you, or Miss Baylor can."

Logan couldn't get the picture of Elizabeth out of his mind, the way her flannel gown clung to all the right places before she put on her robe, how pretty she was in a sleepy state, the way her blond hair hung long and messy when she first jumped off the bed. "I'll feed myself," he answered. "Let Miss Baylor get some rest. We'll leave out again in the morning. I have some men to track down, and I can't let them get too far ahead."

"You'll need more rest than that."

"Can't afford it. I promised Miss Baylor I'd get her valuables back for her. The longer these men are loose, the more likely they will find someone to buy her jewels. In fact, send in Lieutenant Whittaker. I need to know if he's seen the men I'm after. They might have stopped here for supplies."

"I'll see what I can do. Rest easy, at least for today. My wife will be in with that soup."

Logan leaned back and closed his eyes. Damned if he couldn't feel Elizabeth Baylor's soft breast cupped in his hand. Why hadn't she been offended when he did that?

Amy Loomis came in with some chicken broth. She was a pretty woman, one of those who would follow her husband to the ends of the earth if need be. He could tell. There was a properness about her, a bit of a regal air. As she talked about "back home in New York," he knew she'd probably lived a pretty nice life there and missed it. It was hard on any woman coming out to these parts, but for some it was a bigger sacrifice than for others. He found himself wondering what kind of sacrifices Elizabeth would be willing to make for the man she married.

Amy fed him a few bites, but he told her he would finish on his own. She left, and Elizabeth finally came back into the room. She was fully dressed, her face fresh and pink from washing, her hair brushed out and pinned back at the sides. She wore a lovely yellow cotton dress, the curves at the bodice filling out all the right places. Good God, she was beautiful.

"Oh good. You're eating," she said. "Can I help with anything?"

He wanted to yell at her, make her hate him, but there she stood with those big blue eyes and that kind of pouty mouth…a mouth he'd tasted moments ago.

"No, thanks," he answered. "I'll rest a little more today, and we'll head out in the morning."

"That's too soon! You could open your wound, and there is still the chance of infection. And you're in so much pain."

"I've lived through worse."

"Logan, I don't want you losing your life over this. I'll find some way to survive. If you get killed just to get my money back, I'll never forgive myself."

"It's what you *hired* me to do. I doubt you cared much about whether I lived or died then. I was just a bounty hunter who might be able to help you, and that's all I *still* am. Quit blaming yourself for anything that happens."

Elizabeth frowned and stepped back. "Why are you angry? Did I say something wrong?"

"I'm not angry. But you said you didn't know what you'd do if something happened to me. You need to figure that out, because if something happens to me or not, we'll be parting ways once I get back your things." He could tell he'd hurt her feelings, and it killed him to realize it, but he couldn't let her get attached, and he sure as hell had no business letting himself get attached to a woman like Lady Elizabeth Baylor. As soon as she was a rich woman again, she'd head for Denver and build her mansion and make her investments and find some wealthy man who fit her lifestyle.

Before they could talk about any of it, a soldier came into the room, an older man with an air of authority about him.

Logan spoke up. "Lieutenant Whittaker!"

The man grinned and walked closer, putting out his hand. "I had a feeling you'd end up with a bullet in you," Whittaker told Logan. "It's inevitable, considering what you do for a living."

The two men shook hands, and Whittaker turned

to Elizabeth and removed his hat. "Miss Baylor. You look much better today than when we found you."

"Thank you, Lieutenant, for coming along when you did. You finding us was like an answered prayer."

"Well, we keep patrols out there all the time, looking for problems, hunting Indians, helping settlers however they need help." He turned back to Logan. "The doc says you want to know about some men who might have stopped by here."

Logan started to set his tray aside. Elizabeth hurried over to take it from him, and their gazes held for a moment, both realizing there were things they needed to talk about.

"Yes," Logan told Whittaker. "Trouble is, I don't know what they look like. I only know they are led by a man called Chad Krieger, and they're a pretty slovenly bunch. They deal in running guns and stealing cattle and selling women, whichever is most lucrative. I think there might be seven or eight of them. I also think they are after more than Miss Baylor's money and jewels. They are after the woman herself. She won't be safe until I find and deal with these men."

Whittaker shook his head. "Five is one thing—over and above what any average man could ever take on. Now you're talking seven or eight? Do you intend to take on all of *them* on your own, too?"

"If I have to." He noticed Elizabeth turn away. "Miss Baylor thinks she saw them once, back in Kansas City. Says they looked like a bunch of cowboys, a pretty rough-looking bunch. She didn't know then who they really were, but she does now. And she remembers that the one who might be their leader is quite tall, and very blond."

The lieutenant frowned. "Well, I hate to send you into a death trap, but I know you'll keep looking, so I might as well tell you several men who fit that description did stop here for water and tobacco and a few other supplies. I didn't like the looks of them. One of them bragged about how they would soon be rich, but he didn't explain how. I think they said something about Hays City and then maybe Denver—something about meeting some man from England there."

Elizabeth turned, and Logan met her gaze.

"That must mean they don't know about Robert yet!" Elizabeth said.

"Good," he answered. "Then they still have your banknotes and the jewels. They would be trying to sell them by now if they knew Alexander was dead. He'd be the one to tell them what to do with your things. Besides that, they think he'll be bringing *you* to them." Logan shifted in the bed, damning the pain in his leg. "Can you give me any kind of detailed description of any of them?" he asked Whittaker.

Whittaker sat down in a chair at the side of the room. "Well, most of them were your average unwashed, bearded, tobacco-chewing, cowboy types—the kind that all tend to look the same. The only distinction I can make is that two of them were Mexicans. They were all well-armed, Logan, and they looked like they damn well knew how to use their weapons, so you're asking a lot of yourself. I'd advise you to get some help."

Logan noticed the worry in Elizabeth's eyes. She

looked ready to cry again. Damned if the woman didn't do a lot of crying, but he understood why. She'd been through too damn much too fast, and strong as she was, her emotions couldn't quite catch up to everything that had happened to her. Now she was apparently beginning to care too much about one Logan Best. "I'll manage," he told Whittaker. "Do you remember the name Chad Krieger?"

"I do. He seemed to be the leader of the bunch. And Miss Baylor is right." Whittaker rested his elbows on his knees. "He is tall and skinny, had real blond hair, and he wore it past his shoulders. I'd say he was about your age, seemed like the kind who'd left home young and decided he could rule the world—real cocky—know what I mean?"

"I know."

"I'm sure that's the man I saw Robert talking to in Kansas City," Elizabeth told Logan.

"He kept trying to challenge a couple of the men here," Whittaker told them, "made fun of soldiering, told some of the men in the supply store soldiering wasn't near as exciting as riding with outlaws and fu—" He hesitated, glancing at Elizabeth. "Taking advantage of innocent women," he continued, "and riding right into hostile Indian camps with stolen guns, and robbing banks and trains. He wore two guns, one on each hip, and he had a gold tooth right in front. He smiled a lot, like he had the world by the ass. He shouldn't be hard to recognize."

"Logan, the more I hear about these men, the more I don't want you to go after them," Elizabeth pleaded.

"I'm not about to let them go now. They could hurt other innocent people, let alone hurt you."

"What if I fire you?"

Logan grinned, and both men chuckled. "You really think that would *stop* me? I'd just go on without you."

"But they sound so wicked! Logan, there is only so much one man can do against a gang like that."

"Sure there is. You just have to find a way to split them up."

Lieutenant Whittaker sighed and shook his head. "You're one stubborn man, Logan. Big talk for someone lying there in bed with a torn-up thigh. You will not only go after them as one man against seven or eight, but with a painful wound in your leg that is going to be very distracting."

Logan winced as he sat up more. "You totally underestimate my abilities, Lieutenant," he answered with a sly grin. "All I know is we have to catch up with Chad Krieger and his men before they find out the truth about Robert Alexander." He glanced at Elizabeth and saw the terror in her eyes. "Maybe you should stay right here at the fort until I come back."

Her eyes widened. "Never! I'll not let you go on without me. I might be able to help you."

He frowned. "No. I won't let you get involved once we find them. For now, you can keep going with me, but when we're close, I'll find some kind of safety for you. We're leaving at sunrise."

"But, your leg—"

"I'll manage. You must have seen the scar on my stomach when they were working on my leg. That's from a wound far worse than this one. If I lived through that, I can live through anything."

"I advise against it," Lieutenant Whittaker told him.

"I'll be fine." Logan looked back at Elizabeth. "Check all our supplies. You must have left some back there under the dead horse. See what we need and get everything ready."

"Logan, you shouldn't—"

"Just do it. There is no time to waste." Logan answered her as authoritatively as possible, wanting to show no feelings. Elizabeth looked confused, and that was what he wanted. From now on, he had to kill any feelings she might have for him. He probably never should have told her about MaryAnne. He couldn't understand why he'd been compelled to do so, but she was so scared and nervous all the time. He just wanted to explain why she didn't need to be. But now she felt sorry for him. There was nothing that attracted a woman more than feeling sorry for a man and thinking she could mend his broken heart. He turned to Whittaker. "Hays City, they said?"

"I think so."

Logan nodded. "We'll head there tomorrow then," he said. "Thanks for the information, Lieutenant."

Elizabeth turned away. "I'll check our supplies," she said softly.

Logan watched her walk out, hating himself for hurting her.

"She's quite a woman, Logan," Whittaker commented. "Young, beautiful, sophisticated, and totally in love with you."

"What?"

"You heard me. I can see it in her eyes. She was so scared you would die, and she was strong enough to stay for the surgery. She didn't faint at the sight of all that blood. She just held your hand and prayed. If I were you, I'd give some thought to that. It's about time you settled down."

"With an English princess? Believe me, it would never work. Now go through my things over there and see if you can find me a cigarette and a match, then get back to your soldiering and stay out of my personal business."

Whittaker chuckled, finding a cigarette and match and handing them out to Logan. "You've been lassoed, Logan. All that's left now is to pull you in. I'm sure you will kick and plant your feet in the ground all the way, just like a stubborn calf."

Logan lit the cigarette. "Get the hell out of here, Whittaker."

The lieutenant headed for the door. "You be careful," he told Logan. "I don't see you often, but I like you, and after all the doctor's work sewing up that leg, I'd hate to find out it was all for nothing."

Whittaker walked out, and Logan stared at the smoke coming from his cigarette. Again, he couldn't forget the feel of Elizabeth Baylor's young breasts… untouched breasts…just like the rest of her was untouched. Why did it bother him to think of some other man claiming her? It should be a man who knew what he was doing, a man who would be gentle, a man who wouldn't scare her to death…a man she wanted as badly as he wanted her.

It should be me.

She *did* want him. He could see it in her virgin eyes. He felt like throwing something across the room. Finishing this trip was going to be a real bitch. He'd rather face those five buffalo hunters again.

THIRTY-SIX

ELIZABETH TURNED TO GLANCE AT LOGAN'S PANT LEG. She saw no blood stain from where his wound would be, but he kept clenching his jaw as though trying to hide his pain. She could only hope that was the reason he'd been so quiet all morning, both when they packed their supplies and through breakfast with the doctor and his wife. Logan spoke to the doctor but seemed to be ignoring her. And since they'd left Fort Harker, he'd said practically nothing to her other than: *We need to get to Hays City as fast as possible. We've already lost too much time.*

That was it. Elizabeth found his behavior disappointing after how their relationship had recently turned more amiable. She feared he was angry with her for lying next to him the night before last. Had she been too bold? Was he embarrassed he'd touched her?

What bothered her most of all was the fact that she couldn't forget the feel of his hand on her breast. Whether by accident, or if he was thinking about his wife…or if he'd deliberately touched her, it didn't seem to matter, and that surprised her. The touch had sparked something deep inside. He'd kissed her mouth, and she couldn't dismiss the memory of the warmth of his breath, the feel of his lips on hers, so gentle for such a big, rugged man. Robert's kisses hadn't come close to stirring the things in her that Logan's kiss stirred. Now it haunted her in a restless, sexual way that made her embarrassed she was even *thinking* such things. She wanted to be his friend more than ever now…no…much more than a friend. But he was being aloof and had that angry attitude again.

"Are you all right?" she asked aloud. "We've been riding for almost three hours. I know you're in pain."

"I'll survive," he answered quietly.

"What will we do when we reach Hays City?" she asked.

"I'll talk to the sheriff there. I know him. If he knows anything about Chad Krieger, I'll have to decide from there what we do. The important thing is your safety. I should have left you back at the fort."

"I wouldn't have stayed. I would have followed you."

Logan stopped to light a cigarette. "It's two more days after today before we reach Hays City. I have to think about what to do with you, and I don't want any arguments about it. I mean it. I'll tie you up somewhere if I have to."

Elizabeth's heart tightened. He meant it. "Is there a decent hotel there? I could stay in a hotel and let you do whatever you have to do."

"We'll see. It all depends on what I find. And hotel or not, I'll be sleeping someplace else." He rode ahead a little way. "Stay there," he called to her.

Elizabeth literally struggled not to burst into tears and beg him not to sleep someplace else. That "someplace else" likely meant with a prostitute. Why, oh why did that bother her so much? She felt like a child wanting to throw a temper tantrum. *You belong to me, Logan Best!*

He stopped and looked around, then waved her forward. They had only one packhorse now, and it was tied to Suzy's strappings. Elizabeth kicked Suzy's sides to hurry up beside Logan, but she'd urged Suzy ahead too quickly, yanking at the packhorse. She almost lost her balance when the movement caused a hard jerk. She let out a little yelp and hung on to the saddle horn as she started to fall sideways, but managed to stay in her saddle. She straightened before she reached Logan, who looked at her and then back at the packhorse.

"You okay?"

Elizabeth adjusted her wide-brimmed hat. "Yes. The packhorse balked a little."

Logan kept the cigarette between his lips. "Yeah, well, she's female. They tend to get stubborn."

What was that supposed to mean? Was he referring to her instead of the horse?

"I knew there was a pretty good rise here," he told her as he scanned the horizon. "You don't always notice it right away. Good place to see what's ahead of you."

Elizabeth looked out over a huge expanse of green and yellow prairie grass. "It certainly is." She pointed. "It looks like there is actually some kind of stream out there, and some trees. It would be a good place to make camp."

"Too soon. We can make it a lot farther than that before we stop." Logan smoked quietly a moment. "I'm sorry about that thing with the buffalo hunters. I could kick myself for not sensing they were nearby. If I'd been alone, I would have picked up their sound or their scent. We were talking, and the scent of your hair threw me off. Like I said, someone can be just over the hill out here and you don't even know it, but that's no excuse. I had your safety on my mind—too much, I guess. And we're getting closer now to Chad and his men. From now on I'll manage this trip as though you aren't here at all. I have to be more alert."

Elizabeth took a deep breath. She wanted the old Logan back—the one she could spar with verbally. If she hadn't lain down beside him the other night, there wouldn't be this awkwardness between them. That came from not knowing how to behave around a man like him. "Is that why you've been so rudely silent since we left?" she asked.

"Rudely?"

"Yes, rudely. You've acted almost angry with me, and I've been trying to figure out why."

Logan met her gaze, and he looked so damn handsome this morning that Elizabeth wanted to melt into the prairie grass and become a little beetle he wouldn't notice, not the red-faced child she knew she looked like now.

"I think you *have* already figured it out," he told her. "We need to get things finished between us and get on with our lives."

But not together. Elizabeth looked over the horizon again. "I agree."

Logan took a long drag on his cigarette. "I'm not angry with you, Elizabeth, but you need to remember I'm a roaming, uneducated man who hunts men for money and doesn't give a damn what lies around the next corner in life. You are a titled, wealthy, educated, English lady who is as ignorant of the reality of life out here and ignorant of men as any girl your age would be who grew up sheltered like you did. The fact that you ended up with a man like Robert Alexander proves that. I'll get your things back for you, and once I do, you will realize you can have the fancy life you came out here to lead. I'll accompany you to Denver and hang around until you get yourself settled and find the right people you can trust, and then I'll be on my way. You're young and inexperienced and confused and all the things that can lead to bad decisions."

Like lying beside you night before last? God, what a stupid decision that was!

Jasper whinnied and shook his mane, as though sensing his rider was upset.

Elizabeth kept avoiding Logan's eyes. "I'm not a girl," she answered in her defense. "I'm a *woman*, and yes, after I discovered how foolish it was to trust Robert, and after...after he showed his nakedness to me and attacked me, I am no longer ignorant about men."

Logan sighed deeply. "My dear Elizabeth, when I woke up the other morning with you next to me, I just about allowed myself to make my *own* bad decision," he continued, pain in his voice. "So let's get something settled between us or I'll be forced to leave you behind. You and I have not one thing in common and never will have. I feel like an ass for what happened the other morning, and I apologize for it."

Elizabeth hoped a tear wouldn't spill down her cheek and give away her feelings. "You already did," she answered stiffly, "right away. I knew you were in pain and still half drugged from the chloroform, so I was not offended."

"Either way, it was wrong. From here on, it's strictly business, which means no teasing jokes and no wrong thoughts."

Elizabeth held her chin high, afraid to look into his eyes. "What makes you think I had any wrong thoughts in the first place? Apparently, *you* are the one who had wrong thoughts."

"I know women, and I've seen something in those pretty blue eyes that shouldn't be there—ever—not for me, anyway."

"Well, Mr. Logan Best, when I shot Robert point-blank, I decided what men want is something I *don't* want and never will! If you think I had any such thoughts about you, then you are an arrogant, egotistical, condescending, conceited, supercilious man!"

They both sat there silently for a moment. Logan suddenly let out a laugh that was more of a snort. "What was that? Super-something?"

She couldn't help her own smile. Now he was more like the Logan who liked to tease her. "You know what I said," she answered. "I said supercilious."

"Sounds kind of like super silly to me, or maybe super delicious. Maybe I *am* super delicious." Now he laughed harder.

She loved his laugh. Damn him! "I cannot help

it if you are so uneducated as to not understand that word," she declared.

"What was that other one? Condo-something?"

"Condescending."

He snickered and drew on his cigarette. "Well, since you are so well educated, I'm figuring those words probably *do* fit me. And they probably also fit *you*, Lady Baylor, for your own arrogant attitude about education. So there you go. Just another example of how we would fit together like a square peg into a round hole." He smashed out his cigarette. "The fact remains we can't let things get personal. Getting personal led to me being surprised by those buffalo hunters, so let's keep this strictly business and get it over with."

"Well, Mr. Best, I am deeply sorry that I somehow led to you being gravely wounded. I'll keep my distance from now on."

"Good idea." Logan headed Jasper down the very long but gentle slope.

But I liked your arms around me, Logan. I felt safe with my head on your shoulder. Is that such a bad thing? When she caught up, Logan slowed Jasper again. "Maybe, uh, maybe we could at least take a lunch break up there in those trees."

"Whatever you say," she answered. "You're the one who said we have to be strictly business, and I hired you to do a job, so from here on, everything is your decision. I thought it has been since we left Abilene."

He didn't answer right away.

"Abilene seems like months ago," she added. "Isn't that strange? I feel like none of this is real, Logan."

He still didn't answer. He was alarmingly pale. It was then she noticed blood staining his pants leg. "Oh my God! Logan?"

He wiped sweat from his forehead with his shirt-sleeve. "I think I need to get to those trees and lay down."

He never should have left Doctor Loomis's care so soon, but there was no way to stop him. "I told you it was too soon," she said. "Hang on to your saddle horn." She grabbed Jasper's bridle and kicked Suzy into a gentle lope, watching Logan sidelong as she headed for the trees. "Please hang on," she repeated, hoping he heard her. "You're too big and heavy for me to drag you to those trees!"

He looked ready to fall off his horse. Elizabeth slowed, then pulled Jasper alongside her horse and climbed in front of Logan. "Hold on to me, Logan. Put your arms around me."

He obeyed.

God, let me do things right, Elizabeth prayed. She grabbed Suzy's reins and headed for the trees. When they reached the shady grove, she saw she was right about seeing a stream. She led the horses across to what appeared to be a soft, grassy area where it would be comfortable to bed down. She pulled Logan's arms from around and threw her right leg over Jasper's neck so she could slide off the horse. It was a drop for her, but she stayed on her feet when she hit the ground. "Hang on to Jasper, Logan," she told him.

He leaned down and rested his head on Jasper's neck, hanging on to the horse's mane.

Elizabeth quickly untied Logan's bedroll from the

back of Jasper's saddle and spread it out in the grass. She opened it, then hurriedly grabbed some blankets from the packhorse and bunched them up so Logan could use them like a pillow.

"Logan, can you get down? I laid out your bedroll for you. Get down and hang on to me."

"I'll be…all right," he told her.

"No. You are *not* all right! Let me help you down."

"Might…run into those men."

"We're fine, Logan. And you're no good to me in this condition. Let me help you!"

He finally managed to swing his bad leg over and cling to his saddle horn as he let himself down, then stumbled and grabbed Elizabeth. It was impossible for her to hold him up, and her knees buckled as they made it to the bedroll. They both went down, and at least Logan landed mostly on his bedroll. Elizabeth managed to get out from under him and remove his boots, then maneuvered his feet all the way onto the bedding.

She stood there staring at him, not sure what to do next. He muttered something, and she got to her knees and leaned close. "Tell me what to do, Logan."

"Hobble the horses," he said weakly, "then make a fire. Burn it out."

"Burn what out?"

"The…wound." He groaned. "Cut off…my long johns and unwrap the…wound. Make a hot fire and burn it…. Stops…the bleeding."

Elizabeth's eyes widened. *Burn* it? The pain would be awful! "I…I can't do that to you."

He groaned again and grasped her wrist. "Have to or I won't…make it. Cauterize it. That's one big word…I do know…because I've seen it done. Just do what I say. Take the knife…from my side. Heat it in the fire red hot…and hold it to the wound."

"But I—"

He squeezed her wrist. "Do it…if you want me to live."

She looked down at his strong hand on her wrist. She put her own hand over his. Of course she wanted him to live. Her money suddenly meant nothing, if getting it back meant losing Logan Best. Her most valuable possession was her own heart, and Logan Best owned it. She reached around him and pulled his big hunting knife from its sheath at his side, laying it aside as she unbuckled his gun belt and managed to yank it out from under him. She could hardly believe how heavy it was. Thank God he wasn't wearing his extra cartridge belt today. He'd hung it around Jasper's neck.

She rose and moved the gun belt aside, laying the big knife beside it. She hurried over to the horses and unstrapped their saddles and supplies, letting them fall to the ground. She'd watched Logan hobble the horses before. She did the same now and let them graze on the thick grass. She pulled a bundle of wood off the packhorse and walked closer to Logan, doing everything she'd seen him do to make a fire. She got one started, proud of herself for all the things she'd learned already about how to make camp in the wide-open prairie, just like a pioneer woman. She took a small shovel from the packhorse and frantically dug mud from the nearby stream to pack in a circle around the fire to keep it from spreading to the dry prairie grass.

Logan would have dug up the heavy sod instead, but she wasn't strong enough for that, nor did she have the time.

She looked around, never feeling more alone, with nothing for miles but the prairie, three horses, and a man who could be dying. For the next few hours she could not be Lady Elizabeth Baylor from London. She was just Elizabeth Baylor, a nineteen-year-old woman stranded in the middle of nowhere and getting ready to strip a man and hold a hot knife to an ugly wound on his thigh to try to stop the bleeding. She didn't know a damn thing about what she was getting ready to do, but Logan Best had told her to do it, and he knew about survival out here.

"God help me," she said quietly.

THIRTY-SEVEN

BECAUSE THEY CAMPED AMID A GROVE OF TREES, Elizabeth was able to find plenty of kindling to add to the fire. Logan said it had to be extra hot, for heating the knife to a glow. She felt sick at the thought of it as she hurried through what needed to be done.

She finished packing the mud and took off her leather gloves, then hurried to grab a canteen and some towels, carrying them over to where Logan lay…much too still. She hurried to the stream and wet one of the towels, then wrung it out and took it back, kneeling beside Logan and washing his face with it. The coolness made him stir. When she touched his face with her hand she realized why. He was burning up with fever!

She left the wet towel across his forehead. "Logan, can you hear me? It's going to hurt, but I have to pull your boots off." She started with his left leg, which wouldn't hurt, and pulled hard to get his boot off. Then she pulled off his right boot, struggling not to pass out from horror when Logan let out a loud scream. "I'm sorry, Logan! But I had to get your boots off. Now you have to help me get your pants off, too, so I can get to the wound."

"God, it hurts…can't stand…to move."

"I can cut off one leg of your long johns, but I can't cut through these thick cotton pants. I'm not strong enough," she said. She unbuckled his pants belt. All modesty or even concern over what she might accidentally see or touch left her as she unbuttoned the front of his pants and then straddled him, jerking at the pants waist. It took all her strength to pull them over his hips and down his thighs. She struggled not to panic when he screamed with pain again. The bloody spot had dried a little and was stuck to the wound. Grimacing with determination, Elizabeth pulled hard and got his pants down far enough to more easily pull them all the way off.

"Oh God," she muttered, seeing how much blood was on his long johns. How had this happened so quickly? Apparently, part of the stitches had broken open. She reached over to where his pants and weapons lay and took up his hunting knife, then grabbed a hunk of his cotton long johns in her hand and poked the knife into it, tearing at it with the knife. It was thinner material than his pants but still difficult to cut through. She had to cut off the leg of his underwear above the wound so she could pull it away, but then realized she'd better be careful not to cut into something he certainly would *not* want her to cut into!

The night Robert had attacked her, she'd been so shocked and desperate that she hardly remembered what his privates looked like. She wasn't quite sure where everything was down there or how much of it there was. Shocked at her own boldness, she kept cutting, feeling her way to make sure there wasn't more there than just his leg under the long johns in the area she was cutting. She hesitated when she touched something soft and realized it was that forbidden part of man that had horrified her on Robert. Mortification swept through her, but she stiffened her resolve.

If you see something or touch something private, don't be a child about it, Elizabeth Baylor! The man could be dying, she told herself. This was a matter of life and death, and there was no room for formalities and bashfulness. She couldn't get all the way under his thigh for fear of cutting into his skin or something else, so she grabbed the front of the material already cut and sliced down the outside to his foot and through the ankle material so she could completely drape the leg of the underwear away from his leg. Again, it stuck where the wound was.

Didn't that mean it had stopped bleeding? Should she continue or just let it dry up? She leaned close, again bathing his face. "Logan, it looks like the bleeding has slowed. What should I do?"

He just groaned.

"Logan, please don't die. This is all my fault. Tell me what to do. Can you hear me? Do you understand?" She started crying at feeling so helpless. "Logan?"

He swallowed. "Need…water."

Elizabeth hurried to her horse and grabbed a canteen, chastising herself for not thinking of it right away. She walked back to Logan and knelt beside him, lifting his head with her left arm and putting the canteen to his lips. Getting water into his mouth seemed to help bring him around. He grabbed the canteen from her and swallowed a good deal more.

Elizabeth took the canteen from him. "Logan, did you hear me? It's dried a little. Do you still want me to cauterize the wound?"

He looked at her, reached out and touched her arm. "Burn it," he told her again.

Elizabeth felt sick. "First, I have to lay aside the part of your long johns I cut away. It's all stuck, Logan. It will really hurt when I pull it off, and it will hurt even more to get the bandages off."

"I…know that. Give me my belt…something I can put in my mouth to bite down on. Then get… the damn bandages off and heat the blade of that knife good and hot…and I mean hot…like a blacksmith heats a horse shoe…before he shapes it."

"I don't want to hurt you." Elizabeth quickly wiped at tears with the back of her hand.

"It will…be worth it," he told her.

"You have a bad fever," she said, reaching over to bathe his face again.

"All the more reason to burn it," he replied. "It'll burn out…the infection that's causing the fever. Just get it over with. Douse it with whiskey first…and give me some of the damn whiskey to swallow…against the pain."

Elizabeth got up and hurried over to where she'd tossed his belt. She brought it to him. "Here."

He managed to give her a faint grin. "You can do this, Elizabeth. You're…brave enough. I see you even built a damn good fire."

Elizabeth sniffed back more tears. "I did, didn't I?

I even packed it with mud around the outside so it wouldn't spread."

He grimaced with pain. "Let's…get this over with. Bring me that flask of whiskey from my saddlebag."

Elizabeth did as he asked. "This is only for your pain," she said. "I have a feeling it might be best you don't drink any of this when you're feeling good."

He grinned again. "Best for you…you mean. It's hard enough…to be around you sober…can't imagine how hard it would be…drunk. Too bad you aren't ugly."

At least he was back to his teasing remarks and not angry. But this wasn't how she'd wish it to happen. She uncorked the flask and helped him sit up a little, putting the bottle to his lips. He took it from her and downed nearly half of it.

Elizabeth's eyes widened at how easily he'd swallowed so much liquor.

He handed back the bottle. "Don't worry," he said. "I just know…it will take a lot…to stand the pain." He grimaced as he laid his head back down on the blankets.

He was so hot to the touch that Elizabeth feared it was already too late to do anything about the infection. She corked the flask and set it aside.

"Go ahead," he told her. "Cut away…and burn it." He put part of the belt into his mouth and bit down on it.

Elizabeth took a deep breath. She had no choice if she wanted Logan to live. She grabbed hold of the cutaway long johns and took a deep breath, then yanked the material away from the wound. Logan let out a pitiful groan and grabbed hold of a thick bunch of long grass with his left hand. He grabbed hold of her ankle with his right hand, obviously not aware what he was doing. Elizabeth cut into the bandages and ripped those off, too, wincing with pain when he squeezed her ankle so hard she thought he would break it. She grimaced at how ugly the wound looked. Some of the stitches had torn away.

"Hurry." Logan groaned the word through clenched teeth.

"Logan, you have to let go of my ankle. You're hurting me."

He released his grip. Wiping at more tears, Elizabeth carried the knife to the fire, and with a shaking hand, she held it over the flames. Having to hold it there was too close. The heat started to burn her hand, so she simply laid it on the hot coals. She turned back to Logan and picked up the flask of whiskey, uncorking it again and pouring some over the wound. Again, he cried out, this time grabbing more bunch grass with his right hand.

Elizabeth reached for a smaller towel and used it to grab hold of the knife handle. She lifted the knife. The blade glowed red.

"Logan, are you really sure?" she asked.

He looked at her with eyes bloodshot from fever, the belt still in his mouth. She could tell he was literally begging her to get it done. He closed his eyes and looked away.

Do it! she told herself. "Logan, I love you," she blurted out. With that, she pushed the flat side of the knife against the wound. Logan screamed and arched his back, and Elizabeth screwed up her nose at the smell of burning flesh. The horrible hissing sound made it difficult not to let go of the knife, but she held it tight against the wound until she knew it had burned deeply. Logan literally pulled the thick bunches of grass right out of the ground, sod and all, something a man usually had to use a shovel for just to loosen it up.

Elizabeth tossed the knife aside. "I'm sorry, Logan! I'm so sorry!" Because of her tears, she could hardly see what she was doing as she bathed his face again.

He didn't answer. He'd passed out.

THIRTY-EIGHT

LOGAN STIRRED, NOTICING JUST THE VERY TOP OF THE sun was peeking over the eastern horizon. He moved his leg to stretch, and the stiff pain in his thigh reminded him exactly of where he was and what had happened last night. Or was it earlier? He was sure he was looking east, and he remembered it was light out when the pain and light-headedness had hit him. Had he really lain here nearly twenty-four hours?

He turned his head to see his guns lying nearby, as well as his pants, boots, and belt, a canteen, and a flask of whiskey. *Douse the wound with whiskey… Burn it.* He remembered now. He'd ordered Elizabeth to burn out the infection in his wound. What an awful thing for her to have to do!

He looked around further, and that was when he saw her, farther downstream. *Lord, help me!* She had squatted to pee. She stood up, and he could see her perfect, round little bottom. Pain or not, he couldn't help staring at her as she washed herself and pulled on a clean pair of pantaloons, then stepped into her riding skirt.

You ass! he thought, turning away. He'd told her he wouldn't look when she had to pull down her skirt and underthings, and he hadn't...until now. *Shit!* He told himself it was okay because he'd caught her by accident. She probably thought he was still asleep. He noticed the horses hobbled and grazing a few yards away, and the smell of coffee and bacon drifted in the air. Had Elizabeth actually done all this? Maybe someone had come along to help her.

He turned her way again to see her walking toward him with a towel in her hand. Her beautiful hair hung over her shoulders, and he couldn't get the sight of her perfect bottom out of his mind as she approached. She smiled when she saw he was awake.

"Logan!" She hurried closer and knelt beside him, then bathed his face with the fresh, cool rag. "How do you feel?"

He just stared at her a moment. Why in hell did she have to look so fresh and beautiful? She had on a clean blouse, and her full breasts filled it out temptingly. The woman needed nothing in the way of jewels or face paint to be perfectly lovely. Her face was clean, her cheeks pink, her lips full and pouty, her big, blue eyes looking at him with...*damn!*...love?

"I sat up with you most of the night in case you might wake up and need something," she told him.

He rubbed at his eyes. "What time is it?"

"I haven't looked at the time, but it's morning. You passed out yesterday, midday. I was so scared you wouldn't wake up at all."

It hit him then—Chad Krieger! He pushed her hand away and quickly sat up. "For God's sake, Krieger and his men could be anywhere. They could have made off with you in the night, and I never would have known it."

"Don't be silly. Yesterday you told me we're still two days from Hays City. We're fine. Your wound started bleeding again, and you got an infection, Logan. You asked me to burn it out. It's the hardest thing I've ever done, and I'm so sorry it brought you so much pain. It isn't fair that a man as big and strong as you should be brought down by something like that."

Logan ran a hand through his hair, realizing then that he still wore a shirt but no pants. He opened his bedroll to see that the right leg of his long johns was ripped open. A deep, ugly, crusty red scar showed where his wound had been. He looked at Elizabeth again. "By God, you *did* it."

Elizabeth sat down beside him. "I did everything you told me to do. I feared I might vomit or pass out, but I didn't. I told myself I had to be strong for you. Does it look okay? Did I do it right?"

Logan felt around the wound, realizing the ugly pain of infection was gone. "You did damn good."

Elizabeth brightened, turning to the fire. "And see? I kept the fire going and I built a tripod, just like I've watched you do. I made coffee, and I set a fry pan on the fire to cook bacon for you. I'll warm some biscuits for you, too." She smiled. "Aren't you proud of me? I've never made coffee or cooked anything in my life, let alone make a fire out in the middle of nowhere and do such an awful thing as burn out a wound. I took the saddles off our horses and unloaded our supplies. I hobbled the horses, too. They managed to make their way down to the stream for water, and there is plenty of grass for them. All our supplies are neatly stacked and—" She stopped and took a deep breath, refusing to cry. She had to be strong now. "I'm so glad you woke up. I thought you'd die."

She turned away to pour some coffee into a tin cup. "I'm sorry to act like a child sometimes," she said, "but I tend to cry when I'm tired."

I love you. Logan remembered the words she'd spoken just before she'd burned out the wound. Good God, he couldn't let her love the likes of Logan Best. He'd made a huge mistake telling her about MaryAnne, and about his early years as an orphan. That's all it was. She just felt sorry for him because of his past and now being wounded.

"Of course you're tired. You said you were up half the night. And look at all you did. I'm proud of you. You're getting a good lesson in survival, Elizabeth Baylor, and out here that's more important than knowing all those fancy words. Words won't protect or feed you."

"I know that now." She handed him the coffee, then turned to take the bacon from the fry pan and put it on a tin plate she'd left by the fire to warm two biscuits. "We'll share this," she said. "You need to eat and get your strength back."

Logan was amazed at what she'd done, how resilient and strong she was. He'd thought she'd be a pain in the ass on this trip, but in all actuality, *he* was the one who'd been a pain in the ass for sometimes making fun of her and being impatient with her. He drank some of the coffee—too weak, but he wasn't about to tell her that.

She wiped at tears and ate a piece of bacon. "I was so scared I'd do something wrong yesterday and you'd die on me and I wouldn't be strong enough to dig through this sod to bury you and I'd have to figure out how to get you some place to be buried and maybe I'd run into those awful men and worst of all I'd have to watch somebody put you in the ground. A man big and strong and brave as you shouldn't be put in the ground so young. I prayed and prayed you'd wake up and be okay. And I set up camp just like I've watched you do and—"

"Elizabeth!" he said sternly. He reached out and touched her arm. "It's okay. You did as good a job as any woman who is used to all of this would have done. Now let's eat. We've lost too much time."

Their gazes held. Damned if she wasn't telling him she loved him without saying a word. And damned if he wasn't starting to have feelings for her he had no business owning up to. He'd had notions about her sexually, like any man would. But this was different. He wanted her in more ways than that. He wanted her for the brave and earnest woman she was on the inside.

Respect. That's what he was feeling. Respect for how hard she was trying to help, how brave she'd been to burn out his wound. That respect was helping him see that she wasn't just a pretty woman. She had a beauty that came from the inside. He loved her energy and determination, loved her near-childish excitement over learning new things.

He ate more bacon. "I never answered your question about the pain," he told her. "It's much better. Thank you for being brave enough to do that."

"It's okay." She managed a smile. "I had no idea if I was doing any of it right. I just heated that knife and pressed it on the wound like you told me to do. You practically bit your way right through your belt, and you pulled out two clumps of that thick grass with your fists."

Logan grinned. "I did?"

"Oh, you were in such bad pain. I felt so sorry for you, but then later I thought it was pay-back for the times you made fun of me or got angry with me."

Logan chuckled. "I guess it was." He noticed she'd cut away his long johns dangerously close to important places. Lord, had she seen or touched anything? "Let's finish eating. My leg does still hurt some, and I'm a mess from that fever. I need to wash up and get dressed and have a cigarette, so I can think straight."

"Are you thinking of leaving?"

"Yes."

"It's too soon."

"My leg will be okay now. A burn like this runs so deep it kills the nerves and you hardly feel it. I'll be fine as long as the infection is gone."

"If you're sure—"

"I am. Just do as I ask, Elizabeth. When you're done eating, I'd appreciate it if you would get me some clean clothes. I'm going to try to walk down to that stream on my own and wash up and take care of some personal things. And bring me some baking soda so I can clean my teeth. You can clean up camp. We have to get straightened around here and get moving."

They finished eating. Elizabeth did exactly what he told her to do—no complaining. He knew she was dead tired, but she did it anyway. He managed to limp down to the stream and wash up, letting the cool water soothe the burn on his leg. The scab had hardened from the burn being so deep.

They moved methodically then, saying nothing. Logan helped finish cleaning up, then noticed Elizabeth trying to throw her saddle over Suzy. "Let me do that like I always do," he told her.

"You need your strength."

"I *have* my strength, thanks to you. And you're tired from being up half the night." Logan took the saddle from her and put it on Suzy, yanking on the straps to cinch them.

"Are you sure you should be doing all of this?" Elizabeth asked.

"Don't worry about it. I told you I'm not in that much pain now." He jerked at the saddle strap and finished tightening it, then straightened and faced her. "Elizabeth, enough time has gone by that Chad and his men are going to find out what happened back in Abilene. They will be furious they got cheated out of a damn valuable woman they intended to make a lot of money on. And they will also be furious that some little bitch from England—and that's how they'll think of you—dared to kill the man who was behind a lot of the money they made. Believe me, they'll be after you. We have maybe one day to feel safe. We can't rest easy after that. I know you're tired, so you ride with me for a while. You can sleep on my shoulder if you want. I don't want you going to sleep and falling off your horse and getting hurt."

"But—won't that be hard for you? You said I was the reason you weren't alert enough to know those buffalo hunters were following us."

"That was hilly country. I know for a fact that beyond these trees and toward Hays City the land is wide-open again. We'll be okay. Go douse the fire and throw some of that dirt on it."

Elizabeth took the small shovel from the packhorse, and Logan tightened the ropes, securing everything while she shoveled dirt over the fire. *What the hell are you doing, telling her to ride with you?* He felt sorry for her, but it was more than that. She'd changed. She was stronger. She'd literally saved his life. And it wasn't just that. Something had changed between *them*— something he couldn't put his finger on—something that worried him, because that something was growing between them. He was damn well falling in love with the princess from England.

He tied the packhorse to Suzy, then managed to climb onto Jasper with a grunt of pain. Once he settled into his saddle, the pain wasn't so bad. Elizabeth walked up to the horses and slipped the shovel between the ropes of the packhorse, then walked up to Jasper. "Are you sure you can even ride?" she asked Logan.

"Hell yes. We need to get going, and you're the one who was up all night. I got a damn good night's sleep," he told her, grinning. He reached down for her with his right arm.

"Logan, you shouldn't—"

"Get up here."

She grasped his arm, and he lifted her easily, thinking how light and small she was. All this time he'd seen her as snooty and spoiled, and here she was, managing just fine living in the out-of-doors and making camp and saving his life. She settled sideways in front of him, and their gazes met.

That was all it took. He couldn't look at those pouty lips one more minute, not even one more second without kissing them. She damn well didn't resist when he planted his mouth over hers. She threw her arms around his neck and returned the kiss with a passion he didn't know she had in her.

He moved his arms around her, pressing her close and loving the taste of her mouth. He moved a hand along her side, pressing it against the side of her breast...that sweet, warm breast he'd touched three days ago. He wanted desperately to fully grasp it, and he could tell she would have let him, but there wasn't time for this. He took his hand away and put it to the side of her face. "I'm sorry."

"Don't be. I love you," she answered.

Tell her you love her, too. He couldn't. Not yet. Not yet. He had some men to find and kill. The thought of other men touching her only told him what he didn't want to face. He'd fallen in love with her and he wanted to be the man who took her virginity...the right way...the gentle way.

"We'd better get moving." He kept his hand at the side of her face and kissed her eyes, her lips again. How strange that not only did she not resist or act offended, but it all happened as naturally as breathing. It was simply understood that they had to do this. She looked at him with those big blues, lit up with love. He hadn't seen that look in a woman's eyes since

MaryAnne. "I hope you realize you're getting yourself into even more trouble," he told her.

"Some trouble is actually rather fun."

He sighed and kicked Jasper into a gentle walk. Elizabeth put her head on his shoulder, and he kept one arm around her. She relaxed against him, and in minutes, she was asleep.

Logan Best, you're a damn fool.

THIRTY-NINE

Sixty-year-old Hugh Bell watched the motley bunch of men—seven or eight of them—approach the telegraph office, their boots and spurs making a lot of noise as they passed train passengers. A couple of them turned and nodded to the female passengers waiting on the platform. One of them said something that made a woman gasp and turn away. Other passengers watched them with concern, some backing away. The men walked like they owned the town, and Hugh thought maybe Sheriff Bishop should be warned about them. They looked like trouble, and his heart tightened when he realized they were headed for his office.

The old man reached into a ledge under his desk to make sure his gun was there, but he thought twice about whether it would even be worth using it. There were too many of them. He turned when the door opened to watch all of them come inside—all trail-worn, all well-armed, and all with threatening looks in their eyes. Hugh counted eight men.

"Something I can do for you boys?" he asked.

Their apparent leader, who looked hardly more

than a kid, stepped closer. He was tall and skinny, with white-blond hair that hung over his shoulders and icy, white-blue eyes. He grinned, showing crooked teeth, one of them gold. "You the telegrapher?" he asked.

"You see me sitting here."

The kid lost his smile. "Don't get smart with me, mister."

"I'm just answering your question."

"Hey, look how much whiter his hair and mustache look when his face is so red from fear," one of the others said, referring to Hugh.

"Mister, you're a skinny old man who has no chance against us," the man-child told him, "so how about you pull that gun out from under your desk and hand it over?"

Hugh swallowed. He carefully pulled out his six-gun, and one of the others yanked it out of his hand.

"Now, that's better," the leader told him. "My name is Chad Krieger, and you're going to send a little message for me, after which we will stand here and wait for the reply."

"Whatever you want," Hugh told him. "No need to hold a gun on me. It's my job to send and receive messages. I ain't gonna argue about it."

Chad cocked his pistol. "Just do what I say. Turn around and start sending."

Hugh obeyed. As soon as he turned around, he felt cold steel against the back of his neck.

"If I find out you sent the wrong message and warned somebody, I'll come back here and blow your head off. Got that?"

Hugh nodded. "I get you. And what you send is

none of my business. Just tell me what you want to say and get the hell out of here when we're finished."

Chad pressed harder. "I just want to make sure you understand me. Nobody is to know about the message, especially not the sheriff here in Hays City."

"Fine." Hugh tried to keep from shaking. "What is it?"

"Do you know who the sheriff is in Abilene?"

"I do. His name is Adam White."

"Good. You send this to Adam White. And you make it look like it's from Sheriff Bishop here in Hays City. Got that? I'm telling you now if you mess this up, or if you tell Sheriff Bishop about this later, you're a dead man."

"Well, mister, I don't have a lot of years left, so I'd like to enjoy what little there is. Tell me what to say."

"You make it from Sheriff Bishop, like I said. Send it to Sheriff White in Abilene and ask him the name of the bounty hunter who left there with a Miss Elizabeth Baylor."

So, you're those men. Hugh had read the story in yesterday's newspaper. Apparently, these men had read it, too, about some young woman from England who'd been attacked by her escort and had shot him. Turned out the escort was a wealthy man from New York City. All kinds of rumors abounded about the character of the young woman from England and why she was traveling alone with a wealthy widower and why she'd shot him. "I know the story," Hugh told the men. "I don't remember anything about the bounty hunter's name."

Chad poked his neck with the gun again. "That's

why I'm sending the telegram. Alexander probably told that English princess what we're up to—that we were supposed to meet here. That's probably why she shot him. She and that bounty hunter are likely headed this way. The bitch probably thinks one lousy bounty hunter is going to be able to take on all of us."

They all snickered.

"Just wait till that young thing is in our hands," one of them said. "We'll get good money for her, but she won't be any virgin by the time we sell her."

"Forget that!" Chad ordered. "The point is she's headed this way with a bounty hunter, and I want to know who it is so we can be ready." He poked at Hugh's neck again. "Send the telegram! Sheriff Bishop to Sheriff White. Just say somethin' like 'need to know name of bounty hunter headed here with the English woman. Need to warn him about something.' That's all you need to say. Do it right and don't warn neither sheriff about us bein' here, understand?"

"Yes, sir." Feeling damp from nervous perspiration, Hugh began tapping out the message. After a few seconds, he stopped and took his hand away from the telegraph. Sweat broke out under his arms and on his forehead as he sat there with Chad's gun at his neck, waiting for a reply. Finally, the telegraph began ticking away. Hugh wrote as fast as he could until the telegraph stopped ticking again.

"Well?" Chad asked.

Hugh read the note to him. "Bounty hunter is Logan Best, and he's damn good."

"*Logan!*" one of the others said, speaking the name like it was poison.

"*Shit!*" another exclaimed.

"He's one of the best, Chad," a third man told him.

Chad whirled. "Shut the fuck up, all of you! He's one man!"

"You don't know him, Chad," the first man told him. He turned and spit tobacco juice on the floor of the telegraph office. "Me and Galen and Hank do, and Logan Best is five men rolled into one when it comes to gun play."

The three of them looked at one another with deep worry in their eyes.

"Yeah, Chad, Logan took down three men I was with in a bank robbery last year," one of the three told him. "I ain't never seen anybody that fast. He ain't scared of nothin'. Only reason I got away was because one of the tellers was in front of me, and I managed to run out the back. I reckon Best has been after me ever since. That sonofabitch was already trackin' me for somethin' else and rode right in on the bank robbery. That was down in Oklahoma."

"You're all a bunch of chickenshits!" Chad yelled, waving his gun at them. "Eight against one is impossible!"

Hugh watched the one referred to as Galen exchange a glance of fear with the other one called Hank. "Yeah, it's somethin' to see," Galen told Chad. "Me and Hank was together once over in Colorado," he explained. "We didn't do nothin' wrong. We was just sittin' in a card game when we heard a man shoutin' in the street. We all got up and looked out, and we seen Logan Best call out three men he was after—right in the middle of town—Pueblo, I think it was. They was good with guns, but he shot down all three of them like they was nothin' but rabbits. Bam! Bam! Bam! He was fast."

Chad raised his already-cocked pistol and aimed it straight at Galen, a dark, bearded man who glared back at Chad. "Now, you listen to me," he sneered at Galen, before stepping back and waving his gun at all of them, "there are *eight* of us! *Eight!* And we might be able to pick up a couple more in town if we pay them enough. Not only that, but that bounty hunter has the *woman* with him. She'll be a distraction. He'll be busy trying to protect her, but he won't have a *chance*. We'll spread out all over town. We'll take him down and get hold of that bitch who killed Robert Alexander, and we'll fuck her all the way to Miss Betsy's place down in Oklahoma. Any man here who's scared of Logan Best can leave now, but once this is over, I'll by God hunt down the coward who leaves me—for runnin' out on me!"

"How can we even be sure they're comin' here?" Hank asked Chad. "And why horseback? They could end up chargin' right through Hays City by train, headed for Denver."

"The newspaper article *said* they were headed this way," Chad spit at him. "It didn't say what town, but the English bitch probably knows. Besides, Logan Best ain't stupid. He knows the best way to find us is to keep squeezin' us north to Denver. By train he might fly right by us on his way to Denver and lose us, so he'll come by horse, sniffin' us out like a fuckin' bobcat and gettin' his pound of flesh out of that woman the whole way, I expect."

He lowered his gun. "Let's go. We have some

planning to do. Bill, you and Galen know what Logan Best looks like, so Bill, you hang out here at the station to see if they come in by train. Galen, you ride southeast and see if you can spot them comin' in on horseback. If he does make it all the way to town, he'll likely want to take his horses to the livery first. Hank, you go over and keep an eye out at the livery. The rest of us will spread out, most of us at that saloon called The Last Stop." He rested his gaze on Bill. "I know the woman is a pretty blond with an English accent, but what does Logan look like?"

Bill rubbed at stubble on his cheek. "Big man—tall like you but more filled out—lots of muscle. Women think he's handsome."

"You sayin' I ain't strong and handsome?"

"You asked for a description," Bill bit back. "I gave you one. The only other thing I know is that Best is damn good with those guns, and he always travels with an extra ammunition belt. And from what I know about him, I'm guessin' he's right on our tail."

"Good! The sooner we shoot down the sonofabitch and get the woman, the sooner we'll be a lot richer."

Galen and Hank looked at each other. Both frowned in concern, realizing Chad Krieger had no idea what he was up against. Few men cared to tangle with Logan Best.

FORTY

A LOUD CLAP OF THUNDER CAUSED ELIZABETH TO JUMP awake. Logan held her closer.

"Storm coming," he told her. "There's a barn up ahead—somebody's farm. I stayed in there once, and it still looks abandoned. Hang on, and maybe we can outrun the rain."

Elizabeth ducked against Logan's solid chest and wrapped her arms around him to keep her balance while he kicked Jasper into a faster lope.

He'd kissed her! What on earth had just happened to them? He was being so kind. He'd let her ride with him so she could sleep a little, and being wrapped in his strong arms, resting against him—it had all been so relaxing and reassuring that she was able to sleep as well as if she'd been lying in a bed. Being this close to him seemed so natural and right.

Did he realize she loved him? What had changed? And that kiss! Never had she experienced anything like it. Robert's kisses were cold and demanding. She realized that now. They were nothing like Logan's—so warm and deep and gentle. His kisses had stirred something wonderful and erotic, a sweet desire unlike anything she'd ever felt. Responding to his kiss had been as natural as breathing. What was really strange was Logan's kisses were demanding, too, but in a good way—the demands of a man's man who knew what he was about and knew what he wanted, yet she knew instinctively that if she told him "no," that would be the end of it. He would never do one thing she didn't want him to do. She felt not one ounce of fear.

The rain came, dousing them as they headed for the abandoned barn.

"We're almost there," Logan shouted above the rain and thunder.

The skies opened up into a true downpour, and a flash of lightning combined with booming thunder made Jasper balk a little. Logan kicked the horse harder and charged through the rain while Elizabeth hung on for dear life, until they finally reached the barn.

"Oh my goodness!" Elizabeth declared. "I'm soaked as badly as if someone threw me in a lake!"

"Yeah, well, we *both* are soaked. So are the horses and our gear."

Elizabeth straightened and laughed. Her hair was wet, and water ran down her face. "I must look a mess. But you had that wide-brimmed hat. I don't think your hair is wet at all."

He grinned. "Well, the rest of me is. I should have stopped to get out a slicker, but the storm came on so quick I didn't have a chance. And you were sleeping, so I just kept going."

Rain beat on the roof of the barn, and drips of

water sprang through in places, running down walls and into the hay and over the dirt floor.

Logan dismounted and lifted Elizabeth down, only he didn't let go of her right away. The look in his eyes was unlike anything she'd seen there before. He met her lips again, and she thought she might melt right into him. She returned his kiss with fervor, reaching around his neck while he held her with her feet off the ground.

Why was this so natural? Why wasn't she offended? Why wasn't she worried he was just out to have his way with her and nothing more? He could do anything he wanted with her and she'd never be able to stop him…but she didn't *want* to stop him! That was the part she couldn't understand. He moved his hand down over her bottom, and she relished his touch.

He finally let go of her enough to let her feet touch the ground. Rain began to drip on their heads, and Logan looked up. "Let's find a place where the roof doesn't leak and put the horses into stalls. Maybe there's a little hay in here for them. And we need to get out of these wet clothes."

He left her to take Jasper's reins. Elizabeth followed suit, leading Suzy into a stall. She untied the ropes to the packhorse and put him into a third stall. "I wonder who lived here and why they left," she commented.

"All kinds of reasons," Logan answered. He came out from Jasper's stall. "Sickness, a bad year for crops, Indians, outlaws, loneliness—there are any number of reasons why some people just don't make it out here."

"That's sad."

"It's just life."

Elizabeth wondered if he was thinking about MaryAnne. They'd had a farm, too, and she suspected he'd never gone back there after what had happened.

"Get some dry clothes out of your supplies," Logan told her from the other stall. "And some blankets. We'll change and wait out the storm in here. And we might as well eat a little something."

Why did all this feel so natural? It was almost like they were an old married couple just talking and getting ready to…

Elizabeth's heart beat faster. To what? Change clothes in front of each other?

She untied the leather satchel that held a change of clothes and carried it out of the stall to see Logan had laid out some blankets in a different stall that looked clean and dry.

"There is plenty of hay in this one," he said, "and it's dry and not full of mold." He removed his hat and vest and hung them over the wall of a fourth stall, then began unbuttoning his shirt. Elizabeth admired his muscular frame, solid, beautiful like the Greek Gods she'd studied. His muscles flexed in different ways as he removed his shirt. He wasn't just handsome and masculine. He was beautiful.

He caught her looking at him and smiled. "Don't just stand there. Bring our things over here and get those wet clothes off."

Elizabeth suddenly felt like a little girl. "What?" She just stood there like an idiot.

Logan unbuckled his gun belt and slung that over a wall, too. He walked up to her and took her arm, leading her to the blankets. "Need some help?"

"I—"

He took the satchel from her and set it aside, then pulled her leather vest down over her shoulders. Elizabeth just stood there as he unbuckled her gun belt and hung it over the same wall beside his own. He began unbuttoning her blouse. "You need to get out of these clothes," he said. "I don't want you getting sick on me. We've been through enough doctoring." He opened her blouse and pulled it down and off of her, then unbuttoned the waist of her riding skirt.

Elizabeth could not believe she was letting him do what he was doing. He was so sure about it. And to her own amazement and confusion, she trusted every move he made. He jerked down the riding skirt, and she easily stepped out of the wide legs.

"Sit down on those blankets, and I'll pull your boots and socks off," he told her.

Saying nothing, she obeyed. He pulled off her boots and socks. The touch of his fingers against her legs stirred forbidden thoughts. In a moment she sat there in only her bloomers and camisole. Logan removed his boots and pants and stood there in the clean long johns she'd given him just this morning. Thankfully, no blood showed in the area of his wound. She couldn't help noticing the bulge she'd seen yesterday morning was bigger now. For a moment, she remembered how ugly and frightening that part of a man had looked when Robert had exposed himself to her. Why didn't she find it ugly and frightening now? She looked away, not out of terror but out of embarrassment that she'd looked at all, let alone not being appalled or afraid.

Logan sat down beside her and pushed some wet

strands of her hair behind one ear. She wondered if there was something she should do, or say, but decided to wait. Logan Best knew what he was about, and maybe he wasn't even thinking what she guessed he was thinking. She would be mortified if she said the wrong thing.

Logan put an arm around her shoulders and pulled her close against him. "We need to get the rest of these clothes off," he said.

"I know."

"I didn't want to scare you by finishing undressing or forcing you to."

Elizabeth swallowed. "You wouldn't have scared me."

Logan sighed. "Elizabeth, I never thought I'd say this again to any woman, but I love you."

Elizabeth looked down at the lace on her bloomers, hardly able to believe he'd spoken those three words. "I love you, too." She faced him then. "So much."

Logan turned and gently lay her back onto the blanket, moving on top of her. "Do you finally trust me?" He searched her eyes with nothing but love and adoration in his gaze.

Elizabeth felt instantly lost in him, hardly aware of the rain pouring outside and even inside in some places. "In my whole life I've never felt so safe and loved."

Logan kissed her forehead. "For days I have argued with myself all the reasons why a woman like you and a man like me could never get along, but you've shown yourself to be so much stronger than I thought you could be, and—"

"You don't need to explain. It's the same for me.

When we first met, I judged you in all the wrong ways, Logan, but you've turned out to be like a royal knight, brave and sure and—"

"I'm no knight, Elizabeth. I'm just a man who didn't realize how lonely he was until you came along." He kissed her eyes. "I want you right now… more than I've wanted any woman since—"

Elizabeth put fingers to his lips—full lips, delicious lips, soft lips. "Don't say it. Don't even think about the past and all the hurt, Logan. Do you believe in fate?"

He grinned as he stroked more wet hair away from her eyes. "I'm not sure."

"I do. That argument back in London that started all of this…the opportunity for me to come to America… losing my brother along the way…needing help…and then you came along and carried me out of that jail cell." Elizabeth felt like crying. "I think this was all meant to be. You're right about how different we are, but I can't begin to imagine us parting ways after this. I could never, ever forget you, and I've been so scared you would just up and leave when this is over, either because you really don't care, or just because we *are* so different. But there is so much about you to love, and after today, you'll be riding into danger…for me. Tell me all of this has been for me and not just for bounty."

He held her gaze, sincerity in his eyes. "At first it was for the money, but it wasn't long before I realized it wasn't that at all. And if the highborn lady from London will have me, I want you to be my wife."

Elizabeth couldn't hold back tears of relief that this man would not walk out of her life. "I would love to be your wife." She smiled through her tears. "But I

don't want to wait, Logan. You could die when you
go to Hays City, and I'm not letting you go without
you being my first man. I can't begin to imagine any
other man making a woman of me. I don't care how
wrong it is, or how—"

She didn't get the chance to finish. Logan met her
mouth in a deep, possessive kiss. Elizabeth threw her
arms around his neck and returned his ardor with
fervor, whimpering with intense desire to give this
man anything he wanted. This was Logan Best, and he
knew about women and he loved her and he'd rather
die than hurt her. She knew it. She just knew it.

He moved his lips to her throat and licked his way
down to her breasts, untying her camisole and pushing
it open.

"Say 'no' right now, or there is no going back,"
he groaned. He grasped one breast and kissed his way
back up her neck and to her lips, devouring her mouth
with a hint of command. "I'm getting way too close to
not being able to stop," he said softly in her ear. "You
weren't raised for it to be like this. This should be for
your wedding night, so say 'no' right now or there
won't be any choice. Letting go of you now would be
worse pain than this damn leg wound."

"You said you would marry me," she answered.
"I didn't think I could trust any man ever again, but
I know in my heart we belong together, and I know
what I want. I don't want it to be anybody else but
you, Logan, no matter what happens tomorrow."

"As God is my witness, I could never ride out of
your life now."

Elizabeth swallowed, hit with the realization of

what she was about to let this man do to her. The fact
that he'd twice offered to stop was all she needed to
hear. "Say the words again," she said in a near whisper.
"Say you love me, Logan Best."

"I love you. I'll take care of you and protect you
the rest of my life."

"I see it in your beautiful green eyes. And if I told
you to stop right now, it would be a lie just to protect
my honor."

"After today, I'll own your honor, your body, and
your soul." He met her mouth again, savoring it like
something utterly delicious.

Elizabeth couldn't believe how easy it was to
respond, how gently he kissed her, deep and demanding but not at all frightening or forceful. It felt like
fire was making its way through her every vein, every
muscle, every bone, as he raised up a little and pulled
her camisole out from under her, then moved down,
kissing her belly, pulling at her pantaloons.

Elizabeth had never felt so brazen, so wanton, so
eager to be touched by a man. He bent down and
kissed the hairs that hid secret places, and Elizabeth
thought she might faint at the realization Logan Best
was touching and tasting and drinking in the sight of
her naked body. He kissed his way back up to her
breasts and gently fondled them, skimming over her
nipples in a way that stirred a deep ache to please him
in every way.

"My God, you're beautiful," he told her as he lightly
licked her nipples, then suckled her breasts as though
he was tasting the most delicious thing that he'd ever
put in his mouth. He groaned with the want of her.

Elizabeth ran her fingers into his thick, sandy hair. "Logan, I don't know what to do," she whispered. "I want to do this right. I want to please you."

He licked his way up her neck and over her chin, then kissed her again, moaning as he met her lips and searched her mouth suggestively. "You don't need to know what to do," he said softly. "Just being inside of you is all the pleasure I need."

Elizabeth feared she might faint dead away before he finished with her. She felt something hard pressing on her thigh. She knew what it was. Why didn't it frighten her? It was that thing Robert had shown her, that thing she thought was ugly and terrifying. But this time it belonged to Logan Best, and somehow that made it all right.

He kissed her fervently as he moved his hand down over her belly, between her legs, and dipped fingers inside that most forbidden part of her, that place she'd sometimes wondered about, sometimes touched herself but couldn't imagine a man doing it. He toyed with that magic spot where she'd sometimes felt strange urges, then kept moving his fingers back inside of her. She sensed his fingers moving more easily, and she realized his touch was creating juices that made her want to open herself to him.

She whimpered and arched against his touch. Never had she felt so wicked and wild and eager for a man to look at her, to touch her. He licked and suckled at her breasts again, moved to her lips, back to her breasts, all the while making her want him so badly she thought she might scream. What was this wonderful thing he was doing to her—something with his fingers deep inside, something that brought an explosion of aching, wicked desire that literally made her cry out in utter ecstasy?

He moved his kisses down to intimate places, his warm breath arousing forbidden desires. Was she really letting him taste her there? She cried out his name as he kissed his way down her inner thighs, telling her over and over again how absolutely beautiful she was and how much he loved her.

She never knew a man could do such things to a woman, or that she could allow such intimacy, to the point of begging for it if he stopped now.

She was so relaxed, and yet on fire and so ready to let him do anything he wanted with her. In the next moment, a second exotic throbbing deep inside caused her to grasp his hair and push against him, literally begging for more. He moved his kisses back up over her belly as she arched against him.

Was this how it felt to want all of a man, even the very thing that frightened her most? Was this what happened to make a woman want a man to push himself inside of her? He raised up and pulled down his long johns. She again saw that part of a man that had seemed so forbidding and frightening when she saw it on Robert. But Logan was a beautiful man, and she saw his swollen penis as just an addition to all that was man about him. The thought of it fitting inside of her was frightening, but knowing it was Logan who was doing this eased her fears. Logan Best would never hurt her or make it ugly.

Instinctively, she opened her legs as he settled between them and leaned down to smother her with kisses.

"Don't be afraid of the pain," he told her. "It's only the first time. It gets a lot better after that," he groaned near her ear. "I promise."

"I want to feel it," she whimpered in reply. "I want you inside of me."

Logan reached down, and she felt the back of his hand against her privates as he positioned himself. In the next instant, she knew what he meant by the pain. She gasped when he pushed himself inside of her. It was the oddest sort of pain she'd ever known. It was a pain she actually wanted more of as he began invading her in a rhythm that made her arch against him to meet his thrusts. He raised up on his knees and grasped her bottom, pushing deeper, studying her nakedness as he took her for his own. She closed her eyes and allowed the invasion with utter abandon, opening her eyes once in a while to study his godlike body, his solid chest and muscled arms and shoulders. The sweet, erotic throbbing she'd felt earlier enveloped her again, her privates literally pulling him deeper in an uncontrolled spasm that made her emit rhythmic cries of pleasure.

"God, Elizabeth, I can't get enough of you," he groaned. He came down to kiss her almost violently, continuing his thrusts, grunting with each one until she felt a pulsing inside of her. Somehow, she knew what it was. People had babies this way. He'd just planted his life into her deepest being and she didn't care. Maybe she would even get pregnant. She wasn't afraid of it. She actually thought how beautiful it would be if his seed took hold and she bore a child that was beautiful and strong like its father.

"Logan, I love you! I love you!" she cried out, reaching around his neck when he relaxed on top of her.

He moved one arm under her and grasped her hair in his other hand as he kissed her eyes, her cheeks, her mouth. "And I love you," he told her, his penis still inside of her as he settled against her. "Don't move. I want it again."

"What about your leg?"

He grinned and kissed her cheek and neck hungrily. "Believe me, I'm not thinking about my leg right now."

"I can't believe we're doing this."

"Are you okay? Are you in pain?"

Elizabeth kissed his chest. "A little. But it's a nice pain. Does that sound silly?"

He chuckled and kissed her hair. "Yeah, it does, but as long as you're okay with it—"

"I am! You're the finest, gentlest, most caring man I've ever known, and I love you so much I can't find the words to express it."

He kissed her over and over, talking between kisses. "I find that hard to believe."

Kisses.

"How about passionately?" she suggested.

"Kind of simple. I know that word."

"How about, I love you with great fervor? Obsessively? Ardently? How about, I love you with great zeal and adoration?"

"That sounds more like Elizabeth Baylor. There were a couple of words there I didn't understand." He moved fully on top of her again. "And you can apply them all to how much I love you."

Elizabeth met his gaze. "I sure hope this barn really is abandoned. If some farmer comes along and finds us like this, I will be humiliated beyond recovery."

"I've been by here before. No one lives here. And I know we have to be careful, but no one will keep riding in this downpour, and it's late. Tomorrow, as we get even closer to Hays City, we have to stay alert. We won't be able to do this tomorrow, so I intend to make up for all of that the rest of today and tonight."

Elizabeth felt him growing inside of her. He met her mouth again, running his tongue between her lips as he surged into her again, as though to invade every part of her that he could. She was lost in him, lost in the middle of Kansas, lost to the life she'd grown up with…and she'd lost her heart to a bounty hunter. No dime novel could ever tell a story this good.

FORTY-ONE

THEY SLEPT. THE RAIN CONTINUED TO POUR DOWN, making them feel as though they were the only two people on earth. Somewhere deep in the night, Elizabeth awoke to Logan caressing her breasts. He moved on top of her, and they made sweet, quiet, delicious, desperate love again, both realizing that soon Logan would be facing a danger that could take him from Elizabeth forever. He touched her and moved in ways that again created the deep ache to feel him inside of her.

They didn't need to talk. They only needed to touch…and share…and be a part of each other. Elizabeth felt like she couldn't kiss him deeply enough, and in turn, Logan told her he felt he couldn't brand her deeply enough through intercourse. His invasion of her deepest being remained a strangely wonderful pain she couldn't get enough of.

The only sounds through the night were the rain, the occasional shudder of a horse, and their own desperate groans of need and desire and wicked, erotic pleasure. Logan Best made love with the same sureness and strength and commanding power that he used in hunting men and in defending himself…and now he was in complete control of her heart and her body. Elizabeth knew she would never again have to be afraid of anything, not when she lay in these strong arms. She'd lost count of how many orgasms she'd had or how many times Logan had spilled his life into her. The man had gone through so much emotional pain and had lived with a need for revenge for far too long. She didn't doubt he was doing this out of his ache to love and be loved again, and not just for his selfish pleasure.

Somewhere deep in the night, Logan got up and walked out, coming back in with a bucket full of rainwater. He used it to water the horses, then removed their saddles and gear, something he didn't do the night before. It was warm, and Logan didn't bother dressing.

By the dim light of an old lantern they'd found in the barn, Elizabeth drank in every bit of Logan's magnificent body.

She could hardly believe she'd touched that mysterious part of man that used to frighten her. If what they had shared several times over since late yesterday afternoon was love, then she was most certainly in love, far deeper than she'd thought possible.

He lay down with her again after watering the horses and pulled a blanket over them, then pulled her close. "I should have unloaded those horses before we started all of this, but all I could think of was you and how much I love you and especially how much I wanted you."

Elizabeth snuggled backward against him. "I love the thought of being your wife."

Logan kissed her hair. "I want you to know that I don't want anything to do with your money or jewels or anything else once I get that all back for you. I don't give a damn about those things, so don't ever think that's why I want to marry you. I'm not a man to live off a woman. Compared to what you are used to, I am not a rich man, Elizabeth, but I'm damn well not poor, either. When MaryAnne died, we'd had a good year farming. I took the money I'd made and put it in a bank in St. Louis. I figured it was safer in a bank in a bigger town. I have also put most of my bounty money in that bank. You probably wouldn't think it's much, but out here it's plenty—enough to build you a nice place and maybe even get you some housekeeping help—at least at first—till you learn how to cook and such things. And maybe you could teach me how to read. We have a lot to learn from each other."

Elizabeth turned to face him. "Logan, you don't have to be a rich man for me to marry you."

"Maybe not, but you deserve something better than the average settler woman out here. It's just natural because of how you were raised. I'm not even sure where we will end up living, but I'll make sure it's something nice."

Elizabeth ran a hand along his solid forearm. "When did you know, Logan?"

"Know what?"

She studied her handsome lover by the dim lantern light. "That you love me."

"I'm not even sure. Sometimes I think it was

the morning I carried you out of that jail cell, but I fought it. I figured I just felt sorry for you, and your predicament reminded me of MaryAnne. And later, I figured you for a selfish, spoiled, pampered rich girl who could never in a thousand years be interested in a man like me. But something changed when you did all those things on your own the day you cauterized my leg," he said. "I saw the woman in you, the possibility that you could manage life out here and handle it just fine." He kissed her hair. "And I'm tired of being lonely. I guess somewhere down inside I've been needing the love I learned all about from MaryAnne and Lilly. I just didn't want to admit it because it hurt so much when I lost them, and I didn't think I could find another woman I could love that much."

"What will you do when we marry? I don't want you running all over three or four states hunting men, Logan. I'll go insane wondering where you are and if you're all right. And if we have children, they will need their father."

He moved a leg over hers. "I know that. I think I know of a happy medium."

"What's that?"

"You still haven't seen Denver or the Rocky Mountains. Kansas is just a tip of the West. There is so much more to see, and I want to show it to you. I also know what I'm best at, and that's how to use guns and how to hunt men. I'm thinking I can get my money out of that bank in St. Louis, and we could go on to Denver—build a nice house there—something roomy and comfortable enough for you—and I could be a U.S. Marshal. The job has been offered more than once, and I always turned it down because I didn't want to settle in one place. Now I have no choice. We'll use just enough of your money to buy the things you need to live comfortably. I don't need much, and I don't want other people saying I married you for your money."

"Well, at the moment, I am still poor," she reminded him.

Logan laughed lightly. "True. I just want you to believe me when I say this has nothing to do with however much money you do or don't have. If Chad and his boys have already spent or gambled away or lost what's yours, it won't matter to me. That money has nothing to do with the reasons I love you. You're beautiful and strong, and you're willing to learn and adapt." He moved on top of her again. "And when I look into those big blue eyes and taste those pouty lips and feel myself inside of you, I know this is what I want. I'm marrying you for *you*, and nothing more."

Elizabeth traced her fingers over his eyebrows. "You have been nothing but totally honest with me this whole time. I know by your talk and your actions that all you want is love, and I will give you all that I have, Logan Best."

He met her mouth again, then traced his lips to her throat.

"Logan, let's forget about Hays City. My valuables mean nothing to me anymore either. Your *life* is all that matters. I don't want you to go there and face those men. It's too dangerous. I don't want to lose you now."

He sighed, meeting her gaze again. "Listen to me."

He kissed her eyes. "I know men like Chad Krieger. He is going to be out for revenge. And in his eyes, you are his property now. And my name is known among men like that. Krieger and his men will be after *me*, too, because they don't want to have to wonder if and when I'll find them. At the same time, I don't intend to be taken by surprise or expose you to the danger of them catching you alone. Besides that, you deserve to have your mother's jewels back. They are part of that legacy you told me about, which means they will be a part of our *children's* legacy." He grinned and kissed her nose. "See? I remembered that word, but I wouldn't have a clue how to spell it."

Tears filled Elizabeth's eyes. "I'll teach you."

He moved between her legs. "And I'll teach you all the ways there are to please a man."

Her eyes widened. "You mean there's more?"

"You bet." He kissed her. "I am going to make you the most wanton woman alive. But we'll wait on that. After all, we have to save *some*thing for after we're married."

Elizabeth studied the joy in his eyes she'd never seen there since she'd met him…until now. "I don't ever want you to feel alone again, Logan. I feel so sorry for your awful childhood and about your wife and daughter. I can learn to live out here, as long as I have you. And I'll try to make you as happy as you were before you lost your family." She saw pain in his look then, but it quickly passed.

"I didn't think I could let go of it until you came along," he told her lovingly. "And I want you to know that I intend to make sure you live well, and in comfort. I won't have you living out in the middle of nowhere scrubbing my clothes on a washboard."

Elizabeth smiled. "What's a washboard?"

He burst out laughing. "Don't tell me you don't know."

"Well, I have a pretty good idea, but I've never used one."

"I'm sure you haven't, but that's part of what I love about you. When it comes to life out here, you're like a child who needs to learn everything."

"Well, you have things to learn, too."

"Then we'll learn them together when we can spare some time out of bed."

"You mean we can't just stay in bed forever?"

Logan frowned. "I'm getting worried I won't be able to keep up with you."

"We can certainly enjoy finding out," Elizabeth answered. She looked around the inside of the old barn. The dim light of dawn shafted through some of the spaces between the drying boards, and the rain had finally stopped.

Elizabeth reached up and smoothed back some of Logan's hair. "I always thought I'd take a man for the first time in a grand canopied bed with a deep mattress and silk sheets," she said softly. "I'd first walk down the aisle of a huge church, wearing a magnificent wedding gown with a train so long bridesmaids would have to lift the corners for me and help me. My wedding would make all the headlines in London newspapers, and my husband would be a lord or a duke or an earl." She traced her fingers over his full lips. "And here I am, lying on plain blankets with hay for a mattress, and the canopy over me is an old, leaking barn. Instead of maids of honor and groomsmen, I am surrounded by horses." She studied him lovingly. "But my new husband is far more than a duke or an earl. He's a prince—my knight in shining armor, come to rescue me."

Logan frowned. "I think you read too many books."

"Not at all. And I'm glad I read those penny dreadfuls that caused me to come to America. Otherwise, I never would have met you. I would be locked into a boring, meaningless life and probably married to some older man who knows nothing of how to please a woman." She smiled. "Not like you do."

Logan kissed her eyes. "You're not disappointed that you won't have that grand wedding, or that your husband is nothing more than an orphan and a bounty hunter who can't even read?"

Her eyes teared. "You make me happy, Logan Best. I love how you tease me, and I love belonging to you. All the money and grandeur in the world could never replace this moment, these feelings. This old barn will hold more memories for me than anything I ever knew in London or experienced on my way here. All through that trip, fate was leading us to each other. Maybe that means we'll always be together—that nothing will happen to you in Hays City."

"Maybe." Logan met her lips again. Both knew how this could end, and both felt desperate at the thought of it. Their kiss grew deeper and led to more kisses, at times almost violent as they rolled and tossed and tasted and clung to each other.

He took her again. This time he was more posses-sive, more commanding, almost rough with her. This could be their last time for a while. His manly power only made her react with equal fervor, wanting to brand Logan Best as hers alone. She loved the fact that the man could break her in half if he wanted, yet in his arms she was something precious and revered.

Logan Best was her protector, her lover, her owner. He would be her provider, her partner, and soon… her husband.

God, don't take him away from me! Not now!

He finished with her, and they lay there in each other's arms.

"We have to get going, Elizabeth."

"Don't say it!"

"There is no other way. We have to finish what we came here for."

Elizabeth's heart nearly broke at a sign of tears in his eyes. "I don't want this moment to end any more than you do," he said. He rolled away from her, sighing deeply before he rose.

"I'm going to wash and dress," he told her, a resigned sadness to his voice. "I'll make a fire while you do the same, and we'll have a little coffee and something to eat. We have some time yet. I'll resaddle and pack the horses and take them outside to graze on the fresh grass. It finally stopped raining."

They moved methodically, both wanting to pre-tend everything would be all right, both wanting to put off the inevitable. Elizabeth washed and dressed. Logan took care of the horses and made a small fire outside with bundled wood from their supplies.

The grass was so wet he didn't need to dig a trench around the fire. Elizabeth's riding skirt had dried, so she wore it again. She fought tears as she picked up the blankets that had served as the bed in which she'd lost her virginity to the only man she would have considered giving it to. And he'd taken it lovingly, beautifully, gently.

She stared at the scattered hay from under the blankets. This couldn't be happening! Reality began to set in as she thought about what had happened to her there in the stall of an old, abandoned barn. When she'd left London, little did she ever think in her wildest imagination that her journey would lead here…to the middle of Kansas…to be taken by a bounty hunter she'd only known eleven days.

Was it possible to fall in love that quickly? Was any of this real? She walked out of the barn and into the light of a fully rising sun. She tied the blankets onto the packhorse, then turned to watch Logan strap on his gun.

Yes, this was real.

She felt sick when he slung his extra cartridge belt around Jasper's neck and slid his rifle into one boot and his shotgun into the other. This tall, broad, dangerous-looking man had taken her virginity last night, and he over and over again made sure she remembered she belonged to him now, every last inch of her, plus her heart and soul.

Yes, this was real.

Logan Best was all man and then some. He fit every fantasy she'd had about the men of the American West she'd read about in those penny dreadfuls. She couldn't help wondering what Jonathan would think if he saw her now.

Yes, this was real.

She walked to the campfire and poured herself some coffee. It wasn't as hot as it should be, but she needed it to fortify her determination not to fall to pieces in front of Logan. He needed her strength and support now.

Yes, this was real.

Logan started toward her, then stopped and watched in the distance.

"There's a wagon coming," he told her.

Elizabeth walked to stand next him. Logan rested his hand on his sidearm as the wagon drew closer, bouncing and jostling over the clumpy prairie grass.

"Looks like a man and a woman and a couple of kids in the back," Logan said. "They're coming from the direction of Hays City." He moved an arm around her protectively.

Elizabeth breathed a sigh of relief that it wasn't a gang of men coming toward them.

Yes, this was real. And soon the reality of it would slam back at them like a hard prairie wind.

FORTY-TWO

June 8, 1870

A SOLIDLY BUILT MAN, WEARING PLAIN-BROWN PANTS
with suspenders and a plain shirt that looked handmade, drew his wagon to a halt beside Logan and
Elizabeth, shoving his foot against the brake as he
shouted "whoa!" to two of the biggest horses Elizabeth
had ever seen. Both steeds were a golden color with
white manes and tails.

"Hello there!" the driver greeted. "You two need
any help? We don't usually see anybody around this old
abandoned farm. I know it rained awful hard last night."

Elizabeth recognized a slight German accent.

"We're fine," Logan answered.

"Just checking." The man smiled warmly. "My
wife and I are headed home. My name is Lawrence
Bueter, and this is my wife, Florence." He gestured to
the portly woman beside him. She wore a paisley dress
and a gathered prairie bonnet. She nodded to Logan
and Elizabeth. "And these are our sons," Lawrence
added proudly. "Clarence is the oldest. He's fifteen.

Adolf is twelve, and Benjamin is ten. We've just come from Hays City. I traded a bull and two horses there for these two fine plow horses. They are magnificent, are they not?"

"They certainly are," Logan answered.

"Where might you be headed?" Lawrence asked.

"Hays City," Logan answered.

Lawrence and his wife, and even their boys, sobered and looked at one another.

"Something wrong?" Logan asked.

Lawrence looked down at him from the wagon seat. "It might not be wise to go there," he warned.

"Why is that?" Elizabeth asked, grasping Logan's arm.

"Well, there is a lot of trouble in that town right now. We didn't know it when we first got there. Most business owners and the saloons and such are doing business just fine. I managed to make my trade, but I got the family out of there right away. We actually camped away from town last night before leaving this morning to go the rest of the way home. We have a farm about two miles south of here."

Logan moved his arm around Elizabeth. "What kind of trouble are you talking about?"

"Well, sir, there is a gang of men there making all kinds of trouble. The man I traded with acted real nervous, said a bunch of men rode in and kind of took over the place. Sheriff Bishop tried to stop them, and they shot him—shot his deputy, too."

"Oh my God," Elizabeth said softly. She looked up at Logan.

"Any names?" Logan asked, his eyes on the German farmer.

"The trader I dealt with said the leader of the bunch calls himself Chad. Rumor is, they are waiting for some bounty hunter and a woman he's—" Lawrence hesitated. "My goodness! Would *you* be the bounty hunter?"

"Logan, don't go!" Elizabeth told him. "Don't go!"

"That's me," Logan told the farmer. "My name is Logan Best."

Lawrence shook his head. "Well, Mr. Best, I think it's better you stay away from Hays City."

"I can't, especially now that I know they killed the sheriff. Todd Bishop was a good friend of mine. Any idea how many men are involved? Have they accosted any women? Stolen anything?"

"Well, I...I am not sure just who, but the trader said they...well...I don't want to say it in front of the wife and my boys. Let's just say a couple of young women were attacked, and they are holding one of them. They robbed the bank and are making much mayhem at one of the saloons."

"Which one? The Horseshoe or The Last Stop?"

"I believe the trader said The Last Stop. I don't frequent such places, so I am not positive. I left as quickly as I could to protect my family."

"I understand," Logan told him.

"Are you really a bounty hunter, mister?" the boy called Clarence asked.

"I am. And I'm after the men your father is talking about."

"Logan, you can't go there! You can't!" Elizabeth begged. Terror engulfed her.

"How dependable is Clarence?" Logan asked the farmer.

"I'm *real* dependable, mister!" Clarence answered. "I can ride and hunt and all kinds of things! You want me to help?"

"Oh my goodness!" Florence exclaimed. She looked at her husband. "Don't let Clarence do something dangerous, Lawrence!"

"Logan, what are you doing?" Elizabeth asked.

Logan let go of her and gently pushed her aside.

"Why do you ask?" Lawrence asked Logan.

"I need someone these men wouldn't suspect to ride back to Hays City and give a note to a man at a supply store there. He'll get it to a woman who can help me."

What woman? Elizabeth wanted to ask.

"She can hide me until I figure the layout and which men I'm after," Logan told Bueter. "She can also find a few men who might be able to help me. If your son can take one of my horses and ride in casual-like—just a kid come to town to pick up a few things for his ma—something like that—he can get the note to the man at the supply store. The woman I'm talking about is—she lives above the Horseshoe. I'm sure your wife wouldn't approve of the kind of woman she is, but I promise she's good and kind. Your son won't even need to go near the saloon. He just needs to give the note to a man named Dick Elsworth."

"The woman is a *whore*?" Clarence asked.

"*Clarence Bueter!*" his mother exclaimed.

"Well, that's what he's saying, isn't it?"

"I am," Logan answered. "Her name is Brenda

Lake, and she knows me well. She'll know exactly why I sent someone with a note."

Elizabeth's heart fell at the words. Not only was Logan going to ride to certain death, but he was going to be with a prostitute, probably one of his favorites, since he claimed he knew her well. "Logan, what are you doing?"

"I'm keeping you out of danger," he answered.

Before she could reply, Logan looked back at Lawrence. "This is Lady Elizabeth Baylor, from London. She hired me to find some things that belong to her. It's a long story, but Chad Krieger and his gang have what she's after, and I aim to get them for her."

"Logan, no! I changed my mind. It's not worth you dying for." She grasped his arm, tears in her eyes.

He seemed to not even hear her.

"I promise no harm will come to your son, and he won't be walking into some den of sin."

Iniquity! Elizabeth wanted to shout at him. *The word is iniquity! And you're the one who will be walking into it, after which you'll be shot dead, and I'll never see you again.*

"I don't know," Lawrence said with a frown.

"Let me do it, Pa!" Clarence pleaded. "I promise to do exactly what Mr. Best tells me to do. All I have to do is ride into town and give a man a note. Those men won't care nothing about me."

"I'll pay him," Logan added. "Five dollars and the horse I give him to ride into town."

"Holy Moses, Pa! Let me do it!"

"Oh my goodness," Florence fretted.

"There's one more thing," Logan added. "I want you to take Miss Baylor to your farm with you," he told Bueter. "She'll be safe there while I take care of things in Hays City."

Elizabeth's eyes widened in terror mixed with indignation and fury. "*No!*" she exclaimed. "I'll not let you go without me. We are supposed to do this together."

Logan turned and grasped her arms. "*Listen* to me! They are expecting a well-armed man to ride into Hays City accompanied by a pretty blond woman. You will only draw attention we don't need, let alone be a distraction for me. I'll be damned worried they'll somehow get their hands on you, and I won't let that happen. You have to do this for *me*, Elizabeth!"

"No! No! I can't let you ride in there alone. Don't go, Logan! I don't want the jewels and the money."

"I already told you why we have to get this over with. And now that I know they shot Todd Bishop, I can't let this go."

Elizabeth saw the bounty hunter now—the ruthless man she judged him to be when she first met him. All the begging in the world wasn't going to stop him. "But...that woman..."

Logan kept hold of one of her arms and looked up at Lawrence. "You talk it over among you," he told the man. "I need to talk to Miss Baylor alone." He walked off, leading Elizabeth with a firm grip on her arm. He took her inside the barn.

"Logan, please don't do this!" she asked yet again, unable to control her tears.

"I need you to be strong, and I need you to go with Mrs. Bueter and her family. Chad Krieger would never think to look for you there. I need you out of danger, Elizabeth, or I won't be able to think straight. If you don't want me to die, then do as I ask. I can't take you with me."

"Who is Brenda?"

He closed his eyes and sighed. "You know damn well who she is. She's a prostitute and a good friend."

Elizabeth covered her face and wept. Logan kept hold of her arms and shook her slightly. "Look at me, Elizabeth!"

She wiped at tears and managed to meet his gaze.

"I love you. I meant every goddamn word I said to you yesterday, last night, *and* this morning. I *love* you! I want to *marry* you. I'm not going to turn around and sleep with some whore. And believe me, with the job I have ahead of me, that won't even be on my mind. Brenda Lake is a good friend. If I can get a note to her, telling her to watch for me tomorrow night, she'll know what to do. She knows a lot of men who'd be willing to help me. She'll find a way to get word to them; so if you want me to come back from this, you have to write that note for me and you have to trust that I know what I'm doing. Brenda will make sure I don't go into this alone. And I can't go to Hays City with you on my mind. If you love me, you'll *trust* me on this."

Elizabeth couldn't help throwing her arms around his middle. "I can't live without you now, Logan. I can't!"

"You won't need to if you let me do this right." He grasped her hair in his hands and kissed the top of her head. "Last night and this morning were beautiful. *You're* beautiful. It feels good to be loved again. I'm not going to throw that away; and knowing you're with those people out there and waiting for me to come and get you will give me all the incentive I need to get through this. If it weren't for the Bueters coming along, I'd probably be making love to you again right now before we head for Hays City." He kissed her hair again. "Don't cry, Elizabeth. I need you to straighten up and write that note for me. Find that paper and ink pen you insisted on bringing along when we left Abilene."

Abilene. She'd killed Robert in Abilene, and the next thing she knew Logan Best was carrying her in his arms to get help. It felt so good to rest her head now against his solid chest, to feel his strong arms around her, protecting her, reassuring her. How could she let him go into such danger? "Promise me you won't go after all those men without help," she wept.

"I won't. And you have to trust Brenda. She'll respect how much I love you, and she cares about me. She'll make sure I *get* that help. And more than anything, I intend to make sure those men don't get their hands on you, because you belong to Logan Best. Got that?" He grasped her shoulders and gently pushed her away. "You belong to *me*, and I'm coming back for you. If possible, I'll bring a preacher with me. We'll get married as soon as this is over. Now be brave for me. Be brave like you were when you walked up to those Indians and handed them those supplies—and when you shot at those buffalo hunters—and when you burned out the wound in my leg."

Elizabeth studied his eyes. He was her Logan. He'd never lied to her. He'd made love to her, not in a demanding way or because he just wanted what all men wanted. He'd truly made love to her as though she was a treasured object of beauty he wanted to own. His heart belonged to her now, didn't it? And he owned her heart in return.

He met her lips in a burning kiss of desperate promises. She flung her arms around his neck and kissed him hard, wanting to make sure he remembered it. They held each other a moment, her feet off the ground.

Logan finally released the kiss and moved his lips to her ear. "Have you no shame, woman?" he joked. "What do you think the Bueters think of us in here, carrying on like this?"

"I don't care what they think. I don't want to let go of you."

"You have to." He pulled her arms from around his neck. "Write the note, Elizabeth. If Clarence is going to do this, he has to get going so he reaches Hays City before dark."

"Can we spend tonight together again?"

"No. I need a day and night away from you to get my mind off of things that will keep me from being alert. I'll be a different man for a while, Elizabeth. Do you understand?"

She stepped back, wiping at tears. "Sadly, I do," she answered. She had to be strong and brave. He'd praised her earlier for those things. He respected that about her. She couldn't revert to the frightened, simpering, spoiled young woman she was when he first met her. "I'll get the paper and pen," she said.

Everything happened too fast after that. The Bueters agreed to let Clarence deliver the note, saying they felt sorry for Miss Baylor and for Logan, riding into such danger. If they could help, they were willing. Logan took Elizabeth's belongings off Suzy and gave Suzy to Clarence to ride into Hays City.

"Remember to draw no attention," he told the young man. He handed him some money, along with the note. "This is your pay. I want you to go into a supply store called Hays Home Goods and spend some of that money so things look normal. Make it look like your mother sent you to town for flour or cloth or whatever she usually buys. Give the note to Dick Elsworth. He's the owner."

"I know him, Mr. Best. We've shopped at his store before."

"Good. Then you won't look out of place. Tell him Logan Best wants him to put you up for the night and that he should take that note to Brenda Lake. You have to do exactly as I say, Clarence. And make sure none of those men is around inside the store. We can't have one of them overhearing you."

"Yes, sir. I understand."

"Dick frequents the ladies above the Horseshoe, and he knows Brenda. It won't look out of place for him to go see her."

"Okay. I can do it. Thanks, Mr. Best."

Clarence mounted Suzy, and Logan reached up to shake his hand. "One more thing," he told the boy. "You get the hell out of Hays City early the next morning. There will be a lot of shooting going on by late the next day or that night. I promised your parents you wouldn't get hurt. It's tempting for a boy your age to hang around and watch a shoot-out, but if I find out you did that, I'll take back my money *and* the horse. Understand? You get the hell out of town and home so your parents know you're all right."

"Yes, sir." Clarence sobered. "I hope you'll be okay, Mr. Best."

"I will be."

"When it's over, is it okay if I tell my friends what I did and that I know you?"

"Tell them whatever you want. Just don't say a word till I show up at your place alive and well."

The words made Elizabeth feel ill. Clarence rode off, and Logan loaded Elizabeth's things into the back of the wagon, then tied the packhorse to it. He turned and lifted Elizabeth into the wagon. "Remember what I told you. I don't want you anywhere near Hays City. Don't do something stupid and try to ride in behind me, understand? It's important I know you're safe."

Elizabeth nodded through tears. "What will you do the rest of today and tonight?"

"I'll ride in closer—give Clarence time to get there and back. I'll ride the rest of the way to just outside Hays City tomorrow after dark and go straight to Brenda. In between, I'll spend my time trying to get you out of my head and concentrate on what I need to do."

Elizabeth couldn't even answer because of her tears.

Logan took her hand. "Don't make this harder than it is, Elizabeth. I love you. I'll be back for you. That's a promise."

She sniffed and nodded. "I trust you." She leaned down for one last kiss, but Logan stepped away.

"I can't. Just go, Elizabeth." He stepped even farther

away. "Get going, Mr. Bueter. Make sure she stays at your place."

"I will."

"I'll pay you something when I come for her."

Bueter nodded and snapped the reins to his two new plow horses. They got underway. The look in Logan's eyes as he watched her leave tore at Elizabeth's heart.

She watched him turn away then. He took the extra gun belt full of cartridges from around Jasper's neck and slung it around his shoulder, then mounted up. He rode toward Hays City and didn't look back.

Too fast! It had all happened too fast. Elizabeth watched him until she could no longer see him…or the barn where he'd made a woman of her.

"Logan," she whispered.

I'll pay you something when I come for her, he'd told Bueter…*when I come for her*.

FORTY-THREE

LOGAN SAT STARING AT THE FLAMES OF HIS CAMPFIRE, thinking what a good job Elizabeth had done building a fire the night she burned out his wound. He still could hardly believe how fast she'd learned, considering her pampered upbringing.

God, he missed her already. He could see her blond hair spread out on the blankets as he took her, over and over. He couldn't remember bedding any woman that many times in one night. He couldn't get enough of her. Her body was just as exquisite as he'd imagined when he first set eyes on her. Being able to grasp that firm bottom and feel himself inside of her made him ache to make love to her again.

He could see her beautiful smile, her pouty lips, her big, blue eyes, the blond hairs between her legs that hid the sweetest part of her. Yesterday and last night had been just about the most erotic experience of his life. She was everything he'd imagined when watching how her bottom fit into her saddle, the way it swayed and bounced. He knew the moment he learned how strong and brave she was that he wanted her—and when he saw that bare bottom yesterday morning, his ache for her had grown unbearable.

He had to do whatever it took to get back to her. If he didn't return, she'd be devastated beyond measure. She'd been through so much. The thought of what would happen to her if Chad Krieger and his men got hold of her made him crazy. She belonged to Logan Best now, and no other man was going to touch her. He'd tasted and explored every inch of her, and all of it was as soft and sweet and pleasing as he'd supposed it would be.

He'd hated the look in her eyes when he'd sent her away. An innocent young woman could so easily fall into trouble in this land. Being too trusting had led her to Robert Alexander. He would not allow anything like that to ever happen to her again.

Clarence should have delivered the note by now. He drank some coffee and lit a cigarette. Tomorrow night he would sneak into town the back way to Brenda's place. She'd find a couple of men willing to help rid the town of the filth that had invaded it and shot down Todd Bishop.

Damn! He'd liked Sheriff Bishop. The man hadn't deserved to die like that. His wife must be devastated.

His bedroll would seem too empty tonight. He looked up at a black sky full of stars. The heavy clouds from the rain all last night were gone. He remembered that first night with Elizabeth, when they each lay in separate bedrolls looking at the stars, and he'd commented that MaryAnne and Lilly were up there somewhere—watching. "I hope you understand, MaryAnne," he said quietly into the night. "I'll always love you, but I'm tired of being alone. You'd like Elizabeth. She's a good girl. I'll see you and Lilly again when it's my time." He rolled to his side. *If God even lets me in after the things I've done since you and Lilly died.*

The old pain returned to his heart at the thought of his wife and daughter and the horrible way they had died, with him being unable to stop it. That brought back all the old hatred and revenge.

Chad Krieger and his men were not going to rob or rape or kill again after tomorrow night. And they sure as hell weren't going to get their hands on Elizabeth Baylor, even if he had to die to make sure it didn't happen. He would never again let a woman or a kid die right in front of him.

I'm so sorry, baby girl, he thought, remembering Lilly's arms around his neck, her giggles, her bright eyes. What a god-awful way for a little girl to die, screaming for her daddy from inside a burning house. And Logan couldn't help her. He couldn't help her!

He let the tears come, aching for his old family. *Not Elizabeth, too*, he vowed. He prayed for the strength and wit to get rid of Chad Krieger and his men tomorrow night. All he had to do was remember MaryAnne and Lilly…and now Elizabeth. Thinking of them would give him the resolve he'd need to go after several men at once with no fear of the consequences. Men like that had to die, law or no law.

He heard the soft padding of a horse's hooves, somewhere in the darkness.

"Hello there!" someone called out. "May I join your fire?"

Why did the voice sound familiar? Logan grabbed

his rifle and rolled off his bedroll into the darkness. He was still fully dressed except for his boots, and his gun was still strapped around his hips. He knew the danger out there and wasn't taking any chances. "Who is it?" he called out, wiping away the tears he'd just shed over his wife and daughter.

"I might ask the same. Couldn't see you all that good by the light of the fire. I'm just a man headed east and thought maybe I could get a cup of coffee from you, maybe a little food."

This was an odd time of night for a man to be out riding. And where had he heard that voice?

"I'm in no mood to share. Ride on."

"Well now, mister, that's not very hospitable."

"I don't *feel* hospitable," Logan answered. "Get going!"

"Your voice sounds familiar. Might you be Logan Best?"

Logan hesitated. The man knew his name! "I told you to ride on." He heard the sound of a saddle squeaking, the sound of spurs on the ground. The man had dismounted. "I don't think I will," came his voice from the darkness.

Logan backed farther into the shadows but walked quietly over the thick prairie grass closer to the voice, glad his boots were off. He could walk with no sound.

"If you're Logan Best," the man told him, staying beyond the light of the fire, "you'll die either tonight or tomorrow in Hays City. And Chad Krieger and me and the rest of us will fuck that English woman till she's limp as a dishrag. Fact is, it would be better to keep you alive so you can watch."

"Who are you?"

"You don't recognize my voice, Logan?"

The air hung silent. Logan thanked God he'd sent Elizabeth away.

"Where is the woman anyway? You been fuckin' her yourself, Logan? Maybe she's already all used up, and all you're after is her money to keep for yourself. How was she, Logan? You're damn lucky she didn't blow your guts out like she did Robert Alexander's. She's a whore and a murderess, so why are you protecting her?"

Logan did not reply. He quietly crept closer to the voice.

"You must have a soft spot for women," the man continued. "I hear every whore in three states knows you."

Logan's eyes adjusted to the darkness, and he knew his tracker had the disadvantage of looking toward the fire. It would take his eyes longer to adjust if he turned away from the light of the flames. Logan could make out his outline now.

"You don't remember meetin' me up in Pueblo, do you?" the man said. "You got into quite a gunfight there with two or three wanted men. You even had a beer with me afterward—me and Hank Crest. Remember? Me and Hank thought back then how famous we'd be if we had the reputation of shootin' Logan Best. I aim to have that reputation all on my own…tonight. Then Galen and the rest of the boys can rest easy and go find that pretty little gal you've been travelin' with."

Galen Hawk. So, Galen and Hank Crest were

running with Chad Krieger now. If Logan could get the best of Galen, it would be one less man to go after in Hays City. What the hell was he doing out here instead of in town? He must have been a lookout for Chad Krieger.

Logan still did not answer. He didn't want to give away his position. He could see Galen even better now. The idiot was still watching the fire, crouching around it and apparently thinking Logan was still just across from it. The man kept his gun aimed in that direction. Logan raised his rifle and cocked it.

Galen whirled.

Logan fired, deliberately aiming for the man's belly. It took a man longer to die from a belly wound. Galen went down but fired back, little sparks of fire glowing from the end of his six-gun every time he shot it. By then Logan had hit the ground. One bullet whizzed past his ear…too damn close. The other shots went awry.

"Where are you, Logan, you sonofabitch! How'd you get behind me?"

"Because you're fucking stupid," Logan answered. He stepped into the light of the fire and dragged Galen closer. The man screamed with pain, and Logan proceeded to make it worse by stepping on his belly. "How many are there, Galen?"

"You bastard! You belly-shot me!"

"How many?"

"Ride into Hays City…and find out for yourself, you…sonofabitch! Chad Krieger and his men are waitin' for you…all over town. They'll put so many bullets in you…you'll look like…one of them strainers women use…to take the water off their food!"

Logan stepped harder, and Galen's screams echoed out across the prairie. "Give me an answer, and I'll put you out of your misery," Logan growled. "Why in hell are you riding with the likes of Chad Krieger? Just to fuck innocent women?"

"Please! Stop!"

"Chad Krieger has plans for Miss Elizabeth Baylor. I'm here to *spoil* those plans. Now, answer my questions. Otherwise, I can find ways to make you scream all night. How many are there?" He laid the barrel of his rifle against the man's stomach near the wound. "I don't have a lot of patience, Galen."

"No, don't! Don't!"

Logan thought about MaryAnne...and about what these men intended to do to Elizabeth...his beautiful, innocent, trusting Elizabeth. He fired again.

The night sky was filled with Galen Hawk's screams. "Kill me, you sonofabitch!" he begged.

"After you tell me what I need to know."

Galen spit up blood, and his next scream was so hideous Logan almost felt sorry for him. "Seven! There's seven more...besides me. Plus two more men Chad hired to help us. They're...spread out...all over town. I was supposed to...watch for you."

Logan pressed with his foot again.

"No!" Galen screamed.

It was a good thing Elizabeth wasn't here. This would be too hard for her to watch. She might even change her mind about marrying him. "Locations," he barked.

"I...don't know. All...over. Only one I know for sure is...Bill...Bill Dern. He's waiting at the train station…in the telegraph office. And Hank Crest… he's at the livery. That's…the only positions…I know for sure. I swear."

"Bill Dern? I've been looking for that bastard for months!" Logan told him. "Looks like I'll kill two birds with one stone. There's a bounty on Bill." He stepped on Galen's wound again, enjoying the man's screams. Logan shook his head. "You always were pretty stupid, Galen. You should have ridden right back to Hays City once you spotted me instead of thinking you could take me."

"I figured…maybe it wasn't you…'cuz I didn't see…the woman."

"Do you really think I'd put her in that kind of danger? Risk letting the likes of you get your hands on her?" Logan placed the rifle against Galen's forehead. "Thanks for the information."

He pulled the trigger, then stepped back and laid the rifle aside. He brought the man's horse forward, bent down, and pulled Galen's body up. He was a big man and not easy to lift, but Logan managed to lean down and maneuver the man over his shoulder. He straightened and slung Galen's body over the horse. With the rope on the horse's saddle, he tied Galen's feet and ankles together so the body was on tight.

Most horses tended to head back to where they came from and join other horses they were used to being around, so Logan turned the horse in the direction of Hays City and slapped its rump. "Get going!" he yelled. He shot off his rifle. "Hah! Hah!"

The horse took off.

That should give Chad and his men second thoughts,

Logan thought. He felt the wetness of Galen's blood on his shirt. *Guess I'd better change these clothes.*

No more worries about Elizabeth right now, and no more tears and sentimental thoughts about MaryAnne and Lilly. Lady Elizabeth Baylor had hired him to do a job, and he would damn well do it. From here on he was just Logan Best, bounty hunter.

FORTY-FOUR

Elizabeth looked around the kitchen area of the Bueter's large cabin.

So, this was how she might live if she married Logan. He'd promised much better than this, but right now, just being with him was all that mattered to her. The cabin was made of split logs, the floor of wide, wooden planks. A colorful, braided rug lay in front of a big, stuffed chair that was Lawrence's favorite.

Florence Bueter had told her this was much finer than many other settler's homes, some of which were no more than dugouts in the side of a hill or built completely from square-cut chunks of sod.

They have to hang sheets under the ceiling to catch dirt and insects, Florence had told her. *Most have dirt floors. My Lawrence brought these logs all the way out here from a saw mill several miles away where there are enough trees to cut for such things. Before this, we, too, lived in a sod house.*

Elizabeth found it amazing that a woman could live with dirt floors and walls. She'd slept sunken into a feather mattress on a handmade wooden bed last night—Clarence's bed. She'd learned that all three boys slept in the main room and their parents slept in a loft. The whole house wouldn't even fill the entire kitchen in Jonathan's home back in London. And there were no servants, no cooks or maids or laundresses. Florence Bueter did everything herself: the baking and canning, making and mending clothes, scrubbing dirty clothes in a tub outside. She now knew what a washboard was and had actually used it. Florence beat rugs and planted and picked vegetables, killed and plucked chickens, even hunted at times. And she helped Lawrence with the farming. She'd talked about how she had more help every year because *the boys are growing and taking on more responsibilities*.

So, a big family helped. Elizabeth didn't mind that part. She wanted to give Logan as many children as he wanted, but she wasn't sure about being able to do all the other things. Last night, Florence had sat up half the night mending. This morning, she'd cooked ham in a black fry pan that had legs on it to keep it out of the coals and ashes. Elizabeth had learned such a pan was called a spider. It had a very long handle so Florence could turn the meat with a fork that had an equally long handle, both of which kept her from getting too close to the fire.

Now the woman was kneading bread on the home-made wooden kitchen table, using an extra piece of flat wood to set the dough on.

"So, you are in love with the gunman," the woman said aloud.

"He's not a gunman," Elizabeth answered. "He's a bounty hunter."

"Ah, but he is good with the guns," Florence answered in her strong German accent.

Elizabeth ached for Logan. "Yes. He is good with guns." She'd spent most of yesterday answering questions about how she came into her situation, and more questions about life in London, and what did being a "lady" mean, or a duke or a lord. The two Bueter boys who'd come home with them yesterday were enraptured with her, full of questions about life in a mansion in London, with maids and servants and fancy carriages and all. At times, Elizabeth felt a tiny longing for that life, but compared to the excitement she'd found in America, and the passion she'd found in Logan Best's arms, she could never go back now.

Still, could she manage a life like this one? It seemed Florence's work was never ending.

"Would you like to learn to knead bread?" Florence asked her.

"I…yes, I think I would."

"Come over here, and we will get started," Florence said.

Today, Elizabeth wore a blouse and her riding skirt. She didn't want to soil the simple, yellow paisley dress she'd packed. It had a lace-trimmed, square-cut neckline, and she'd brought only one slip, figuring she wouldn't need more than that. Too many clothes wouldn't fit, and since she had only the one dress, she wanted to save it in case something came up that she'd need to look extra nice for Logan. *Perhaps a wedding*, she thought. First Logan had to return—alive and well.

She tried to smooth the wrinkles in her blouse when she stood up from a nearby chair.

Florence smiled. "I can teach you how to iron out those wrinkles," she told Elizabeth. "And how to churn butter and make your own clothes, and how to cook over a hearth." She nodded toward a metal door at the side of the fireplace. "That is the oven where we will bake the bread. I can also show you how to make fruit pies and cakes. Would you like that? I do a little of all those things every day. Tomorrow I will wash clothes outside with a tub and scrubbing board. If you are still here, I can teach you that, too. I am sure you have never done these things."

Florence kept pounding and turning the dough as she spoke. She was a heavyset woman with big, strong hands. Elizabeth came around to stand beside her. Florence stopped for a moment to retrieve another kneading board, and she set it on the table in front of Elizabeth. "Put on the apron hanging over there on the wall," she told Elizabeth. "Then come and put flour on your hands."

Elizabeth obeyed. Florence took more dough from a big wooden bowl on the table and slapped it onto the extra kneading board. "Just watch me and do as I do," she said. "You need strong hands. I am not sure yours are strong enough."

Feeling challenged, Elizabeth took some flour from a big can on the table and sprinkled it onto the dough, then powdered her hands with it. She began pounding and turning the dough, following everything Florence did. They were the only two in the house this morning. Lawrence Bueter had announced this morning that the boys had spent so much time visiting and asking questions yesterday that they were far behind on their chores, especially with Clarence still gone. Elizabeth could tell Mrs. Bueter was worried about the older boy.

"Don't be concerned about Clarence," Elizabeth told her. "Logan would never let anything happen to him. I'm sure he's on his way home right now." *But where is Logan? Will he be shot down tonight?*

"Yes, I am hoping," Florence answered. "And you did not answer my question. You and Mr. Best were kissing in the barn, and you did not want him to go to town. Will you marry him when he returns?"

"Yes," Elizabeth said. "I am very much in love with him."

"He seems a man who lives with much danger. It will not be an easy life. You are young, and you know only a good life, with servants and money. What if you have to live like this? In a cabin, cooking over an open fire? Do you know *how* to cook?"

Elizabeth kept kneading, embarrassed to answer. She never thought it would bother her to not know how to do these menial things. "No," she finally said. "I will appreciate anything you can teach me."

Florence smiled. "It is a good life, Miss Baylor, once you are used to it. It is easier, of course, when you grow up with it. I was helping my mama cook when I was just a tiny girl. It is sad women like you are not taught such things. There could always be a time when you need to know for your own survival, especially in land like this."

"Oh, I have definitely learned that lesson. I have already learned how to make a camp on the open prairie, how to cook over a campfire, sleep on the grass. If I can do that, I can learn this, too. And I guess you could say I know how to make coffee and bacon over an open fire, and how to use a knife to open a can of beans."

Florence chuckled and turned to face her, a kindness showing in her brown eyes. "I think that the bounty hunter will make life easier for you than this. I saw much love in his eyes when he let you go with us. He will make sure you do not have to live quite this hard. He will not want to ruin your beautiful skin or make you do work that will spoil your slender hands. He knows how you lived, and that doing the things most settler women do would be hard for you. I think he will want you to know how to cook, but he will find a way to help you with other things."

Elizabeth wanted to cry with worry over Logan. She kept kneading the bread, wanting something to do that would help keep her from envisioning Logan in a wild shoot-out in Hays City. "He did promise a nice home and some help. If he gets my jewels and money back, we will be very well set."

"It is the man you want back, not your valuables. Am I right?" Florence returned to kneading the bread.

"Yes," Elizabeth told her.

"A woman will usually give up everything she loves for a man. That is just how things are."

"Yes, I suppose it is," Elizabeth answered.

The tears started coming then and dripped into the bread dough. Elizabeth stepped back, wiping her hands on her apron. "I'm so sorry," she told Florence. "I want to learn all this, but I'm so worried about Logan." Her tears came harder. and she sat back down in the chair near the fireplace.

Florence stopped her work and faced Elizabeth. "Mr. Best is a very able man, and he seems to have a plan," she said. "But if the worst happens, we will make sure you get wherever it is you want to go. We promised to look after you, and we will. But you should not cry. There are too many reasons to shed tears in this life, Miss Baylor, so save them for when you know you truly have a reason. Worry will not make things turn out the way you want. It will only make you even weaker when you must face reality, and you do not yet know what that reality might be. Think how happy Mr. Logan will be if he comes here and is able to eat some wonderful, fresh bread you baked yourself." She turned back to her work. "Come, finish kneading the bread. It will have to rise and be kneaded again several times before we bake it. While it is rising, I can tell you how to make the dough, and I will let you help cook our supper and learn to use the fireplace crane, and how to keep the fire where you want it—not too small, not too large. I will keep you very busy so there is no time to worry."

Elizabeth realized Florence was trying to find ways to help her through this. She thought about the snooty, gossiping friends she'd had back in London, who thought of nothing but outdoing one another in their jewels and attire to attract the most available bachelors. Mrs. Bueter would never understand such behavior. And Logan would never be attracted by fancy clothes and fluttering eyes. Bravery and resilience were what attracted him. Beauty without the help of face paint and fancy hairdos attracted him. And yes, she suspected that when he returned, he'd be thrilled to know she'd kneaded and baked the bread he was eating.

She began kneading the bread again.

"Have you ever peeled potatoes, Miss Baylor?"

"I'm afraid not."

"I will show you. You can peel some for our supper. They will be boiled in a wire basket. You just lift them out when they are done, and we can use the water they were cooked in for vegetables and meat. Out here, you learn to reuse cooking water and not throw it out. Water is not something to be wasted. And I will show you how to mash the potatoes. We will make gravy from meat drippings I save. Men love mashed potatoes and gravy. I am sure your bounty hunter would like that, too."

Elizabeth lifted the heavy wad of dough and turned it. "I hope I can remember all this."

"There now. You are already thinking about how to learn things instead of worrying, right?"

Elizabeth smiled. "Yes. Thank you."

"Clarence will be back later today, and we will know he delivered the note to Mr. Elsworth. Then you will know Logan will find help. He will be fine, Miss Baylor. Good will win over bad. It always does. And tonight, you will entertain us with more stories about what is like to live in mansions and go to grand balls. You have my sons excited and dreaming. And when Clarence gets here, he will be equally excited and full of questions. You are our entertainment, Miss Baylor. I hope you do not mind. We feel honored to have you here."

"Thank you. And I don't mind." Elizabeth pounded

the dough. How was she going to get through another night or two without sleeping in Logan's arms, not knowing what was happening to him? She decided she most certainly *could* live this way if it meant Logan Best coming back alive and well. She would do anything to have him in her bed every night.

She smiled at the thought of handing him a warm piece of homemade bread and telling him she'd baked it herself. Eating meals cooked and served by someone else seemed so frivolous now, so boring. Now here she was, helping a settler woman in the middle of Kansas, learning how to cook in a fireplace and to make the food they would eat. It was just another experience she'd once fantasized about but never thought would really happen. Her dime-novel life was becoming all too real. There wasn't much left when it came to living the reality of those little books.

The only thing left was for a royal "lady" from England to marry a "knight" of the American West and ride off into the sunset with him. Surely she would know that reality, too. It was like riding into one of those books and getting lost between the pages, never to be found again, except perhaps in one of those hand drawings that showed a muscular, Wild West cowboy carrying a fainting woman away on his horse.

I'll be that fainting woman, she thought with a smile.

FORTY-FIVE

BRENDA LAKE JUMPED NERVOUSLY WHEN SOMEONE tapped on the window behind her. She turned and gazed out, then quickly opened the window. "Logan Best! You really did come," she said as Logan climbed inside.

She leaned out and looked around before quickly closing the window and pulling curtains over it. She turned to Logan and threw her arms around him. "When I got your note, I was terrified for you! There's a whole gang of men in town looking for you." She stepped back and grasped his arms, talking quietly. "But I guess you know that. What on earth is going on? Those men say you have a woman with you. They're after both of you."

"It's a long story. Did you manage to get a couple of men together?"

"Yes. Dick Elsworth is waiting for me to signal him. I just have to set an oil lamp in the window and turn it way down. And the bartender downstairs is ready, too. Those filthy men came here three days ago and started fights and broke the place up pretty bad— broke the big mirror behind the bar."

Logan removed his hat and sat down in a chair at her dressing table. Brenda stood there in a gown and robe, looking plainer and older than he remembered because she wore no makeup. Her bleached hair hung long and straight.

"What about you?" he asked. "You okay?" It was then he noticed bruises on Brenda's face and arms. The light was so dim in the room, he hadn't seen them right away. "Shit!" He stood up and took her face in his hands. "Was it those same men who did this? How many are there?"

Brenda urged him to sit back down, then knelt in front of him. "It doesn't matter. This old gal has been the brunt of these things too many times to count, Logan Best. All that matters is you get rid of those men without getting yourself killed. They murdered Sheriff Bishop and his deputy, and they're holding poor Rebecca Peterman over at The Last Stop. She's the daughter of the couple who run a small restaurant in town. She's only sixteen. Somebody needs to kill them, Logan, so they can't do this anymore."

"That's why I'm here." Logan touched her bruises. "I'm sorry, Brenda. I've been trailing them. If I had gotten here sooner—"

"Don't be worrying about me. I just sure don't want to see you die. There's at least nine of them, Logan. Three are at The Last Stop. Two are hanging out on rooftops, and one is at the livery, figuring if you come by horseback you'll take your horses there when you arrive. There are two more who move around a lot, and one is over at the telegraph office waiting to see if you come in with the woman by train." She frowned. "Where *is* the woman?"

"I sent her someplace where she'll be safe. She's a young woman from London who got mixed up in all of this by trusting someone too much. They want *her*, and I'm not about to let them touch her with a twelve-foot pole."

Brenda studied his eyes. "Don't tell me you've grown attached to one of your clients."

Logan managed a grin in spite of the gravity of his situation. "Attached is the word, and not just emotionally."

Brenda shoved his shoulder. "Go on with you!"

"I'm going to marry her, but first I have to get through this mess."

Brenda shook her head. "She must be something."

"She is."

"My rough-and-tumble Logan Best—hooking up with a proper high-born lady from London! Now *there's* a good one for gossip." Brenda laughed and shook her head. "How did you get into town without being noticed?"

"I left my horse and gear tied a good half-mile away—figured I wouldn't be noticed if I snuck in at night with just my six-gun. I have just two hand guns, one in my holster and one behind my back. That likely won't be enough. Get word to Dick Elsworth. He needs to pretend to come visit you so I can talk to him about how he can help."

"Sure." Brenda grabbed an oil lamp and hurried over to set it in a front window. She turned down the wick and closed the curtains behind it. "I'll go downstairs and work my usual job," she told Logan. "I'll tell Max—that's the bartender—to find somebody else to tend bar and come up here to see what you want him to do." She touched his shoulder. "They're ready to help, Logan, but you're the real gunman. All Max and Dick know are hunting rifles, and they aren't used to using them on men."

"All I need is for them to bring down two or three of them. I can take care of the rest." He removed his boots and stood up. "You get word to Max. I'm going back out the window and pay a visit to the one at the telegraph office."

"Logan, what if they see you? You're a big man."

"I can be invisible when I want to be. And I took off my boots. A man makes a lot less noise with his boots off."

"Where's the woman who's the cause of all this? What's her name? If something happens to you, she should be told."

Logan felt a stab at his heart. He never thought he could be so much in love again. "She's Lady Elizabeth Baylor, and she's staying with some farmers about ten or twelve miles south of here. Bueter is their name."

"I know of them." Brenda smiled. "Titled, is she? That sure doesn't sound like the kind of woman you would marry. 'Lady' Elizabeth. I'll bet you've made sure she's no lady when she's around you."

Logan grinned. "She's beautiful. And she *is* a lady, in every way. But she's also mine, and when this is over, I'm going to find a preacher to marry us. We're as different as night and day, but we'll find a way to make it work." Logan walked to a second window on a darker side of the room. "Get those men over here. We need to make plans. I'll go take care of the one in the telegraph office."

"A gunshot will bring them all running," Brenda warned. "They're already edgy, because one of them they left out on the prairie to watch for you came back into town, his dead body thrown over his horse." She put her hands on her hips. "That was you, wasn't it?"

"It was."

"My God, Logan, he was shot to pieces, part of his guts hanging out!"

"Just part of the job."

Brenda looked him over. "Remind me to always stay on your good side."

Logan couldn't help a smile. He leaned down and kissed a bruise on her cheek. "I'd never lay a hand on a woman," he said. "Thanks for your help. I figured you'd know what to do if you got that note. If I can take care of the one at the telegraph office and at the livery, that's two more out of the way, and we're down to six. If your friends can get a couple more, I only have to deal with four of them."

Brenda's eyes teared a little, and she reached up to touch his face. "You be careful, Logan Best. I'll cry a river if something happens to you."

He grasped her wrist and squeezed it. "Nothing is going to happen. Get those men up here with their rifles. I'll be back." He walked to the second window and opened it. "Is there a porch roof under this window, too?"

"Yes."

Logan ducked out the window.

Brenda put a hand to her chest, hurrying over to the window and looking out again. She could see nothing. In the saloon below, a man hired to play piano plunked away at a bawdy tune, and men talked among themselves. The whole town was in an uproar, yet everyone was terrified to do anything about Chad Krieger and his vicious gang.

But not Logan Best, she thought. *He's not afraid of a damn thing.* She felt sorry for the English woman if she should have to tell her Logan Best wasn't coming back for her. He'd never said it outright, but she had no doubt Logan had already branded her in the only way a man like that branded a woman. He'd be easy to fall in love with, and the young Miss Elizabeth Baylor was likely totally smitten.

"God be with you, Logan," she said quietly, wondering if God even listened to a woman like her, or cared about a man who killed other men for money.

FORTY-SIX

BILL DERN SAT IN THE TELEGRAPHER'S CHAIR, HIS HEAD hanging back, his mouth open, the room filled with the sound of his heavy snoring. Old Hugh Bell slept on a cot nearby. He'd been ordered not to leave the telegraph office and to read aloud every message sent and received in case there was news of Logan Best and the English woman.

Both men jumped awake when the door suddenly burst open. Before Hugh could blink, a big man had put a gun deep into the folds of Bill Dern's beer belly and fired it. The shot was muffled by the outlaw's belly fat.

Hugh sat there with his mouth open while Bill made grizzly choking sounds and stared wide-eyed at the shooter.

"Logan…Best…how did you…" His body slumped sideways. Logan pulled him out of the chair and dragged him to a corner of the room. "Let him bleed to death," he told Hugh. "And do me a favor. Send a telegram to Sheriff Adam White in Abilene. Tell him Sheriff Bishop has been murdered by the men Logan

Best was hunting and that Best will take care of things. Tell him to send someone to clean up the mess and help bring some law and order back to Hays City. He'll know what to do."

"You're that bounty hunter they've been waiting for?"

"I am."

"There's an awful lot of 'em."

"I'll manage."

Logan went back out the door, and Hugh stared into the darkness. Stunned, he got up and walked to the chair to send the message. He grimaced at blood on the chair. The back rungs were blown out, the bloody pieces lying several feet away.

"Jesus," Hugh muttered.

Bill Dern made an ugly, groaning sound, and a pool of blood began growing under his body. Logan Best had said to let him bleed to death. Hugh Bell decided to oblige the man. He sat down at the telegraph.

Logan made his way to the livery. The big doors in front were closed. Brenda said one of Krieger's men was waiting there to see if Logan showed up. The man probably also slept, never figuring Logan would show up so late at night. Thanks to Galen Hawk, Logan already knew the man in the stable should be Hank Crest.

He snuck around back and looked through a window but saw nothing. The window had no glass. It was just a cutout for air, which was ripe with the smell

of manure. A closed-up livery smelled pretty bad…
and fast. Logan figured there was likely a window on
the other side for a cross breeze. There was too much
light at this window, so he made his way around to
the other side. His eyes adjusted to the dark, and he
found the second window and climbed through it.
He landed in a horse stall. The horse nickered, and
Logan put a hand over its nose. "It's okay, boy," he
whispered soothingly into the horse's ear.

"Who's there?" someone called out.

Logan said nothing. By the dim light of the
lantern left lit, he could see the man. He stood in
the middle of the livery, hat off, rubbing tired eyes.
His gun was drawn. "Who's there?" he called again,
turning in a circle.

Hank Crest. Logan recognized him now. He
vaguely remembered that Hank and another man he
now knew as Galen Hawk, had challenged him after
the shoot-out in Colorado. They'd changed their
minds and had a beer with him instead.

So, you're running with Chad Krieger and his bunch.
Logan quietly lifted a horseshoe from where it hung
over a nail on a nearby post. Taking aim, he flung
it, hitting Hank in the head. The man grunted and
went down.

Logan opened the stall door and walked out, taking
Hank's gun and tossing it aside. He took his hunting
knife from its sheath on his belt and leaned close.
Hank seemed to be out.

"Sorry, but I can't take the chance of you coming
around before I'm finished with the others," Logan
said. He sliced his knife across the man's throat,

wiped it off on Hank's shirtsleeve, and put it back in its sheath.

He turned and left through a back door and made his way in the darkness back to the Horseshoe. He climbed onto a barrel he'd used earlier to reach the edge of the porch roof, then pulled himself up and climbed into the second window of Brenda's room. He heard someone cock a rifle and saw two men standing there, aiming guns at him.

"It's Logan," Brenda told them.

Logan climbed the rest of the way inside and nodded to Dick Elsworth.

"This is Max, from downstairs," Brenda said, indicating the second man. He was big and bald and looked like the kind of man someone wouldn't want to cross.

"I appreciate what you two are doing," Logan said. "The one at the telegraph office is dead. So is the one at the livery."

Both men looked at him in surprise. "How in hell—"

"No time to worry about that," Logan interrupted. "Do either of you know where the ones are who Chad Krieger planted on the rooftops?"

"Everybody knows where they are," Dick Elsworth said. "They're all scared to walk down the street for fear they'll get shot by one of them."

"One is above The Last Stop," Max said. "The other one is down the street over a supply store."

"What about the two from town they paid to help them?"

"They chickened out," Max answered. "Some of the townspeople cornered them over by the train station and told them if they helped the bastards who killed Sheriff Bishop, they'd damn well hang them. Told them earlier today to get out of town or else, so they left on the next train."

"Good."

"Logan, there's blood on your shirtsleeve and on the front of your shirt," Brenda told him.

Logan looked down. Blood must have squirted onto him when he slit Hank Crest's throat. "It's not mine," he answered. He faced Dick and Max. "I need you two to sneak out of here somehow and get yourselves into position to shoot the ones on the rooftops. Do you think you can do it?"

"If it means getting rid of those bastards, we can," Dick declared. "They've got Rebecca Peterman over at The Last Stop, Logan. If you go charging in there, she could get hurt."

"I intend to call those who are inside the saloon out into the street. They'll likely leave her inside when I do that."

"Logan! There will be at least three of them, and they've been waiting for you," Brenda reminded him. "They're scared of you, so they won't give you a fair chance. They'll come out shooting."

"I know that." Logan pulled out his six-gun and checked it to be sure every chamber had a bullet in it. "You two go ahead. I'll give you ten minutes to get into position. It won't be easy, because it's dark. Try to draw the rooftop men into standing up or hurrying down to help Krieger and the others once the shooting starts. I just need you to keep a bead on them and take a shot when you're able."

"We will." Max reached out to shake Logan's hand. "Good luck."

"Thanks. I'll need it." Logan shook his hand, and the two men left, heading down a back stairway. Logan headed for the window again.

"Logan!" Brenda called to him. She walked closer. "Does your English lady know you're a crazy man?"

Logan grinned. "She knows." He ducked out the window and headed through a back alley to The Last Stop, then leaned against the back wall and waited, giving the other two men time to track down the men on the rooftops. He could hear talking and laughing inside, and a girl crying.

That was the trigger. He saw MaryAnne again, bloody and crying, giving him that helpless look. Any worry he'd had about making this work left him. All thoughts of Elizabeth left him. He was filled now with one need, and that was to draw out Chad Krieger and the other two inside and kill them for hurting the girl.

He started to head for the street, but something slammed into the right side of his head, sending him sprawling into the alley. He felt someone pull his gun from its holster and yank his second gun from the back of his belt. "You must be that fucking Logan Best!" someone growled.

Logan scrambled to gather his thoughts. He heard a gun being cocked as he lifted his head slightly and saw a bloody brick lying nearby.

"Thought you'd sneak up on us, did you?" came the same voice. "You didn't think about maybe one of us would need to come out back to take a piss? Stand up and face me!"

Logan managed to get to his feet. He could feel blood running down the side of his face. He had to wipe some of it out of his right eye to see better. There stood a tall, skinny man with long, blond hair. He was aiming Logan's own gun at him. *Chad Krieger!*

"Where's the woman, Logan?" the man sneered.

Logan noticed Krieger stood there in his long johns—no gun of his own. The bastard had probably just raped the girl inside, or he'd decided to undress and get some sleep. Logan made no reply.

"Answer me, you sonofabitch!" Krieger said. "Or I'll take you inside, and me and my men will do things to you that'll *make* you talk!"

Logan knew he had to be quick, but the wound on the side of his head was making his thoughts swim and his ear ring so badly that Krieger's voice sounded muffled. He had no choice but to take this skinny bastard by surprise. Risking getting shot point-blank, he dived at Chad's thighs. A gun went off, and Logan felt a sting in his left side. He paid no attention. He slammed Krieger to the ground and rammed a fist straight into his nose. Krieger cried out, and Logan kept hitting him, smashing his nose and knocking out some of his teeth. All he could think of was the men who'd so horribly abused MaryAnne and the possibility that these men could do the same to Elizabeth. He kept up the beating until someone shouted.

"Hey! It's Chad! Somebody has him down!"

Logan quickly grabbed his gun out of Krieger's hand and fired it into Krieger's head. A bullet whizzed past near his ear, and Logan whirled and put a bullet in a man who'd run out the back door at the sound of gunfire.

There came more voices then. Shouts. Men running. Shots fired. Logan got to his feet and ran inside The Last Stop. Men scattered, all but one, who stood there staring at him. The man's gun was drawn. He raised his hands at the sight of Logan facing him, bloody, a gun in hand.

"Don't shoot!" he begged, dropping his gun.

There came more gunshots outside, and Logan knew Max and Dick were shooting at the men who'd been on the rooftops. Apparently, one or both had missed, because the shooting continued. Suddenly, a man ran inside the saloon, panting and bleeding. "Where's Chad?" he yelled.

"He's out back," Logan said flatly.

The man who'd run inside looked at him in surprise, eyes widening. "You Logan Best?"

Logan raised his six-gun. "I am. And you'll never get your hands on Elizabeth Baylor!" He fired, opening a hole in the man's forehead. The man fell, and the first man started to run. Logan fired, shooting him in the back.

Everything became a blur then as the blow to Logan's head began to take its toll. He wasn't even sure what he'd been hit with, but dizziness overwhelmed Logan, and he felt himself going down. He heard shouts of "Get him! Let's hang the bastard!" Men ran out of the saloon. In the deep recesses of his mind, Logan figured one of the rooftop men was still alive and captured.

There came a couple more gunshots. Someone

picked Logan up. He felt himself being carried down the street and up some steps. They laid him on a bed. He heard Brenda's voice.

"Logan, you'll be okay."

I have to be okay. I have to get back to Elizabeth. "Suitcase," he muttered, not sure if he was thinking the words or speaking them. "They have...a suitcase. Elizabeth's jewels...banknotes..."

"We'll find it, honey," Brenda told him.

Everything went black.

FORTY-SEVEN

ELIZABETH SAT ON THE PORCH IN FRONT OF THE BUETER cabin, watching the horizon while peeling potatoes. She looked down at her hands. They were red, and her palms had blisters on them from helping Florence Bueter churn butter the day before. She was actually proud of those blisters. She'd never dreamed so much work went into preparing food. Back in London, she'd taken all of it for granted. Her meals had just appeared in front of her when it was time to eat. Now she knew that while she was in her room being pampered by a personal maid so she could dress properly for a meal, the kitchen help was slaving away *preparing* those meals, and likely for menial wages. She'd never asked Jonathan what he paid the help.

Learning so many things helped keep her mind off of what could be unbearable news. It had been five full days since Logan had left her and headed for Hays City. She refused to think the worst. She would fall apart and never recover if she allowed those thoughts, but it was becoming more and more difficult to think positively.

Lawrence had promised that if Logan didn't show up today, he and Clarence would ride into Hays City tomorrow to learn what had happened. He refused to take Elizabeth with him in case Chad Krieger and his gang were still looking for her. *I promised Mr. Best I would watch out for you,* he told her, *and now you have become like a daughter to us.* Elizabeth thought the Bueters were some of the kindest people she'd known, and she thanked God they'd come along when they did.

Today she wore the yellow dress she'd been saving, wanting to look as pretty as possible for Logan if this was the day he returned. Clarence had come home the day after he'd ridden into Hays City. He'd told them there were men with guns all over the place. He'd not seen Logan anywhere on his ride home.

A tightness gripped Elizabeth's stomach every time she considered what looked more and more like the truth. Logan wasn't coming back. He would never hold her again. A good man had died for her valuables...valuables she didn't care about anymore. She fought tears as she kept peeling the potatoes, forcing herself to stay busy. And "busy" was an understatement for a woman who lived in this lawless, lonely land.

She dipped another potato into a bucket of water to wash it off and put it into a pan with the others, then looked up at the sound of horse's hooves. Clarence was riding Suzy hard toward the house from a distant field where he'd been hoeing weeds. He charged up to the porch. "He's coming!" he said excitedly. "Logan is coming, and he's got people with him!"

Elizabeth set her knife and the potatoes aside and jumped up. "Give me your horse!" she told Clarence.

"Yes, ma'am." Grinning, he jumped down from Suzy and handed her the reins.

"Should I head north? Is that where he's coming from?" Elizabeth asked.

"Yes, ma'am. Go out toward the field where I was working, and you'll see him coming! From here it's a low hill, so you can't see him yet."

Elizabeth pulled Suzy to the porch steps so she could climb onto the familiar horse easily. She heard Clarence running into the house and yelling to his mother that Logan Best was back. After quickly arranging the skirt of her dress to cover her legs, Elizabeth kicked Suzy's sides and headed for the field Clarence had indicated. In minutes, she saw them—three men riding horses, and another man and what appeared to be a woman in a buggy, all coming toward the farm.

"Logan!" she yelled. She recognized Jasper's buckskin color and black mane, but even if Logan had been on a different horse, she would have known that the man in front of those coming was Logan. No one sat a horse as tall and sure as he did.

She kicked Suzy into a harder run, and in minutes, she reached him. She didn't even look at the people behind him. She saw only Logan. One side of his face was black and blue, from his temple down to his jaw, and there was a deep cut on that cheek.

"Logan, you're hurt!"

"Right now, that's the last thing I care about," he said rather sadly.

Elizabeth felt alarm at the look in his eyes—a look she couldn't quite read. He seemed so hesitant. He winced with obvious pain as he slowly dismounted and told the others to go on ahead to the Bueter cabin.

One of the men on horseback winked at Logan. "You were right, Logan. She's a looker!" He tipped his hat to Elizabeth and rode on with the others.

Logan walked around the other side of Jasper. Elizabeth quickly jumped down from Suzy as Logan came back around and handed something out to her.

Elizabeth gasped. "The suitcase!"

"It's all there—your jewels and your banknotes. You are now a very wealthy woman again."

Elizabeth felt the tears coming as she reached out and took the suitcase, not even caring about looking inside. Logan had kept his promise as a bounty hunter to find her valuables. She dropped the suitcase and met his gaze. In his eyes, she saw something that was almost like the look of a lost little boy.

"You have your money now," he told her. "And you need to think twice about marrying me."

"*What?*" Elizabeth couldn't believe her ears.

"I just want you to be sure, Elizabeth. Look at the things in that suitcase and give it some thought. When I saw the money and the jewelry in there, it hit me just how rich you really are...and titled and educated and...beautiful. You belong with a doctor or a lawyer or a banker or—"

Elizabeth choked back tears. "Logan Best! How can you even *think* I wouldn't want to marry you!" she interrupted. "I *belong* to you now. I gave my love and my heart and my body to you, trusting that you loved me and would make me your wife. And if you don't hug me right now, I'll…I'll…I don't know what I'll do!" The tears came then.

A slight grin showed as Logan studied her lovingly. "Look at you. You look like a real pioneer woman, apron and all."

"I *am* a real pioneer woman!" she blurted out, lifting her apron to wipe at her tears. "Mrs. Bueter taught me so many things, Logan. Look!" She showed him her blisters. "I got these from churning butter."

He broke into a bigger smile. "Don't hug me too hard. I took a bullet in my left side. Just a flesh wound, but it bruised a rib," he said.

Elizabeth's tears came harder as she reached out for him. Logan pulled her into his arms and buried his face in her hair. "I wasn't sure, Elizabeth. Now that you have your things—My God, Elizabeth, there is fifty thousand dollars' worth of banknotes in that suitcase, let alone the jewels!"

"I don't care about that!" she said, burying her face against his chest and breathing in the scent of him. "You can throw them in the creek if you want. Logan, I've learned how to knead and bake bread, how to churn butter and peel potatoes and make stew and cook over a fireplace." She looked up at him, and he kissed her tears. "I even helped Florence clean a rabbit! I just want to stay with you and be your wife. I love you. I was dying inside at the thought that you might never come back. I'll do anything I need to do for us to be together." She touched his bruised face. "Oh, Logan, what happened?"

"We'll save that for when I get to the house and

can rest. Let's just say Chad Krieger and his men are all dead. A couple of them were hanged by the townspeople. I would have been back sooner, but this blow to the side of my face left me so dizzy for a couple of days that I couldn't stand up for ten seconds without falling down again. Plus, I have stitches in my side. I had to wait till I could ride a horse before I could get back to you."

Their gazes held. "Tell me you love me, Logan, and you still want to marry me."

He put a hand to the side of her face. "You know damn well I do. I brought a preacher with me and his wife. I even got you a ring. It's just a plain gold band for now, but I'll get you a prettier one when we get to Denver."

"A plain gold band is good enough for me."

Logan shook his head. "You are Lady Elizabeth Baylor. You deserve better. Maybe we can have a ring made from the stones of some of your jewels. I'll bet your mother would like that."

"Oh, Logan, that's a wonderful idea!"

"The men who came with me are from Hays City. They wanted to see the beautiful lady from England." He pushed back some loose strands of her hair. "And she *is* beautiful, even with her hair plain and not an ounce of color on her face or one piece of jewelry."

"And if you don't kiss me right now, I'll die!" Elizabeth told him.

His smile moved into a bigger grin. He gently grasped the sides of her face and leaned down, meeting her mouth in a sweet, hungry kiss that suggested much more to come once they were married. Elizabeth

reached around his neck and returned the kiss with
fervor. Both of them could taste her tears. In spite of
the pain in his side, Logan drew her closer, keeping
one hand at the back of her neck while he grasped her
bottom with his other hand and pressed her against him.

"I can't wait to be inside of you again," he groaned
next to her ear.

"It's all I've thought about since you rode away
from me the other day," Elizabeth wept.

"Don't cry. It's over now." He kissed her hair. "All
the ugly stuff you went through is over too, and I have
to accept the same thing about MaryAnne. I want a
life with you, Lady Elizabeth. I want to make things
nice for you, and I want you to have my babies. And
I'll damn well enjoy helping *make* those babies."

"I might get fat."

"I don't care if you get as big as a house. You'll be
home to greet me every time I come back from whatever my job requires, and you'll be in my bed every
night that I'm home. I'll never get enough of you."

They kissed again, a sweet, long, deep kiss of
promise.

"If we were alone and I wasn't in all this pain, I'd
lay you down right here in the grass and make love to
you," he told her softly.

Elizabeth looked up at him again. "Let's go back to
that old barn for our honeymoon."

Logan frowned. "That's not good enough for your
wedding night."

"We don't have any choice. We certainly can't
gambol in the Bueter's bed in their loft. We'll be
making far too much noise."

Logan chuckled and kissed her eyes. "*Gambol?* Where do you come up with those crazy words?"

"It means—you know—cavort—frolic."

He grinned and shook his head. "Jesus, woman, can't you ever talk in normal words? Why not just say 'have sex'?"

Elizabeth kissed the hairs of his chest that showed through his open shirt. "That sounds so risqué."

"See? You're doing it again."

"Risqué means naughty."

"Oh, I intend to be *very* naughty, Miss Baylor, in spite of a sore rib and jaw."

She reached up and ran her fingers into his hair. "I'll be gentle, Mr. Best."

He smiled wickedly. "I can't promise the same."

He kissed her again, a beautiful, deep kiss of true adoration. Elizabeth thought about how she'd left London a spoiled, pampered, innocent, ridiculously trusting young "lady," wanting to experience the American West. Now here she was in the middle of Kansas, and she'd realized nearly all the things she'd read about, including finding her handsome knight. The only difference was, his horse wasn't white. It was roan colored. His weapons were not swords and shields. They were rifles and six-guns. And he didn't wear armor, or dress in a suit and top hat like a duke or a lord. He wore a wide gun belt packed with cartridges and a six-gun, dusty boots and pants, a leather vest, and a scarf around his neck…and a wide-brimmed cowboy hat. And he was just as grand as any highborn English man.

There was no going back now. Not ever.

EPILOGUE

April 1871

SOMEONE KNOCKED AT THE DOOR OF THE WELL-groomed white house with green shutters. It was surrounded by a white picket fence. Small, freshly planted rose bushes decorated the inside of the fence, but there was only sand and gravel for a lawn, because water in Denver was still much too hard to come by to waste it trying to keep grass alive.

Denver was still growing, wildly sprawled out below and in need of city planning. In spite of its small size, the home of Logan and Elizabeth Best was one of the nicer dwellings above the town, although some of the "new rich" were building Victorian mansions at even higher elevations.

"Shall I get the door, Mrs. Best?"

The question came from Lizzy Tate, the wife of a miner. Lizzy needed the extra money she made cleaning Logan and Elizabeth's house once a week and coming in daily to cook and to help with little William, Logan and Elizabeth's new son.

"No. I will," Elizabeth said. She pulled little William from her breast, where he'd fallen asleep during a feeding. She'd named the boy in memory of her brother, whom she would miss the rest of her life.

"Your husband said to always be careful who you let in because of his job, Mrs. Best," Lizzy reminded her.

"It's okay. Logan will be back any minute. He just rode down to the tobacco store to get more cigarettes." Elizabeth rose from the breakfast table and handed the baby to Lizzy. "Put him down, will you?"

Lizzy took William, and Elizabeth buttoned her dress and headed for the door, where she first pulled back a lace curtain to see who was there. Instantly, she gasped and opened the door. "Jonathan!"

There stood her older brother. He removed his top hat and looked around the tidy living room of the frame house with disdain. A buggy rattled by in the street. When Elizabeth glanced at it, she noticed a much fancier carriage parked at her gate. Of course, Jonathan would put up with nothing less than the best rental carriage Denver had to offer.

She looked up at Jonathan and almost stepped back because of the look in his eyes as he came inside.

She just stared at him a moment, in shock. Jonathan looked her over rather scathingly, as though she were no more than one of his servants.

"So, this is what you've become."

Elizabeth closed the door. "Become?"

Jonathan looked around the living room again, frowning as though it were a poor man's hovel. "Do you know what I have gone through trying to find you?" he asked in a bitter tone.

Elizabeth folded her arms and shrugged. "I don't really care, Jonathan. You didn't need to find me at all." They both walked farther inside. "Are you and Caroline all right?"

"We are both well. I was very upset to hear about William, of course."

"Why? *You* kicked him out of the house, remember?"

Jonathan frowned. "I certainly didn't mean for him to *die*! If it weren't for your ridiculous dream of coming to America, he would still be alive."

"You don't know that! Any number of things can happen to a man—or woman—in London, just the same as here in America." Elizabeth refused to let him intimidate her. "At least he believed in my dream. He had a *heart*, Jonathan. You have one physically, but you never had one spiritually."

"Still the obstinate little brat, aren't you?"

Elizabeth closed her eyes and shook her head. "Why are you even here, Jonathan? It's quite a trip to Denver, Colorado, all the way from London, England. You don't truly care what happened to me after I left, so why are you *really* here?"

Little William started to cry, and Jonathan glanced at the doorway to the downstairs bedroom.

"That's your nephew," Elizabeth told him. "As I'm sure you know by now, since you did whatever investigating you did to find me, I am married to Logan Best. He was a bounty hunter who saved my life and my virtue when my fortune fell into the wrong hands after I got here. He's a U.S. Marshal now."

"I know the whole story. When you murdered Sir

Robert Alexander, it made all the papers in London eventually. Plus, the sordid details. You can imagine the scandal, learning you were alone in a Pullman car with that man! Things don't get much more private than that. And then you turned around and ran off with a complete stranger. A *bounty* hunter, no less, a man who kills other men for money."

Elizabeth couldn't help a smile. "It didn't happen anything like you are thinking. But you can believe whatever you want, Jonathan. Logan Best is the bravest, most skilled man I've ever known, and he got my jewels and my money back for me. He risked his life doing it, let alone risking it more than once on the trip we took to find those men. He's a good man, and we fell in love and married. This is our home. We could have a mansion, but neither of us wants that. And I've never been happier. If that's what you came to find out, you have your answer. I am perfectly fine, and I am where I want to be. I'm glad to have seen you again, and I can't say I'm sorry for the scandal, because you could have avoided it if you had not abandoned your brother and sent him away."

Jonathan sighed and waved an arm around the room. "How can you live like this?"

"Because I am *loved*, truly *loved*. It's a wonderful feeling, Jonathan. You should try it some time. And I am married to a real man, one who knows how to take care of a woman and who appreciates her independence and strength. I'm not just something on an old man's arm, to be put on display by day and pawed over at night. I didn't marry for position and wealth. I married for love and nothing more."

"And nothing more is right. How can the pay a lawman gets out here satisfy you?"

"I have my own money, and we are spending it wisely. And Logan had quite a nest egg of his own when we married." She smiled. "As far as being satisfied, believe me, I am *very* satisfied."

Jonathan looked her over as though she were a harlot. "I cannot believe what you have become."

"I have become Mrs. Logan Best, a wife and a mother and even a homemaker. I know how to cook and sew, and I do my own cleaning when necessary. But Logan understands this new life isn't easy for me. He insisted I have a woman come in and help me with all those things, especially since I have a new baby to look after." She raised her chin with an air of confidence. "You still haven't told me the real reason you made the long trip to find me. But knowing you, I am guessing you don't care one whit about my well-being. You are after William's share of the estate. Money is the only thing that would make you do this."

Jonathan drew in his breath. "William is *dead*! That money belongs back in the estate."

"You'll not get one dime of it. After Tyler issued us that money, we went right to another solicitor and had a note drawn up in which William named me his beneficiary. I reciprocated. We didn't trust Tyler not to tell you about that part of it, because he's been in the family too long, so we used someone else. And most of the money is in a bank in Saint Louis. Denver is still a bit wild and lawless, and we don't trust putting too much money in a bank here yet."

Jonathan's dark eyes turned even darker. "William had no right—"

"It's *done*, Jonathan." Elizabeth wanted to cry at the realization he didn't give a damn about her or William. He was only after William's money. Other than the dreadful crimes Robert had been guilty of, Jonathan was not much different from the man when it came to a high opinion of himself and caring only about money and status. It gave her the shivers that she'd almost married such a man. "Don't you even want to see your nephew, Jonathan?" she asked.

Jonathan glared at her. "As far as I'm concerned, he's an illegitimate bastard. You lay with Robert Alexander like a harlot and then married a commoner, who, I am told, is not even educated and can barely read. And how do you know that child in there doesn't belong to Alexander?"

Elizabeth gasped at the suggestion. "Because I *killed* Robert before he could touch me. That boy belongs to my *husband*! How dare you accuse me of such crude behavior!"

The door opened then, and Logan walked in. He stood still a moment, other than removing his wide-brimmed hat and tossing it onto a chair. He glanced at Elizabeth. "What's going on here?"

Elizabeth looked up at Jonathan, wishing she could hit him. "Logan, this is my brother, from London." Elizabeth walked closer to Logan. "Jonathan, this is my husband, Logan Best."

Jonathan looked Logan over almost scornfully, his eyes resting on the marshal's badge on Logan's vest, then down to the wide gun belt and six-gun on his hips. Elizabeth could tell her brother had mixed emotions—thinking of Logan as a commoner, and yet a bit intimidated by Logan's size and weapons.

"So, you are the man-killing scoundrel who has soiled my sister's reputation!"

Elizabeth's jaw dropped at the remark, and she didn't need to touch Logan to know that every muscle in his body immediately tensed. "No," he answered, stepping a little closer to Jonathan. "I'm the man-killing scoundrel who fell in love with Elizabeth and *married* her—*legally*. This is my house, and Elizabeth sleeps in my bed and wears the ring I bought her—and she's given me a son. Her reputation is just fine, and I don't appreciate any man, brother or not, coming into my home and insulting my *wife*."

Elizabeth swallowed, knowing how easily riled Logan was. He deliberately put out his hand almost tauntingly. "Nice to meet you," Logan said coolly. "Since we are brothers-in-law, I will withhold myself from knocking your teeth right down your throat and instead, welcome you to our home. It's no damn mansion, but it's full of love, which I'm told can't be said about the Baylor estate in London."

Jonathan ignored Logan's outstretched hand. He let out a snicker of disgust as he turned back to Elizabeth. "You've lost your mind. This wild, lawless land has messed up your thinking and caused you to marry this…this brute of a man!"

Elizabeth stepped closer to her brother. "On the contrary, it made me think very clearly about what does and doesn't matter in life. And I would appreciate it if you shook hands with my husband and apologized for your insults. Logan Best is respected as a law officer and an honest man who—"

"You don't need to speak for me," Logan interrupted. He set aside the paper bag that held his smokes, keeping his gaze directly on Jonathan. He stepped even closer to the man. "Your brother knows damn well you have a good life here," he told Elizabeth. "He just doesn't want to own up to being the cause of William's death and the hell you ended up going through. And I'm guessing he came here looking for William's share of the estate, not because he cares anything about you. Am I right?"

"You're exactly right," Elizabeth answered. "He isn't even interested in seeing his nephew."

Logan stepped to within inches of Jonathan. He was as tall and intimidating as Jonathan, who finally stepped back. "I don't want this man laying one hand on my son," Logan continued, his gaze drilling into Jonathan's.

Jonathan stiffened, turning again to Elizabeth. "How can you be so sure this man didn't marry you just for your money?"

"If he'd married me for my money, we would be living in a mansion, and Logan wouldn't be working at a dangerous job just to provide for us," Elizabeth answered. "We live in this simple but warm and comfortable house because this is how we *choose* to live. I'll not raise my son the way *I* was raised—and the way *William* was raised—with the attitude that we are better than other people. And Logan will never be the tyrant to our son that you were to me and William. The minute we walked out of that dark, boring mansion of yours, William and I never felt freer or happier. Go back to London, Jonathan. You found me, and you know I'm all right, so just go home. Denver, Colorado, is *my* home now, and if Logan gets transferred someplace farther west, I'll follow him, and *that* will be home. Home is where the people you love are, Jonathan, not the house you live in."

"You're an ignorant fool, Elizabeth."

"Get the hell out of my house," Logan told Jonathan before Elizabeth could answer. "*Now!* Before I lose my temper fully, and believe me, that's something you don't want to see."

"You took advantage of my sister!"

Logan stepped back a little and glanced at Elizabeth. She knew exactly what he was thinking. His sense of humor had kicked in for the moment, and he grinned. "I sure as hell did. And she sure as hell was *willing*."

Jonathan's face grew red with rage. "You pompous, obtuse, lawless, uneducated, murdering bastard!" Jonathan spit at Logan.

Logan frowned mockingly and turned to Elizabeth again. "Pompous?"

"It means arrogant—haughty," she told him.

"How about obtuse?"

Elizabeth swallowed, not really wanting to answer that one. "It means…simple-minded—thick-headed."

Logan's frown turned darker as he returned to Jonathan. "Well now, pompous, uneducated, sometimes murdering bastard—those I will accept. But not obtuse." He suddenly gave Jonathan a shove that sent him sprawling into a stuffed chair. "You are pressing your luck, Lord Jonathan Baylor. I'm still considering that you are Elizabeth's brother, worthless as that connection is. But I'm real close to risking Elizabeth's wrath for knocking the hell out of you all the way back to London."

A red-faced Jonathan looked at Elizabeth again. "This is your last chance to come to your senses and withdraw your inheritance and come back to London with me. You can leave that bastard baby here with its father, so no one will know what you've done."

Elizabeth was shocked he would suggest such a thing. "You are the most reprehensible man I have ever known!"

She'd barely finished the sentence before Logan yanked Jonathan out of the chair. He dragged him to the front door and took his top hat from the nearby hat tree. He slammed it on the man's head, then opened the door and began shoving him outside.

"Get the hell out of my house," Logan growled. "Any man who would suggest a woman abandon her own baby is the lowest of the low. I should *kill* you for calling my son a bastard."

Jonathan, just as big as Logan, tried to shove back, but to no avail. Logan kept pushing him until both men were on the wooden steps outside. Logan pulled back a fist and slammed it against Jonathan's jaw, sending him sprawling down the steps and onto the ground below.

"I want you off my property!" Logan roared. "Move quick, before I beat you bloody and throw you in jail for trespassing!"

Jonathan rolled to his feet and straightened, shaking dirt from his cape and brushing off his pants. He rubbed at his jaw and at the blood that began to trickle from his lower lip. He stepped over to where his hat lay after flying off his head when he fell and picked it up, brushing it off before putting it back on. He glared at Elizabeth then. "You've made your choice. But I guarantee that someday you will regret this."

"Just go, Jonathan," she told him, tears in her eyes at the fact that her brother actually thought she would leave her own baby behind. "I've never been happier that I left home, in spite of all the awful things I suffered after that."

Jonathan glanced at both of them once more before turning and walking through the gate. He climbed into the fancy buggy he'd rented and drove off.

Logan, still tense with anger, turned to Elizabeth.

"I'm so sorry, Logan," she said.

"For what? The man is a selfish, arrogant sonofabitch. I'm surprised you turned out the way you did, growing up with a man like that."

"But he insulted you so badly. And to suggest I would leave William behind—"

Logan breathed deeply to control his temper, then leaned against a porch post. "Jesus, Elizabeth, do you really think insults affect a man like me? I've been called every name in the book, some you've never heard of and some that would shock you onto a fainting couch. It was what he said about William and his insults toward you that made me want to kill him."

Logan turned and paced across the porch for a moment, glancing out at Jonathan to make sure the man was still headed away. Finally, he sighed and faced Elizabeth, his hands on his hips. To her surprise, he smiled again. "At least I learned a few new words."

Elizabeth couldn't help smiling in return. "I love you so much, Logan Best."

"And that's all that matters." He stepped closer, pulling her into his arms. "By the way, what's that you called Jonathan? Reprehensible?"

"Yes. It means inexcusable, shameful, unacceptable."

Logan shook his head. "Why didn't you just call him a sonofabitch?"

She laughed lightly. "*You* called him that. But that's Logan talk. I'm not about to start using the kind of words *you* use. If I did, people would think I was some kind of saloon woman."

"Just as long as you don't mind *behaving* like a saloon woman when you're in bed with me."

"Oh, I don't mind that at all." Elizabeth looked into his bright, yellow-green eyes—disturbingly handsome eyes that reminded her of a clever, prowling wolf about to pounce on its prey—and she was his prey.

Logan met her lips with a delicious, searching kiss. "Lady Elizabeth, you are now doomed from ever going back to your old life in London. You belong to me, and here is where you'll stay."

"Here is the only place I *want* to stay," she answered. She turned her head to see Jonathan's carriage moving farther away. *Goodbye, Jonathan.* Her days in England were done. She was in her wonderful American West now, and in Logan Best's arms.

She thought how, in a way, she'd written her own dime novel. What could be better than that?

AUTHOR'S NOTE

I hope you have enjoyed my story. I would love to write a sequel to *Logan's Lady*, so I hope you will contact me at rosannebittner17@outlook.com, through my website at rosannebittner.com, or visit me on Facebook and Goodreads. Let me know if you, too, would like to continue reading about Logan Best and his "Lady" Elizabeth. After all, they are settled in Denver, Colorado, now, in a growing city full of gold miners and those who would steal their claims; ranchers and those who would steal their cattle; corrupt businessmen and bankers and those who would show them up for what they are; outlaws and those who would seek them out—and men like Marshal Logan Best, eager to right the wrongs. Logan and Elizabeth have just started their journey through the American West Elizabeth grew to love in those dime novels.

Thanks to all my readers for their continued support of my sixty-eight published novels about Native Americans and America's wild, untamed "Old West." You can bet I will keep writing exciting Western romance for you to enjoy!

ABOUT THE AUTHOR

USA Today bestselling novelist Rosanne Bittner is highly acclaimed for her award-winning love stories about the American West and other facets of American history. Known for the historical accuracy in her books, Rosanne's epic and adventure-filled romances span the West—from Canada to Mexico, Missouri to California—and are often based on personal visits to each setting. She lives in Michigan with her husband, Larry, and near her two sons, Brock and Brian, and three grandsons, Brennan, Connor, and Blake. You can learn much more about Rosanne and her books through her website at rosannebittner.com and her blog at rosannebittner.blogspot.com. Be sure to also visit Rosanne on her Facebook author page and through Twitter and Goodreads! Rosanne loves hearing from her readers and often runs contests on Facebook and for her Street Team, through which readers can win free books and other prizes!

ALSO BY ROSANNE BITTNER

Stand-alone Novels
Wildest Dreams
Thunder on the Plains
Paradise Valley
Desperate Hearts
Logan's Lady

Outlaw Hearts
Outlaw Hearts
Do Not Forsake Me
Love's Sweet Revenge
The Last Outlaw
Christmas in a Cowboy's Arms anthology